# SISTER'S CHOICE

# Books by Judith Pella

*Beloved Stranger*
*Mark of the Cross*
*The Stonewycke Trilogy**
*Texas Angel*

## Daughters of Fortune

*Written on the Wind*
*Somewhere a Song*
*Toward the Sunrise*
*Homeward My Heart*

## Patchwork Circle

*Bachelor's Puzzle*
*Sister's Choice*

## The Russians

*White Nights, Red Morning*

*with Michael Phillips

PATCHWORK CIRCLE

# SISTER'S CHOICE

A NOVEL

JUDITH PELLA

BETHANY HOUSE PUBLISHERS
*Minneapolis, Minnesota*

*Sister's Choice*


Cover design by The DesignWorks Group, Jason Gabbert
Cover photograph by Steve Gardner, PixelWorks Studios, Inc.
Cover quilt created by Grace and Peace Quilts, Saddleback Church, Lake Forest, California



Published by Bethany House Publishers
11400 Hampshire Avenue South
Bloomington, Minnesota 55438

Bethany House Publishers is a division of
Baker Publishing Group, Grand Rapids, Michigan.

Printed in the United States of America

**Library of Congress Cataloging-in-Publication Data**

Pella, Judith.
Sister's choice / Judith Pella.
p. cm. — (Patchwork circle ; bk. 2)
ISBN 978-0-7642-0134-9 (pbk.)
1. Quilting—Fiction. 2. Courtship—Fiction. 3. Trials (Murder)—Fiction. I. Title.

PS3566.E415S57 2008
813'.54—dc22

2007035136

This is dedicated to my small
quilt groups who bring me
laughter, inspiration, therapy,
and wonderful friendships.
Thanks to each of you!

Sew Much More
Thursday Nighters
So & Sews
Novel Quilters

JUDITH PELLA has been writing for the inspirational market for over twenty years and is the author of more than thirty novels, most in the historical fiction genre. Her recent novel *Mark of the Cross* and her extraordinary four-book DAUGHTERS OF FORTUNE series showcase her skills as a historian as well as a storyteller. Her degrees in teaching and nursing lend depth to her tales, which span a variety of settings. Pella and her husband make their home in Oregon.

VISIT JUDITH'S WEB SITE:
*www.judithpella.com*

# ONE

## Columbia County, Oregon
## August 1882

Maggie Newcomb stood on the front porch of her house gazing idly into the yard. The day was sunny with some dots of white clouds in the blue late August sky. Dad said it might rain later in the week to usher in September, but now summer was holding on nicely.

Maggie sighed as she peered across the yard and down the road. She felt as if she were looking for something but couldn't think what. Surely not for the guests to arrive for Mama's quilting bee. She'd hardly noticed the two quilt frames set up in the yard. No, she really wasn't anticipating the gathering. And it wasn't because she was jealous of her sister, Ellie, for whom Mama had arranged this bee so they could finish her twelve wedding quilts.

Maggie did feel blue, but she was sure it wasn't because of the quilting party for Ellie or because her sister was engaged to be married to a handsome, wonderful man. Maggie didn't want her sister's quilts, or her man—though Maggie had in fact proposed marriage to that very man, to Zack Hartley, but that was when he had been the minister William Locklin. In truth, Maggie hadn't wanted him even then. She'd just been stupid and silly, wanting to get back at everyone who thought she was too young and too immature to snag the much-sought-after new minister. All she had ended up proving was just how right they were. She had been childish and immature. Maybe she still was a little, but in the last weeks since all the upsetting events, she had changed some—for the good, she believed.

The cause of her present melancholy wasn't jealousy. It was . . .

She couldn't pinpoint the exact cause. She felt as if she were floating around aimlessly in a fog. Everyone else seemed to have a purpose in life. They were moving ahead to exciting futures. Well, at least Ellie and Zack knew where they were going, and so did her older brother, Boyd, who would marry in October after he finished the season in the lumber camp where he worked. Her younger brother, Georgie, had school to look forward to, even if he didn't always like it. They all had a reason to get up in the morning: wedding plans, new home plans, even schoolwork.

All Maggie seemed to have were chores. Was she just bored, then? Did she merely want some excitement? No, she simply wanted to know that there was more ahead for her than mucking out the barn or helping Mama peel potatoes or hang laundry. She had recently turned eighteen; surely there was more out there for her to look forward to.

"Maggie! Maggie!"

Mama's voice abruptly intruded into Maggie's reverie.

"Come on, now. Everyone will be here soon."

Maggie gave another long-suffering sigh and turned toward the house.

Mama was standing in the doorway with an armload of quilts. She and Ellie and even Maggie had been hard at work getting Ellie's quilt tops ready for the quilting. Mama and Ellie had marked four or five of the quilts, as that's all there had been time for. Then these had been sandwiched with wadding and backing and basted—this is what Maggie had helped with. Some of the ladies would work on marking the other quilts while the marked ones were being quilted. Maggie, of course, hadn't been involved in the marking, for marking the quilting patterns was exacting work, far above her meager skills.

"Take these and set them carefully on the blanket I spread out by the frames," Mama said.

Ellie had twelve quilt tops ready to be quilted. Maggie could not imagine the women finishing them all today. If they just finished the five that were basted, that would be something. Mama said when she was a girl she had been to quilting bees where it was common for all twelve to be done in a day. But there might be three or four frames set up and twice as many ladies stitching. There were nine members of Mama's Sewing Circle; however, a few extras would come today, including some of the older daughters of the Circle women, some of the very girls who had vied with Ellie for Zack. There were no hard feelings among the girls, especially since it turned out Zack hadn't been a real minister. Ellie was the only one who had fallen in love with the *man*, not the "office."

Maggie set the quilts where instructed and then returned to the house. Ellie was slicing the bread Mama had spent two days baking. All the women would be contributing food, but Mama felt, as hostess, she had to make sure there was enough, since both lunch and supper would be served. The menfolk had been invited to join the ladies for supper. Lewis Arlington and Kurt and Clyde Lambert might even bring their instruments to provide music for dancing later.

"Ellie, why don't you let me finish the bread," Maggie offered, "so you can get started loading your quilts onto the frames."

Mama and Ellie both started at Maggie's suggestion, and her cheeks suddenly heated.

"Well, I can be helpful once in a while," she added defensively.

She could see both Mama and Ellie were suddenly embarrassed at being caught with their surprised expressions.

"We're sorry, honey," Mama said. She seemed about to say more but remained quiet.

"It would speed things along if the first two quilts were loaded," Ellie suggested.

"And that's best left to you," said Maggie. "I'm far better at slicing bread." She nudged her sister away from the cutting board and slipped the knife from her hand.

"Thank you, Maggie. But you are going to do some quilting today, aren't you?"

"You don't want my toenail catchers in your beautiful quilts."

"But I do—well, that is, I don't . . ." Ellie sputtered. "That is, your stitches aren't that bad, and I want my sister to be part of this. I truly do!"

"Well, I guess—"

"Of course Maggie will add some quilting!" Mama spoke up. "I'll help her, and her work will look fine."

As the back door shut behind Ellie, Maggie bit her lip to keep from groaning, or worse, from spouting a cross retort. All she needed was to be the only one getting quilting lessons like a child. That's what nearly got her into trouble with Zack. Why couldn't she be equal with the women, or at least with those her own age?

The answer was clear. They were all skilled stitchers, and she wasn't. Since she could never measure up, she would always be inferior. No one seemed to care much about her other talents. Why, she was good at—

What was she good at? As she sliced the bread she searched in her mind for her accomplishments and came up quite blank. In school she'd always been good at arithmetic, but no one cared if a girl was good at that. What else? She could ride, but so could Ellie. She could fish, but even Ellie could learn to fish if she put her mind to it.

Let's face it, Maggie, you have no real talents. You are just a big lump.

"Ow!" she cried suddenly. Because she hadn't been paying attention to her work, the knife came down and nicked her finger instead of the bread. She thrust her wounded finger into her mouth.

"Oh, Maggie, what have you done?" exclaimed Mama.

"Nothing!" Maggie retorted angrily. "I can't do anything! I am just a . . . lump." Her voice caught on the final word, and to her surprise tears sprang to her eyes.

Mama tore a strip from a clean rag and handed it to Maggie. "Wrap this around it." Mama looked closely at her. "What is it, Maggie?" she said more gently.

Maggie sniffed. "Nothing."

"You've been out of sorts all day. What's troubling you?"

"It's just what I said." Maggie's voice trembled over the words, but she just couldn't keep her feelings in any longer. "I'm not good at anything. I'm a lump of plain nothingness."

Mama took Maggie's injured hand and examined the cut finger. It was still bleeding a little. She wrapped the piece of cloth around it. "Surely you can't believe that," Mama said.

"I dare you to name one thing I can do."

"Well, you are good at arguing."

Maggie grimaced at that.

Mama smiled. "You are young, dear. You will find your niche in life, I promise." She put her arm around Maggie. "You said you are a lump—well, that doesn't have to be a bad thing, you know. It's like the lump of dough that made this bread. It starts out as not much, but before you know it, it turns into this wonderful bread."

"I can't even make bread," Maggie groused.

"You know what I mean, though, don't you? You are a late bloomer, Maggie, but you will bloom. I believe it with all my heart. You will bloom into a beautiful flower."

"I'm eighteen, Mama. That's kind of old to be a bud." Maggie dashed a hand across her eyes to wipe the tears still dripping. Mama took a handkerchief from her apron pocket and gave it to Maggie.

Maggie wiped her eyes and blew her nose. Mama was about to say more when Ellie called from outside.

"Mrs. Donnelly and Mrs. Renolds are here!"

Mama hesitated, clearly torn between her duties as hostess and her need to comfort her daughter.

"Go on, Mama," Maggie said. "I'll be okay."

"We'll talk more later, all right?"

Maggie nodded. Mama went outside, and Maggie returned her attention to the task at hand. She tried hard not to think glum thoughts for the rest of the day, but that proved almost impossible because every little thing seemed to conspire against her efforts.

Right off she was reminded of another reason for her melancholy when she glanced out the kitchen window and saw Mrs. Donnelly. Immediately she thought of the woman's son, poor Tommy Donnelly, languishing away in the St. Helens jail. He was never far from her thoughts, not only because he was her friend but also because she held a secret that could, if revealed, probably get him convicted of murder. A few weeks ago Tommy's father had been found dead. Tommy had eventually confessed to shooting his cruel, good-for-nothing father. He'd said it was because he had feared for his own life, but shortly before the shooting Tommy had made remarks to Maggie that could be construed as threats against his father's life. Zack had advised Maggie to keep quiet about these matters unless the sheriff asked her point-blank. So far, no one had given her a second thought, but if there was a trial, she could be called, Zack had said, as a character witness. Then she would most likely have to reveal her secret.

And that wasn't all. Maggie had not gone once to visit Tommy in jail. She felt terrible about it. She knew she was about his only friend. Some friend! She was a coward, afraid if she got in the same room with the sheriff, she would panic and blurt out everything. She'd been avoiding Mrs. Donnelly, as well, for weeks, not an easy thing, since she was Mama's best friend.

Maggie finished cutting the bread and went outside to join the quilters. Just then Florence Parker arrived with her usual grand flourish, this time all excited about a letter just received from her son, Evan, saying he would be coming home soon for an extended visit. He was away in Boston, attending Harvard University. But Maggie was far more interested in another bit of news. Emma Jean Stoddard mentioned they would be having a houseguest, as well, a young woman from Portland. She and Sarah Stoddard had become friends in finishing school. Mrs. Stoddard said her name was Tamara Brennan, daughter of Dr. and Mrs. Curtis Brennan, who apparently were hoity-toity Portlanders.

Upon hearing the Brennan name, Mrs. Parker gasped. "Well, it is a small world, isn't it? Evan attended Harvard with the Brennans' son. We met them in Boston last spring when we attended Evan's graduation."

Maggie was dying to know what this girl Tamara was like. Colby Stoddard was, after all, still a very eligible bachelor, and now that Ellie was taken, Maggie had been thinking she might finally have a chance with the handsome young man. She hated to think that new competition was going to be close by.

Mama was speaking to Mrs. Parker. "I thought you said Evan was going to work for a big law office in Boston."

"He's had offers from several *very* prestigious firms back East," Mrs. Parker replied. "But he misses his family, you know. I am sure he will be able to take up any of those offers when he is ready. He was fifth in his class at Harvard and is much sought after."

Maggie had heard Mrs. Parker brag about that fact several times since the graduation, and she thought she saw her mother roll her eyes just now. Well, Mrs. Parker and Mama were not the best of friends. They were brought together only through the Sewing Circle. Otherwise they probably wouldn't give each other the time of day.

By noon two quilts were finished. Everyone was having a grand time chatting and exchanging gossip. Maggie had managed to avoid quilting all morning. She helped with the basting of some of the other quilts but was even criticized for that. Mrs. Stoddard came up, turned over the section Maggie was working on, and said, "Dear, you didn't catch the backing in your stitches. You will have to re-do that."

"Yes, Mrs. Stoddard. Sorry," Maggie said contritely through gritted teeth. She couldn't antagonize Colby's mother if she hoped to have any chance at all with him.

After lunch, however, Maggie was railroaded into a seat at one of the quilt frames. She knew how much Ellie wanted her to participate, so she tried to do the task with good grace. It was just her luck that Mrs. Stoddard took the seat right next to her, and Mabel Parker sat down across from her. Someone to criticize her *and* someone to compare her work to. Mabel, along with Ellie and Sarah, were the best young stitchers in Maintown. Nevertheless, Maggie worked doggedly on her section, which happened to be a fairly intricate feather design with some cross-hatching. Every now and then she could feel Mrs. Stoddard's incisive eye upon her, and that was usually when she would prick her finger or bungle in some other way. Though she did her best, most careful work, her stitches were uneven.

After about a half hour Maggie was ready to scream with restlessness and boredom. She decided she had done enough to satisfy Ellie. Nonchalantly she rose and stretched.

"I need to take a little break," she announced to no one in particular.

"We have barely gotten started," Mabel said.

True, the women would go far longer, taking brief moments to stretch and flex their hands. "Well, nature calls, you know," Maggie said with a nervous chuckle.

Mrs. Stoddard's eye arched at Maggie's indelicate words.

Maggie hurried away toward the outhouse. She didn't really have to use it, but she couldn't bear to sit quilting another moment. She had to get away, if only for a few minutes. After visiting the outhouse she started back toward the quilt frames but with an ambivalent step. Then she stopped dead in her tracks. From where she stood, she could see that Mrs. Stoddard had scooted into the chair Maggie had occupied, and she was taking out Maggie's stitches!

Why weren't Mama or Ellie stopping her? And though she could tell both of them were occupied elsewhere and unable to see what was happening, Maggie knew they would be happy someone was repairing her rotten work. Tears sprang to her eyes.

She hated to cry, and she hated herself for it and the weakness it indicated. But she couldn't help herself. She'd tried so hard to do her best work. And to have Mrs. Stoddard be the one to note and fix her work was the worst kind of insult. At least no one had seen her return from the privy, so she spun around and quickly headed to the barn. She wished she could have instead gone to the house and locked herself in her room with a book, but to do so she'd have to walk right by the women. There'd be little to do in the barn, but it was her only safe retreat.

She spent the rest of the afternoon there, alternately crying and fuming over the fact that no one came looking for her. They hadn't even noticed she was gone!

She brushed down the horses and doled out hay. Several of the guests' horses were housed in the barn, so fussing over them kept her busy and helped divert some of her dismay. The horses also presented amiable sounding boards for the venting of her ire.

"The nerve of that woman ripping out my work!" she told the family saddle horse, Buster. "Without even asking me! I hate that woman!" she declared, then suddenly realized the full implication of her words. If she wanted Colby, he came with a mother. If she won Colby, that woman would be her mother-in-law! Maggie groaned.

"Buster, be thankful you are a horse. It simply stinks to be a girl thinking about marriage. But the hard fact is, I'll have to go through *her* to get to Colby. He's not really a mama's boy, but everyone in his mama's life is under her thumb. He may try to fight it, but that is still the cold, hard fact."

Maggie plopped down on a mound of hay. "Oh, what's the use! I think I'll just be an old maid like Iris Fergus. Maybe I'll go to the big city and work in an office." She had visited an office in Portland once with her father and had been impressed by the female secretaries in their starched, white, high-collared blouses and trim dark skirts, sitting with refined postures at their desks and primly typing. Maybe that's what she would be good at, typing on those fascinating machines. How quickly those ladies' fingers flew over the keys, just like—Maggie grimaced—just like the quilters' fingers flew in their stitching.

Okay, so that might not be for her. She couldn't stand wearing a starched white blouse, either. Though it scandalized her mother, Maggie usually wore her brother's overalls, except for church and other special occasions. She was wearing them now, having slipped past her mother's scrutiny.

There had to be something out there to give meaning to Maggie's life. Mama promised!

Only when Maggie began to hear male voices outside did she realize just how long she had been hiding in the barn. It must be close to suppertime if the men were beginning to arrive. Glancing up at the loft opening, she saw the afternoon sunlight had dimmed, and it was pushing on toward evening. Now someone would come looking for her because they would need help getting supper on. That's all she was good for—slave labor.

# TWO

"There you are, Maggie!" Mama exclaimed the moment Maggie came into view. "It's time for supper."

Maggie looked around. The quilt frames had been taken down, replaced by tables—well, actually boards set over saw-horses. They were covered with tablecloths and lined with benches Mama had borrowed from the school. The ladies had been joined by several men. There were at least thirty folks in the yard now. The men were standing in knots talking to one another. No doubt they had done the heavy work of removing the quilt frames and setting up the tables. The women were busy carrying out food and dishes and all that was needed for supper. No wonder no one had looked for Maggie. They hadn't needed her labor—for a change.

Maggie also noted that the girls her age had been busy doing something else. They must have brought clothes to change into for dancing, because now they were dressed in pretty party frocks. All the girls, with the exception of Sarah Stoddard, were decked out in their finest. The husband hunting never seemed to end. Even Ellie had on her pretty yellow-and-blue sundress, but that was for Zack. Sarah had worn a dress to the quilting, just a drab everyday dress. She was not interested in finding a husband, though, more likely, she was scared stiff at the prospect and was trying her hardest to remain invisible. Maggie envied her.

At this moment Maggie was painfully aware of her own garb. She was in her usual overalls and shirt. Mama had argued with her that morning about wearing something more "presentable" because they were having company. Maggie said she'd change before the ladies arrived but kept putting it off until Mama was so busy she either didn't notice or didn't have time to argue further. Now Maggie regretted her stubbornness. If she had changed, at least now she would have had on a decent everyday dress.

Well, it wasn't too late. Glancing quickly around, she noted Colby hadn't arrived yet. She started toward the house.

"Where are you going?" Mama asked.

"I'm going to change."

"But we are about to start supper."

"I'll just be a minute."

Mama looked on the verge of giving Maggie a much deserved "I told you so." Then she paused, sighed, and said, "All right. We'll wait for you."

Maggie realized that would be worse than being the only girl in overalls—having everyone waiting on her! She'd have to make some grand entrance with everyone seeing she'd made a desperate bid to make up for her earlier bad taste. And they would know, at least Mabel, Iris, and Mrs. Stoddard would know, she had changed for the benefit of the young men, placing her in league with the husband hunters.

She gave a shrug. She was who she was, and if they didn't like that, she didn't care.

"Never mind, Mama," she said. "Let's just eat."

"There's time," Mama said. "And you'll want a dress on for the dancing later, won't you?"

"Do I need a dress, Mama?" she snapped angrily. "You think that will help me?" Her voice shook, and she felt tears sting her eyes once again. Fortunately she and Mama were standing apart from the crowd, so she hoped no one heard her outburst. With an embarrassed scowl, Maggie added, "I'm not hungry anyway, and I've got a stomachache. I'm just going to go to my room to lie down—"

"Oh no, you are not!" Mama's former gentleness turned suddenly to steel. "You are not going to ruin Ellie's day by acting like a child. You will join us for supper and the party afterward. You can do so in overalls or a dress, but you will be sitting at a table in ten minutes. That is that!"

Maggie could feel herself pouting, even though she knew her mother was right. What was wrong with her?

"And you will smile!" Mama added.

Maggie wanted to retort in protest, but it wouldn't help. She thought if she ran into the house and up to her room, Mama might let her go rather than cause a scene in front of company. But it would still ruin Ellie's party, not to mention that it would make Maggie look worse than ever.

So plastering a smile on her face, she turned, went to a table, and plopped down on a bench. It was just for show because, as the daughter of the hostess, she couldn't be the first to sit. She waited until her mother got busy with something else, then rose and went to the kitchen to help with the food. As it turned out, she could have changed her clothes—it was fifteen or twenty minutes before the meal was actually served—but she didn't, probably out of sheer orneriness, as her dad would say. Let them accept her as she was or not at all.

She wavered in this resolve when Colby showed up. She had wondered if he would come to what might be construed as an "old folks" gathering. But he rode in with three other Maintown eligible bachelors—Elisha Cook, Able Jenkins, and Stew Weatherby. They must have heard there would be unattached women present and decided it would be worth a visit.

Of the four young men, Colby stood out for his remarkable good looks. In Maggie's estimation, he was practically perfect. The fact that he was twenty and still single was merely because he'd had eyes only for Ellie for so long. Most everyone assumed they would marry eventually. How did he feel about being spurned for another man? He didn't look brokenhearted. He was laughing with his companions as they dismounted and tied their horses at the watering trough. Maybe he was hiding his feelings; maybe he was just relieved not to have to make a marriage commitment.

Maggie had always thought it was a terrible state of things that at nineteen or twenty a girl was considered an old maid if she wasn't married. But a man could wait as long as he wanted. A man never had to face the shame of being an old maid. It wasn't fair.

Maggie had always said she didn't care about such things, but in truth she wasn't as much against marriage as she often preached. Mama said that once she loved a man, she would understand the beauty of marriage and the joy of companionship it offered. And when she loved a man, she would find much pleasure in bearing his children and loving them, as well. That's what Maggie wanted, what she hoped for.

Since supper was served almost immediately after the young men's arrival and Ellie and Zack wanted Maggie to sit with them, she didn't have a chance to say much to Colby. But the other girls certainly made up for her absence. With the eligible new preacher out of the picture, and with Ellie taken by that same ex-preacher, Colby was now fair game, and the girls wasted no time. They flocked to him like vultures on carrion. The other young men also received a good share of the attention. Even Mabel was still flirting, and rumor had it she had a new beau who lived in Astoria!

"Would you rather sit at the other table, sis?" Ellie asked, obviously noting Maggie's gaze wandering in that direction.

"Good heavens, no!" Maggie replied. "I'm just feeling a little sorry for those poor young fellows. At least when you were available, Zack, they could breathe some."

Zack laughed. "They don't look like they are suffering much."

"Well, anyway," said Maggie, "I've had quite enough of all that. The last thing I want to do right now is throw myself at a man."

Zack gave her a more careful appraisal.

"Don't worry, Zack. Like I told you before, you didn't break my heart. I didn't really want you, and I meant it. I like you much better as a friend and soon-to-be brother-in-law."

"Just so you know, you are the prettiest girl I ever turned down," Zack said with a grin.

"And just how many girls have you turned down?" Ellie asked with playful indignation.

"A few," Zack replied evasively. "But it is only the one I *didn't* turn down that matters!"

Smiling, Ellie linked her arm around Zack's and snuggled close to him. She seemed not at all aware of the discomfort that gesture caused Maggie. Maybe she was a bit jealous, not of Zack, but of what he and Ellie had together.

By the time dessert was served, Maggie had decided that she was her own worst enemy. She was stubborn and childish.

And, as her mother always said, a pouty face isn't pretty. She ate a few bites of cake, rose from her seat, and quietly slipped into the house, determined to rectify the situation.

When she stepped back into the yard fifteen minutes later, not only had her attitude changed but so had her appearance. She usually needed Ellie's help getting dressed up, so she knew she didn't look perfect. But neither was she unsightly. Her light green dress, which was her second-best dress, had a skirt that was fuller than the current fashion, and was ideal for dancing. The demurely scooped neckline was trimmed in ecru lace as were the short puffed sleeves. She had tied a burgundy ribbon around the fitted waist and a matching ribbon in her hair. She had left her brown curls loose except for the sides, which she tied at the back of her head with the bow. She'd pinched her cheeks good and hard to give them roses, wishing Mama would let her wear a touch of rouge like Mabel Parker sometimes did. Wearing the gold locket that Dad had given her for Christmas a couple years ago, she thought she looked quite fetching indeed.

Her stomach flipped a bit when she reentered the party. She feared everyone would notice her and think her silly for going to such trouble. It was quite natural for the other girls to don party dresses, but she knew she would stand out like a pig in a parade. However, it was too late now. To her surprise and relief, all heads didn't turn toward her, and mouths didn't gape with astonishment at her transformation. Unlike some girls, she didn't care to be noticed . . . well, not much anyway.

The sun had set, making way for a lovely summer evening. Lanterns strung around the yard gave a warm, inviting light to the festivities. The tables had been cleared and pushed aside, though one table remained, laden with Mama's good punch bowl and all the desserts Mama and the other ladies had made. Lewis Arlington, with his guitar, and Clyde and Kurt Lambert—father and son—with their fiddles were playing a lively turn. All the young people were lining up for a reel. Maggie realized that in her absence most appeared to have already paired up. Colby was with Mabel.

Feeling a sudden wave of shyness, Maggie contented herself with standing on the sidelines, tapping her foot and clapping her hands in rhythm to the music. She didn't want to be noticed too much, but she wouldn't have dressed up if she hadn't wanted to attract *some* attention. Even if Colby didn't notice her, surely one of the other boys would! It didn't help that all were already taken.

When the reel was over, the dancers stopped, out of breath and laughing. Zack came up to Maggie. He was breathing hard after dancing with Ellie.

He held out his hand gallantly. "Do me the honor of the next dance, Maggie."

Maggie's eyes shot quickly to Ellie standing a short distance away.

Ellie smiled and nodded. "I need a rest. Zack can dance nonstop all night if you let him."

Maggie knew it was a pity invitation, but she accepted anyway. It was better than feeling foolish just standing there, and she had noticed her mother saying something to Georgie. Dancing a pity dance with Zack would be better than dancing with her little brother!

She quickly got over her self-consciousness as she became caught up in the dance. She began to laugh and enjoy herself. Then, when she took Zack's hand and progressed down the line of dancers, she was relaxed and almost her old self again.

When the dance ended she was out of breath but smiling a real smile. She had barely thanked Zack when Stew Weatherby came up to her.

"Do you want some punch, Maggie?" he asked.

Surprised but suddenly aware that she was parched after the exertion, she nodded. He hurried away to the refreshment table.

Then Colby was there.

"Hi'ya, Maggie," he said with his usual winning grin. "You sure do clean up pretty!"

"Thanks, Colby." Her stomach fluttered, and her cheeks grew warm. He had noticed her!

"Why, I'd say you're the prettiest girl here."

She gave his arm a playful shove. "Oh, go on with you!"

"I would not lie about such a thing."

Just then Stew returned with two cups of punch. Taking one, Maggie gulped down half—a pretty dress and a ribbon in her hair couldn't completely refine her manners! But instead of worrying about that, she was noting a bit of a scowl on Stew's face as he glanced at Colby. Stew was a nice fellow, two or three years older than Maggie. He had blond hair that seemed to always fall into his blue eyes. He was nice looking, or would have been if he were standing alone, but in close proximity to Colby, he looked plain indeed.

"Maggie, would—?" Stew started.

Colby cut in. "I've just asked Maggie to dance. Hold this, Stew." He thrust the cup Maggie had been holding into the hapless fellow's hand, then grabbed Maggie's hand and tugged her—though she didn't resist—back to the dancing area.

Were two men competing for her? And was one of them actually Colby? It must be true, since here she was dancing with him. But he didn't monopolize her for every dance. Stew finally asserted himself, and she danced with him and then with a couple of others. But Colby got her back for the last dance, a waltz, the only waltz of the evening because some of the older folks were old-fashioned and thought this pairing off of dance partners was scandalous. But Mama and Dad never saw the harm since the partners didn't hold each other any closer than in a reel, though, of course, it was sustained for much longer. Mama thought it was a beautiful dance anyway and enjoyed watching it.

Ellie, who had learned to waltz at her finishing school, had taught the dance to her sister. But Maggie had never danced the waltz with a male partner before. She thought it was more than mere coincidence that her first real waltz should be with Colby. It must be a sign of things to come.

As they glided over the straw-covered ground, she felt his gaze upon her, and when she lifted her eyes and squarely met that gaze, he smiled with a warmth to melt her heart. There seemed to be a sincerity in his expression that she had seldom seen in him. Was he seeing her as if for the first time? And liking what he saw? Were all her dreams going to be realized sooner than she had ever thought possible?

Had she known all it would take was donning a frilly party dress and a ribbon in her hair, she would have done it much sooner.

The evening almost ended on this splendid note. Then Mrs. Stoddard made her presence known. Maggie was standing near Ellie with their parents, bidding the guests good-bye. Mrs. Stoddard made a beeline right to Ellie, not only completely ignoring Maggie, but practically shouldering her out of the way.

"Ellie, dear, you know that block pattern I was telling you about, that unusual snowball and nine-patch combination? I will send Colby over tomorrow with it."

"Thank you, Mrs. Stoddard," Ellie replied politely, looking a bit bemused, probably not understanding the need for such urgency. "There's really no hurry. I can get it the next time we see each other."

"Who knows when that will be? We can't even count on Sundays anymore until we get a new pastor. Colby will be happy to bring it by."

"Mother," Colby put in, having overheard the exchange, "I need to fix that damaged fence tomorrow. It will probably take all day."

"I'm sure you'll be able to spare a few minutes to drop by the Newcombs'," Mrs. Stoddard said.

What was the woman's game anyway? Maggie had been thinking the upcoming visit by Miss Tamara Brennan was in reality a bid to match her with Colby. Now Mrs. Stoddard seemed to be attempting to push Ellie and Colby together. Was she just trying to pad her options? Of course, she wouldn't even consider Maggie as one of those options!

But even for a domineering matriarch like Mrs. Stoddard that kind of behavior was peculiar. She knew very well that Ellie was engaged to someone else. Even Mrs. Stoddard couldn't be that uncouth. Nevertheless, Maggie thought this the perfect time to assert her own cause. In one gesture she could place herself into a position of seeing Colby *and* at the same time show Mrs. Stoddard what a thoughtful and generous person she was.

"Mrs. Stoddard," she said, "I happen to be going out your way tomorrow"—she really wasn't, but that was beside the point—"why don't I pick up the pattern?"

Without even a glance at Maggie and in her most dismissive tone, Mrs. Stoddard responded, "Oh, I suppose it isn't that important. Colby will bring it by another day soon, Ellie."

Maggie fumed inside. It had to be obvious to this woman, who kept her children under her thumb and was surely aware of all their actions tonight, that Colby had spent most of the evening in Maggie's company. How could she be so blatantly rude to her? Or perhaps that was the exact reason why she was so rude. If she ignored Maggie, perhaps her son would take her lead and do so, as well.

Unfortunately, Maggie feared he might do just that.

# THREE

This must be the season for parties, Maggie thought as her dad pulled the wagon into the Parkers' yard. She reasoned that the community probably needed some festivities to help get over the rough events of late. Houseguests were as good a reason for socializing as anything, though Evan Parker wasn't exactly a guest, since this was his home. In any case, Maggie was less concerned about him than she was about another houseguest who would be in attendance at Evan's "welcome home" party.

Tamara Brennan, the Stoddards' guest, would also be at the Parkers' tonight. Tamara was the same age as Ellie, and they, along with Sarah Stoddard, had been in the same class at Mrs. Dubois' finishing school in Portland. Maggie had wheedled all the information she could out of Ellie about Tamara. Ellie had tried to downplay her qualities.

"Oh, I guess she is pretty, in an ordinary sort of way. Yes, she has a graceful manner about her, but anybody can learn that."

Maggie read between the lines and knew Tamara was beautiful, graceful, sophisticated, and accomplished. All the things Maggie wasn't.

Well, now she was about to see for herself. She was as prepared as she could be. She had worn her best dress, a rose-colored lawn with matching lace yoke and sleeves, and a dark purple satin ribbon tied around her waist. She felt far more "got up" than she had at the quilting party. Ellie had fixed her hair, taming her wild curls into ringlets, some falling around her shoulders, some tied at the back of her head. She felt on display in the most brazen, horrible way. Ellie tried to reassure her that everyone would be dressed up and had worn her best dress to prove it. Mrs. Parker had told everyone it would be a formal evening. Perhaps, then, everyone would be as uncomfortable as she was. After all, they were farm folk, not city socialites. Dad, in his Sunday suit, was running a finger around his stiff collar. Even Mama looked a bit out of sorts in a navy linen dress that Maggie had seen her wear only twice before, years ago. It was better than even Sunday best. Georgie was complaining about having to wear his Sunday duds on a Friday.

Before Dad had knocked on her door, Maggie had prepared herself for a boring evening. A far cry it would be, she was certain, from the relaxed barn dance held at her house last week.

They were not the first to arrive. More than a dozen folks were already standing around the Parkers' large parlor. Maggie noted the furniture had been rearranged so that chairs now lined the wall, but there didn't appear to be enough room for dancing, which was too bad. She had hoped for another chance to dance with Colby. She craned her neck but did not see him. She supposed this would be one of those boring parties where everyone just stood around and talked and ate.

"Welcome!" Mrs. Parker said, scurrying up to them as they handed their wraps to Mr. Parker, who apparently was in charge of opening the door and taking care of coats. Affluent as they were, they did not have servants.

Mrs. Parker was smiling and flushed, obviously excited about the festivities. She took Mama's hand warmly, as if there were no animosity between them.

"We have been looking forward to the evening," Mama said, also in a congenial way.

"Come, let me introduce you to my Evan," Mrs. Parker said.

"But we already—" Maggie began to state that of course they already knew him, even if it had been years since he'd been home for any length of time.

"Evan, dear, come see who is here!" Mrs. Parker called.

Maggie saw Evan standing by the refreshment table, and just as his mother called, he popped a big piece of cake into his mouth. When he turned upon hearing his name, Maggie had to restrain a chuckle. He looked like a chipmunk hoarding his winter meal. He hurriedly tried to swallow, his Adam's apple bobbing in an even more amusing manner.

Evan was four years older than Maggie, so her memories of him were vague. Yet she recalled that he had always been an odd sort. The other boys his age tended to make fun of him. Even Boyd, who was the same age, had done so. They called him four-eyes because he wore glasses, and teacher's pet because he always made good marks. Maggie remembered Mama scolding Boyd for it, telling him that the boys were just jealous of Evan because he was so smart. He'd won every prize in school and most of the county prizes, as well. Only the educational ones though, not the athletic prizes. They usually went to Colby or Boyd or a couple of the other more popular boys.

Evan now came over to greet the Newcombs. He politely shook Dad's and Georgie's hands—Boyd was absent, still working at the lumber camp. Then he gave a small bow to the women. When he smiled, Maggie noted there was a bit of chocolate cake stuck to his front tooth. Other than that, she did think he had a nice smile, even if it did twitch nervously a little. He was about as tall as Dad, not quite as husky, but certainly not slender. His complexion was ruddy, his hair a carpet of tight blond curls cut short, probably to prevent a wild mass like Maggie's long curls. His eyes were brown, and he wore wire-rimmed spectacles, no doubt because he'd ruined his eyes with all his studying.

"My goodness, what fine manners they taught you back there in Boston," said Mama.

Maggie thought the little bows were a bit old-fashioned, even silly, but she kept that to herself.

"We are so very proud of our boy," gushed Mrs. Parker. "He graduated law school at the top of his class!"

The other day he'd been fifth in his class, but Maggie wasn't about to quibble with a proud mother.

"So you are a practicing lawyer now?" Dad asked.

"I am licensed to practice law," Evan replied. There seemed a peculiar edge to his response, as if there were more behind his words than he was saying.

"Maybe you can give Earl Cranston some competition," Maggie said. "We can sure use a lawyer around here that isn't in the saloons half the time."

Dad arched a brow. "What do you know of Mr. Cranston?"

"Well, he—"

Just then the door was opened again by Mr. Parker, and new guests arrived—the Stoddards. Excusing herself, Mrs. Parker flitted over to them, calling for Evan to join her. The Newcombs made their way into the parlor, but Maggie lingered in the foyer for a moment. She was delighted to see Colby among the new arrivals. Unlike all the other men in the crowd, he actually looked marvelous in his Sunday suit, but then she always thought he looked wonderful. Colby was simply at ease in any situation, as a gentleman, a farmer, a lumberjack, or whatever guise he chose.

Next to him was obviously Tamara Brennan, a dark-haired beauty if ever there was one. Just as Colby outshone every man in the room, Tamara made every female appear pale and dowdy in comparison to her. And to see her and Colby standing side by side as though they belonged together made Maggie's stomach queasy.

Even in her dismay, however, she noted something else. Evan Parker had turned red as a beet. Had he just realized his teeth were covered in cake? It couldn't be the presence of Sarah Stoddard, who was all but hiding behind her brother. No, that wasn't it. Evan was looking right at Tamara and looking a lot like Maggie did when she looked at Colby. Was he merely flustered by her beauty? Then Maggie recalled Mrs. Parker mentioning that Evan and Tamara's brother had been classmates at Harvard. He must already know Tamara, and by the look of it, he must have a crush on her.

Everyone was now moving into the parlor, and Maggie joined them. She said hello to Colby and was a little perturbed that he barely acknowledged her. Still, she lingered in the little circle that formed with Tamara, Colby, Evan, and herself as they continued to exchange pleasantries.

"Well, Evan, how are you adjusting to our little backwater burg after the big city?" Colby asked.

"I am happy to be home," Evan replied.

"I loved Boston when I was there this spring for the graduation," Tamara said. "The tall old buildings, the traffic on the streets, the shopping—we have nothing like that here."

"But you live in Portland," put in Maggie, to keep in the conversation.

"Portland may seem grand if that's all you know, but once you see a really big city, you realize what you are missing."

"They are the ones missing something," Evan said. "I mean—uh—if you ask me."

He added this because he'd obviously realized his contradiction might offend Tamara.

"I guess Boston had many good points, too," he added a bit lamely.

"Like what?" Maggie asked. She probably shouldn't have put him on the spot like that, but it irked her that he had clearly changed his opinion in order to support Tamara.

"Well, uh . . . history . . . yes, history. So much there."

"That's what I was saying," Tamara said.

"I never could take too much history," said Colby.

"Neither could I," Maggie chimed in quickly. And though her statement was true, she realized she was doing just what Evan had done, lining herself up with Colby by supporting his statement.

"You'd think differently if you could stand and look upon the very harbor where they had the Boston Tea Party," Tamara said, her eyes alight with enthusiasm. "It is not the same as reading history in books."

"That would be interesting," Colby said. "The Boston Tea Party was one of the few exciting stories I recall from school. I was always amused to think of our forefathers dressing up like Indians and sneaking onto British ships. They were quite the rebels of their day."

Maggie laughed. "Put that way, it is funny!"

No one else laughed quite as heartily as Maggie, and there followed an awkward pause in the conversation.

Finally Colby broke the silence. "I am parched. Can I get anyone punch?" When both Tamara and Maggie said yes, he responded, "I'll make two trips."

"I'll lend a hand," offered Evan.

The two men went to the refreshment table. Maggie searched her mind for something to say to Tamara, mostly because the silence was uncomfortable, but also because she wanted to know more about her . . . rival?

"I hear you were in the same finishing school class as my sister, Ellie," Maggie finally said.

"Oh yes. What a dear girl. I hear she is to marry."

Glancing to where Ellie was standing across the room, Maggie noted Zack was beside her. He must have already been there when they arrived. "That's him next to her," Maggie pointed out.

"He's very handsome." Tamara paused, seeming hesitant, then asked, "Is it true, what Mrs. Stoddard was saying . . . ?"

"I'm sure it is." Maggie laughed. "Yes, he pretended to be our minister so he could hide from a gangster who was after him. He was actually a very good minister."

"How positively . . . well . . . interesting."

"So, Tamara, you live in Portland?" Maggie asked.

"Yes. My father is a doctor there."

"You must be engaged yourself, to be married, that is?" Maggie asked hopefully. It seemed possible that a beautiful girl like Tamara would be taken.

"No, I'm not. My mother says I best make a choice soon, or I will be considered an old maid."

She smiled pleasantly, the kind of smile that made Maggie certain Tamara Brennan wasn't a bad sort. In fact, she was rather friendly, and maybe Maggie could become friends with her. But first she had to know if Tamara had designs on Colby.

"It's too bad you had to interrupt your husband search to come here," Maggie said. "You must have many suitors in Portland and Boston."

"I broke off an engagement two months ago. He—well, it didn't work out. My mother thought a change of scene would do me good."

Colby returned holding two glasses of punch. Maggie reached out her hand, but Colby didn't see it and gave one of his glasses to Tamara. He might have handed the other to Maggie, but just then Evan arrived. He was still a couple steps away when the toe of his shoe caught on the edge of the carpet. He leaped forward, right in Maggie's direction, and the contents of the two glasses of punch he was holding flew into the air. The red punch made a perfect arc. Everyone else nearby scurried out of the way, but Maggie was a step too late. The punch splashed upon her, right in the middle of her bodice and down the front of her skirt.

"Oh my!" exclaimed Evan as he caught his balance. "Look what I have done!" Juggling the two now empty cups in one hand, he plucked his handkerchief from his pocket with the other and tried to blot up the mess on Maggie's dress. Realizing how unseemly that was, he turned as red as the punch and became more flustered than a fox caught red-handed in the chicken coop.

"It's okay," Maggie tried to assure him, taking the hankie from him to finish the blotting.

"I've ruined your dress," Evan lamented.

"Not at all. Look, it is practically the same color as the punch!"

Mabel Parker came up to them. "Come with me, Maggie, and I will help you clean up." She put an arm around Maggie and led her from the parlor.

Maggie didn't think she needed any help, but Mabel probably thought it her duty, since this was her home and it was her brother who had caused the mishap.

They went upstairs to Mabel's room, and Mabel produced a bottle of clear liquid she said was a good stain remover. She dabbed it on the worst of the spill, then used clear water to clean up the rest. Though there probably wouldn't be a stain, Maggie would have a big wet spot down her front during the rest of the evening.

"It'll dry quicker than you think," Mabel said, being unusually considerate.

For a country girl Mabel had always been rather snobbish, Maggie thought. She was sophisticated and charming in her store-bought clothes, but she had always made Maggie feel like a silly child. Maggie wondered how she had turned out as she did because her parents, though rich, came from farming roots, and though her mother did at times "put on airs," she was, in dress and manner, just like everyone else in the community. And now Maggie saw that even her brother, for all his years in the city, was just as unrefined as his parents.

"There's nothing more to be done, but thanks for your help, Mabel."

"You're welcome." Mabel's brow knit.

"Is something wrong?"

She seemed hesitant to respond, then said, "I'm worried about my brother."

"He's probably just nervous about being the guest of honor," Maggie suggested.

"If only that were it, but you wouldn't understand, dear."

This was the kind of statement that always irked Maggie. Mabel could be so condescending.

"Are you worried he'll have his heart broken by Tamara Brennan?" Maggie asked, just to prove she might understand more than she was given credit for.

Mabel blinked in surprise. Maggie had hit it exactly right.

"What do you know of that?" Mabel asked.

"Well, it's obvious. He turns red every time he looks at her, or worse, trips all over himself when she is near. That's probably why I got punch spilled all over me."

"And he hasn't got a chance with her because she is here to snag Colby."

"What!" That was what Maggie feared most.

"You are so perceptive, I am surprised you didn't guess that, as well."

"I guessed," Maggie admitted, her stomach sinking. "Has . . . has Colby spoken for her?"

"Both the mothers are manipulating matters, though I am sure Tamara and Colby know the real purpose of the visit."

"That can't happen!" gasped Maggie. Just the other day at Ellie's quilting party it seemed as if Mrs. Stoddard was trying to push Colby and Ellie back together. That hadn't bothered Maggie too much because she knew Ellie's love for Zack was solid. What was Mrs. Stoddard's game? Hedging her bets all around?

"What do you mean? Oh, of course. You have a little crush on Colby, don't you?"

"How—?"

"It wasn't hard to guess. Every girl in town has been after Colby at one time or other."

"What about you?" Maggie asked.

"Even me." Mabel shrugged. "I gave it up when I saw how serious he was for your sister."

"Now that he's free . . . ?"

"No . . ." She got a dreamy look on her face. "Stanley Driscoll is paying court to me. You probably don't know him, but his father owns the Driscoll Steamship line. I met him last summer when we were in Astoria."

That was indeed a perfect match for Mabel—a rich city fellow. But Maggie was surprised she hadn't heard anything but vague rumors about this. The gossip from the Sewing Circle always managed to drift down to the daughters eventually.

"I hadn't heard, Mabel," Maggie said, then added politely, "Congratulations."

"It's not official yet, and Mother wants to keep it quiet until . . . well, just for a bit." Then Mabel went on, returning to the earlier direction of the conversation. "You won't have much of a chance for Colby with Tamara around."

Maggie nodded dismally.

"And my brother won't have a chance at Tamara with Colby around."

Feeling suddenly reckless and honest, Maggie said, "I'd be happy to remove Colby from the field."

"You could, you know." Mabel gave Maggie a careful look. "All dressed up like you are, you could give Tamara some competition."

"Ah . . . no . . ."

"Honestly, you could." Mabel rubbed her chin thoughtfully. "You and Evan should join forces. Of course you would have to do the lion's share of manipulation. Men can be so dull regarding romantic matters."

"I don't like the sound of that," Maggie said. "I'm no good at it, for one thing. I tried when Zack was the minister, and I failed miserably. I'm glad I failed because he and my sister belong together, but still, I know I'm not good at scheming."

"I wouldn't call it *scheming*. But if opportunities were *encouraged* for Evan and Tamara to be together and likewise for you and Colby, what is wrong with that? It's just like giving nature a little push."

"How well does your brother know Tamara?" Maggie asked, growing uncomfortable with Mabel's suggestions, though intrigued at the same time.

"Her family went to Boston last spring, as did we, for the Harvard graduation. Apparently the Brennans had visited their son in Boston on a few other occasions. Evan had opportunity at these times to socialize with Tamara, because he and Tamara's brother, being from the same state and all, had become friends. Poor Evan was besotted with her but too shy to do more than bask in her presence."

"Did she give him any encouragement?"

"They were friendly to each other, but she was being courted by a man at home. My brother must not have made a strong enough case for himself, for she became engaged to this other man upon returning to Portland. It didn't last. I haven't been able to ferret out the reason, but the engagement was broken off. When Evan found this out, he gave up all his Boston prospects and hurried home."

"Does he realize the mothers are trying to match Colby and Tamara?"

"I'm sure he does, but if you haven't noticed, Evan isn't what I would call an aggressive sort. Nor has he the kind of charms that would woo a girl from the likes of Colby."

Maggie thought about the clumsy, average-looking fellow who had dumped punch on her dress and had to agree. "I suppose he could use some help."

"Do give it some thought, Maggie. You could benefit, as well."

Maggie wondered what was in it for Mabel to see these matches succeed but could only discern that she truly wanted to see her brother happy with the woman of his dreams.

"We best get back to the party," Maggie added. She wasn't ready to make a commitment.

Back in the Parker parlor Maggie kept thinking about her conversation with Mabel and grew more and more intrigued. As they were leaving for the evening, she thought of a way to get to know Evan better and perhaps search him out about these matters.

"Evan, may I speak with you sometime about a friend of mine who is having some legal problems?" she asked.

His momentary hesitancy concerned her, but then he replied, "Yes, of course. I could come by your house sometime, if that would be convenient."

"Thank you. How about tomorrow?"

"I have some family obligations, visiting some relatives and such who couldn't make it tonight. I will be gone several days to Scappoose and Columbia City. Would sometime next week work?"

"That would be fine." Maggie tried to hide her impatience with waiting, but she couldn't very well badger the man. She also remembered that her family had received a letter from Mama's mother that morning. She would be arriving on Monday, and Maggie shouldn't make other plans until Grandma had been here at least a day or two. "How about after lunch on Wednesday, then?"

Giving his spectacles a push up the bridge of his nose, he said, "I will look forward to it."

Maggie wondered what she was getting herself into. Could she really maneuver, or as Mabel put it, "give nature a little push," in this situation? Tamara was obviously not interested in Evan, since she had spent very little time with him all evening. And Evan appeared helpless to rectify the matter. Could Maggie help him? It seemed she had no other choice. Though Tamara hadn't been with Evan, she *had* all but monopolized Colby.

# FOUR

There were other things in life besides husband hunting. Maggie knew that while she had lately been spending an embarrassing amount of time on just that, she'd been putting off something far more important, and now she must rectify the oversight.

She had to visit Tommy Donnelly in jail. Dad didn't like the idea. He'd never had a high opinion of Tommy. He only saw that Tommy had picked up many bad habits from his father. Dad couldn't see, as Maggie did, that Tommy had a good heart and wanted to do right. The fact that he'd returned to Maintown after first fleeing following the death of his father proved his good intentions. Maggie only hoped it didn't get him hanged.

Zack mentioned as they were leaving Evan's party that he had the next day, Saturday, off work at the sawmill. He said it would be a good time to go see Tommy, which they had been talking about doing for some time.

Maggie told her parents about her plan to visit Tommy when they got home from the party last night. Since Mama supported Maggie's plan, Dad agreed, as long as she didn't go alone. She quickly informed them that Zack had agreed to accompany her. She would rather have Zack's company than her father's because Zack knew her secret and he was Tommy's friend. Ellie asked if she could come along.

"Not because I don't trust you with my fiancé," she had added quickly. "I just need some things in town."

Maggie laughed. "I was hoping you'd come. It'll be fun."

The next morning, before Zack came, Mama almost wavered in her encouragement of the visit. Tommy's mother might be Mama's best friend, but she still didn't like the idea of Maggie visiting the jail.

However, when Mama voiced her doubts, Maggie reminded her of Grandma Spooner's visit in a couple of days and pointed out that the flour bin was getting low. That got Mama thinking of all the other things they would need for Grandma's stay. Now the trip to town became imperative, for Mama had a long list to fill.

It had been a long time since they had seen Grandma Spooner. She lived over in Deer Island, practically on the other side of the county. She had said in her letter that she regretted missing Ellie's quilting bee, and though Ellie's wedding was months away, she hoped she could help out with preparations for it and for Boyd's wedding, as well, which was next month. Besides, she wanted to meet Ellie's fiancé.

"But she's already met Zack," Maggie said. He'd been the minister of Grandma's church in Deer Island, after all.

"She knows Reverend Locklin," Mama said. "Now she wants to get to know *Zack*."

Maggie didn't think there was that much difference between the two, but she knew some folks disagreed. Though most liked Zack as much as they had liked Reverend Locklin, there were still many who thought he had to prove himself. He had, after all, pretended to be a minister, deceiving them for months.

Grandma added in her letter that she wouldn't be able to wait for a reply to her letter because her friends, the Busfields, were going to visit their daughter in Bachelor Flat and had offered her a ride, since Maintown was not far away from their daughter's place. They planned to arrive Monday in the late afternoon.

Maggie didn't know why Mama was in such a dither over the visit. Grandma Spooner was not the critical type, unlike Grandmother Newcomb, Dad's mother. Grandma Spooner wouldn't care if the house was clean or if the larders were full. Mama was probably just excited.

Zack came early. Maggie was a little groggy after being out late at the Parkers' the night before, but she was excited, as well, not so much about seeing Tommy—that made her a bit nervous—but the outing with Zack and Ellie would be fun.

The morning started off cloudy and chilly. Maggie feared rain might interfere with their plans, but the clouds had dispersed a little by the time Mama fed Zack breakfast. Dad threw a canvas tarp into the back of the buckboard, just in case. At least they could cover their purchases. As for the passengers, well, they were Oregonians and weren't afraid of a little moisture. There were a few sprinkles during the six-mile drive to St. Helens but not enough to deter their plans.

Rain was the least of Maggie's worries as they neared town, and nerves assailed her. Would Tommy hate her for waiting so long to see him? Zack had visited him a few times and tried to assure her that Tommy held nothing against her. What would she say to him? As friends they had fished together, hunted together, swam in the pond, hiked over the countryside. But they had never *visited* each other. And most of the things they had done never involved much talking. Tommy was, well, rather a simple-minded boy. Most of the kids in school called him far worse than that—*dummy, bonehead, moron* were among the kinder names. He'd never done well in school, probably couldn't read beyond the first primer. Same with all the other subjects. Maggie had first befriended him when Mrs. Donnelly had asked her to help him with arithmetic in third grade. He never could get long division or fractions.

Tommy was not a refined conversationalist. The few times he talked to Maggie about anything of consequence, he complained about his father. Tom Donnelly was a drunken, ill-tempered layabout. He regularly beat Tommy and ridiculed him. It seemed Tommy could only please his father when he drank with him and shirked responsibilities. No wonder Tommy got such a bad reputation, but he had only been desperately trying to please his father.

Zack parked the wagon in front of Dolman's General Store, where Ellie went to begin the shopping. Since she didn't know Tommy that well and her presence might make him uncomfortable, she'd shop instead. Maggie was glad that Zack had agreed to go with her to the jail. She not only wanted his company during the visit but hoped that his presence would give her courage should the sheriff be there and think to question her.

Thankfully, only the deputy was present, and he wasn't interested in asking questions. He led Maggie and Zack back to the cells—he didn't even bother to search them first! He did take a look under the covered basket Maggie held, and his eyes glinted at the sight of the plump muffins Mama had baked for Tommy.

Tommy jumped up from where he'd been lying on his cot when he saw his friends.

"Hey, Maggie, Zack!" he said, clearly thrilled to see them.

"Now, you remember who brung your friends in when you open that there basket," the deputy said.

"What basket?" Tommy asked.

"Mama made you some muffins." Maggie held out the basket.

Tommy grinned. "Thank you very much." He glanced at the deputy. "Come on back later, Chet, and I'll give you one. Mrs. Newcomb is the best cook ever, 'sides my mama, that is."

The deputy let the visitors into Tommy's cell and locked the door behind them. With an apologetic shrug he said, "I gotta lock it." Then he shuffled away.

The other cells, three in all, were empty. St. Helens was a fairly peaceful town.

There was one chair in the cell, and this Tommy offered to Maggie, doing his best to be a proper host. He and Zack sat on the cot, which sagged with their weight.

"Maggie, I am mighty happy to see you," Tommy said, "but I sure don't like seein' a well-brung-up lady like you coming to a place like this. You know, a jailhouse and all."

Maggie laughed, relaxing a bit seeing that Tommy was still the same old Tommy. "Whatever gave you the fool idea I was a lady?"

" 'Course you are! Ain't she, Zack?"

"Yes, she is," Zack agreed. "But she is also your friend and is concerned about you."

"I'm sorry I didn't come sooner, Tommy."

"I didn't expect it. Like I said, this ain't no place for a lady, even one who wears overalls."

"How are you doing?" she asked.

"It ain't so bad. They feed me real good. The food comes from Welton's boardinghouse, and that Mrs. Welton is a fine cook." Tommy scrunched up his face in thought, as though wanting to give a thorough reply. "It's mostly bein' cooped up inside that's hard. And I get fearsome bored. Chet plays checkers and cards with me—he owes me five dollars, but I told him it's just for fun, and he don't have to pay me."

Maggie imagined how someone with Tommy's limited interests could be bored absolutely silly in this situation. If she were in jail, she could read and even sew if it got really bad. Everything that interested Tommy was outside.

"Have they set a date for your trial?" Zack asked.

"They said the next time the circuit judge comes through. He was here last week, but my lawyer still weren't here from Portland yet, so they had to put it off. I still don't like my mama spendin' so much on a fancy city lawyer. But Mr. Cranston has a bad touch of ague and ain't up to a trial."

Mr. Earl Cranston was the only lawyer in the county, and even Maggie knew he wasn't someone into whose hands you'd want to place your life. He spent too much time in the local saloons, so it was a blessing he was sick. Maggie wondered, however, if there was more to his reluctance to take Tommy's case. Maybe he didn't want to fight a losing battle. That worried her. She thought of Evan with his law degree from a fancy school. Maybe he would agree to help, but she decided not to say anything to Tommy, so as not to raise his hopes.

"Your mother can afford it," Zack said, "so don't you worry."

"Yeah, ain't that somethin'? Who'd a thought my pa had stashed away so much cash while we lived like poor folks?" He shook his head, looking bemused, then his eyes hardened. "I ain't sorry he's gone."

"That may be so, Tommy," Zack said, lowering his voice and looking to the door that led from the office to the cells, "and no one has a right to blame you for feeling that way. But

Chet gets bored and has a habit of eavesdropping, so it might be prudent to not say things like that before your trial."

"Prudent?" asked Tommy. "What's that?"

"Smart," explained Maggie. "It means the smart thing is to be careful what you say. Folks who don't know you like we do might take it wrong."

"I should lie, then?"

"No. Don't lie about anything," Zack replied. "But . . ." He glanced at Maggie. Apparently he was perplexed about how to explain the fine line between lying and simply not incriminating oneself. "Look, Tommy," Zack went on when he saw Maggie couldn't help him, "don't talk to anyone about your pa or what happened to him—except to your lawyer when he comes. Mr. Werth will know what to do and who to talk to."

"I guess I can do that. I don't care to talk much about it anyway."

Taking that cue, Maggie launched into a report of Maintown news. She told about the various visitors. Tommy didn't remember much about Evan, except that he was real smart. Thus, with Zack's help, she managed to fill the next half hour with conversation. She hated to admit it, but she was relieved when the deputy came in to say their time was up. She hugged Tommy and Zack shook his hand; then they were led back into the office. Maggie wasn't thrilled to see that the sheriff had returned and was seated at his desk.

"Good morning, Mr. Hartley," said Sheriff Haynes. He cast a critical glance at Maggie. "I don't like to have children come into my jail," he added sternly.

"I'm not a child!" exclaimed Maggie, momentarily forgetting her trepidation.

With more of a voice of reason, Zack added, "I'm sorry, Sheriff, but Maggie is eighteen, not really a child."

"Does your father know you have come here?"

"Yes . . . sir," Maggie replied, finally remembering her manners and the fact that she didn't want to give this man any reason to question her further.

Zack asked, "Sheriff, do you know why Tommy's lawyer hasn't come to see him? His mother and I went to Portland two weeks ago to speak with him and hire him."

"Haven't heard a word from him. Our backwater town is probably low on his list of priorities."

"Well, it isn't right that Tommy should languish away in jail waiting on the sluggish wheels of justice. I see no reason why you can't release him into my custody until the trial starts."

"You see no reason, Mr. Hartley?" Haynes's tone was laced in sarcasm. "Only a few weeks ago, you came very close to getting arrested yourself. Perhaps you've forgotten that you are no longer the respected circuit preacher."

Maggie wanted to rise up in defense of her friend, but as awful as the sheriff's words were, they were true. She couldn't argue against them, but she could offer an alternative.

"My father could take custody of Tommy," she said.

Haynes arched a brow. "Your family is closer to Tommy than I thought."

Maggie gulped. Now she was in for it.

"Well, it doesn't matter," the sheriff added quickly. "Tommy ran once. I won't risk his running again."

Maggie and Zack wasted no more time there. They were both anxious to get away from the sheriff, Maggie for her secret, and Zack probably because he feared the man might find a reason to arrest him after all.

They found Ellie in Dolman's. Everything on Mama's list had been carried out to the wagon, and now Ellie was looking through some of Mr. Dolman's catalogues.

"Maggie, I have to show you something," she said excitedly as they entered the store. "Zack, you can't look. Okay?"

He smiled. "I'll just go out to the wagon and see that everything is secured."

When he was gone, Ellie opened one of the catalogues to a page of wedding gowns. She poked her finger at one in particular. "That's it. That's the gown I want."

"It's really beautiful," Maggie said, trying to make her enthusiasm equal her sister's. She was, in fact, glad to have something to take her mind off the trip to the jail. "Do you think Mama will let you buy a store-bought dress?" She saw that the price was thirty-five dollars and fifty cents! That was more than a month's wages at the sawmill.

"Of course not, and I wouldn't ask for something so extravagant. But Mama can surely make a pattern from this picture, and if not, Grandma definitely can. Mr. Dolman said this catalog will be replaced with a new one in a few weeks and I can have it after that. Until then, I've made a sketch to show Mama."

"Wow, Ellie!" Maggie said, her voice slightly rough with emotion. "You are really getting married! I'm going to miss you."

"It's not as if I'll be leaving Maintown."

"But everything will change."

"It won't be long before you'll be married, too." But Ellie looked a little uncertain herself, as if the excitement of *getting* married had made her forget what *being* married meant.

Maggie was worried they both might start to cry right there, so she quickly added, "Have you found me a bridesmaid dress?"

Ellie flipped over a page in the catalog. "What about this? Perhaps in pink?"

"Ellie, you really wouldn't make me wear something so frilly!" Maggie forgot her previous melancholy. "It looks as if they used every inch of lace in the country to make it."

"Oh, but my heart is set on it," Ellie beseeched.

"Well . . ."

Ellie burst out laughing. "Even I wouldn't wear that dress," she said between giggles.

Maggie gave her sister a playful punch in the arm. "I guess you got me good."

"It doesn't happen often. Your mind must be elsewhere. Oh! That reminds me. I have a thought about—"

Just then Zack poked his head into the store. "You ladies about ready?"

They were in the buckboard and headed home when Ellie returned to the thought she had left incomplete earlier. "Maggie, I was thinking about what you said last night, you know, about how you'll never get around Mrs. Stoddard to get to Colby—"

"Ellie!" Maggie gave a quick, uncomfortable glance in Zack's direction. She and Zack could talk about a lot of things, but never about her romantic troubles.

"Zack already knows about you and Colby," Ellie stated matter-of-factly. "I didn't think you'd mind. Zack and I talk about everything."

"She didn't have to say much," put in Zack. "It's pretty obvious how you nearly melt when he's around."

Maggie groaned. "I suppose everyone knows! Even Colby. I'm such a fool."

"Only those who know you well can tell," Ellie said. "It's really not that obvious." She gave a sideways glance at Zack.

"Not at all," Zack recanted, but rather lamely. "I could tell only because I already knew."

With a shrug Maggie asked, "So what were you thinking, Ellie? I obviously need every bit of help I can get."

"There is one thing that will surely impress Mrs. Stoddard—your sewing ability."

"I'm doomed, then. If you and Mama couldn't teach me, then it is impossible."

"You are forgetting the one person who can teach you to sew if no one else can—Grandma Spooner." Ellie grinned triumphantly, as if it solved everything.

"I don't know . . ."

"She'll be able to teach you. I know," Ellie said.

"What if I'm just a sewing dunce?"

"You have never learned because you were never properly motivated. You never cared about learning. You've got some motivation now, don't you think?"

"Maybe." Visions leaped into Maggie's mind of her making a fabulous quilt of fancy laid-on work with tiny stitches that would make one cross-eyed trying to find them. She saw Mrs. Stoddard's eyes light up with admiration, immediately nudging her son into Maggie's arms. The fantasy was enough to raise her hopes a little. "Do you really think so?"

"Yes, and I think it is meant to be with Grandma coming now."

"Does Tamara Brennan sew?" Maggie asked, though she was pretty sure of the answer.

Ellie replied honestly. "We learned needlepoint at Mrs. Dubois', and she was very accomplished at that."

"I'll never be able to learn before she gets her clutches into Colby."

"You've got to try."

"I guess it wouldn't hurt to ask Grandma."

# FIVE

Mama probably didn't like the fact that she was a younger image of her mother, just as Maggie wasn't thrilled when everyone also told her that she, Maggie, was exactly like her mama. It wasn't that Maggie didn't love and admire her mother and even aspire to many of her finer qualities, but like anyone else, she wanted her own identity, wanted to be unique. Not to mention the fact that she and Mama were constantly butting heads. Could it be they argued so much *because* they were alike? Had Mama and Grandma argued a lot when Mama was younger? They seemed to get on well now.

"Maggie, you are being unusually pensive," Grandma said.

"Huh?" Maggie replied, pulling her thoughts back to focus on the activity in the Newcomb kitchen. She was just in time to catch her mother casting a peculiar glance in Grandma's direction, like an unspoken signal or something she hadn't intended for Maggie to see. What was that all about?

"Goodness! I am so happy to be here." Grandma reached across the table and patted Maggie's hand. "I have missed my grandchildren."

"Too bad I'm the only one around right now," Maggie said. Grandma had arrived that afternoon. Not knowing exactly when Grandma would come, Ellie had run into Maintown to get thread at the general store. She would be home soon. Boyd was working up at the lumber camp and wouldn't be home until Saturday. Dad was out in the field harvesting their potatoes, and Georgie was helping him—Maggie would have been there, too, except Mama thought there ought to be some kind of welcoming committee to greet Grandma. So it was just Mama and Maggie on hand for Grandma's arrival.

"I am going to make it a point to spend some *alone* time with each one of you this visit." Grandma Spooner was the kind of grandmother whose statement like that didn't make you cringe. Maggie had always enjoyed her company. And, now that she thought about it, if Mama was like Grandma and Maggie was like Mama, then it stood to reason that Maggie was also like Grandma. That wasn't such a bad thing after all.

But Maggie sure didn't feel like Grandma, who was kind, thoughtful, and even serene. She always said the right thing, was never selfish, and, of course, was very skilled in all the womanly pursuits. Maggie wondered what the woman had been like when she was younger. Had she argued with her mother about things? Had she felt out of step with other girls her age? And clumsy with boys? Surely not.

"Grandma," Maggie ventured, "since that's what you'd like to do, may I suggest something you and I might do?" She suddenly felt shy and awkward. If she continued, both the older women at the table would question her motives, and it would be embarrassing to explain.

"Of course."

Maggie forged ahead. "Well, I was wondering if . . . well, if—that is, if there is time. I mean, there probably won't be, and I would understand. In fact . . ." Her resolve crumbled with each word. "I know there won't be, time, that is. It would take forever—"

"Why don't you let me decide if there is time?" Grandma said. "Tell me what you'd like to do."

"Maggie, I have never known you to be so tongue-tied," put in Mama.

Now there definitely were going to be questions. Maggie rolled her eyes at her own stupidity. But she made herself go on. "Okay, I-I'd like you to teach me to sew," she finished in a rush.

"I'd love to," Grandma enthused.

Mama opened her mouth to speak, but Grandma shot her a glance, kind of an unspoken signal as Mama had done earlier, but this was also like a mother hushing her child. Mama clamped her mouth shut. It was almost as if they already knew Maggie's motives, but they couldn't possibly know. Only Ellie and Zack knew about Colby. Mama may have guessed, but she couldn't have said anything to Grandma. They hadn't been alone since her arrival.

Maggie was relieved there wasn't going to be an interrogation about her request. She had feared Mama might take offense at Maggie's going over her head to get help from Grandma. But maybe she understood that Maggie's case was hopeless enough to warrant outside help.

Before they had a chance to discuss Maggie's request further, Ellie returned from town, Dad and Georgie came in from working in the fields, and the house was full of bustle. Grandma fit into it all very easily, as if she had always been there. Indeed, Mama would love nothing more than to have Grandma come live with them, but she feared if that happened Grandmother Newcomb would want the same arrangement, or at the least she'd have her feelings hurt by being left out. The irony was that Grandmother and Granddad Newcomb would have jumped at the chance to live with their son and his family, while Grandma Spooner steadfastly insisted on keeping her own home. Mama had once said, when she didn't think anyone was listening, that Mother Newcomb only wanted to live with them in order to make Mama's life miserable.

When dinner was cleared away and the dishes done, Grandma sat at the kitchen table and asked Maggie to join her.

"Shall we talk a bit about your request to learn to sew?" Grandma asked.

"What do you mean?" Maggie was suspicious. Now the questions would come.

"I just want to get an idea of what you want to learn, of where you'd like to start."

"From the beginning, I guess."

"I don't think we have to go that far back, do you?"

Maggie glanced over at her mother seated in her rocking chair by the hearth, a sewing project in her hands, her concentration on her work. She didn't appear to be listening to the conversation at the table.

"Mama has tried hard to teach me," Maggie said, just in case her mother *was* listening. "I probably know the basics, but I never paid close attention."

"Who's to say you will pay attention now?"

"Ellie said I would because I am more motivated."

"That is a good start. It will certainly make a difference. May I ask why you are more motivated now than you were before?"

That, of course, was the very question Maggie didn't want to answer. But maybe she should be honest, get it all out in the open. It was still no less embarrassing. Perhaps a version of the truth would suffice.

"I am all grown-up, Grandma. I am going to have a home and family soon. It is just time I learned, don't you think?"

Grandma smiled, a small smile, more a twitch at the corners of her mouth. It was as if she was restraining a big grin so Maggie wouldn't feel silly.

"Would you like to make clothing, or knit—"

"I want to make a quilt," Maggie replied emphatically. "Not some simple nine-patch, either, but something spectacular. A Feathered Star or Mariner's Compass or Rose of Sharon."

"Eventually, yes."

"I need to make it now, before you leave!"

Maggie heard a noise by the hearth, and her head jerked in that direction. Mama was looking at her. She *had* been listening. But she quickly glanced away, and Maggie chose to ignore the moment, as well.

Now Grandma made no pretense of a smile, instead letting one bend her lips unrestrained, showing the gold tooth she had in front. "There is one thing a teacher loves, and that's an enthusiastic student!"

Ellie strolled over to the table. "My first quilt was a four-patch."

"You were five," Maggie said.

"No matter a person's age," Grandma said, "you simply can't get ahead of yourself, Maggie. If you bite off more than you can chew, you could become discouraged and give up."

"I won't give up, Grandma." Maggie's tone was full of solemn determination. She was grateful Grandma didn't smile this time but took her words seriously.

"Why don't we take a look at some of your previous work?" Grandma suggested. "Then I can get an idea of where you are in your skills."

"I don't know if I can find anything right off," Maggie hedged. In truth, she didn't know where any of her unfinished projects were, and she certainly had no *finished* things to show. Usually she would start something, then get frustrated or bored and toss it aside, eventually losing track of the thing.

Mama quietly rose from her chair and went to the chest in a corner of the front room where she kept special things. Her wedding gown was in that chest, each of her children's christening gowns, a few photographs, and a couple of quilts that had been passed to her from her grandmother. She lifted out a fabric-covered box and carried it over to the table. Opening the lid she took out some items Maggie recognized.

"Those are mine?" Maggie half questioned, though she knew the answer.

"I kept everything," Mama said.

Maggie was amazed that when she had thoughtlessly cast something aside, her mother had found it, rescued it, and stored it away. Mama proceeded to spread out several quilt blocks that were in various stages of completion. A nine-patch, with only eight patches; a Log Cabin with several logs missing; a Bird in the Air block that Maggie must have tackled when she felt unusually confident because it is a tricky pattern of triangles. She had only done a couple, and those were crooked and puckered. There was half a doll quilt of which Maggie had only completed four patches. She hadn't even been able to finish something as simple as that.

When Mama had emptied the box, Maggie saw that the things were not just from when she was young. One block, a Churn dash, had been started about a year ago. Not only was the sewing bad in this, but the cut pieces were skewed, throwing off the entire block.

"Oh, Mama," lamented Maggie, "please put them away! I'm so embarrassed!"

"I didn't mean to embarrass you, dear," Mama said. "Anyway, you are among family. No one is going to judge you."

Maggie couldn't resist a quick glance at Ellie.

"I won't judge you," Ellie said earnestly.

"It is still embarrassing." She glanced again at the pile of lopsided, catawampus, puckered attempts at stitchery. Even she knew she could have done at least a little better, especially on that most recent piece. She just hadn't cared to. "I'm hopeless, aren't I?" she asked, even though she knew what they would answer. Maybe she was looking for an escape. Maybe she wasn't as motivated as she thought. Yet when an image of Colby leaped into her mind, her resolve strengthened. She just had to win him.

Gritting her teeth, she added, "Okay, where do we start?"

"It is a bit late to start tonight," Grandma said.

"Oh, I can do it. I'm wide awake," insisted Maggie.

"But your grandmother has been traveling all day," Mama said.

"We need to be fresh for this," added Grandma. "We will start in the morning after breakfast."

They didn't start right after breakfast the next day, for all the morning chores had to be done first, but finally Grandma called Maggie to the table. Maggie had thought she would dread this moment but was surprised to realize she had actually been anticipating it.

Grandma's sewing basket, which she always brought with her when she visited, sat on the table. She also brought a box of scraps that she could trade with Mama.

"I wish I had known we were going to do this," Grandma said, "because there are a few other things I would have packed, but we will make do. Come and sit down, Maggie."

As Maggie took a chair, Ellie wandered over to the table. Maggie glanced in her direction.

"Ellie," Grandma said, "I know you are interested in this, but you won't mind if Maggie and I do this alone, will you? It might make Maggie nervous to have someone looking on."

"I guess not," Ellie replied.

"We will do something together, you and I, later."

Mama called Ellie into the kitchen to help with the laundry, which had been put off on Monday because of Grandma's arrival.

Grandma turned to Maggie. "Now, this is the template we will work with." She picked up a cardboard piece, about four inches square, that she had taken from Mama's pattern box. "We are going to start with a nine-patch—"

"But, Grandma—"

"Now, Maggie, if this is going to succeed, you must promise you won't argue with every instruction I give—"

"But—"

"What do you say, dear?" Her tone was gentle but firm. Of course Grandma knew Maggie's propensity for debate and was trying to nip that in the bud.

"Okay," Maggie said, trying not to pout. She was an adult and must act like it if her grandmother was going to take her seriously.

"You may think a nine-patch is simplistic," Grandma went on. "But I have seen many quilts made with only the nine-patch that are stunning because of the placement of light and dark fabrics. The same is true of the Log Cabin block."

Maggie's brow creased, but she tried hard not to protest. However, she knew a nine-patch would not impress Mrs. Stoddard.

"Don't worry," Grandma assured, almost as if she had read Maggie's thoughts. "We will only do one nine-patch. That will be the first block in the sampler we will make. Each block will teach you a new skill and will be progressively more difficult."

"Can I pick the fabrics? I mean, the colors that I like?"

"Of course. What would you pick?"

"Red, mostly, but also green—but I don't want it to look like Christmas. Maybe blue—but not so it looks like a Fourth of July bunting."

"You could have different colors in each block but with some red in all to unify it. Let's take a look in the scrap box to see what we have."

They brought over both Mama's and Grandma's scrap boxes. There weren't many scraps of red in them, much to Maggie's disappointment, but she was able to pull out several other colors that were plentiful enough and that she would like to use in the nine-patch. Much to her surprise many of these were browns and golds. She hadn't thought of using these with red but found she liked the combination very much. As she and Grandma were spreading the pieces of fabric on the table and checking them against the template to make sure they would fit, Mama went to her sewing cupboard. Maggie's jaw nearly dropped when she brought over a length of red calico material.

"I bought this a while ago," Mama said. "I thought I might use it but just haven't gotten around to it. If you like it . . ."

"Like it? It's perfect!" Maggie exclaimed, almost, but not quite, speechless about her mother's offering. It was a Turkey red cloth with tiny gold and brown flowers on it. "This accents the colors I've chosen perfectly."

"That is exactly the best way to choose colors for a quilt," Grandma said. "Use one fabric you love and draw your color palette from it."

"Palette? Like an artist uses?" Maggie asked.

"Exactly. I have seen many quilts that are truly pieces of art."

"Zack has said just that," interjected Ellie, "when he saw some quilts. He compared them to works by famous artists like Leonardo da Vinci."

For a fleeting moment Maggie thought of creating a masterpiece like one she remembered Grandma had done of appliquéd vines and leaves and flowers surrounding a medallion of a large basket of flowers. Or like either of the wedding quilts Mama had made for her and Ellie. But she forced herself back to reality. If she could just *finish* a quilt and have it halfway presentable, it would be a great accomplishment for her. That would have to be enough to impress Emma Jean Stoddard.

"Mama," Maggie said, remembering herself, "thank you so much for the fabric. I hope I don't mangle it up too much."

"You will make a beautiful quilt, Maggie. I know it."

Mama looked a lot more confident than Maggie felt.

# SIX

Maggie tried to hurry through her sewing lesson the next morning so she could finish her chores before Evan arrived. But her grandmother scolded her and questioned her dedication, especially after she'd had to rip out her nine-patch three times.

"I know you can do better, Maggie," Grandma said, her patience stretched nearly to its limit. "I thought you *wanted* to do better. I'll let this work pass if you are satisfied with it."

But Maggie knew this was mock leniency and that her grandmother expected her to reject the work. She looked at the puckered, crooked stitches and sighed. Her chances with Colby were slimmer than ever, so her stitching might be all that stood between her and happiness. With resignation she picked out the stitches.

"Follow the line we drew on the square," Grandma reminded Maggie.

"You have been in a hurry all morning," Mama put in. "Are you going someplace?"

Maggie had purposely not said anything about Evan's visit because she wasn't certain how her mother would respond.

Mama had never had a problem with Mabel Parker or even with Mr. Parker, but then, Maggie and Ellie had never been close to Mabel, and Dad was not a close friend of Nathan Parker. Therefore, little socializing had taken place between the families. But more than that, Maggie didn't want to answer any questions Evan's visit might raise. Nevertheless, she probably should say something before her silence was perceived as suspicious.

"Didn't I tell you?" Maggie said as casually as she could. "Evan Parker is stopping by later. I wanted to talk to him about Tommy's legal case."

Mama set down the dish she was drying and picked up another. "Why would you want to do that?" There was a slight edge to her tone.

"Well, I think it could be handled better. Do you know his lawyer from Portland hasn't even come to see him yet?" As Maggie spoke, she realized this visit with Evan was a good idea for more than one reason. Maybe he really could help Tommy.

"Do you think that is your place?" Mama asked, but it wasn't really a question. "Isn't it Mrs. Donnelly's concern?"

"I thought it would be best to talk to Evan first. If he can't help, then it won't raise Mrs. Donnelly's hopes."

"Well, I guess if you have already invited Evan, it can't be helped. But just remember, Maggie, Tommy may be your friend, but it would not be appropriate for you to get too involved in these matters."

"Ouch!" Maggie had been trying to talk while she sewed and now stabbed her finger with the needle. "This is hopeless!" she grumbled, tossing the nine-patch onto the table.

Grandma picked it up, turned it over, and examined it. "This is actually very nice, Maggie," she said of the new stitches. "Don't give up so easily."

Appreciating the encouragement, Maggie took the item back in hand and looked at the seam she'd just sewed. It did look rather good with straight, even stitches. She only had seven more patches to go to finish the block! At this rate she and Evan could say good-bye to happiness with the mate of their dreams. They would probably be stuck with each other. But she was making progress, so maybe there was some hope yet.

Maggie laid the next patch against the ones she had just finished to make a row. She knotted her thread and, with intently pursed lips, began sewing again. In the background Mama was putting away the breakfast dishes and humming a little tune. Grandma was working on her own sewing, a six-inch patch consisting of a curved piece in blue, topped by a muslin piece. It was a pattern she called Drunkard's Path. Maggie could hear a dog barking outside. She thought Gypsy had gone with Dad to the potato field. Normally, she would rather be outside playing with the dog or following some other more active pursuit. Today was Ellie's turn to help Dad. They were giving Maggie some leeway for her sewing lesson, which only proved where Mama's priority was and how much influence she wielded in the family. Maggie would have to help Dad later, though.

It surprised Maggie to find she was rather content at the moment sitting in the kitchen, listening to the common household sounds, and sewing her patchwork.

"Maggie," Grandma said, "did I ever tell you the story of how your grandfather and I got together?" When Maggie nodded, a little bemused because of course she had heard this story, Grandma added, "I mean the whole story?"

"Well, you and Grandpa grew up together. You and his family were close friends, and the two of you did everything together," Maggie replied.

"Yes, that is part of it, but there is more that I haven't shared because I thought it would be more suitable to do so when you were older."

"Grandma, don't tell me it's risqué!"

Grandma laughed. "Hardly that. Do you want to hear about it?"

"Of course," Maggie said eagerly. In her youth she had always thought family stories were so boring, but she was grown up now and before long would have children of her own to whom she would want to pass on these stories.

"Well," Mama put in, "I have heard this, so if you don't mind, I have to sweep the porch and water some plants."

When Mama was gone, Grandma continued, "You are right that your grandfather and I were playmates, almost like a brother and sister. I certainly never imagined having romantic feelings toward him. In fact, when I was about sixteen I set my cap for another, a boy named Raymond. But I did so for all the wrong reasons. You see, his mother had made a beautiful quilt that was laid-on work in a pattern of flower wreaths. To this day I have not seen the like, it was so fabulous. She said it would go to her son's bride. I wanted to be that bride so I could get that quilt."

"Grandma, how shocking!" Maggie said, half teasing but also truly a little shocked that her grandmother could ever have been so frivolous.

"Most girls in my day did not marry for love, Maggie. Many marriages were arranged by their parents for economic reasons. It wasn't as shocking as it might seem to you for me to seek a man for whom I felt nothing."

"For a quilt?" Maggie thought of all the hullabaloo this last summer with the girls thinking a quilt could win the minister. Maybe Grandma's story wasn't so farfetched.

"You should have seen that quilt." Grandma smiled and seemed to be looking at it in her mind's eye. "And Raymond was not opposed to my advances. I could have won him, if I do say so myself."

"What happened, then?"

"One day your grandfather and I were out in the field picking berries. I happened to glance at him. He was popping a nice juicy berry into his mouth, which was already stained purple because he was eating far more than he was putting into his bucket. My heart started racing. Grandpa always said later it might just have been an attack of the vapors, but I know differently. I saw him as if for the first time and was smitten with what I saw, stained lips and all. I thought the feeling would go away. I *hoped* it would because I still wanted that quilt, but even I knew I couldn't marry one man when I was falling in love with another."

"What made you suddenly fall in love with Grandpa?"

"I had begun to think that if I married Raymond, I would not be able to continue being friends with your grandfather. A married woman could not associate with another man in that way, and I knew my heart would break if I had to give up Joey."

Maggie had never heard her grandfather Joseph called Joey. It made her really able to think of her grandparents as youngsters.

"I knew," Grandma added, "that was the kind of love that was worth a hundred quilts."

"That's a nice story, Grandma," Maggie said. She thought a moment and added, "What is the moral to the story?" She knew Grandma's stories almost always had deeper meanings.

"Oh, I don't know. Maybe that life doesn't always turn out as you think it will."

Maggie glanced out the kitchen window and saw Mama busily sweeping the porch. "Can I tell you something, Grandma? Please don't say anything to Mama or she might get all in a dither. She has been a little touchy about some things since all the business with the fake minister."

"You mean matters of romance?"

"Yes, that's it exactly. She seems okay with Zack and Ellie—we all love Zack. But . . . I don't know. Mama doesn't talk a lot about it, which is odd for her."

"Yes, that is odd. So you are afraid of sharing your romantic notions with her?"

"I don't want to upset her. That's all."

"If I thought you were doing yourself harm, I would certainly have to tell your mother," Grandma said, reasonably enough.

Maggie thought her grandma's and mother's ideas of what was harmful might be different from her own. Still, Maggie knew these quilting lessons were, or could be, for a far greater purpose than simply learning to quilt. Grandma had a bounty of wisdom that even Maggie should not take lightly.

"This isn't anything harmful," Maggie replied confidently. "It is just that I want to win a fellow, and I know I first have to win over his mother because she pretty much rules the roost at his house. He's a very manly man, don't get me wrong, but she would probably be able to rule even the president of the United States."

"Must be Emma Jean Stoddard's boy." When Maggie's jaw dropped, Grandma added with a chuckle, "Well, she does fit your description. And even I have noticed over the years how moon-eyed you are around Colby."

With a disgusted snort, Maggie said, "Everyone seems to know how I feel but Colby himself."

"Oh, men are so blind in such matters."

"Is it bad to try to win the mother in order to get the son?"

"I see no reason why. Sooner or later a girl is going to have to win over her future mother-in-law or live to regret it."

"Like Mama?"

"Your mother never had a chance with Agnes Newcomb. That woman was not going to like any woman who married her sons. It is the same with your Uncle Martin's wife." Martin was Maggie's dad's brother.

"You get along with Aunt Silvia's husband." Silvia was Mama's older sister who lived in Rainier.

"It is different with daughters. I had a bit of a problem with Uncle Homer's wife. But we eventually worked it all out and now get along fine. I think mothers have a harder time letting go of their sons because they resemble their husbands. That is all I can think anyway." Pausing thoughtfully, Grandma went on, "Your mother does love Kendra, your brother's intended. No doubt she has learned from the strife with her own mother-in-law."

Maybe Grandma saw that Maggie was starting to lose interest now that the conversation had veered from her own problem, because she added after a moment, "So Maggie, I think you are fine trying to impress Mrs. Stoddard. Just keep in mind that it may not be possible."

"Should I give up even trying? Maybe Colby would defy his mother's wishes—"

"I couldn't support that idea entirely," Grandma replied. "Maybe Mrs. Stoddard loves her son enough to bend her will to allow for his happiness. When a mother sees that her son loves a woman strongly enough, she is hard pressed to stand in the way of their bliss."

"Doesn't mean she won't bring in some stiff competition." Maggie got a sour look on her face as she thought of Tamara Brennan.

"At that point, even before, for that matter, the best thing is to leave it in God's hands. Though it wouldn't hurt to continue to do your best to help your own cause." Grandma's gaze fell on the sewing in Maggie's hands. "Look at that. While we have been talking, you have been sewing along very nicely. Your stitches are much improved!"

"Maybe there's hope for me after all!" Maggie exclaimed.

"I have no doubt of it," Grandma said. "And, Maggie, I don't think your mother would be upset if you shared with her all you have with me."

"Maybe so," Maggie replied noncommittally.

Maggie was enjoying her lesson and especially her conversation with Grandmother. Unfortunately, she couldn't spend all day sewing, not that she would have had the patience for it anyway. There were other chores to be done if she wanted to be ready for Evan's visit after the midday meal.

Ada watched Maggie stride out to the chicken coop. She moved with such surefooted steps. Funny how a few months ago Ada was so worried her younger daughter would never settle down to serious thoughts of marriage. Maggie had been such a tomboy of a girl that it had seemed, despite her prettiness, she would never attract the romantic interests of the young men in the community.

On the other hand, Ada had been quite sure about Ellie's prospects. All the fellows had wooed Ellie, Colby Stoddard most earnestly. Ellie was a refined young lady, especially for this backwater town. She was mature and levelheaded beyond her years. There had never been a doubt that she would make a good match.

How things had suddenly flip-flopped! Ada found she wasn't all that worried about Maggie any longer. It seemed the pieces had fallen into place for her. She was finally embracing the necessity of homemaking, and if she still enjoyed fishing and hunting and climbing trees, Ada saw no problem. She was a country girl after all.

Now it was Ellie whom Ada fretted over. Ada loved Zack as a person and even as a son. In just a few weeks since his profession of faith, he was proving to be serious and sincere about his growth as a Christian. He earnestly read his Bible and frequently asked questions. He was working hard to be honest and responsible in his choices and in seeking to right past wrongs. Why, just the other day he had asked Ada her advice about seeking out his own mother. Zack had left home when he was twelve years old and never attempted to keep in touch. His mother must have worried terribly about her son, never knowing if he was alive or dead. No wonder Zack wasn't sure she would care to see him after he had neglected her for so many years. Ada had assured him that, as a mother herself, she was confident his mother would be deeply thrilled to hear from him.

Yet she still could not shake her discontent over her daughter's choice of a mate. Would it be terrible not to be heartbroken if the marriage plans fell through? She felt like a most evil woman for such thoughts. If only Zack had better prospects and wasn't so much in debt. She wished they would wait at least until summer before marriage and had hinted at this to Ellie, but thus far her daughter seemed determined to forge ahead with the December wedding. That was less than four months away.

Ada didn't want to be like some members of the community who were taking it slowly in accepting Zack back into their good graces. That was their right, for he had duped all of them. Yet Ada truly believed Zack's heart was pure in its intent toward God. She felt he deserved her full forgiveness.

Ada propped the broom against the back door and went inside. Wednesday was bread-making day, and her mother had begun the task, a job Ada was happy to let her take over, since she made the best bread. Ada brought over the large basket of mending and sat at the table. The large window above the sink provided nice light for the task. She picked up one of Calvin's shirts that had a large hole in the elbow. My goodness, that man was hard on clothes! There was always a good deal of mending. They couldn't afford to buy new shirts every time one was torn. That's the way all country folk were. Frugality was simply inborn. Even Florence Parker, with all their money, did mending, though Ada had seen some of her rags and probably would not have discarded them into the rag box so soon.

This line of thought made her remember what she had been mulling over earlier.

"Mama, what do you think of Zack?" she asked. Ada's mother had had a chance to get to know Zack a little better, because he had been to supper both evenings since her arrival.

"He's a nice young man. I am especially impressed how his faith has grown."

"He is quite sincere about it," Ada said. "He has become like a member of the family."

"I can see that. Calvin seems especially taken with him."

Ada nodded. That fact only made Ada's reservations even more puzzling. Calvin was usually such a good judge of character. Ada hated questioning that.

"Mama, do you think . . ." Ada hesitated, then gave her head a shake. "Never mind."

"You must have doubts about the young man," her mother said.

"I hope it isn't that obvious. I don't have doubts about him. I am quite fond of him. It is just that . . . I worry about his prospects. I worry about his ability to provide for Ellie. Is that terrible?" She glanced toward the stairs and then remembered Ellie was out in the fields with Calvin. She would not want her daughter to overhear this conversation.

"What does Ellie think of these doubts?"

"I am reluctant to speak to her about them. She is so happy, and they are so much in love." Ada's hands moved deftly over her work as she spoke. "I have encouraged my children to make their own choices in these matters. I know Ellie well enough, and if I interfere, she may act in order to please me instead of following her heart."

"You and I both know that a girl will most likely follow her own heart, even an obedient child like Ellie." Mama Spooner's hand paused as it stirred the bread dough. A thoughtful look creased her brow.

Ada wondered if she was thinking of when Ada had been a girl and in her own romantic quandary.

"But more than that, Ada, you must trust that God is directing Ellie. The hardest thing for me as a parent was to remember that my children had their own relationship with God and that God was speaking to them quite apart from me. Ellie has a stronger faith than many children."

"I appreciate your reminding me of that. A mother spends years as the center of her children's lives, directing them, even—dare I say?—controlling them. It is very hard to step out of the picture."

"If it were me, I'd be more worried about Maggie than Ellie."

"Truly?" Ada frowned. She didn't like to think she'd been mistaken about both of her daughters. "Did she say something to you?"

"She did say some things in confidence. Nothing to raise a huge alarm, but still I fear she may be hurt by her romantic pursuits."

"How so?"

Mama Spooner dumped the dough out on a floured board. "By setting her sights on the wrong young man."

"Do you mean Colby Stoddard?" Mama frowned again. "He has always been a childhood infatuation of hers, but I don't see the harm in her pursuing him. He's a good man, if a bit wild. Of course, I wouldn't envy Maggie having Emma Jean for a mother-in-law."

Mama Spooner shrugged as she gently kneaded the heel of her hand into the dough. "You know better than I do. I haven't seen the lad in a year."

Ada laughed. "If I am supposed to know better than you, Mama, I am in trouble."

# SEVEN

Maggie had about an hour to clean out the chicken coop before the midday meal. She wished she had given Evan a more specific time than "after lunch." Would he come at one o'clock, or two? Most of the farm families had their big meal of the day around that time. But the Parkers were not farmers anymore, so they practiced the city schedule of having what they called luncheon between twelve and one.

Well, she would eat quickly to make sure she had enough time to clean up and change before the visit. Besides her determination to learn to sew, Maggie was also trying to improve her appearance. No overalls except to work around the farm—well, she might also wear them for fishing or hiking in the woods. But for receiving guests, she intended to dress like a proper lady.

As she walked out to the coop she noticed a flash of black and white dart out from behind the barn.

"What're you doing here, Bob?" she mused, then called, "Hey, Bob." It was the Donnellys' dog. That must have been the dog she'd heard barking earlier. When the animal loped up to her, she reached down and ruffled its shaggy head. "What're you doing so far from home? You bored?" Zack was helping Dad and Georgie and Ellie with the potato harvest, and Mrs. Donnelly was probably busy in the house. "I'll bet you are missing Tommy, aren't you? I wish I could play with you, but I have work to do. Gypsy is off with the men in the field. You ought to go find them."

The dog was jumping around too excitedly to listen. Finally Maggie found a stick and tossed it. Bob raced after it, giving her a moment to get inside the chicken yard. When Bob came up to the gate, gripping the stick between his teeth, Maggie felt sorry for him. She couldn't open the gate because he wasn't as well-trained as Gypsy to be trusted around the chickens.

"Okay, I'll play with you as soon as I finish in here," she promised. "But only for a minute. I have a busy day today."

Bob, of course, made Maggie think of Tommy. She ought to go visit him again. She also would definitely see if she could enlist Evan's help. She did feel a little guilty pursuing her romantic notions while her friend languished in jail, but there really wasn't much else she could do.

Turning her attention to the chickens, she opened the door to the coop and was met with a chorus of squawking hens and crowing roosters. Though they were happy to get out of the chicken coop, they did need a little added enticement, which she provided by sprinkling feed from the coop to the enclosed yard. They fluttered down to the ground from their roosts and followed the trail into the yard. Maggie then got the wheelbarrow, pitchfork, and shovel and proceeded with the messy task of cleaning the coop.

Both she and the chickens were making so much noise she didn't hear the sound of boots crunching over the dirt yard.

"*A-hem!*" uttered the newcomer.

Maggie started and nearly dropped the pitchfork when she looked up and saw Evan Parker standing in the door of the coop.

"What're you doing here?" she blurted in a most unsociable way.

"I—uh, thought you asked me to come," he replied.

"You're not supposed to come until after dinner."

"Are you sure? I thought you said—" Breaking off, he smiled apologetically. "I am sorry. I must have made a mistake."

"Well, it's okay, I guess," Maggie replied, regaining her manners. "I just didn't want to be all covered with hay and muck when you came."

"I don't mind. That is, I mean, you look fine. Really, I didn't expect this to be a formal visit."

But Maggie saw that he was dressed in a suit, a stylish well-fitted woolen sack jacket with only the top button closed—the current fashion—revealing a matching vest under it, both of a charcoal gray, as were the trousers. His shirt was white with a buttoned, turned-down collar, and his light gray tie barely showed under the vest. He wore a jaunty black Derby style hat, which he seemed to now remember, and he doffed it politely. He looked formal indeed for these parts, but Maggie supposed he was still dressing in Boston fashion.

Before she could say another word, the racket from the chickens rose to an almost deafening crescendo, accompanied by the barking of a dog.

"The gate!" she exclaimed, seeing it was gaping open.

Several chickens had wandered out, and Bob was gleefully chasing them around the yard. Maggie ran toward the gate.

"I'm so sorry," Evan said, joining her.

Maggie hardly heard him as she ran after the dog, waving her arms and calling his name. Right now he was having fun, but if he caught one of the chickens and killed it and got the taste of blood, it would be the end of him, because a dog that started killing the livestock would have to be shot. The dog was Tommy's constant companion, and it would devastate him if anything happened to the animal. Zack should be giving him more attention, but Maggie couldn't really blame Zack. He was working day and night to pay off his debts and save a little nest egg for his marriage.

"Come on, Bob!" Maggie called in a cajoling tone, which didn't fool the animal at all. Bob nipped at a fat hen and nearly got her.

Maggie looked around to see what Evan was doing and saw that he, too, was chasing after one of the chickens. And he was grinning, seeming to enjoy the fracas he had started by leaving the gate open. She had never seen anything more than a nervous or apologetic smile on Evan's face, but this was a full, gleeful grin, like a kid having the time of his life.

"I'll get Bob," Maggie said. "You try to get the chickens back in the pen."

Evan nodded and went for one of the chickens. But his foot came down on the stick Maggie had tossed to Bob earlier. He lost his balance and went down, spread-eagled, into the dirt. He was still grinning!

He jumped up and finally got his hands on a chicken and quickly deposited it back into the pen. Maggie grabbed the stick, thinking Bob might be enticed by another game of fetch.

"Bob, go get it!" She tossed the stick.

Bob would have none of it. He went for another hen, nipping its fluttering wing.

"What's going on out there?" Mama's voice came from the house.

"Nothing," Maggie called back. "Some chickens just got out."

"Sounds like the whole henhouse is loose."

Her guess was not far off. By now all but a couple of their fourteen hens and three roosters were out, but Evan was making headway getting them corralled once again.

Maggie went after Bob. Figuring that last time he hadn't gotten a good look at the stick, she got it again and this time waved it right in his face.

"Go get it, Bob!" She heaved the stick into the air.

Now Bob took the bait and leaped in pursuit of the stick. While he was thus engaged, Maggie hurriedly gave Evan a hand with the chickens, stopping only when Bob returned with the stick. It took about three stick tosses before they finally had all the chickens in.

Evan was still grinning.

"You enjoying yourself, Evan?" Maggie asked dryly.

He suddenly seemed self-conscious, and his grin turned nervous.

"Well . . . uh . . . there weren't any chickens to chase in Boston," he finally said.

Maggie laughed. "I guess not! But you got your pretty suit all dirty."

"Makes up for me getting your pretty party dress all wet the other evening." He gave his duds a slap with his hands, sending up a little cloud of dust.

"I didn't mind," she said.

"Neither do I—I mean about my suit. I still feel awfully bad about your dress."

"Don't give it another thought. Mama said it would be good as new once it's washed." Then she added, "I worked up a mighty thirst. Come on up to the house. I know we have some fresh buttermilk because I did the churning myself."

"My favorite," Evan said, seeming more at ease, "and nothing quenches a thirst like buttermilk."

He gave his suit a few more pats to get rid of any remaining dust, and they trooped up to the house.

They took tall, frothy glasses of buttermilk out to the porch and sat there to enjoy the cool afternoon breeze. Bob was still prancing about in the yard. Maggie supposed she would have to take him back up to the Donnelly place later.

"That's Tommy Donnelly's dog, you know," she said by way of broaching one topic of conversation she intended to discuss with Evan.

"I heard what happened to him," Evan said. "It is very sad. I kind of remember Tommy. I felt sorry for him. I guess I know what it feels like to be made fun of. The irony is, they made fun of him for being slow-witted and of me for being too smart."

"You just can't please people," Maggie said.

"It is best to be yourself and hope for the best."

"That's what you did, Evan, and it worked out okay. And I admire you for it. You went on to a big Eastern college, got high marks, and became a real success."

With a self-deprecating shrug, Evan replied, "I did in part, but looks can be a bit deceiving."

"What do you mean?"

He hesitated, then said, "I remember you were Tommy's friend, probably his only friend. You never made fun of him, or me either, for that matter."

"I never could see the point. I know I'm not perfect, so who am I to berate another?"

"I'll tell you something about myself. That is, if you'd like to hear it?"

"Of course I would."

"Well, I did very well at Harvard. I passed every theory course with flying colors. I stumbled a little over the practical elements, mock trials, that sort of thing, but it didn't detract from my standing because my arguments were all sound and compelling, even if my delivery . . . ah . . . faltered. For the most part I managed to conceal the fear I felt when I made court presentations. I passed the bar exam easily and was invited to join an important Boston law firm. I enjoyed the work until I had to appear in court. Then the fear was always there. That's why I left Boston—well, one of the reasons. I don't think I am cut out to be a lawyer."

"But you did so well in school."

"I enjoy the law, but I guess my nerves don't." Pausing, he sipped his buttermilk. "This is very good. I missed this kind of thing in Boston. Oh, they have chickens and buttermilk at farms out in the country in Massachusetts, but I wasn't around any of it. I missed home and farm life."

"Were you that happy here?" she queried. "Even though some made fun of you?"

"They were just kids—granted, the very kids I wanted to accept me." He gave an ironic smile. "The odd thing is, I never fit in much in Boston either."

Maggie nodded. "I know that feeling."

"You?" He looked truly astonished. "But the Newcomb children were always the most normal, well-rounded of all the kids. How I envied Boyd!"

"Yes, Boyd and Ellie and even Georgie are pretty normal, though I could tweak Georgie's ears sometimes. But you try being a girl who hates housework and sewing in a world where that's the only thing that matters for girls. It is every bit as bad as being the smartest kid in the county."

With seemingly sincere understanding, he said, "Yes, I can see that. You really don't like sewing or housework?"

She gave a disgusted roll of her eyes. "And you really don't like talking in front of people?"

He laughed and she cracked a smile, as well.

"Shall we discuss why you invited me here?" he asked. "I assume the friend you mentioned is Tommy Donnelly?"

"You are smart," she said wryly. "But now I hesitate to ask for your help."

"Help in what way?"

"Well, Tommy has been in jail for weeks waiting on his lawyer," Maggie replied. "His mother hired a fellow from Portland who must not think we backwater farmers are very important."

"If Tommy has engaged another lawyer, it would be improper for me to interfere."

"Would you be willing if the other lawyer was gone, I mean, fired or something?"

Evan didn't answer for a long time. Maggie could tell he was giving his response thoughtful consideration. Finally he said, "Even if I wanted to help, I already told you I doubt my competence."

"If there was a trial, you wouldn't have to get up in front of fancy Eastern people, only us common Columbia County folks. You could do that."

"I don't know . . ."

They sipped their milk in silence for a while. Maggie didn't want to pressure him.

"I have no real trial experience," he added. "To start out on a murder trial, of a young boy to boot—I don't know. . . ." He shook his head. "I just don't know. . . ."

"Listen, Evan, you have something the Portland lawyer doesn't have. You know Tommy, and you know the folks here. And I think you care a long sight more, too. That counts for a lot. Maybe it is even more important than experience and confidence." She took a breath and stopped, feeling herself getting a bit pushy. She did add, "Couldn't you at least talk to Mrs. Donnelly?"

"That wouldn't be ethical."

"Could *I* talk to her?"

"I guess I have no control over whom you talk to." There was no guile in his tone, just a statement of fact.

She liked that about him. He was so straightforward. It inspired her to be likewise.

"Evan, there is something else I wanted to talk to you about." He nodded for her to continue, but her resolve wavered as she realized she was venturing into a very delicate area. "It is a bit personal," she hedged.

"If it is too personal, I will tell you so. Okay?"

"All right, then . . . well, it is about Tamara Brennan." She waited a moment for him to stop her. His expression was unreadable except for a slight twitch at the corner of his right eye. He didn't stop her, so she continued, not confidently, but with determination. "Mabel told me that you cared for her."

"I wish she hadn't done that, but I didn't tell her in confidence," he said. "I suppose I should have known that with her penchant for gossip, she couldn't keep it quiet."

"I, too, have a secret crush on a fellow—" She stopped when she saw his brow arch in surprise and realized he might take her words wrong. "It's on Colby Stoddard," she quickly added.

"Ah . . ." he mused.

She saw he was intelligent enough to put some of her intent together. "I suppose you are aware that Colby's mother and Tamara's mother are conspiring to match them with each other."

"I guessed that at the party—and Mabel also enlightened me." He shrugged and fidgeted a bit with his spectacles. "They make a fine couple."

"So that is it? You came all the way from Boston to give up so easily?"

"Truly, Maggie, do you think I have half a chance against Colby Stoddard?"

"You are not an unsightly man." She studied him a moment and knew she could say that sincerely. While his looks weren't stunning, they were pleasant, enhanced by the strength of his character. Just in the short time they had been talking she could tell he was decent and upright.

"Maggie," Mama called from inside the house, "dinner is almost ready. Make sure you invite Evan." Her voice was unusually sweet.

Maggie looked over at Evan, who replied, "I don't want to impose . . ."

"There's always plenty," Maggie assured him.

"I'd like that, then," he said, his voice loud enough so Mama would hear.

"Very good, Evan. We are happy to have you." Mama's voice was uncharacteristically syrupy. She was probably just trying to be sure Florence Parker would hear later that she was an excellent hostess to her son.

"Mama," Maggie called, "can I help with anything?" It wouldn't hurt for Mrs. Parker to also know Mama had raised a proper daughter.

"Oh no. Grandma is here to help. You just entertain your guest."

Hearing Mama's voice made Maggie a bit self-conscious about her previous conversation with Evan. Mama wasn't prone to eavesdropping, but still, she'd feel better not seated so close to the kitchen window.

"Evan," she said, "I promised Bob I'd play 'fetch' with him. You want to join me?"

"Sounds like fun."

Maggie remembered how he appeared to be having fun chasing the chickens. She got the feeling he wasn't accustomed to having that kind of amusement.

Walking out to where Bob was now sprawled out in a patch of sunlight by the barn, Maggie asked, "You didn't much like Boston, did you?"

"At first it was exciting," he replied. "But that wore off quickly. While I had my studies to keep me occupied, I was fine, but after graduation I thought more and more about home and the farm. I'll admit I was never much of a farmer. My parents had me away at prep schools in Portland, then college, so I never could learn much of farming. And, of course, my father is a lumberman not a farmer, but I thought of the life here in general. Perhaps I romanticized it."

Maggie picked up a stick and called to the dog. "Fetch, Bob!" Bob was up in an instant, tail wagging as he raced after the stick. Maggie commented, "I think you surely did romanticize it. Farming is hard work. And constant work. Dad and Mama never seem to stop working."

"At least they are in the wholesome outdoors. In the city the air is close and fetid. Regular working folk are holed up in dim, dirty factories all day." He wrinkled his nose with his distaste. "And it is hardly much better being shut up in an office all day."

"I don't remember your being such a nature lover," Maggie said.

Bob came up with the stick, and Maggie reached to take it, but he clamped his teeth down on it and pranced before Evan. When he grasped the stick, Bob released it. Evan gave it a toss.

"Bob likes you." Maggie grinned.

"I'm not a bad sort," Evan replied with a touch of wryness in his tone.

"I know that." Maggie was completely sincere.

"And about being a nature lover," Evan added, "that is a more recent manifestation. When I was living here, that is, when I was home from school, I spent most of my time studying and reading rather than being outdoors. That was because I had few friends. It was a bit of a vicious circle—the boys made fun of me because of my studying, and I studied to protect myself from their ridicule. For that reason, I was happy to leave for school in the East. I thought it would be different there."

"Mama always says you can't run away from your problems."

Bob returned with his stick, and this time he made it clear he wanted Maggie to toss it. She complied.

"It was very brave of you to come back here after Tamara."

"Foolish, I would say."

"All is certainly not lost yet," Maggie insisted.

"Tamara broke my heart once. I was a fool to come and give her the chance to do it all over again." Evan fidgeted with his spectacles, a habit she noted he seemed to do whenever he was nervous or distressed.

"Did you propose to her in Boston?"

"I was ready to. I stupidly thought she returned my feelings."

Bob returned again and was impatiently wagging the stick in front of Evan, but Evan looked at Maggie instead.

"For someone who took top honors in school, I am quite stupid. And yet . . . she seemed to enjoy my company. I should have known all was lost when she told me she thought of me as a big brother. Maggie, don't ever tell a man that. Spit in his face first." His bitterness was clearly evident.

"I'm surprised you don't hate her."

"She didn't mean to hurt me." Pausing, he took the stick and gave it another toss. "It was just God's will. That's all. As perhaps it is His will for Tamara and Colby to be together."

"I believe in doing God's will, too, Evan," Maggie said. "But God doesn't expect us to sit on our haunches doing nothing, does He? Last school term Georgie was doing poorly in arithmetic. He told Mama it must be God's will that he made a D. Mama said it didn't mean he was going to stop studying and trying to bring up that grade. She said he wasn't going to use God's will as an excuse to quit."

"It is easier to quit and blame the results on God."

Bob brought back the stick, but they had tired of the game. Evan gave the dog a pat on the head instead, then turned to Maggie. He took off his spectacles, and she saw a determination in his eyes she hadn't noticed before.

"All right, Maggie, I'll do it," he said.

"Do what?"

"I expect you are leading up to our somehow joining forces in order to further our individual causes with Tamara and Colby."

Much to her surprise he had perceived exactly what she was thinking.

"Perhaps you are wanting me to feign romantic interest in you in order to get Colby's attention."

"Hmm . . ." Maggie mused. "I hadn't thought of that, but it wouldn't work—"

"Naturally," he quickly interjected, uncertainty once more returning to his gaze, "for who would believe I'd have a chance of winning a girl like you—"

"Evan, stop it!" Maggie exclaimed. "Stop belittling yourself like that. That sort of thing would definitely put off a girl."

"I'm sorry. I don't even realize it. I—" He gave a shrug to complete his meaning. "I don't know why I do it. Maybe I am fishing for compliments."

Sighing, Maggie went on, "I was going to say that it wouldn't work because it wouldn't help further your cause if Tamara thought you were interested in me. There are other means, however. For instance, I could befriend Tamara and build you up to her, and you could do the same with Colby."

With a harsh laugh Evan said, "I doubt I could ever be friends with Colby. He was always my chief tormentor. Though he was younger, he still had the temerity to make fun of me."

"He's changed." Maggie hardly realized how defensive her tone was.

"He must have, for you to be interested in him."

"He isn't a bad sort. Sometimes he doesn't think before speaking is all." Not wishing to keep to that vein, Maggie changed the subject. "Evan, you could help me by showing me how a real lady behaves."

"Me?" He laughed. "What do I know of such things?"

"You've been around city ladies. You know more than I or most folks around here do. Ellie knows some, but I need every bit of help possible. A man's perspective wouldn't hurt, either."

"And you'll help me be more like Colby?"

"If that's what you want."

He was not quick to respond. She couldn't understand his hesitancy. Didn't every man want to be like Colby? Maybe he realized it might be impossible. Almost as impossible as it might be for her to become a housework-loving, expert-stitching, proper lady.

# EIGHT

Ellie slipped into her bedroom, lit a lamp on a table by the window seat, and took up her sewing basket. The family was still downstairs. Their guests, Evan and Zack, had left a little while ago.

Zack had left earlier than usual. Ellie had been happy to see him but worried a bit because he looked somewhat peaked. She feared he was burning the candle at both ends. Though he boarded at the Donnellys' and helped work the farm now that Tom was dead and Tommy in jail, for the most part he only slept there when he wasn't working. When there wasn't farm work to do, he filled in at the sawmill. He had Sundays off and the occasional Saturday. Any other spare moments he spent with Ellie, taking most suppers with the Newcombs and sitting on the porch visiting in the evenings.

This evening he looked especially haggard. Last night he had spent several hours sitting with Elisha Cook's ailing mother. Ellie knew that many of the folks he had served as a pretend minister still valued his—well, she supposed it had to be called "ministrations." There was a contingent, growing more each day the denomination failed to send a replacement, that continued to think of him as their minister. Zack insisted he was only visiting as a friend and neighbor, no more. But when he and Ellie talked about it in private, he admitted to enjoying that role. Mrs. Cook had actually told him he should be a real minister now that his faith was real. Ellie had heard others express this idea, as well. Even her father supported the idea.

Ellie tried to remain neutral on the subject except to let him know he must do this for God, not to please her or anyone else. He was aware that she had once dreamed of being a minister's wife but now only dreamed of being *his* wife. She believed he truly understood this, yet worried that his desire to please her might color his ultimate decision.

Thus, with all the work, courting her, and fretting about his future, Zack was wearing himself out.

Ellie picked up her current project from her basket. It wasn't the hexagons she often worked on when she was feeling melancholy. The new project was a quilt for Maggie. Ellie had often thought she had plenty of time to make a wedding quilt for her sister, but lately she was feeling time might be shorter than she imagined. Why, it was very possible that she would "tie the knot" before Ellie and Zack. Maggie had set her sights on Colby and seemed serious about it, so things could happen very quickly. It would be sad if Maggie had no finished quilt tops in her hope chest for a quilting bee.

Ellie turned the half-completed quilt block over in her hand. Grandma had let Ellie raid her box of scraps, and so had Mama. She was using muslin in the background and for the main part a different color fabric in each block. The pattern she had selected was a design called Sister's Choice. It was a nine-patch surrounded by triangles that made it look like a star. She thought it was perfect for Maggie, not only because she was coming close to making a choice for a husband, but also because, knowing Maggie, her choice might surprise them all.

Ellie was happy and excited for Maggie, and when she imagined that she and her sister might marry and enter this new phase of their lives together, it simply thrilled her. Despite the fact that they were so different, they had always been close, and the prospect of sharing the adventure of marriage and having babies together was wonderful to look forward to.

Ellie prayed nothing would upset this dream. It wasn't Maggie who worried her as much as herself. Ellie's mind rehashed the reason Zack had left early that evening. It hadn't been entirely because he was tired. She had mentioned that he didn't need to spend so much time at her house. She enjoyed his company but not at the cost of his health. He'd taken it all wrong.

"All right, I'll go if you are bored with me," he had replied with a hurt tone.

"That's not what I said, Zack. You just look so tired—"

"Why don't you let me decide when I am tired?"

"I don't know why you are getting so touchy."

"Oh? Perhaps it is because you as much as told me to leave," he had snapped. "That really does make a fellow feel good."

She couldn't help her devastated expression.

Then he'd been sorry and tried to apologize. "I'm sorry, Ellie! Maybe I am tired, too tired to think straight. And maybe it's true what everyone says—I mean how can a girl like you continue to have patience with a man who has a dark future and few prospects?"

"What?" she'd gasped. "Who is *everyone*? Oh, never mind. I can't believe you'd think such a thing."

"Well, it's true I have nothing to offer you, and you are so much better than me—"

"Stop speaking such hogwash!" she'd cut in sharply, scolding him as Mama might scold her children.

"Maybe it is the first time I am being sensible," he said, his tone more even. "The one thing I would truly like to do is become a minister, but what kind of life is that for you? You have dreamed about it but not in a practical way, not considering the life of near poverty, the days and weeks you would be alone while I rode a circuit. Think of it, Ellie! What kind of life is that?"

"It's the perfect life if that's what God wants for us," she replied. Maybe her response was idealistic, but how could it not be the truth?

He ran a hand through his hair, sighing. "I don't know. Maybe it is just fatigue. My mind is just . . ." He let his words trail away, unable to find the words to complete his thought.

Gently, she said, "Go home, Zack. Sleep is probably all you need."

"And the one thing I can't seem to find."

Now she understood, and her heart ached for him. "Zack, know this—I fall asleep every night praying for you."

"That is what I truly need," he said. "Thank you. I suppose I will go home."

She walked him to his horse, and he gave her a hug, but she felt a distracted aspect to the embrace, as if his fears were still grasping him.

No wonder she worried that Maggie's wedding day might come before hers. It didn't help to know that Mama had reservations, too. Mama was mostly concerned about Zack's being able to support a family by Christmas. Who else had doubts? Obviously someone had been saying things to Zack to make him doubt.

Ellie welcomed the distraction from her thoughts when Maggie came in later. Ellie quickly tried to hide the work in her hand. She wanted the quilt to be a surprise.

"What's that?" Maggie, ever perceptive, asked.

"Oh, nothing."

"Looks like something new."

Ellie had to smile. "Time was you never noticed stitching. You are changing, sis." When Maggie came over to take a closer look, Ellie decided to be honest. "You can't see this," she said, tucking it under the hexagons in the basket. "It's a surprise for you, and that's all I'm going to tell you."

"For me? A quilt?"

"A wedding quilt."

Maggie chuckled. "You have a lot more confidence in my prospects than I do."

"You might beat me, Maggie."

Maggie blinked, then her brow creased. "Don't tell me you and Zack had your first fight. I thought he left kind of early this evening."

"It wasn't exactly a fight. He's worried about his future prospects and his ability to support me."

"Well, a girl's gotta eat," Maggie said flippantly. Then, when Ellie gave her a frown in response, she added, "You two will be fine because you are meant to be. You are perfect for each other. I don't care what Mama says."

"What did Mama say?"

"Oh, nothing . . . well, I overheard her talking to Grandma the other day. She worries about your having to struggle. But all mothers worry about such things."

"I suppose . . ." Ellie wanted to believe this. It was important that her parents supported her choice. She thought of something else. "Maggie, I wouldn't care if you married before me. Some have the notion the elder sister has to marry first, but I don't hold with that. You have my blessing—"

"Whoa!" Maggie exclaimed. "Let's not get the cart before the horse. First I have to snag the man, and that won't be so easy. Which reminds me, I spoke to Evan today, and he's going to help me—you know, he wants Tamara, so if we join forces, we each might have half a chance."

Ellie listened as Maggie chattered about her big plans to win Colby. She had reservations about all this maneuvering, but Ellie was also happy to immerse herself in her sister's love life so as not to fret so much over her own.

# NINE

The next day Maggie made Ellie go with her to the Stoddards'. She remembered accompanying Ellie on a few visits to "Reverend Locklin" back when they were trying to woo the minister. So Ellie owed Maggie, though Ellie was happy to help anyway.

Maggie wasn't exactly certain what she expected from this visit. She was starting to feel a little uncomfortable about it.

"Evan Parker seems like a nice fellow, doesn't he?" Ellie said as they walked down the road on their way to the Stoddards'.

"Yes, he is. We had a nice talk." She had told Ellie all about their conversation.

"I'm still surprised he agreed to help in breaking up Colby and Tamara—"

"They are not even together!" Maggie broke in defensively. "They are not engaged or even courting. So there is nothing to break up. I wish you would support me for once!"

"I was supporting you before it got so complicated." Ellie paused.

Maggie wanted to say something to interrupt her train of thought, but just as she opened her mouth, Ellie went on.

"Maggie, I won't be a party to deception."

"Now you are going to be Miss Goody-Two-Shoes!" Maggie said disdainfully.

"I would hope you would have some moral fiber in this matter, as well."

Oh, how Maggie hated it when her sister got so high and mighty. She hated it more when Ellie was right. "I am not going to be deceptive," Maggie assured her sister, her ire dampened by her own conscience. "It is only natural that we pay a visit to welcome Tamara. Mama even suggested it."

"After you brought it up."

"Still, it is the neighborly thing to do."

"I don't want you to pretend to be friends with Tamara just to undermine her."

That statement, spoken with a superior tone, as if Ellie was her mother, sent Maggie's ire soaring once more. "If you don't have the stomach for this, then you can go back home!"

"Maggie . . ." Ellie beseeched.

As usual, Maggie needed her big sister's approval. And she truly did not want to be deceptive. "I'm not going to pretend," she appeased. "She seems like a nice girl that I could easily be friends with."

"I think you should tell her right off about your interest in Colby."

Maggie gasped. "I couldn't!"

"What would it hurt? Maybe she would put aside any designs she might have on Colby."

"Why would she do that?" Maggie argued. "And what of Mrs. Stoddard's designs? Once she learns of my interest in her son, she will think me a brazen hussy."

"Hardly. She might even like the idea of Colby matching with a local girl."

Maggie replied with a skeptical sidelong look.

"Okay," Ellie conceded. "You might not want it to get back to Mrs. Stoddard, but couldn't you get Tamara alone and tell her in confidence? Even if she chooses not to step aside, you will have been honest."

"This is not one of those times when honesty is the best policy," Maggie insisted. She knew Ellie's intractable moral sensibilities might have a difficult time with that idea, but Maggie believed you could be quiet about something and not be deceptive. "I don't care if Tamara steps aside or not. My main intent is merely to present Evan in a good light to her. That wouldn't be deceptive because I think he is a fine person. She just needs to realize that the brotherly affection she felt for him is more than that, like how Grandma realized it about Grandpa."

"Okay, Maggie, I'll go along," Ellie said. "And if I see things get out of hand, I will say something."

"I can always count on you to be my conscience," Maggie said sarcastically.

They reached the Stoddards', and Sarah welcomed them at the door. They weren't expected, but visits were always welcome in the little community. Mrs. Stoddard, Sarah, and Tamara were busy at work in the kitchen. Three bushels of apples were sitting on the floor, and Sarah and Tamara were paring and coring them while Mrs. Stoddard was slicing them up to place on drying racks. Ellie and Maggie offered their help and were immediately given paring knives.

"We haven't got our apples yet," Ellie said, "but Mama warned us we will be busy next week."

"Soon as this batch is done," Mrs. Stoddard suggested, "we will do some apple butter."

"You do make the best apple butter, Mrs. Stoddard," Maggie put in. She didn't care if it was shameless flattery. No one but Ellie would guess.

"I have so enjoyed all the domestic chores since I've come here," Tamara said. "I have never dried an apple or cooked hardly anything."

"Never cooked?" Maggie asked, clearly astonished. "What do you do with yourself all day in Portland?"

"Maggie, don't be rude," reproved Mrs. Stoddard, as if she were Maggie's mother.

"That's all right," Tamara replied. "She has a right to be surprised. It does sound terribly lazy, and I am rather ashamed."

"You have many other talents, my dear," Mrs. Stoddard said.

"Tamara is an accomplished pianist," Sarah put in meekly. "She is also an excellent violinist."

"Really?" Maggie knew she couldn't compete with that because she could barely carry a tune much less play a musical instrument. "Do you stitch?" Maggie held her breath waiting for the dreaded answer.

"I do a little needlepoint. My mother says all refined ladies should be handy with a needle. I don't make quilts like Mrs. Stoddard and Sarah. They have shown me some of their work, and I am simply in awe. I practice my music all the time, so there is little left for other pleasures."

Maggie searched Tamara's tone for signs of bragging or arrogance but found none. "My grandmother is helping me refine my stitching," she said. It was time she sang her own praises, though they be few, just so Mrs. Stoddard would know what she was up to.

"Sarah began learning to stitch when she was five and was quite accomplished by age nine," boasted Mrs. Stoddard.

Maggie shrank down in her chair. Maybe her grandmother was right, and it was impossible to please some people.

"Maybe I could learn with you," Tamara said enthusiastically. Then she added quickly, "I'm sorry, I didn't mean to be presumptuous."

"Maggie, isn't that a wonderful idea?" Ellie agreed, much to Maggie's surprise. "I'm sure Grandma wouldn't mind."

Part of Maggie thought this would play into her scheme perfectly, but another part, taking her by surprise, was reluctant to share her time with Grandmother. Also, her stitching, such as it was, appeared to be her only edge over Tamara. If Tamara learned to sew, and no doubt she would excel at it, Maggie's hopes would be diminished that much more. What had Ellie been thinking in encouraging this? Surely she wasn't trying to sabotage Maggie. But now that the subject was raised, Maggie would appear ungracious if she rejected Tamara's request.

"I'll mention it to my grandmother," Maggie said, but she couldn't quite match Ellie's enthusiasm.

Mrs. Stoddard actually offered, though unwittingly, a reprieve for Maggie. "If I had known you were interested in learning to stitch, Tamara, I would have offered to teach you myself."

"That is kind of you, Mrs. Stoddard, but you have done so much for me already. And you are so busy with your household duties, especially with Mr. Stoddard taken ill lately. I wouldn't want to impose further. I thought since Maggie's grandmother was already teaching and might have more time on her hands while she is visiting . . . but maybe it is a bad idea."

"My feelings would not be wounded if you sought out Mrs. Spooner's expertise. She is quite an adept stitcher and could teach you much," Mrs. Stoddard said.

Groaning inwardly, Maggie didn't think the afternoon could get worse after that, but it did when Mrs. Stoddard sorted through a bowl of sliced apples both Ellie and Maggie had filled.

"Girls, I don't know how your mother likes it," she scolded, "but I like my apples sliced thinner, please." She was holding in her hand several that Maggie had done. And Maggie had the feeling they all knew it was she and not Ellie who had cut those apples.

When the apples were done, Mrs. Stoddard suggested the girls go into the parlor and listen to Tamara play her violin. Colby came in just then from working outside, and Mrs. Stoddard herded him into the parlor, as well. Tamara acted embarrassed at being on display like this, but once she started playing, she seemed to forget that and became caught up in the music. She cajoled Sarah to accompany her on the piano so that she wouldn't be the lone performer.

Maggie was bored with it and glanced over at Colby. She was gratified to see a very bored look on his face, too.

When Tamara finished, Maggie patted the divan where she was seated with Ellie. "Colby, come sit. You must be dog-tired after working all day."

"I'm too dirty to sit on Mother's good furniture," he said.

He looked rather rakish and certainly handsome standing with an arm propped up on the mantel. Even in patched dungarees he took Maggie's breath away.

"In any case," he went on, "I must leave you ladies to your visiting. I came in for only a moment to bring Mother some potatoes for supper. Tamara, thank you for the entertainment."

"You are so welcome, Colby," Tamara said. "But you have no doubt gotten your fill of music these last few days."

"We can use more culture around here," he said.

"Tamara," Sarah asked, "can you show me once more how to hold the bow?" Apparently Tamara was teaching Sarah to play. Sarah was already an excellent pianist, but she loved music and Maggie guessed it was a kind of escape for her, as books often were for Maggie.

"Good afternoon, ladies," Colby said as he exited. A chorus of parting words followed him.

While Sarah and Tamara were engaged in examining the violin, with Ellie observing them, Maggie waited a few moments and then slipped out of the parlor. She exited the house by the front door so Mrs. Stoddard wouldn't see her and found Colby striding across the yard.

"Colby!" she called. Hurrying over to him, she racked her brain to think of a reason for waylaying him. It had been purely an impulsive action, and she only knew she had to use any chance she could to get near him.

He turned and her heart fluttered. This must be love!

"Hi, Maggie," he said with a dazzling smile. "Did you have to escape the boredom?"

"Yes, sort of," she replied. "What do people see in that kind of music? Give me a guitar and fiddle anytime."

"Toe-tapping music!"

She grinned, knowing in her heart that she and Colby were meant to be. "You must be bored to distraction having Tamara and her music around all the time."

"Mother has talked about buying a violin so Tamara and Sarah can play all the time. Where she'll find the money for it, I don't know." His expression dimmed momentarily. "But Tamara isn't such a bad sort to be around when you get rid of the music."

"Really?" Maggie's heart began to sink.

"Don't you like her?"

"I hardly know her, but she seems nice." Not liking the direction of their conversation and having come up with a reason for following him, she added, "I'll bet even Tamara would enjoy the kind of music we had at the quilting party last week."

"I sure did."

Was he thinking about how he and Maggie had danced together? Encouraged, she went on, "We are going to have another party next Saturday. I wanted to make sure you knew."

"I'll be there. But you have to promise me a dance."

She was ready to promise him her life, but with as much aplomb as she could muster, she replied, "Of course I will, Colby."

# TEN

Maggie was hard pressed at supper that night to talk her mother into holding another quilting party. She mentioned that Kendra had quilts to be quilted before her wedding.

"Two parties in one month!" Mama had exclaimed. "You'd think this was some big city."

"I'll help with everything, Mama," Maggie said.

"I'll help, too," put in Ellie.

Maggie was surprised at this. She had expected Ellie to be opposed to the idea. She was so contrary lately.

Finally Grandma said, "I'll be here to help, as well. It sounds like fun. I was so disappointed to miss Ellie's party."

In the end Mama agreed to talk it over with Nessa at the Sewing Circle on Sunday.

When supper was finished and the dishes cleared, Zack and Ellie went outside to sit on the porch. Maggie joined them, as was often her habit. She had slipped into the role of chaperone when the couple wanted to be alone. Maggie's presence satisfied Mama and Dad, and Zack and Ellie were fairly at ease with Maggie around. It was a suitable arrangement for all except perhaps

Maggie, who didn't much like having to pretend to be invisible while Zack and Ellie talked, sharing all the sweet nothings couples usually share. Maggie didn't complain because it did indicate her parents trusted her and, at least in this instance, perceived her as an adult.

Tonight, however, Zack and Ellie were quieter than usual. There seemed to be some tension in the air. She'd missed sitting with them last night because she'd been entertaining Evan. Now she wondered if they had had an argument of some sort and thought they might appreciate it if she broke the ice. "Ellie, thank you for offering to help with the party."

"I do think there should be a quilting for Kendra. She is going to be married first. She may have only three or four tops done, but I know she will appreciate getting them quilted before her wedding. Mrs. Wallard is probably too shy to mention it."

Maggie was disappointed Ellie hadn't said anything about the real purpose of the party. She'd hoped her sister was finally on her side. Ellie had been understandably surprised when Maggie had announced the party to the girls at the Stoddard house after returning from going after Colby. But she had not said anything about it on their walk home.

"Do you still think I am trying to be deceptive?" Maggie asked bluntly.

"I don't know," Ellie answered evasively. "But you only want to have the party in order to get close to Colby. You don't really care about Kendra."

"That's not true!" Maggie retorted. "Kendra is going to be my sister-in-law, and I do care about her. Maybe she, at least, will support me once in a while."

Then Zack asked, "What's wrong with having a party?"

Ellie looked at him sharply, perhaps perceiving his words as unsupportive toward her. "You of all people, Zack, should see how manipulating people never works out."

"This is different from what I did," Zack replied, his tone a little tense.

Though Maggie knew there had been some bumps lately in Zack and Ellie's road to happiness, she had not believed it anything serious. She certainly had never heard them have an argument. She wasn't pleased to think she'd started one now, so she jumped in, trying to soothe their ruffled feathers. "Maybe Ellie is right. I didn't think it would hurt anything, though."

"Did you know that in England," Zack said, "the upper classes have something they call the 'Season.' For several months each year parties or balls are held almost every day to allow young women to 'come out' to society. The purpose is to provide opportunities for the girls to find husbands. It is too bad that the girls here have to resort to more illusive means."

"I imagine that even in England the young people must resort to subtlety in these matters," Ellie said. "As in the case when two girls want the same man."

"That is a fact of life, Ellie," Zack stated, as if he'd just won the argument. "Romance is often a path fraught with twists and turns. Even someone as straightforward as you, Ellie, didn't have a completely unfettered path in your quest for a husband."

"I haven't a husband yet," she said solemnly. Then her frosty expression melted, and she smiled. "Oh, I guess you are right. I just hate to think someone might get hurt—especially you, Mags."

"That's what I love about you, Ellie," Zack exclaimed. "You have the tenderest heart I have ever seen."

Maggie took the cue of Zack's moon-faced expression to melt into the shadows.

Later, after Zack had gone home, Maggie's sense of vindication prompted her to broach another prickly topic.

"Ellie, why did you support Tamara's interest in learning to sew?" Seeing that her sister might take this as a challenge, she quickly added, "I really want to know because I value your opinion."

"Well, when Tamara brought it up, I saw it as a perfect way for you to get to know her better."

"My first thought was that I might lose my only edge over her," Maggie said.

"I honestly didn't think of that," Ellie replied.

Maggie knew that was true and inwardly repented of her thought that Ellie had some evil ulterior motive. Zack was right. Ellie had a tender heart and did not have an evil bone in her body. Perhaps there was indeed some higher reason behind the whole idea of Tamara learning to sew. Perhaps God's hand was in it, and Maggie ought to just let it happen and see where it led. Ellie was far more sensitive to godly matters than Maggie.

So Maggie asked her grandmother about it, and she said she'd be happy to teach Tamara.

Maggie had other business to take care of the following afternoon. She was beginning to feel like a juggler she'd once seen at a fair. He had been juggling china dinner plates, five all at once, in the air. Mama had been appalled at how careless he was being with the fine china, but Maggie had been fascinated and a little disappointed when all the plates didn't eventually crash to the ground. She wasn't so certain she would have as good success in her own dealings.

At least her trek to Mrs. Donnelly's place had been successful. Mrs. Donnelly had not considered the idea of asking Evan to represent Tommy, but it seemed a good suggestion to her. She was growing quite impatient with the Portland lawyer. She immediately sat down and wrote a letter, releasing the Portland man from his contract and including some money in the envelope to pay for any services rendered. Then she asked Maggie to join her when she went into Maintown to pay a visit to Evan.

Evan seemed surprised to see them pull up to the Parker home in the wagon. Maybe he had not believed anything would come of Maggie's suggestion. But she would not forget about Tommy, no matter what.

As they sat in the parlor, Evan was still reluctant to take the case. "Mrs. Donnelly, I must tell you I am completely inexperienced with murder trials. I never seriously considered taking on criminal cases in a law practice. I leaned more toward business matters, contracts, that sort of thing."

"Now, Evan," put in Mrs. Parker, who had joined them, "don't depreciate yourself. You passed all your courses with flying colors."

"Then you did learn about criminal law in school?" Mrs. Donnelly asked.

"He most certainly did," answered Mrs. Parker. "The Boston firm that wants to employ him was very impressed with his credentials. When he returns to Boston to take up that position, I have no doubt he will rise to great heights."

"You can't be anxious for him to leave," commented Mrs. Donnelly.

"I'm not, of course," Mrs. Parker replied. "But it is a sacrifice I am willing to make for my son's advancement."

"Yes . . . well . . . um . . ." Evan said, clearing his throat delicately, obviously unsettled by his mother's words. "In any case, Mrs. Donnelly, while my marks were good, litigation was not my . . . ah . . . forte."

"But you *know* the law?"

"Yes." There was self-doubt in his response. "I know the theory of law quite well."

"Will you defend my son to the best of your ability?"

"If I took the case, I would." Now his voice held confidence.

"I should like to hire you, then."

"You should give it a few days to ensure your lawyer receives the letter of release."

"I hate to wait that long," Mrs. Donnelly said. She had been holding up well during the visit, but now her lips trembled. "Tommy dearly hates to be locked up. It has been so long already. I would go into Portland myself, but it is the middle of harvest, and even though my neighbors are helping out, I need to be at the farm."

"I will go into Portland and speak with your lawyer—Mr. Werth, isn't it?" Evan asked.

"You would do that?" Tears welled up in Mrs. Donnelly's eyes.

"A good lawyer does everything he can for his clients."

"Then you will take Tommy's case?"

"I will." Evan looked a little surprised himself about his decision.

Mrs. Donnelly took both his hands into hers. "Thank you so much!" She gave Evan the letter she had yet to post so that he could deliver it to Portland personally.

When Mrs. Donnelly was ready to take her leave, Maggie told her to go on ahead, for she wanted to speak with Evan a moment longer.

Sensing perhaps this would not be a conversation they would wish to have in the parlor with his mother near, Evan suggested they take a walk. "I am in need of exercise," he said for his mother's benefit.

Maggie noted mother and son exchange a look that implied deeper meaning.

"Now, Evan," Mrs. Parker said, "you needn't worry about your lack of industry. This is a vacation for you before you return to your real work in Boston."

"I still need exercise for the sake of a fit constitution," Evan rejoined.

"Oh, you are too young to worry about such things, but take your walk, if you must." Mrs. Parker rose and then turned to Maggie. "I should get back to my sewing. Maggie, you must tell your mother that I am almost finished piecing an entire quilt top on my new sewing machine. I hope to bring it to the Sewing Circle on Sunday to show."

"I'll tell her, Mrs. Parker." But Maggie would do no such thing. The last thing she wanted was to get in between the two rivals.

She and Evan went outside. Maggie had been so busy that day she'd barely noticed what a fine September day it was. It was the middle of the month and summer was still holding on, but leaves were already starting to turn on some of the trees.

Evan suggested he walk her home, so they headed in that direction, taking a shortcut from the edge of town, where the Parker house was located, over a back road that wound between the Briggs' place and the Lamberts' farm.

"I might do Mrs. Donnelly more good if I helped her with her farm," Evan commented.

"I didn't think you were much of a farmer."

"And I never will be if my parents have their way," he replied with emotion. "They are appalled that I would even consider giving up the law. They won't let me work at the mill. My father is probably the only man on earth who is less than thrilled at the prospect of his son following him in business. Mother continues to hang on to the hope that I'll return to the influential Boston job."

"They put a lot into your education and don't want to see it wasted."

"Maggie, I just took upon myself a case in which a young man's life is in my hands. I don't know if I am up to the challenge."

"You are, Evan."

"How do you know? You don't even know me."

"I think Mrs. Donnelly saw, as I do, that there is more to you than meets the eye and more than you want others to see. You can't let yourself be stopped by fear."

"I'd guess you have never been afraid of anything in your life." He arched a brow when she started to protest.

She shrugged. "I don't think about it much. Maybe that's your problem. You think about things so much you get worked up into a lather over it."

"Yes, that describes me to a tee." He chuckled wryly. "Maggie, why don't you help me with the trial?"

"Me? What could I do?"

"In the Boston law office there were clerks who did research and other kinds of footwork required during a trial. I clerked there during my schooling. If there is one thing I am sure about, it is that I will need a clerk for this case."

"Could I do that and still be a witness?"

"Why would you be a witness?"

Maggie realized she might have said too much. She had not thought whether or not she would reveal to Evan what Tommy had told her before his father's death. Maybe she should worry more about things like Evan did. Perhaps then she wouldn't be caught by surprise.

"Well," she replied, "to witness as a friend. To tell people what a good person Tommy is."

"A character witness," he said. "I will have those, but I wouldn't call a young woman unless absolutely necessary."

She might have argued the point. She was slightly insulted that because she was a young woman her testimony might not be valued. But she decided to accept it as a reprieve for now, though she would soon have to make up her mind about what exactly to tell Evan about Tommy.

Changing the subject seemed her safest move. "Evan, I wanted to tell you that we are going to have a party next Saturday. And this one will be fun—I mean . . ." She fumbled, realizing the implied insult of her words. The last party had been at his house. "That is, there will be dancing. You and Tamara can dance, and Colby and I—" She stopped upon seeing he'd suddenly gone pale. "What's wrong?"

"I can't go!" he blurted, almost desperately.

"What do you mean? I'm planning this party for us, for our causes, you know."

"It doesn't matter if I'm not there, does it?" He fumbled with his spectacles, nearly knocking them off his face.

"Yes, it does matter. You have to be there. You will keep Tamara occupied while I keep Colby occupied. Don't you get it?" She couldn't help the sarcasm in her tone. Was she pinning her hopes on a dullard?

He let out a sharp, frustrated breath. "I can't dance!" he admitted.

Somehow his statement didn't really surprise her. "There must have been parties in Boston. What did you do then?"

"I didn't go."

"Even when Tamara was there?"

"There were a couple parties when she came to visit. I . . . uh . . . managed to find some excuse or other to bow out. Once I feigned an injured foot."

"No wonder she didn't fall passionately in love with you! She probably thought you didn't want to dance with her. That tends to put a girl off."

"So would crushing her delicate toes under mine."

She nodded with a wry smile. "Yes, I can see your point. Well, I'll just have to teach you to dance."

"In one day?"

"The party isn't tomorrow," Maggie said patiently. "It is *next* Saturday."

He gave her a look that meant, "So what does it matter?"

"Even you can learn to dance in a week," she said confidently.

# ELEVEN

The next day, Tamara came to the Newcombs' for her sewing lesson. She was dressed prettily in a day dress of pink, printed with little red flowers. It was nice enough to be a party dress. And Maggie was in overalls! She had completely forgotten her resolve to dress for company, but then she hadn't really considered this a company occasion. If she dressed for Tamara's visits, she was going to have to dress up all the time!

Maggie had finished her nine-patch block. The browns and golds she'd chosen complemented the red nicely. The block had turned out well. It was actually square! And no puckers, either.

Would Tamara begin her lesson with a nine-patch? If so, Maggie was ahead of her right from the start. She tried to convince herself this wasn't a competition, but it was hard not to think of it in that way. Grandma did tell Tamara her first block would be a nine-patch. She asked Maggie to show hers, and Tamara was very complimentary of it.

"What will I do next, Grandma?" Maggie asked.

"A log cabin."

Maggie groaned. She had been hoping to finally do something more intricate.

"The log cabin may seem easy," Grandma explained, "but this is a pattern in which you must sew a very uniform seam. Because the log cabin has so many pieces, any variation will show. You must learn to make a uniform quarter-inch seam before you move on to more intricate patterns."

"I love your colors, Maggie," Tamara said. "Mrs. Stoddard let me choose some of her scraps to use in my project."

"Let's see them," Maggie said.

Maggie wasn't surprised when Tamara took from her basket some fabrics in pastel colors—pink, lavender, pale blue, buttery yellow, all very feminine.

"You are welcome to look in my scrap box, as well," Mama offered, calling from the kitchen, where she was washing up after breakfast. Usually Mama left during the sewing lessons, but no doubt she was staying around to be sociable toward Tamara.

"This is very exciting," Grandma said. "You are both going to make the same quilt, but since you are using such different colors, they will each be unique."

"The same quilt?" Maggie couldn't help the disappointment in her voice. It was bad enough that she'd been roped into sharing her sewing lessons; now there would be nothing special about her quilt.

"Trust me, Maggie," Grandma assured her, "they will look like two completely different quilts. And, as you become more proficient, perhaps I will let you choose different blocks that more suit your tastes. How is that?"

Maggie nodded, not entirely convinced but determined to stick with her promise not to argue. When Grandma made her next suggestion, that Maggie actually teach Tamara the nine-patch, Maggie just shrugged and accepted her fate. Grandma said teaching others was the best way to learn.

They chatted while they sewed, just like the women in Mama's Sewing Circle.

"I understand you are from Portland, Tamara," Grandma said.

"Yes. My father is a doctor."

"And what do you enjoy doing besides sewing?"

"I hope I will enjoy sewing," Tamara replied. "I've only done some needlepoint. I keep busy practicing my music."

"You should hear her, Grandma," Maggie said. "She plays the violin really well. I mean, as far as I can tell. I don't know much about music. And she plays the piano. But no one around here plays the violin like she does."

"Mrs. Stoddard says she is saving for one for Sarah," Tamara said. "Sarah excelled in piano at school—ouch!" Tamara had stuck her finger with her needle. Maggie couldn't help feeling just a little gratified by this.

"You should have chosen red like me," Maggie said lightly, "then the blood won't show as much!"

Tamara laughed. "I hadn't thought of that."

"Just remember that your saliva will get your own blood out if you dab it on quickly," Grandma suggested.

"Ick!" said Maggie and Tamara together.

It was not long after that incident that Maggie realized she was actually enjoying the session, enjoying Tamara's company. Tamara wasn't some rich snob, which was how Maggie had wanted to perceive her. She was a nice person. Maggie wondered if she should be honest with her about Colby. Well, she wasn't ready to do that just yet, but she'd give it some thought.

Grandma asked Tamara how she happened to be visiting the Stoddards.

"Sarah and I attended finishing school together," Tamara answered.

"Ellie was also in their class," put in Maggie.

"But our parents were friends before that. Mr. Stoddard grew up in Portland and attended school with my father. So here I am." Pausing, Tamara concentrated on her work for a moment, then went on, "I guess the main reason I've come is because my mother thought I needed a change of scene after . . . after my engagement ended."

"I'm so sorry, dear," Grandma said.

"I suppose it wasn't meant to be." Tamara sighed.

"Did you decide you weren't ready to get married?" asked Maggie.

"Not actually." Tamara hesitated, then added, "He jilted me."

"How awful!" Maggie exclaimed. And she truly meant it. It was a sad thing to happen even to a rival.

"I keep trying to tell myself that it was God's will."

"And it surely is," said Grandma, "but that still doesn't prevent it from breaking your heart. It will get easier. How long ago did it happen?"

"I went to Boston last spring for my brother's graduation from Harvard. When I returned home, I learned Jeffery had found someone else. I guess he realized he didn't miss me as much as he should."

"What a cad!" Maggie said.

"Now, Maggie," said Grandma, "Tamara may still have feelings for the young man."

"But he was terrible—" Maggie started to protest. Then she realized how advantageous it might be to her if Tamara did still love this fellow. Yet she wouldn't wish even her worst enemy to be matched with someone so calloused.

"It's okay," Tamara said. "I don't suppose I care about him anymore. He was my parents' choice in the first place. Oh, I came to care for him, but not . . ." Her words trailed away, and she concentrated on her work.

Perhaps she realized she was sharing too much with people she hardly knew. But Maggie wanted to know more. "You didn't love him?"

"Well, I'm nineteen years old. I didn't want to be an old maid!" Tamara blurted the words like a painful confession.

"And now your parents want to match you with Colby Stoddard?" Maggie ventured boldly.

Grandma stirred but said nothing. A few dishes rattled from her mother's direction. Maggie had the feeling she'd get scolded later for her bluntness, but she'd worry about that later. Now she needed to know Tamara's intentions.

"You know about that?" Tamara smiled a self-conscious smile. "Everyone must know."

"Girls, we must concentrate on our sewing for a moment," Grandma put in. "I've noticed you are having some difficulty threading your needles. We all have heard about wetting the end of the thread, and that often does the trick. I have another little hint—try wetting the eye of the needle." She demonstrated with her needle and thread. It did work well.

The conversation didn't get back to Tamara's love life after that. Maggie had a suspicion that Grandma had purposely diverted the direction of the discussion. Maggie knew she had pushed too far. Tamara would probably never come back now and that, surprisingly, disappointed Maggie. Not only because of her schemes, but because she liked Tamara and also felt a little sorry for her. It must be hard for her to have her parents so dictate her life. Maggie complained often enough that her own parents, especially her mother, were always telling her what to do, but in reality, they were fairly lenient. Her mother made comments about her need to get ready for marriage, but never did she push her toward any one person. The closest she had come to doing that was when she had supported the idea of marrying the new minister. She'd learned her lesson from that and now was more reticent than ever on the subject of marriage.

After about an hour Grandma declared the lesson over for the day. She encouraged them to work on their projects on their own when they had a chance. She also welcomed Tamara to join them again. Tamara thanked her but made no firm commitment.

Maggie followed her outside. "Are you sure you want to walk home?" She knew Mr. Stoddard had brought Tamara and that she'd told him she would be happy to walk home. "It's a good two miles to the Stoddard place."

"Exercise will do me good."

"We could lend you a saddle horse."

"I don't ride well."

"You could ride with me. I don't mind."

"Thank you very much, but I'll be all right."

Maggie detected a coolness in her tone. "Tamara, I am sorry if I offended you earlier. Mama tells me I'm too curious for my own good."

Tamara seemed surprised by the apology. "Don't worry about it. Truly. Though it is a touchy subject . . . I thought I might want to talk about it, but in the end I was too embarrassed. My reticence had nothing to do with you. Honestly."

"There's nothing to be ashamed of," Maggie assured her. "It's that fellow Jeffery who should be ashamed."

"You have to be jilted yourself, Maggie, to know how it feels." Her tone was slightly defensive, but it held no accusation. "You feel that when a man leaves you, it must be your fault, that you failed him in some way. And you fear that other men will find you objectionable, as well. I guess that's why I jumped at the chance to come here where I wasn't known. Yet that didn't work out. My past has followed me."

"It's a small town." Maggie wanted to say something to lift her spirits. "I'll bet Colby doesn't care about that other fellow. He seemed very attentive to you the other night."

"But to know my mother was desperate enough to push me toward someone who, in her estimation, is beneath me is, in itself, humiliating!" When Maggie opened her mouth, about to defend Colby, Tamara added, "Don't get me wrong. I don't think he, or anyone, is beneath me. But my mother would have wanted someone of more financial affluence though she likes the idea of a match with the son of an old family friend."

"The Parkers have lots of money," Maggie found herself saying. As much as she was conflicted about scheming, she couldn't let this prime opportunity go.

Tamara rolled her eyes. "So everyone knows about Evan Parker, as well. He was never a real suitor because I was engaged at the time we were together in Boston."

"Well, Colby isn't the only eligible bachelor in these parts." Maggie was only speaking the truth. There couldn't be anything wrong with that.

"Evan was sweet. But Colby . . ." A blush of pink rose in Tamara's cheeks. "He's so marvelous." She giggled.

With a sinking feeling, Maggie realized Tamara was already starting to fall in love with Colby.

# TWELVE

Ada wondered if everyone would be at the schoolhouse for the Sewing Circle. Their usual day had to be changed to this the third Sunday in September because last Sunday Pastor Barnett had been able to come to Maintown and hold a service for the folks. It was kind of him to occasionally fit the Maintown Brethren of Christ Church into his schedule, even though they were of a different denomination.

Ada felt a bit awkward when she arrived at the schoolhouse for the Sewing Circle to find only Emma Jean present. She wondered how much Emma Jean realized about Maggie's designs on her son. She also debated about whether to say something. Ada would like nothing more than to see her daughter and Emma Jean's son get together. It hadn't worked out with Ellie, but now there was a chance with Maggie.

Jane Donnelly had told Ada the other day that she had been talking to Hilda Fergus, who said she had heard from Emma Jean herself that she had invited Tamara Brennan specifically for the purpose of orchestrating a match between her and Colby. The conversation during Tamara's sewing lesson seemed to confirm that. If that were so, Emma Jean would hardly wish to support a match between Maggie and Colby. Ada hoped it wasn't the case because it would likely break Maggie's heart.

"Good morning, Ada," Emma Jean said as she arranged chairs around the frame.

Ada grabbed a chair and helped out. "Hello, Emma Jean. How are you?"

"I was hoping you were Nessa, that is, since we are doing her quilt for Kendra. We need to get it on the frame. That wedding will be here before you know it."

"So very true! But you and I are early. I'm sure Nessa will be here in plenty of time." Ada made a bit more fuss over the arrangement of the chairs than necessary just to have something to do.

"Miss Stowe did not do a very good job sweeping the floor on Friday." Emma Jean bent to pick up a sliver of wood kindling. "I best get the broom."

"I'll put another log on the fire," Ada offered. The room was chilly, indicating the morning air was cooling off with autumn just around the corner.

Emma Jean found the broom and, as she swept, said, "Oh, I have been meaning to mention how kind it was of your mother to agree to teach Tamara to sew. I offered to do it myself, but she felt I was too busy. I suppose I am with Albert taking to his bed more and more lately."

"I'm so sorry to hear that, Emma Jean." Ada knew Albert Stoddard had resigned from the Board of Deacons because of his health, but she hadn't realized it was so serious. "Is there anything I can do?"

"You are busy, as well, with two weddings fast approaching and your mother visiting."

"I could send Georgie over—"

"He's already helping the men with the harvest, and soon school will start. His education should come first." She paused as she bent to sweep the floor leavings into the dustpan. "We'll manage."

"Emma Jean, honestly, don't be so proud." Emma Jean could be difficult at times, but seeing her friend's need helped Ada warm toward her. "The Sewing Circle will not stand to see you in need and not give a hand."

Emma Jean sighed, and her usually steely demeanor softened. "I forget what good friends I have."

After a moment of awkward silence, Ada said, "We enjoyed Tamara's visit. She's a sweet girl. She told us she has just ended an engagement."

"There are no secrets in this town, are there?" Emma Jean gave a little roll of her eyes. "Yes, it is true. But I hope to rectify that situation."

"How is that?" Ada queried as casually as she could.

"I have a perfectly eligible son, don't you know?"

"Colby is courting Tamara?"

"Not yet, but it is only a matter of time." Emma Jean dumped the dustpan into the woodbox. "They make a fine match."

"I am surprised Colby has not set his sights on a local girl."

"You know very well he did," Emma Jean said stiffly. "But when Ellie turned down his proposals, I suppose he was shy of courting other girls right away. Enough time has passed, I think—"

"What are you saying, Emma Jean?" Ada's mind was reeling. "Colby proposed marriage to my Ellie?"

"I'm not surprised you didn't know. I didn't learn of it myself until recently."

"They must have thought there was no need to say anything, since nothing came of it," Ada reasoned. Yet she did feel a little hurt that her daughter hadn't confided such a momentous event to her. What else was she in the dark about regarding her children? Was she so critical of them that they feared to tell her things? That might be the case with Maggie, who often warranted more criticism, but Ellie?

Ada was glad when the other ladies began to arrive to distract her worries. She would have to give this more thought later. She did not wish to put her children off from her.

Once the other women arrived, Ada welcomed the soothing process of quilting and visiting with her friends. Nessa decided they should put a pretty green-and-pink quilt in the Double Irish Chain pattern on the frame first. Nessa and Kendra had marked a feathered wreath quilting design in the large spaces that were of muslin. Because it was an intricate design, they were likely to get only the one quilt done that day, but Nessa said Kendra wouldn't mind if this was her only finished quilt. It was her favorite.

Ada took that as the perfect opportunity to bring up the quilting party. Nessa was so thrilled they would do that for her daughter that she turned as pink as the fabric in the quilt. Nessa never expected people to pay attention to her, so it didn't take much to please her.

At midday the ladies took a break. They rose, stretched, then took their lunch pails and sat in a circle to eat. Ada had noticed that Florence Parker was quieter than usual. She had not arrived with her usual fanfare, nor with some tale of an escapade to share. Ada had felt certain she would bore them to death with more bragging about her son or her daughter's recent engagement to a wealthy Astorian.

Mary Renolds must have noticed this, as well, because she asked, "Is everything all right, Florence? You have been quiet all morning."

"I don't want to cause a stir. That's all." Florence's gaze flickered in Ada's direction.

"What are you talking about?" Emma Jean demanded. "Now you've got us all curious. What is going on?"

Florence sighed heavily. "It's my son. I'm just worried about him."

"Just the other day you were proud as a peacock over him," said Polly Briggs.

"Of course I am still proud of him," Florence said. "But I fear he will throw away all his talent and education by remaining in this obscure, backwater town."

"I should think you'd be thrilled for him to be close to you," Mary said.

"Not when it means his giving up all that Boston has to offer. Harvard graduates go on to far more prestige than country lawyers. They rise to the highest pinnacles of power. Now he is talking about giving all that up and staying here."

"Perhaps he could become a lawyer in Portland or Seattle," offered Emma Jean. To most of the folks here, Portland and Seattle were high enough.

Florence merely pursed her lips disdainfully at that comment. Ada remained quiet. Though Evan had been to their house for dinner, she didn't feel she knew the boy well enough to make comment on his future. Thus her shock when Florence lifted her gaze to squarely meet Ada's.

"Ada, it doesn't help that your daughter has manipulated Evan into taking Tommy Donnelly's case."

Ada's jaw dropped. "Maggie?" She was so shocked at being suddenly thrust into the middle of this that she could think of nothing to say.

"Yes. She put it into his head to do this." Florence glanced at Jane Donnelly. "Please don't take me wrong, Jane. I don't begrudge Tommy the best legal counsel there is, but if Evan takes cases here, he will never return to the Boston firm."

"You can't blame Maggie for this," Ada said when she found her tongue.

"She's the one who orchestrated it," Florence said.

"Maggie had the best intentions," Jane Donnelly replied. "She wanted to help Tommy. But if this upsets you, I will go back to the Portland lawyer."

"That wouldn't help now," Florence replied with frustration. "Evan is set on taking Tommy's case. And if he knew I had interfered—"

"Looks to me like you are already interfering." Ada's voice trembled in belated ire. "And I'll dare you to try to cast blame upon my daughter! It is entirely Evan's fault if he is so weak as to be led around by a mere girl!"

"Ladies, please!" Emma Jean tried to intercede.

Florence cut her off. "If you want to begin name-calling . . ."

Ada was horrified at how quickly the matter had escalated. It had been a long time since she and Florence had squared off like this. Now she understood the wisdom in their careful avoidance of each other.

Quickly she said, "Florence, I am sorry. I didn't mean to degrade Evan. I was just a mother protecting her cub. Forgive me."

"All right," Florence responded, still an edge to her tone. "But perhaps it would be best if those two didn't see so much of each other."

"I try not to dictate my children's friends—and I assure you, it is nothing more."

"I never thought it was!" Florence as much as implied that Evan was far too good for the likes of Ada's daughter.

Ada nearly bit her tongue in trying not to make a caustic retort.

"Let's get back to our quilting," Mary suggested.

"We have quite a bit more to do," Emma Jean put in.

But the afternoon never returned to its semblance of peace. The silence between Florence and Ada was deafening. The others tried to fill it with their usual conversation. Ada had been on the verge of leaving after the confrontation but decided to remain. She knew that once she departed under such circumstances, it would be hard to return next time. And if she kept away, Jane and a few others might do so, as well, to support her. Ada knew that the pain of her Sewing Circle splitting would be far greater than the tension she felt around the frame today.

If she stuck it out now, the conflict would probably blow over before the next time they met. She hoped and prayed so.

When Ada returned home from Sewing Circle, she said nothing about the confrontation. She certainly was not going to forbid Maggie from seeing Evan. Never in the past had the differences between her and Florence spilled over into their families, and she wasn't about to let it happen now. If Florence chose to take that route, the repercussions would be on her head.

When Ellie appeared to note her mother's pensive demeanor, Ada brought up her concern about the Stoddard family since Mr. Stoddard's illness, as though that accounted for her melancholy. She suggested the possibility of Maggie helping out and was pleased with her daughter's positive response.

She was also pleased with herself for making the suggestion. Though Maggie would have been willing to help a neighbor in need, there was a little more in her expression than merely doing a good deed might warrant. Helping at the Stoddards' might also give Maggie opportunity to visit Colby.

Ada couldn't help herself. Why shouldn't she play matchmaker in her daughter's interest? How much good it would actually do with Colby out in the fields most of the time, she didn't know. But it was something, and Maggie was resourceful if nothing else.

When Maggie smiled, Ada found she liked the feeling of not being at odds with her younger daughter, as she had seemed to be so often lately.

"Oh, and by the by, I spoke with Mrs. Wallard about having a quilting for Kendra on Saturday, and she was tickled about it. All the ladies will be there and, of course, later the menfolk."

As much as Ada was enjoying helping Maggie for a change and seeing good results, she prayed that soon her daughters would be married so she could be finished with all this romantic tomfoolery. And that did remind her to be diligent in praying in the real sense for these things. God had surely worked for good the mess with the false minister, and He would do the same regarding Maggie.

# THIRTEEN

Evan could not get to his dancing lesson until Tuesday afternoon. He'd been to Portland Monday and spoken with the lawyer who was happy to release Tommy's case. Evan said the lawyer had been busy with other clients, though Maggie thought there might be more to it. However, she was too anxious to get to the dancing to question Evan further.

She'd enlisted Ellie's help, and Mama had let them move aside some of the furniture in the parlor. Mama had wondered why they couldn't use the front room, and Maggie said she thought Evan might not feel comfortable practicing in front of the whole family. At that hour in the afternoon it would be only Mama and Grandma, but still, that might put him off a bit.

"Evan, we are going to learn a couple of reels today," Maggie began, just as a schoolteacher might begin a lesson.

He looked relieved. She supposed he'd been worried about waltzing. Wisely, Maggie thought they should start with something easy.

Ellie was going to keep the beat for them and dance when needed.

"It's going to be hard to learn a reel with only three people," Maggie said, "but I've lined up some chairs that will represent the other dancers." She noticed Evan casting the chairs a skeptical look. "Honestly, Evan, this is easy. You can't mess up a reel." She held out her hand. "Come on, let's stand at the beginning of the row."

Obediently he moved to the head of the chairs, standing on the right, in the "men's" line, with Maggie on the left in the "ladies' " line. Ellie clapped the beat.

"Right hands," Maggie instructed. "Turn your partner."

Evan grasped Maggie's right hand with more force than was necessary, and in the process somehow got his foot caught on a chair leg. He lost his balance, tottered a moment, tried to grasp the chair, missed, knocked the chair over, and nearly went down himself. Instead, he stumbled back until he plopped on the nearby sofa. The overturned chair, however, made a terrible racket as it banged against the other chairs.

"What is going on in there?" Mama called from the kitchen.

"Nothing's broken, Mama!" Maggie replied, then glanced at Evan. "You're okay, aren't you?"

Clearly humiliated, Evan scrambled to his feet. "This is a mistake!" he mumbled. "I am too clumsy for dancing."

"It's just because you are nervous," Ellie consoled.

"You don't have to be nervous around us," Maggie assured him. "We're friends."

"I get nervous around everyone, but mostly around women!" he confessed.

Maggie could just imagine what a spectacle he had presented in front of Tamara, a woman he really cared about.

"It is different with friends," Maggie insisted. "We're going to like you no matter what. Isn't that right, Ellie?"

"That is what friends do," Ellie agreed.

"Truly?"

"Haven't you ever had a friend, Evan?"

"Not many," he replied hesitantly.

"Tamara's brother? Wasn't he a friend?"

Fiddling with his spectacles, he said solemnly, "I'd probably call him more of an acquaintance. You know how it was here . . . well, that's how it has been my entire life. It is easier to read a book than get to know someone."

"That's got to change," Maggie insisted. "You are a great person. Tamara thinks you are sweet."

"Sweet? She said that?"

"Yes, she did, right in this very house. I am not kidding." To her surprise, instead of this information encouraging him, he got a sick look on his face. "Now what's wrong?" she asked a bit impatiently.

"What man wants a woman to think he is sweet!" Evan shoved his spectacles up the bridge of his nose. "That's as bad as being 'like a brother.' "

Maggie turned to Ellie for help. "You think Zack is sweet, don't you, Ellie?"

Caught by surprise, Ellie stumbled. "Sweet . . . ah . . . well, yes . . . I suppose so."

"I have met Mr. Hartley," Evan said. "I doubt most women would describe him as *sweet*. Dashing, handsome, charming, yes. And what of your Colby, Maggie? Do you think he is sweet?" His frustration gave more force to his voice than usual. For once, he sounded like he could be a lawyer orating in a courtroom.

Maggie was reminded of how Tamara had finished her comment about Evan, saying Colby was "marvelous." That Colby had won in the comparison had been clear.

"Well, then, if you don't want her to think that about you," Maggie said decisively, "you'd better learn to dance. Take my hand and let's try this again."

Doggedly he complied. He bumped a few more chairs, nearly crushed Ellie's foot once, and tripped Maggie a couple of times, but they made it through the reel. It was like trying to lead a bull through a patch of daisies without crushing a flower, but the whole patch was pretty well crushed by the time they finished. Evan looked ready to bolt.

"One more time!" Maggie demanded.

He wanted to protest but didn't. Instead, he grasped her hand, wearing the look of a man stepping out on a gangplank.

"Right-hand turn!" Maggie called. "Left-hand turn! Do-si-do with your partner!" There was a bit of a mix-up as they went around each other back to back, but it was better than before. "Sashay down the center! Evan! You are doing great!"

His confidence grew as they proceeded to "reel the set." His intense frown of concentration relaxed into a slight smile. He and Maggie hooked elbows, turned once so that she was facing the "men's" line and he was facing the "ladies'." They were each to pretend to turn an imaginary partner. Evan had just swung out of turning Maggie and was moving fluidly, seeming finally to be getting the hang of it. Then, moving a bit too fluidly with an imaginary person on his arm and turning too quickly, he stumbled toward the fireplace mantel and bumped a china vase—Mama's precious vase she had bought in Portland a few years ago. Maggie watched helplessly as the vase toppled from the ledge. She was too far away to do anything, but Ellie saw it and leaped forward, catching the precious thing before it hit the floor.

Evan stared, mortified. He knew that in a simple farmhouse, such a knickknack was highly regarded.

Ellie held the vase up to show no harm was done.

"Good catch, Ellie!" Maggie laughed. Then noting the look on Evan's face, she said, "All's well, Evan."

"I think that's enough for today," he groaned miserably. "We'd better quit before I destroy your house."

"Oh, pshaw!" Maggie replied. "We're just starting to have fun. We can move out to the barn where there is more room."

"You will stay for supper, won't you, Evan?" Ellie asked. "Zack will be joining us."

"That is kind of you. If your mother won't mind," Evan replied politely.

"Zack can help us with the dancing," Maggie said, hoping that was the encouragement Evan needed. "It will go much better with two couples."

He merely shrugged, lacking the enthusiasm she had expected, but at least he hadn't bolted.

After supper the lessons moved out to the barn. With two couples, the instruction went easier. Georgie joined them for a while and clapped the beat, but with the fall term of school now on, he had to leave after a short while to do his homework. The dancers lit a couple of lanterns and continued practicing until well after dark. Finally exhaustion signaled the end of the "party." They collapsed onto some bales of hay, panting and laughing.

Evan laughed as much as everyone. At some point during the evening, Maggie could not tell exactly when, he had forgotten his inhibitions—and his two left feet!—and had begun to have fun.

It was Zack who reluctantly drew himself up and said, "With a little breather, I could go on all night, but I've got potatoes to harvest bright and early in the morning."

"There'll be another lesson tomorrow," Maggie announced.

"Do you think I still need help?" Evan asked, a bit chagrined.

"You've got the reel down fine," Maggie replied. "Now you have to learn to waltz."

A stricken expression flickered across his face.

"Don't worry, Evan," Zack said, "the old folks don't allow much waltzing. Many think it's scandalous."

"But there has to be at least one waltz," insisted Maggie. "And with only one chance, you have to do it perfectly."

Evan pulled a handkerchief from his pocket and blotted the drips of perspiration from his brow. He cast a beseeching look at Zack. "You'll be here for the lesson, Zack?"

"Wouldn't miss it," Zack answered.

Evan looked relieved. It would have been awkward if it was just Maggie and Evan practicing the waltz, even if they were only friends. Dad probably wouldn't allow it anyway.

"Thank you," Evan said. "And thank you for this evening. I don't know when I have had such enjoyment with . . . friends."

He seemed to honestly mean it, and Maggie believed him. Here he was, twenty-two years old and experiencing friendship for the first time. It made her appreciate her own friendships, though in truth she didn't have oodles of friends either—Ellie, Zack, Tommy, and . . . now Evan.

Zack and Ellie left the barn, but Evan lingered behind with Maggie.

"You have been so kind to me," he said.

"You know well enough I have an ulterior motive," she replied.

"But you did say we were friends?"

"I did, and I meant it. I like you."

He smiled. "Do you think it's possible I never gave others the chance to get to know me? Was it my fault I never made friends?"

"That could be. I think anyone who got to know you would like you."

They sat back on the hay bale, and Evan reached up and straightened his spectacles.

"Why are you doing that?" Maggie asked.

"Doing what?"

"Fiddling with your spectacles. You do it when you get nervous." His surprised expression indicated he had not been aware of that.

"I don't know. I suppose it makes me nervous to be too happy."

"Whyever so? Is it like waiting for the other shoe to drop?"

"Perhaps."

A thoughtful silence ensued. Then Evan said, "I went to Portland yesterday and spoke with Mr. Werth, the lawyer. He released the case to me. Then I visited Tommy and told him I'm taking his case."

"How is he?"

"He seems all right, physically, that is. He also appeared rather melancholy. I, of course, don't know him well enough to judge, but that was my impression. The sheriff said he had been very quiet and sullen of late. I feel there can be no more delays for Tommy's sake. We must have the trial the next time the circuit judge comes through. That will be in about two weeks, I believe."

"The sooner the better," affirmed Maggie.

"Sooner, if it turns out well," Evan said thoughtfully. "I am still uncertain about the exact direction of our defense."

"You don't think self-defense will work?"

"Without any eyewitnesses that defense is dependent on the mood of the jury. Almost all is based on Tommy's word, and . . . well . . ."

"He doesn't have the best reputation around here," Maggie finished glumly.

"There is the possibility of proving legal insanity—"

"Evan, no!" Maggie gasped. "That would ruin Tommy's life more than hanging."

"It doesn't have to imply that Tommy is a lunatic," Evan explained. "The classic approach is defining insanity as the inability to distinguish right from wrong. In Tommy's case this approach would not work, since it is obvious he does know right from wrong. But there are other more subtle definitions. The most plausible one is 'irresistible impulse.' This allows that a man might know an act is wrong but is driven to it by some uncontrollable—irresistible—impulse and thus cannot be held responsible for his actions. I can cite a precedent in *The State of Iowa versus Felter*."

"It still says Tommy is crazy."

"Only at the moment the crime was committed. But, yes," Evan admitted, "the insanity defense can be tricky. Psychiatry is hardly an exact science. I was able to be present to observe the trial of Charles Guiteau last fall—"

"That name sounds familiar." Maggie's brow creased in thought. "That was the man who killed President Garfield, wasn't it?"

"Yes. His defense lawyers tried an insanity plea, but though the man was obviously deranged, there was no chance that the killer of the president of the United States would avoid hanging. Nevertheless, they might well have made a plausible case had the victim been any other than the president."

"I guess you know what is best, Evan." Maggie tried to sound confident, despite the fact that it made her cringe to think folks would believe Tommy to be insane on top of all else.

"I am not saying that is the best strategy," Evan said. "I suppose I am merely playing devil's advocate. Out here in the country folks do not have as deep an understanding of insanity as they might have in the city. It is a defense that could easily backfire. I plan to stick with self-defense, hopefully finding enough witnesses who can support the idea that Tommy had reason to fear his father."

"Everyone knows his father beat him a lot. I don't know how Mrs. Donnelly put up with it."

"You must not blame her too much," Evan said. "I've spoken with her and I believe she was kept in the dark somewhat about this, not only by her husband but by her friends, as well. Even Tommy tried to protect his mother."

"What a sad situation," Maggie said.

"You could help me, Maggie, by identifying folks who would be the best prospects as witnesses. Another thing, Tommy wouldn't talk much to me when I spoke with him the other day. That didn't surprise me, since he doesn't know me well, but I need him to open up to me and tell me his story." He reached for his spectacles, realized what he was doing, and self-consciously dropped his hand. "He might be more willing to talk if you were present during the questioning. I hate to ask it of you, but could you come into St. Helens with me tomorrow—"

"Of course I'll come. I told you I'd help."

"Can I come for you after breakfast, say around eight?"

"I'll be ready."

"Should you ask your parents first?"

"Oh, they won't mind," she said boldly. What she really meant was that she would somehow talk them into it.

Evan returned to the house with her to thank her parents for dinner and take his leave. Maggie had suggested he not mention the trip to St. Helens. She wanted to talk to them by herself.

It was her father who had reservations about the trip, but not for the reasons she'd imagined.

"I don't want you getting any more mixed up in Tommy Donnelly's affairs," he said.

"But, Dad, Tommy needs all the help he can get," she argued. "He needs the help of the community, his neighbors. And Evan needs my help."

"You mean a man who graduated from a fancy Eastern college needs the help of a simple farm girl?" He arched his brow skeptically.

"Tommy won't talk to a stranger, which Evan is to him, even though they grew up in the same town. Evan thinks it will help Tommy relax more if I am there. Tommy knows me and trusts me."

"Calvin," Mama put in, "I went to see Jane the other day and found her sitting at her kitchen table weeping. She tries to put on a brave front at Sewing Circle, but this is tearing her apart. If our Maggie can help Tommy . . . well, I know how you feel about the boy, but think of poor Jane."

Sighing, Dad rubbed his face in defeat. He couldn't win over both Mama and Maggie, but he did have another ready argument. "And what of you spending hours on the road alone with a single young man?"

Both Mama and Maggie laughed at this. Even Mama knew Evan was not threatening to a girl's honor.

"I don't see what's so funny," huffed Dad.

"Dad, Evan is in love with Tamara Brennan. My honor is safe with him."

"That is one young man who can be trusted, Calvin," Mama agreed.

"Even though he is a Parker, Ada?"

"Florence and I have our differences," Mama said, "but one thing we would both agree on is that we raised decent children."

"Well," Dad said with reluctance, "I'll permit it this time."

"Thank you, Daddy!" Maggie gave her father a jubilant hug and ran up to bed.

# FOURTEEN

It had rained all night before Maggie and Evan's trip to St. Helens, but it cleared a little with the dawn, and by the time they departed, there was only a light drizzle. Evan had his father's rockaway, which had a roof and curtained sides, so they would stay fairly dry. Maggie wore a blue cotton print shirtwaist. She thought a trip to town warranted dressing up. Evan was, as usual, in a wool three-piece suit. Maggie wondered what he would look like in dungarees and a chambray shirt. But that didn't matter because Tamara would no doubt prefer a suit on a man. However, Tamara was taken with Colby, who seldom wore a suit except on Sundays.

"Evan, have you ever worn dungarees?" she asked as they drove along. Her curiosity had just gotten the best of her.

"When I was a kid," he replied.

"Do lawyers have to wear suits?"

"In Boston they certainly do." He wrinkled his brow pensively.

She liked that he thought things over before speaking. It seemed to indicate he took her seriously.

"I think even in the West a judge would expect a man of the law to respect the court well enough to dress properly. You don't want to get on a judge's bad side. Judge Olsen, the county circuit judge, has a somewhat bilious reputation. I attended some of his trials when I was younger, and he never failed to find reason for complaint against the litigators. Although he gave me a recommendation for law school, I never had the feeling he thought much of me, either."

"Do you think that will hurt Tommy?"

"Despite his quirks, Olsen is fair and impartial. He simply puts up with no silliness in his court—and his interpretation of silliness is broad."

Maggie pulled back the curtain on her side of the seat and looked out. The rain had stopped, but the road was muddy. She had wondered how they would pass the two-hour drive into St. Helens. She knew from their previous encounters that Evan was an interesting person. Though reticent to talk about himself, he needed only a little encouragement to do so. As they drove, she got him to talk more about Boston and learned that though he hadn't been entirely happy there, he had seen much of the city and was willing to share about the broader world. Her own existence was so narrow, confined to Columbia County with only one trip to Portland, that she was an apt listener, prompting Evan to share even more.

This led to a surprising discovery. They had a common interest in reading. He enjoyed the same kind of adventure fiction that Maggie loved. They were both avid fans of Mark Twain. Having both read *The Adventures of Tom Sawyer*, they spent some time discussing the parts they liked best. Evan had brought from Boston a recent novel by Twain titled *The Prince and the Pauper*, which he said he'd loan to Maggie when he finished it.

They each had different reasons for their love of literature. For Evan, it provided insulation from a harsh world; Maggie, however, read to escape into new and exciting worlds.

Evan had visited London with his family years ago, and she questioned him thoroughly about that. "If I had known you were this interesting," she said, "I would have made friends with you when you were a kid."

"When I was twelve, you were just an eight-year-old kid," he commented. "But I appreciate the sentiment."

In what seemed like no time at all, they were trotting into the main street of St. Helens.

"Do you want to stop by Dolman's before or after the jail?" Evan asked.

Mama had not been able to let a trip to St. Helens pass without giving Maggie a list of items to pick up at the store. Mrs. Parker had given Evan a list, as well.

"Let's go to the jail first." She didn't want to say it, but she preferred getting what was sure to be an unpleasant experience over with first.

When they arrived, Sheriff Haynes led them back to the cells. This time one of the other cells was occupied by a man who was sprawled out on his cot snoring loudly.

"Sheriff, I would like to confer with my client in private," Evan said.

"Aw, that fellow's out cold, sleeping off a mighty hangover," the sheriff replied. "He won't hear nothing."

"That isn't good enough," Evan insisted.

Maggie was impressed by the authority in his voice.

The sheriff looked for a moment as though he might argue, then, with a shrug, went to the drunk prisoner's cell and unlocked it. "He's slept long enough anyway," the sheriff commented. "Now the city don't have to pay for his breakfast." He gave the prisoner a hard shake.

Groaning and mumbling, the man woke up and, with some prodding, was finally escorted from the cell.

Tommy was awake and called out a greeting to Maggie. He paid little attention to Evan.

After the sheriff let them into Tommy's cell and exited, Maggie smiled and held out another basket of baked goods for him. This time the sheriff had inspected the basket before letting her bring it in.

"Tell your ma thanks again," Tommy said, taking the basket and setting it aside. "Don't you look pretty, Maggie! Did you get all gussied up just for me?"

Maggie didn't know how to respond to that. It wasn't exactly the case, but she thought an affirmative would give him a much-needed boost.

"I know you like blue, Tommy," she said. Then thinking it was time for Evan to be acknowledged, she added, "You remember Evan Parker."

" 'Course I do," Tommy said, a bit more guarded. "Just saw him the other day. Ma says he's my new lawyer and I should cooperate. She was here to see me yesterday."

Maggie knew Evan had spoken to Mrs. Donnelly after his first unproductive visit. "That's true, Tommy," she said. "And Evan is going to do good by you. You saw how he stood up to the sheriff just now."

"I saw that." Tommy eyed Evan.

Maggie had the feeling that if Tommy'd been a dog, he would have sniffed him just to see if he really could be trusted.

"Shall we sit down and talk?" Evan suggested. "Maggie is going to help me on the case, so anything you say will be held in confidence by her."

"I know that 'bout Maggie," Tommy said. "It's you I ain't sure about."

"As an officer of the court, I am *sworn* to keep your confidence. Confidentiality is one of the highest duties of an attorney."

Tommy glanced at Maggie for assurance. She nodded enthusiastically, saying, "Tommy, you've got to tell Evan everything. That's the only way he can get you free."

Tommy looked at Evan. "You'll get me outta here?"

"If you are innocent, I will get you out of jail."

"But I ain't innocent!"

"I believe, from what I know of your case, that there are extenuating circumstances that would make you innocent in the eyes of the court."

"Ex—what circumstances? First off, you gotta speak English to me, Mr. Parker. Didn't no one tell you I ain't the smartest turnip in the field?"

Patiently Evan explained, "I think things may have occurred that would have given you good reason to shoot your father. But before we proceed, that is, before we go on, I do need to hear your story. I have to know what exactly happened the day your father died. And you have to tell me the truth."

"I don't like talking 'bout it."

"I know, Tommy."

Evan's tone was so gentle and understanding, Maggie knew no other lawyer would have cared as much about Tommy as Evan did.

"It must have been a terrible day for you."

"Couldn't Maggie tell you? She knows most of it."

"I wasn't there," Maggie said.

Just then there was a shuffling at the door that led from the cells to the office in front. The deputy appeared, holding a broom. "I want to sweep out the cell that was just vacated," he said.

"That will have to wait," Evan said. "I'm conferring with my client now. Didn't the sheriff tell you?"

"He left and I got work to do."

"I'll let you know when we are finished."

The deputy left, probably happy to have a good excuse for idleness.

"I know it is hard for you," Evan said, returning his attention to Tommy, "but you are the only one who knows exactly what happened that day."

"I kilt my pa!" Tommy murmured, his voice trembling." He sniffed and tried to get control over his emotions.

"But you didn't want to, did you?" Evan prompted.

When Tommy hesitated, Maggie knew that was not a good sign.

Again Tommy looked at Maggie. "I tole you, didn't I? That I wasn't gonna take it from my pa no more, that if the preacher could whup him, so could I. I tole you, Maggie, if he pushed me, I'd push back."

Evan glanced at Maggie but made no comment. The little instinctive groan she emitted was probably all he needed to hear.

Evan asked, "Is that what happened that day, Tommy? Did your pa push you?"

Tommy ran a hand over his face. For the first time Maggie really noticed how imprisonment wasn't sitting well with him. His face appeared sallow instead of ruddy as it had before from his being constantly outdoors. He also looked several pounds lighter than he had weeks ago.

"Okay," Tommy said with resignation, "this is what happened, and it's the truth, I swear. Me and Pa was goin' out to hunt pheasant. He brought along a jug of moonshine, like usual. Well, there weren't no pheasants, so we got to drinkin' instead."

"And you each had a weapon?"

"Pa had his shotgun. I didn't have none 'cause I was working out in the field when he come and got me. I didn't figure it was worth goin' back for it 'cause it was late in the afternoon and we weren't likely to find no pheasants. I just went along to be sociable."

"You did not have a weapon?"

"That's what I said."

Maggie knew this was significant. If Tommy didn't bring a rifle, it meant he had not planned the crime. She felt great relief. Yet if the sheriff knew this, why hadn't he dropped the charges?

"Tommy, did you tell the sheriff about the gun?" She had not wanted to interrupt but couldn't help asking.

"I think I did when they had that hearing way back when they first arrested me." He rubbed his chin. "Is that important?"

"It could be very important," Evan replied. "But go on with your story. What happened after you started drinking?"

"Well, we got drunk, of course!" Tommy chuckled, probably thinking his reply had been quite clever. "After that," he went on more seriously, "Pa started to rail at me 'bout going to church and becoming a religious sissy. I tried to tell him that religion couldn't be all that sissified 'cause the preacher sure wasn't no sissy. That got Pa real riled up. I kind of enjoyed that 'cause I knew he still had a real tender spot about that whuppin' he got from the preacher. Then he jumped up—my pa, not the preacher, of course—and he started yellin' at me and callin' me a girl and a nancy and all sorts of mean stuff. He yelled,

'I'm gonna make a man outten you once and for all.' Then he started shootin' at me."

"Was he trying to kill you?"

"He might not a been, but he was drunker than a skunk and not aimin' too straight. That shotgun could do some damage, that's for sure."

"You were afraid for your life?"

"Well, what'd you think?" sneered Tommy. "I didn't have that much moonshine and wasn't drunk enough not to be afraid. I ain't ashamed to admit I was shakin' all over and yellin' and cryin' for him to stop."

"What happened next?"

"I started running, and he chased after me, still shootin'. Then Pa tripped and the gun went flying. I got my hands on it and aimed it at him, thinking to give him a taste of his own medicine. He got up and came toward me, still yelling and calling me names. Then I fired and fi—" Tommy's voice shook, and tears welled up in his eyes. "I kept pulling the trigger till the gun was empty. Then I kind of woke up, or something, and realized what I'd done." The tears spilled over the rims of his eyes and streamed down his cheeks. "I didn't mean to! Maybe there was times I thought about killin' him, but I didn't mean to then. I really didn't. You gotta believe me!"

"I do believe you, Tommy," Evan said with quiet assurance.

"You gonna make the sheriff and everyone else believe it?"

"During your trial, you will get to tell the jury your story," Evan said. "I'm sure once they hear just what you have told me, they will believe it, as well."

"What's this jury thing?"

"Do you know how a trial works?" Evan asked.

Tommy shook his head.

Evan explained, "One day soon we will be in court. There will be two lawyers. One will be me, defending you, and another lawyer, called a prosecutor, will speak for the state. His job is to prove your guilt. Our system of justice works on the premise that you are innocent until proven guilty. Thus the burden of proof is on the opposing side. Both sides will bring in witnesses that will help prove their case. We will also pick twelve jurors—that is, local folks who show that they can be fair and impartial. These folks will listen to both sides and then decide whether you are guilty or innocent."

"Will these be folks I know?" Tommy asked. "Can Maggie be one of them jurors?"

"No. Maggie couldn't be impartial because she is your friend—"

"But my enemies couldn't be fair, either!"

"They won't be your enemies. They will be people who aren't attached to you in any way."

"But if they don't know me, how they gonna know I'd never do anything like this on purpose?"

Maggie thought that was a very good question. She didn't understand the workings of the legal system much more than Tommy did, but it did seem cockeyed to have strangers judging a person.

Evan replied, "It is the fact that they are strangers that will make them fair. They will have to go by the evidence, that is, the facts presented in the trial. That's what they must base their decision on—the facts, not whether they like you or not. My job is to present the best possible case to convince them of your innocence."

Tommy looked at Maggie and asked plaintively, "Can he do that, Maggie?"

"I believe he can," she replied with confidence.

"Okay, then," Tommy said. "How much longer do I have to wait for this trial?"

"The circuit judge will be through here in about two weeks. We have a lot of work to do before then. We need to come up with some witnesses on your behalf."

"But ain't no one seen what happened."

"We will find people who can attest to your character—"

"No one likes me much around here. Ain't that true, Maggie?"

"There are a lot of people who will say you'd never hurt your father on purpose," Maggie replied.

"Like who?"

"Me, for one," said Maggie. "And my . . . well, my mother."

"And my ma, too!" Tommy brightened with the thought that there were at least three people who liked him.

"Not your mother," Evan interjected. "People figure a mother has to support her son, so they would discount her testimony."

"My ma would never lie!"

"I know that. Don't worry. We will find enough witnesses without her." Evan rose. "We will take our leave for now, but I will come back soon to see you."

"You, too, Maggie?" Tommy asked hopefully.

"I'll try," she said.

"I miss you an awful lot." There was an intensity in Tommy's voice that made her uncomfortable, but she said nothing. He most likely needed to cling to their friendship more closely than before.

Since no one had bothered to lock them into Tommy's cell, she and Evan let themselves out of the cell area. As they exited, Maggie noticed that the adjoining door was ajar. The deputy hadn't closed it all the way when he'd been there before.

She glanced at Evan and noted that he had made the same observation.

Once in the office he questioned the deputy, who was still alone and seated at the sheriff's desk, feet propped up, chair leaning against the wall, his ear not three feet from the door. "Deputy, were you listening to our conversation?"

"No. What'd you mean?" The deputy leaned forward, letting down his feet.

"The door wasn't shut all the way."

"Oh, I was just letting in some ventilation."

"Where did the sheriff go?" Evan asked.

"I dunno. Maybe home for dinner."

"Come along, Maggie," Evan said, striding to the front door. Maggie hurried after him. Once outside, he walked down the plank sidewalk a short distance from the jail, then said, as if to himself, "I don't much trust that deputy."

"He seems harmless to me," Maggie replied.

"Maybe so."

They headed to Dolman's, and while the shopkeeper was filling their orders, Maggie noticed a perplexed look still knitting Evan's brow. When their purchases were loaded into the backseat of the rockaway, Evan took the reins in hand and coaxed the team into an easy trot out of town.

# FIFTEEN

It had started raining again in earnest while they had been visiting Tommy, but the inside of the carriage stayed fairly dry. Maggie had brought a basket of food for their midday meal. She'd thought they might find a spot to picnic at on the way home, but the rain curtailed that idea.

"Are you hungry?" she asked, breaking the silence. Evan had been quiet since leaving the jail.

"Yes, I suppose so."

"I thought we could have a picnic if it didn't rain, but we could just pull over and eat in the carriage," she suggested.

"How about when we get out of town?"

"Evan, is everything all right? Are you worried about Tommy's case?" After hearing the entire story from Tommy's lips, Maggie felt better than ever about his chances. She didn't know why Evan had been so solemn.

He didn't answer for a long moment, no doubt thinking over his response, as usual.

"Maggie, I am concerned about that deputy," he said finally. "And I am concerned about something Tommy said about you."

"What's that?" She tried to sound guileless, though she knew what was coming.

"He said he'd told you he was not going to put up with his father's abuse anymore. Is that true?"

"Yeah, I guess he did."

"It couldn't have been long before the murder if he said it after Zack beat up Tom."

"I don't see it is all that important," Maggie reasoned. She didn't say that this had been eating at her for weeks, a very large matter indeed.

"If anyone knows about this, it could be used against Tommy. Do you see that?" His patience and lack of any accusation whatsoever broke down Maggie's defenses.

"Oh, Evan! I'm sorry I didn't tell you! Zack said I needn't tell unless I was asked, and no one ever asked." There, she'd said it, and she was glad she had finally told someone besides Zack. She took a steadying breath. "But it can't be that important. Tommy was always saying things against his father. He even told me once or twice that he could kill him, but he never meant it. It was just blowing off steam."

"I think you realize it could be very important," Evan replied, still with that steady, calm tone. "Especially if the opposition knew about it."

"Will you make me tell them?" Her lip trembled.

"No, of course not," he soothed. "I am not required to do any such thing. But if the prosecution called you to the stand . . ."

"They can't! They just can't. I'll lie if they do."

"You cannot lie." His tone was firm and unyielding. Then his voice softened. "I won't let it come to that, but it means I can't call you as a character witness."

"Who else will you find?"

"There will be someone else in the community, I am certain."

Maggie wasn't so certain. Many tended to lump Tommy and his father together in their esteem. If Maggie's own father, who was the most fair-minded man around, had ill feelings about Tommy, how would anyone else be found to stick up for him in court?

They drove in silence for a while, all thought of food gone. Maggie concentrated on the sound of the carriage wheels splashing through the mud. She thought she heard a funny thumping sound in a wheel but forgot all about that when Evan spoke again.

"Maggie, forgive me if this seems indelicate," he said, "but it could be pertinent in Tommy's case—it may even give the prosecution cause to call you to the stand as their own witness, though a hostile witness to be sure." He paused, then continued. "Is there more between you and Tommy than friendship?"

"What!" Somehow it bothered her more than ever that Evan, of all people, could think she'd have romantic feelings toward someone like Tommy.

"Stranger things have happened," he said defensively.

"How do you mean *stranger*?" she challenged.

"Well, ah . . ." He paused awkwardly before continuing. "You are intelligent, bright, and beautiful, while Tommy is, you have to admit, a bit slow-witted. He hardly seems your type of man. Yet you do seem very attached to him."

"I'm beautiful?" she asked, for the moment forgetting all else.

"Of course you are." He swallowed, perhaps flustered that he had even noticed, much less admitted it. "Please, forgive me for my forwardness!"

She still was unsure how to respond to Evan's compliment, so she chose instead to recall his other words and respond to them. "I've always felt so sorry for Tommy. The kids made such vicious fun of him. He desperately needed one friend."

Evan nodded. "Somewhat like you have been with me."

She wanted to make a ready protest, but she saw how he might interpret it in that way. Yet it was also very different. "I never felt sorry for you," she tried to explain. "I feel more equal with you, Evan. In fact, I feel almost as if we are like me and Tommy only in reverse. I am Tommy and you are me because you are far above me in so many areas."

He laughed ruefully. "That is an interesting analogy but hardly true. I may have had more education, but it doesn't mean I am smarter than you. However, I will accept the notion of our being on equal footing. I like you a lot, Maggie, and I would hate to think you only felt sorry for me."

"Banish that thought! I like you, too. Hey, how about that food?"

As Evan was directing the team to the side of the road Maggie heard that strange thumping sound again. She was about to mention it to Evan when the wagon lurched. Then suddenly the entire rear of the carriage tilted. Evan sharply pulled the team back, and as if in protest, both horses reared. He tried to control them, but that was almost impossible, and the carriage continued its tilting slide. Maggie hung on to her seat, bracing herself for the whole rig to overturn. Her fingers could not get a good grip on the leather seat, and she slid down the seat, stopping with a hard bump against Evan. He nearly dropped one of the reins but managed to save it with a finger and loop it back around his hand.

Then, as suddenly as it had begun, the movement stopped. The horses were still restive, and Evan had to keep a tight hold on the reins.

"Are you all right?" he asked Maggie, directing a concerned gaze toward her.

"Yes," she said, though her voice was slightly shaky. "I hope I didn't bruise your shoulder."

"That is the least of our worries." He pulled aside the curtain on his side and looked out. "We've slipped into a ditch and lost the left rear wheel. That was the odd sound I heard a while ago. It was probably coming loose."

"Maybe we can fix it," she said.

He looked at her as if she were crazy. Then, when she pulled her curtain aside and started to climb out, he seemed to remember himself. "You sit tight! I'll look at it." He handed her the reins, though the horses had finally calmed since the initial mishap, and climbed out.

"Make sure the horses are okay, too," she said. Maggie didn't like just sitting while he did the dirty work, yet she belatedly realized that a lady, as she wanted to be, would let the man fix the problem. Besides that, it was raining, and she did have one of her better dresses on.

After a few minutes he called, "The horses are fine."

A few more minutes passed. She heard him sloshing around. The carriage shook once; then she heard a yelp.

"Evan, are you okay?" she called.

When there was no immediate response, she slid down the rest of the way on the seat to the driver's side. The carriage tottered, and she realized it might have been a mistake to disturb the vehicle's precarious balance. She paused a moment until the movement stopped, then jumped out. At least the rain had let up a bit. Just as her boots hit the mud, she heard Evan.

"I'm . . . I'm okay," he said, his voice gritty. When she turned toward the sound, she saw why. He was clawing his way back up the ditch, his mouth and indeed his entire face caked with mud, his spectacles hooked over one ear, held up only by his nose, and the front of his suit covered with brown ooze.

Maggie thought he looked quite funny but wisely restrained the laugh that rose to her lips. "Oh, you poor thing!" she said as sympathetically as she could. "Let me help you—"

She took a step toward him.

"Careful!" he warned.

But regardless, her feet slipped out from under her. She landed on her behind and just kept going, sailing down the side of the ditch as if she were a ship on a brown sea.

"Yowl!" she cried, not entirely from distress. It was really rather exhilarating.

"Maggie! Maggie!" Evan cried, his voice registering true distress. "I'm coming for you!"

"Stop!" she yelled as she thumped to the bottom. But it was too late. In a moment Evan was at the bottom of the ditch beside her. He landed with a muddy splat! She could no longer restrain her mirth and nearly rolled in the mud laughing.

Evan stared, mystified. He was obviously unable to see the humor in this state of affairs. Filled with an evil desire to break through his seriousness, Maggie grabbed a handful of mud and tossed it at him like a snowball. She had a very good aim for a girl and struck him square in the nose.

"What—!" he sputtered.

She was practically howling now. In her amusement she closed her eyes for a moment, not aware of what a perfect target she made and certainly not expecting that the solemn Evan would react until a wad of mud suddenly filled her mouth.

She gagged, spitting and sputtering.

Bubbles of laughter finally escaped from Evan. Maggie gave him a shove, but she was laughing again, as well.

"Guess we don't have to worry about getting dirty anymore." Maggie giggled.

"I don't think you were worried much about that in the first place," he said dryly.

"I haven't had this much fun in an age," she replied, amusement still rippling through her voice.

"Still, I've ruined another one of your dresses."

"I think I'll go back to wearing overalls. You should, too," she said. "Think of the fun we could have then! I'll take you fishing and berry picking—I know a patch up by the pond that is good and ripe—" She stopped, seeing a very peculiar look on Evan's face. "What's wrong?"

Suddenly he was more flustered than when he'd had a mouthful of mud. "Nothing!" He scrambled to his feet. "We better see to the carriage." He held out his hand for her, and as he drew her to her feet, his expression still looked strange, as if he'd gulped down more than mud.

After several attempts, they made it up the slippery ditch. Evan had to straddle the edge of the ditch precariously in order to examine the wheel shaft. Maggie stood close by on more level ground, her hands ready to steady him should he lose his footing again.

He scratched his head. "To be honest, Maggie, I haven't the slightest idea how to fix this. We may have to walk the rest of the way home. Do you mind?"

"I don't know," she deadpanned. "I might get dirty."

"At least it has stopped raining," he offered.

"I say we eat something before we go. There's a good four or five more miles to home."

Using a jug of water that was kept in the back of the carriage and some napkins Mama had packed in the picnic basket, they cleaned some of the mud from their hands and faces. The meal of bread and cheese and apples was eaten with a liberal helping of grit, yet Maggie thought it was one of the best meals she'd ever had. They ate standing up in ankle-deep mud with the basket sitting on the floor of the tilted carriage. They talked and laughed some more over the incident, and when they finished eating, Maggie suggested they ride the carriage team home, since they were going to have to unhitch the horses and bring them back anyway. She almost regretted her suggestion. The five-mile walk with Evan would have been enjoyable. But the ride was almost as good and more of an adventure because Evan hadn't ridden a horse bareback since he'd been a boy. He was having so much trouble making his horse, who wasn't accustomed to carrying riders, go in the right direction that finally Maggie suggested they ride double and lead the second animal.

It was hard to tell under all the mud still caked on his face, but Maggie thought he got a bit pale at the idea of riding double.

"No," he said, "I refuse to let this beast win." And with renewed tenacity, he managed to get the animal to obey his commands.

It started to rain again, and by the time they arrived home, they were wet to the skin. Maggie would have liked to invite Evan to supper, but that was impossible. He needed to get home and take a bath and then see to the carriage. He did accept her invitation for the next day to have another dance lesson and supper afterward.

As soon as Evan departed, Mama set up the tub on the back porch and began heating water for Maggie's bath. Standing by the fire in the hearth with a quilt wrapped around her shivering body, she thought about the day. Though it had gotten off to a shaky start with the visit to Tommy and his slip about what he had told her before his father's death, it had ended rather pleasantly. If only Colby had been there instead of Evan! Yet if so, would she have had the same fun with Colby? Had she *ever* had such fun with him?

No, she couldn't remember ever having such a day with Colby. She'd never even gone on an outing with him except to events where large groups of people were in attendance. Surely those couldn't count. Besides, he'd always been pursuing Ellie, and Maggie had always been in too much of a dither around him to even begin to have a good time.

Here she was about to spend another day with Evan when it should be with Colby. But she couldn't ask Colby. What if he said no? Moreover, it made her shaky inside just thinking of it.

When the tub was full, Maggie shed her muddy clothes and slipped into the nice warm bath. The back porch was covered, so it was protected from the rain, and Mama set up a folding screen to give her privacy. The Parkers had an indoor bathroom with a fancy claw-foot tub. Evan was probably using it right now. Suddenly Maggie turned red at the thought of Evan taking a bath.

Ellie poked her head around the screen. "Here's a towel for you—what are you all red for? Is the water too hot?"

"Must be," Maggie said, grasping at the ready excuse.

Ellie laid the towel over the back of a chair. "You sure had a miserable trip to town."

"I don't know. It was actually kind of fun."

"That's right. You don't mind getting dirty. Evan must have been upset to ruin his expensive suit."

"He was more worried about my dress. And he wasn't that upset. We . . . well, it was fun. He's a lot of fun when he stops being so serious."

"Oh really?" Ellie arched her brow, a knowing glint in her eye.

"What's that supposed to mean?"

"Well, you have been spending a lot of time with Evan lately."

"And you know why." Maggie gave her head a shake, knowing her wet hair would spray all over Ellie.

Ellie squealed and jumped back. "Maybe you are barking up the wrong tree, Mags."

"Oh, please!" Maggie laughed at the outlandish implication of her sister's words. "Can you imagine the cow Mama would have if I took up with Florence Parker's son?" She laughed harder. Around her giggles she added, "Almost as bad as if I took up with the fake minister." The words were no sooner out of her mouth than she realized how insensitive they were. The stricken look on Ellie's face didn't help. "Ellie, I'm sorry! You know I was just joshing you. Mama loves Zack."

Ellie took a shaky breath, then plopped down in the chair. "Do you really think she does? Oh, I think she does love him, but I'm not so sure she loves the idea of him being her son-in-law. The other day she questioned me about our future, and I didn't have many good answers for her about how we would live, especially with his debt. She got that look, you know, the one where she really disapproves but is trying to hold it in."

"I never liked *that* look." Maggie soaped up her hair and gave her head a good scrubbing. "Do you love Zack?"

"I love him more each day, and I like him more every day I get to know him better!" Ellie said emphatically. "I talked to him about what Mama said, and he feels we should wait to marry, maybe a whole year, at least till next summer."

"And you were hoping for a Christmas wedding."

"Perhaps Christmas of eighty-four," Ellie said glumly.

"You sure don't want to be poor as church mice when you marry," Maggie said, surprising even herself at her practicality. "You're going to want children, and you don't want to live like the Arlingtons. Poor Louise looks ten years older than her twenty-five years. She works harder than anyone I ever saw—taking care of three kids, practically running the farm all the time because Lewis has to go away for work so often to make ends meet. I doubt even Mama and Dad had it that hard when they first married."

"To hear such wisdom from you, Mags, makes me truly think twice." She looked pale but smiled all the same. "You really are maturing, aren't you?"

"Maybe where other people's love lives are concerned." Maggie dunked her head into the water, massaging the soap out of her hair. When she lifted out her head, Ellie handed her a towel to dry her eyes. "I can't seem to get it right with Colby. I'm spending all my time with Evan to help him win Tamara in order to get her away from Colby. In the meantime Tamara and Colby are probably spending tons of time together."

Maggie groaned. "Everything I do only makes it worse!" She grabbed the towel and wrapped it around herself as she stepped from the tub.

"Maybe the party Saturday will help," Ellie offered hopefully.

"I hope so. I am running out of ideas."

# SIXTEEN

Maggie was a domestic wonder for the next two days. Besides Evan's dancing lessons and sewing lessons with Tamara, she worked with Grandma and Ellie baking for the party. Mama helped with this, as well, as Maggie knew she would. Maybe the delicious smells wafting through the house also motivated Maggie with her sewing. She finished the first three blocks for her sampler, and they looked quite nice—perhaps nicer than Tamara's, though Maggie would never say so.

The day of the party was perfect. It was one of those beautiful September days that made you think it was still summer. The earlier rainy days had cleaned everything off, leaving a sparkle to the landscape. It was sunny and warm enough to hold the festivities outdoors, and like the previous party, the quilting frames were set up outside. The ladies would quilt all day and then later, when the party began, the refreshment table would be set up outside, as well, with lanterns strung around the yard for light.

The quilting bee for Kendra's wedding quilts got the day off to a great start. With Maggie seated at a frame beside Grandma, and Tamara on the other side, Grandma instructed them both on their quilting stitches.

When Mrs. Stoddard walked by, she actually paused and complimented Maggie's work. Maggie swelled with pride, and hope. The fact that Mrs. Stoddard's comments about Tamara's work weren't quite as enthusiastic didn't give Maggie as much pleasure as she would have imagined. In fact, when Tamara asked Maggie for help, Maggie gladly gave it. She didn't mention that she had been practicing on the sly in her free time. Ellie had given her a doll quilt she had started years ago but hadn't finished, and Maggie had been working on it, her quilting stitches getting smaller and more even with each try.

When the dancing started later in the evening, her confidence was soaring. The first reel was announced, and the men fanned out to ask girls to dance. Maggie had her eye surreptitiously on Colby and was certain he was heading in her direction. But before he could reach her, Evan appeared at her side.

"May I have this dance, Maggie?" he asked.

Out of the corner of her mouth, she murmured, "What are you doing? You're supposed to ask Tamara."

"I . . . ah . . . thought just a little practice dance first," he stammered. "You know, to make sure I have it right."

"You'll do fine," she said with forced patience. But she saw Colby change his direction and now head for Tamara. It was too late. "Okay, one dance." She gave Evan her hand.

The dancers lined up, there being enough for two sets of six couples. Maggie made sure she and Evan were in the same set with Colby. At least she would get to dance some of the moves with him.

The music started. Evan turned her right hand, then turned her left hand. He did very well, though his expression was etched with deep concentration and his lips moved slightly as he silently counted the beats.

"Do-si-do!" called one of the musicians. Evan stepped on her toe once, but she pretended not to notice. He became flustered and almost did it again. This time she laughed and skipped out of his way as if it was part of the dance. When it was their turn to sashay down the middle of the line, she whispered, "Evan, smile. Act like you're having a good time."

"I am having a good time."

"You look like you're being tortured."

"Oh." He plastered a smile on his face, and though Maggie couldn't say the stilted expression was an improvement, at least he was trying.

When it was time to "reel the set," Maggie worried about letting Evan be on his own. However, there was no choice. It was their turn to hook elbows and dance a turn with new partners all the way down the row. She uttered a silent prayer that he wouldn't hurt any of the girls. She heard a couple of feminine yelps, but when they met back in the middle, he smiled at her. Apparently he hadn't done too badly.

After the dance Maggie made sure she and Evan were standing next to Colby and Tamara so that when the next dance began, there would be no mistake in the pairing up. Even at that she had to give Evan a covert elbow in the ribs to remind him to ask Tamara. He finally did, and it was quite natural, since they were both right there, for Colby to ask Maggie.

Everything started going wonderfully for Maggie. When another reel started, Maggie managed to nudge Colby over to the refreshment table while Evan and Tamara lined up for the dance.

"All that dancing works up an appetite," Maggie said.

"That's the truth!" Colby agreed. He grabbed a couple of plates, handed one to Maggie, then began piling food onto his. "Besides, my feet are killing me. I've been working twelve, fifteen hours a day between the farm and the mill. Don't know how I found the strength to dance anyway."

"You poor dear!" Maggie said with doting sympathy. They went to sit on one of the benches Dad had set about the yard. "I have been meaning to mention that I want to come to your place and lend a hand with the chores. The families of the Sewing Circle want to help out until your father gets back on his feet."

"That's awfully kind of you, but with Tamara and Sarah, Mother has plenty of help in the house—"

"I was thinking of helping you, Colby," Maggie said quickly. "I can help with feeding the animals, cleaning out the barn, whatever you need."

He smiled. "I guess I almost forgot, with you wearing dresses lately, that you are as good as any fellow on the farm."

She thought that was a compliment and smiled back. "I can come over Monday, and you can show me what needs to be done."

They concentrated on their food for a few moments, but Colby's earlier statement about all the work he was doing gave her another idea.

"Colby, you know the old adage, 'All work and no play makes Jack a dull boy.' Not that you could ever be dull, but I expect you might need some fun, too."

"This party sure fits the bill!"

"Yes . . . well . . ." She hesitated, knowing what she was about to ask was terribly brazen, but she'd begun to think that her working at the Stoddard farm wasn't going to be enough to grab Colby's romantic interest. "This weather isn't going to last forever," she went on in a rush. "I think you—uh—we, need a picnic. You aren't planning to work tomorrow, are you? It's Sunday."

"Just the regular chores."

"Then how about it?"

"Will you bring your mama's apple spice cake?" he asked with a grin.

"You can count on it!" She grinned back at him. A picnic with Colby! Could life be more perfect?

When she looked up, Evan and Tamara were approaching with plates of food. Maggie had been so absorbed with Colby she hadn't even noticed that the reel had ended. Tamara didn't look too distressed, so it must have gone well with Evan. However, though they were walking side by side, they did not appear at ease, especially Evan, who seemed rather stiff, until he saw Maggie. Then he smiled.

"May we share the bench with you?" Evan asked.

There was room for four on the bench, but Maggie was loath to give up her time alone with Colby. Scooting closer to Colby, she consoled herself with the fact that she and Colby would have all afternoon tomorrow together. Evan sat in the space next to her, and before she could get Colby to move over, Tamara had taken the space on the other side of Colby.

Did she have to do everything for Evan? He should have assessed the situation and made sure he sat next to Tamara.

Tamara fanned herself. "Goodness, I haven't danced so much in ages! This is such an enjoyable party."

"Say, I've just had a terrific idea," Colby said. "Maggie and I were talking about extending the fun into tomorrow by having a picnic. Why don't you join us?"

Maggie nearly dropped her plate. Her mind raced, trying to think of reasons why Tamara shouldn't join them, but she came up blank.

"Oh, I'd love to!" Tamara enthused.

"Of course, you must come, too, Evan." It was all Maggie could think of to salvage the disaster.

Maggie was up the next morning while it was still dark in order to make apple spice cake. When Mama came down an hour later, she was greeted by a cloud of flour dust in the air, pans and bowls everywhere, and Maggie up to her elbows in flour and batter.

The look on Mama's face indicated she'd been awakened by the clatter and wasn't happy about it. "What is going on? You are going to wake the dead."

"I'm making spice cake for the picnic," Maggie said, unconsciously lifting the wooden spoon she was using to stir the cake batter and spewing batter all over, just missing Mama.

"What picnic?" Mama asked, moving quickly out of the line of fire.

"Uh . . . some friends and I are going on a picnic today."

"We have church today. What friends?"

"After church," Maggie said, hoping to deflect Mama's final question. "I wouldn't miss church. It was so nice of Reverend Barnett to include us again in his circuit this month."

"Well, I am of the opinion he is merely attempting to proselytize us, but your father believes we should support his kind offer."

Maggie knew her parents had had a disagreement about this matter. Since the Brethren of Christ back East still hadn't come up with a new minister—and they could not promise one in the near future—many of the Brethren folk were seriously considering switching churches. Mama and Dad, like the community itself, were somewhat divided on the issue. Mama had been raised in the Brethren of Christ church while Dad had grown up Methodist. Dad felt, and Maggie had to agree, that the two denominations were alike enough that it made little difference which church they attended.

The county board of deacons for the Brethren of Christ, of which Dad was a member, had decided that they must be unanimous on the issue so that there would be no split in the church. Because of this, no definite decision had been made about whether to meld the Brethren with the Methodists. However, there was another contingent that felt they ought to reinstate Zack as their minister. Dad and Zack had talked about it at supper one night.

"If you felt a true calling from God in this, Zack," Dad had said, "there would be no reason why you couldn't be our real minister."

Zack had stared back in shock. He had known about the growing interest in having him return to the duties of minister but hadn't placed much stock in it. "I don't see how I could do it, Mr. Newcomb. People would want to get married and baptized and all manner of things that I avoided doing before because I wasn't a real minister."

"I have written to the denomination headquarters," Dad said, "and laid out our situation here. I mentioned you and how the folks felt about having you as their minister. I haven't heard back yet, but I don't think it is as impossible as you might think. With the shortage of ministers, a man with a Call could be accepted and certified—I think. We'll have to wait the final word from back East."

Plaintively Zack had asked, "How does a man know if he has a Call from God?"

"Best way is to pray about it, I reckon."

Zack glanced at Ellie, who had kept her eyes focused on her hands. She had been remaining studiously impartial on this issue. She loved Zack as he was and would never want it to seem he was doing this for her.

"I've been doing that, sir," Zack had replied.

Nothing more had come of it since that conversation. Of course Maggie hoped Zack would be their minister. Wouldn't it be grand if he could preside over her and Colby's wedding? But as wedding bells began chiming in her head, she remembered Mama standing there and the messy kitchen to be dealt with.

Mama sighed. "Did you follow my recipe exactly?"

"Yes, I tried. Goodness, this isn't an easy cake to make. Apples to grate, a half dozen spices to measure, butter to cream. Where is your cake pan?" She was glad she didn't have to give more details about the picnic. She didn't think Mama would mind who was going, but it might come out that she had asked Colby, and Mama wouldn't like such forwardness in her daughter.

Mama got a pan from a cupboard and then went to the stove. "You'll need more wood on the fire to get the oven hot enough," she commented as she spread lard on the pan.

"Well, aren't we early birds this morning!" Grandma said, coming down the stairs.

"Maggie got it in her head to make a cake," Mama said.

"Why don't you two work on that, and I'll start breakfast," Grandma offered.

"I'll go gather the eggs and get a ham from the smokehouse," Mama said. "Maggie, will you want some for your picnic?"

"That would be nice." Maggie gave Mama a big appreciative smile. She knew her mother was giving her great latitude, for egg gathering was usually Maggie's job.

Mama walked to the back door, then paused. "By the way, who is going with you on this picnic?"

"Oh, just Tamara, Colby, and Evan," she replied casually.

"Hmm." Mama nodded thoughtfully and went outside without another word.

"That's a nice thing to do with your friends," Grandma said as she rummaged about the kitchen for breakfast preparations.

"I had hoped it would be just me and Colby," Maggie said. "But the others ended up tagging along."

"It would have been unseemly for you and Colby to go alone. Your parents would not have permitted it, so you should be thankful the others are coming, as well."

Scraping the cake batter into the pan, Maggie sighed. "I guess so. I do wish things with Colby could move along faster."

"I may be old-fashioned in these matters, but taking time to get to know a beau can never hurt." Grandma cleared a space on the table where she could peel potatoes.

"I've known Colby all my life. Isn't that enough?"

"How have you known him, Maggie? He was your older brother's friend, then your sister's beau. Have you really had a chance to know him? What kinds of things do you talk with him about?"

"Talk?"

"Yes. What do you talk about after church or at parties and such?"

Maggie shrugged. "Things," she said vaguely. "Grandma, can you tell if the oven is ready?" she asked, glad for a diversion from the uncomfortable direction of her grandmother's questioning.

Grandma checked the oven and nodded for Maggie to go ahead and put the cake in. "Maggie, I know this is hard to hear, but don't rush things. Try to get to know Colby."

"How do I do that? I hardly ever see him."

"You are going to see him today. It doesn't matter if Evan and Tamara are there. Engage Colby in conversation. Learn his interests and your mutual interests. This is one of the responsibilities of the new way of things. In the olden days when marriages were arranged, this burden was lifted. No one cared much if they had anything in common. But now, if you wish to marry for love, it comes with certain strings attached. And one of those strings is discerning true love from infatuation."

"Is that what you think?" Maggie asked defensively. "That I am just infatuated with Colby?"

"I don't know, dear. But isn't it something you'd want to know before you marry?"

That did infuriate Maggie about Grandma. She never railed and insisted, like Mama sometimes did. Rather, she put things in the form of reasonable questions. So instead of getting mad at her, Maggie was forced to think about what Grandma said. But she didn't want to think too much about things—it took the fun out of it.

Or was she simply afraid to think too deeply about her feelings for Colby?

She recalled something that happened at the party last night that had disturbed her. It was during the first and only waltz of the evening. She had made sure Colby asked her, mostly by covertly urging Evan to ask Tamara before Colby could.

She thought she would simply melt with happiness at being so close to Colby. Instead, she found her attention wandering from him, searching the dancing couples until she found Tamara and Evan. Maggie watched them nearly the entire time. She told herself it was because she was worried Evan would mess up the dance steps. But a tiny little part of her just didn't like Tamara—beautiful, charming, beguiling Tamara—holding Evan in such a familiar way.

It was only that she didn't want to lose a friend to Tamara any more than she wanted to lose Colby to her. That's all it was.

# SEVENTEEN

Sunday turned into a crisp fall day with a pale sky stippled with clouds. Not as perfect as the previous day, but certainly not a day to discourage hearty Oregonians. The picnickers wore their Sunday clothes so as not to waste time going home to change. They also had coats and plenty of quilts.

Maggie had packed a hamper with thick slices of ham, a couple of loaves of bread, the apple cake, of course, fresh apples, and plenty of cider to drink. Tamara brought a basket, as well, with a jar of Mrs. Stoddard's pickles, some muffins, and a few hard-cooked eggs. Maggie noted there was nothing in Tamara's basket that was made specially by her, which made the fact that her cake had turned out well even better.

They rode in the Parkers' rockaway, now repaired, out to a favorite meadow near the Baxter place and along Dart Creek. The road only went so far, and they had to hike in about a half mile. Their destination was little more than a clearing in the middle of a thick stand of timber but a nice covering of grass gave them a soft floor on which to spread a quilt.

"I'm starved. Let's eat!" Colby said, hardly giving them a chance to alight from the carriage.

Besides being hungry, he was probably glad they had arrived and he no longer needed to converse with Evan. Maggie and Tamara had sat in the backseat of the carriage and had chatted about this and that, mostly their sewing progress. But Colby and Evan had seemed uncomfortably quiet in the front. At first Evan had tried to engage Colby in conversation, but Colby's responses were brief, not as if he were mad, but rather as though he weren't interested.

"How was your harvest?" Evan had asked.

"Good," Colby replied curtly.

"My father says the price for potatoes is holding steady this year."

"Uh-huh," Colby grunted.

"Dad is happy to have the farmers return to the mill now that harvest is over," Evan said. "They should be busy all fall."

"That's good."

Finally Evan fell silent. Maggie couldn't understand what was wrong with Colby. He had no reason to be upset about anything. She realized she'd never heard Colby have a lengthy conversation. Mostly he joked, made wisecracks, or when with girls, he flirted.

Well, a man didn't have to talk, did he? Colby had many other good attributes. Why did she feel she had to defend him anyway, especially in her own mind? It was Grandma's words still bouncing about in Maggie's head that made her notice Colby's behavior today. Why didn't Grandma just yell and insist on her way, instead of asking sensible questions?

Reclining on one of Mama's old quilts, they ate their dinner. Maggie received raves for her spice cake, which she modestly said was a little dry. Still, she hoped that either Colby or Tamara would go home and mention to Mrs. Stoddard what a good baker Maggie was.

Conversation among the foursome was a bit stilted. Finally, shortly after finishing the meal, Evan rose, stretching his legs.

"I'd like to do a bit of exploring," he said.

"Oh, that sounds lovely," Tamara said, rising also.

Maggie waited a couple of heartbeats to see what Colby would do.

"I'm feeling lazy," he said. "I've been working hard all week."

"I'll keep you company," Maggie said politely, though inside, her heart was racing. Some time alone with Colby at last!

Evan and Tamara trooped off toward the woods. Evan cast one backward glance at Maggie, as if to give her one last chance to join him. What was wrong with him? Didn't he realize this was a chance for him to be alone with Tamara?

Maggie gave him a "You can do it!" nod, though in a way she would have preferred a hike to sitting sedately on a blanket.

After Evan and Tamara disappeared among the trees, Maggie fussed for a few moments, packing up the picnic things.

"Do you want some more cake before I put it away?" she asked Colby.

"Don't know where I'd put it," he replied with a contented pat on his belly.

She wrapped the cake and placed it in the hamper. When the job was done, she started to feel restless. Colby had stretched out on the quilt. Not wanting him to fall asleep and ruin this wonderful opportunity to get to know each other, Maggie began talking.

"What did you think of the church service today?" She had tried to talk about this before when all four of them were there, but the topic hadn't developed because Evan and Tamara, being newcomers, had little opinion of the little Maintown controversy.

"It was okay," Colby murmured, still lying back, eyes closed.

"Do you think we will really change over to the Methodists?"

"Six of one, half dozen of the other."

"Maybe, but there must be some differences for there to have been two denominations in the first place. But the thing is, we have always been Brethren of Christ. You and I were born in that denomination."

"Uh-huh."

Seeing that he wasn't much interested in that topic, she tried a different tack. Maybe she could get him to talk about himself. Men seemed to love that.

"Colby, is everything okay with you? You've been kind of quiet today."

"Really? I hadn't noticed."

"I almost thought you were miffed at Evan." She laughed dismissively. "But how could that be? You hardly know him."

"Don't need to know him to know that spending all that time in the big city has gone to his head," Colby said.

"What?" This truly astounded Maggie, for she'd felt the exact opposite about him. She knew no man more modest than Evan. "He seems rather humble, if you ask me, considering all his education and experiences and family affluence."

"Not from where I'm looking. He's all the time using those big fancy words and wearing those expensive suits."

Maggie simply could not believe what she was hearing. "What do you want, Colby, for him to talk gibberish and be unclothed?"

"Sounds like you're defending him." Colby rolled onto his side and, propping his head with his hand, focused a challenging gaze at Maggie.

"No. But maybe you just need to get to know him better."

"He always acted too good for the rest of us."

"Is that why you made fun of him?" Maggie rejoined sharply.

"Had to do something to put him in his place."

"Colby, I must say I am shocked at what you are saying."

Colby studied her a moment. "Sounds like you might be sweet on him. And here I thought your heart belonged to Tommy Donnelly." His tone mocked her.

Now she was furious, not only at his words but because he was ruining what was supposed to be their time alone, her time to woo him.

"I am not sweet on Tommy or Evan or anyone!" she railed. "But at least neither of them would belittle another person, not like you've done to both of them. Colby, I never thought you were a malicious person, but now I must wonder."

"Aw, I was just having fun with them," he defended himself. "Like I said, Evan asked for it, and Tommy . . . well, you know Tommy."

"But you hurt them both."

"I didn't know that." He paused, then added with a sincere tone, "Guess I'm sorry I hurt their feelings. But I was a kid and didn't know better."

"Maybe you should apologize to both of them."

He arched a brow as if she was asking for a million dollars. "Maybe so," he replied, with little enthusiasm.

They were quiet for a couple of minutes. Maggie tried to cool off. She wished Colby had been a little more emphatic about making an apology, but he might come around with time.

Finally Colby asked, "Hey, Maggie, did you mean it when you said you weren't sweet on anyone?"

She knew she'd been given another opportunity, and Colby might even be fishing for some encouragement. But she surprised even herself when she replied, "Maybe not."

"Not a single person in this whole county?" he prompted.

She shook her head.

"You mad at me for what I said about Evan?" Colby asked.

"A little."

"What could I do so you won't be mad at me?"

"Does how I feel about you truly matter to you, Colby?"

"Kinda does."

She was about to make a concession and try to get back on a better footing when sounds of laughter drew her attention to the tree line. A moment later Evan and Tamara burst into the clearing.

"I thought we would be lost forever!" Tamara said through her giggles.

"I figured we couldn't be too far from our party." Still chuckling, Evan swiped a sleeve across his damp brow.

"You were worried for a minute," Tamara taunted good-naturedly.

"Don't tell me you two got lost a couple of feet from the clearing?" Colby said, perhaps unaware of how derisive he sounded.

"Well, out there all those trees look alike." Evan laughed.

"That's what happens when you send two city folks into the woods," Colby said.

"One of us should have gone with you," Maggie offered, now, after the fiasco with Colby, wishing more than ever that she had.

Tamara laughed. "What? And miss our little adventure? When I looked up and saw Evan staring around, trying to pick out one tree from another—"

"I must say, I did panic for just the smallest moment," Evan admitted, and the two laughed again.

Maggie listened, not with amusement but with—what was it? It struck her like an anvil when she realized she was jealous. Now Evan and Tamara had a funny adventure to share, like her own muddy adventure with Evan. They had a private moment to share a laugh over that only they knew about. And it irked Maggie.

"Getting lost for a moment in the woods is nothing compared to what happened to Evan and me the other day," Maggie found herself saying. "Did you tell her about the mud, Evan?" She laughed. "My goodness! The carriage broke down, and we slipped into the mud." Maggie threw back her head and howled.

Evan chuckled. "Yes, it was quite a mess. That is one trip to St. Helens I will never forget."

"You two went to St. Helens?" Colby asked.

"Yes, to visit Tommy," Evan replied.

Maggie put in, "Evan is going to be Tommy's lawyer." She couldn't help the pride in her tone.

"You sure you want to get mixed up with that one?" queried Colby. "He was always a bad seed, but now that he's a murderer, you'll want to steer clear of him."

"Every man is entitled to a defense under the law," Evan said, growing more serious.

"But he has admitted to murdering his father."

"He is innocent until proven guilty," Evan rejoined.

"But he ain't innocent."

"I can't discuss the particulars of the case, but one must keep in mind extenuating circumstances."

Colby looked at Maggie. "There's what I said about them highfalutin words." He made sure, as he spoke, that he sounded more like a country bumpkin than he ever really did.

Again, Maggie wasn't happy about the direction things were taking, so she tried to change tack. "You two must be hungry after your hike. There's lots of food left."

"Perhaps we ought to be heading back," Evan suggested. "It is getting dark earlier these days."

Before Maggie knew it, they were seated in the carriage and on their way. The idyllic picnic, or *imagined* idyllic picnic, with Colby was over. And she had nothing to show for the afternoon except a big knot in the pit of her stomach.

Evan drove Colby and Tamara to the Stoddard place first and then drove Maggie home. On the way they were silent for a time, and Maggie knew the conversation that had ended their picnic was still weighing on their minds.

"Evan," she began, trying to broach the delicate subject, "I don't know what got into Colby today."

"I don't think he likes me very much," Evan replied matter-of-factly.

"You know, all those years of he and the other boys making fun of you," she said, "I really do think they were jealous of you."

"I never gave them cause." A hint of the hurt he'd felt then and now was evident in his voice. "I couldn't help that I was smart or that my family had money and could send me to fancy schools. I probably wouldn't have gone away to those schools if I had fit in here."

"I know, and Colby shouldn't hold it against you. But he does."

"I will try to overlook it, because that is my Christian duty," he said. "And because you care for him, I will try to see his good side."

"I think he would like to apologize for making fun of you all those years ago," she ventured. "But he's got that male pride."

Evan nodded.

She knew Evan had his share of pride, as well, but his sense of duty to God was stronger. Bits from their youth came back to Maggie's memory. She recalled an incident that occurred shortly after she had started going to school. It involved Evan and the older kids, mostly the boys. Evan would have been about ten years old, and he had just gotten his spectacles. It was quite a novelty around there, since most families couldn't have afforded them. If a child had bad eyesight, he just learned to live with it. But Evan had come to school that day with his new spectacles, and now Maggie realized how that act alone had been brave of him. He'd already had a hard time fitting in, and now the spectacles made him stand out even more. The boys called him four-eyes, and one boy—could it have been Colby?—snatched the spectacles from Evan's face, and all the boys played "keep away" with them.

Did Evan cry and rail at his abusers? No, he hadn't. Did he run to the teacher? No. He'd attempted to reason with them instead. He explained that the spectacles weren't toys and were expensive and if anything happened to them, he'd be in trouble. He had told them they could try them on and see what they were like. All the while he kept trying to get them back as the boys tossed them around.

She remembered thinking how stupid those boys were. If she'd been given the chance, she would have tried on the spectacles, for she had been very curious about them. She had thought Evan was being quite generous with his offer.

Now in the carriage she turned to Evan. "Do you remember that first day you wore your spectacles to school?"

"It's not one of my fondest memories, but you tend not to forget the more humiliating days of your life," he said dryly.

"Was it that awful?"

"I was the only child in school with spectacles. And the boys didn't let me forget what a freak that made me."

She told him then how she remembered the event and ended by saying, "I thought you were brave and very lucky—I mean to have those fascinating spectacles! The other boys were stupid. I wanted to try on your spectacles."

He smiled appreciatively. "I went home and bawled. I swore I would never wear them again."

"But you didn't cry in front of the boys."

"I wanted to. But of all the names they called me over the years, crybaby was never one of them."

"You must have hated them."

"No." He seemed surprised at the idea. "I often hated myself for being odd, but never them. I wanted to be accepted. I wanted to be like them. Sometimes I would pray so hard to God for Him to make me less different. I don't know why He never did."

"That's easy," Maggie said. "God doesn't want us all to be alike. I know sometimes it bothers me that I don't fit in with the women, yet, on the other hand, would I really want to be just like them? How boring!"

"You are quite right. I will try to keep that in mind."

Evan pulled into the Newcomb yard. Gypsy ran up to the carriage barking. Ellie and Zack were sitting on the porch, waving and calling out a greeting.

Maggie had thought she would be happy to see the afternoon end, since it had not fared well between her and Colby. Now she practically forgot all about that, realizing instead that she wanted to keep talking to Evan. She invited him for supper, but he declined because his parents were expecting him. She asked when they could return to St. Helens to see Tommy. He said he needed to research the case further and begin interviewing prospective witnesses before meeting again with his client.

Thus he drove away with no plans made for them to see each other again soon.

Evan Parker was not sure about a lot of things in life. In fact, life in general often confused and befuddled him. For instance, how stupid it was of him not to conjure up some pretense for seeing Maggie again! Why had he just now met her invitations with practical and true reasons for refusal? It wasn't until it was too late and he was driving away that he realized his stupidity. He could have—should have!—come up with something, some reason to see her again.

There were probably only three things he could say at the moment that he was certain of. One, without question, was his faith in God. Even if God hadn't answered his youthful prayers to make him more like the other boys, he knew it was God who had given him the strength to endure a difficult childhood.

The second certainty, which at this juncture was definitely questionable, was his intelligence. He knew the law backward and forward, could quote pages from law books, cases, and precedents. He'd tutored half his classmates and had even taught his instructors a few things they didn't know. He'd excelled in science and mathematics and had been courted by the School of Medicine but had opted for the law because he had no stomach for blood.

The third certainty was just now dawning upon him, but it was no less certain. He was in love with Maggie Newcomb.

This did not make him as fickle as it sounded. Yes, he had once thought himself in love with Tamara. But time had passed since she had so blithely, if unknowingly, rejected him. Now, considering the depth and breadth of his feelings for Maggie, he wondered if he had ever truly loved Tamara. And as for the rumor, which he'd allowed to spread, that he had come home in order to be close to Tamara—well, it wasn't exactly true. He let his family think that because he'd been too ashamed to admit that he simply was not cut out for the life of a big city lawyer. The only person he had even come close to admitting that to was Maggie herself.

However, as was his sorry habit, he had made quite a mess of things. How could he have embroiled himself in a plan to bring Maggie and Colby Stoddard together? When he had first agreed to this, he hadn't been certain of his feelings for Maggie. Though even then he'd been very keen on getting to know her better and had jumped at what might have been his only chance to do so.

He'd felt something that first moment he had looked upon her at his welcome home party, had looked upon her and doused her with his punch! The fact that she had not held that faux pas against him endeared her to him more.

Nevertheless, it wasn't until they had been mired in mud and she had laughingly flung a handful at him that he had known without doubt his heart belonged to her.

What a quandary he was in now! Though the scheme to pair her with Colby was giving him a perfect excuse to be with her, it was also working against him. There was the opportunity provided by her interest in Tommy Donnelly's trial, but he could not in good conscience use that to further his romantic pursuits.

Should he simply tell her of his feelings? He was fairly certain what would happen if he did so. She, like Tamara, would be forced to tell him that she cared for him only as a brother. There was another possibility. He could attempt to push Colby and Tamara together. Yet that might only break Maggie's heart and place a wedge between them. The last thing on earth he wanted was to hurt Maggie.

Moreover, he was not comfortable with all the scheming.

If he had but a small sign of encouragement from Maggie, he would come clean to her. He knew that God liked to give His children the desires of their hearts. Surely God would not want to see him rejected twice. He could only pray and hope God would choose to bless him thus.

# EIGHTEEN

On Monday morning Maggie went to the Stoddards' place to work, as she had promised Colby, but she was disappointed when Mrs. Stoddard greeted her at the door, informing her that he was not there.

"He's working in the orchard today," his mother said.

"I've come to help out a bit, if you need me," Maggie offered. She couldn't very well back out, even if the object of her generosity wasn't present.

"Well . . . I suppose I could find something around the house for you to do." Mrs. Stoddard was understandably hesitant if she thought Maggie had come to do housework.

"I was planning to help Colby with his chores—but if you need me, I'm here for you, as well. I just want to be useful."

"Come in. And it was very thoughtful of you to think of us. We can use help."

Mrs. Stoddard slowly warmed to the idea of Maggie's help. Would she have been more receptive if it had been Ellie at her door?

Maggie entered the house. It was very much like her own home, one big room downstairs with bedrooms upstairs. Sarah and Tamara were in the kitchen doing the breakfast dishes. She exchanged greetings with them. Tamara mentioned that she hoped she could come by Maggie's house tomorrow for another sewing lesson.

Mrs. Stoddard, garbed in an apron over her work dress, had apparently been tending a large pot on the cookstove. "I must keep stirring this," she said, returning to the task. "I am starching some of Colby's and my husband's good shirts."

"I can do that if you want," Maggie said, trying to be as helpful as possible.

"No, thank you. It must be done just so." Mrs. Stoddard paused in apparent thought. "There are so many things to do. Let me give it a moment's consideration."

Maggie knew she wasn't the most perceptive person in the world, but even she could notice the tension in the Stoddard kitchen. Had she offended in some way? Or had the tension been there before her arrival? Then it began to come clear when she heard the sound of floorboards creaking. Maggie glanced up and saw Mr. Stoddard coming down the stairs. She remembered he hadn't been in church yesterday and it had been a week or two since she had last seen him. In that time he seemed to have aged noticeably. She'd always thought him handsome for a man of his age. Colby had obviously inherited his father's good looks. Now Mr. Stoddard was pale, the lines on his face standing out like the markings on the relief map at school. There were dark circles under his eyes, too. Maggie knew that he had been ailing for months, but for the first time she realized how serious it must be.

Mrs. Stoddard also heard the boards on the stairs creak. "Albert, what are you doing?" she demanded.

"My water pitcher is empty." With a wan smile he held up the pitcher.

"Why didn't you use the bell I gave you? You must not come downstairs." She spoke to him as if he were an errant child.

"Aw, I feel silly ringing that bell," he replied.

"I don't care. Dr. Leetham said you were to stay in bed." She strode up the stairs to where he stood and took the water pitcher from him. "Now, you march back up to bed this instant!"

Like a child who had been soundly scolded, Mr. Stoddard obeyed and turned around. He didn't exactly *march* up the stairs but plodded slowly like an old man.

"That man is going to be the death of me!" Mrs. Stoddard grumbled as she filled the pitcher from the kitchen water pump. Then, still mumbling to herself, she headed upstairs.

Both Maggie and Sarah had the same idea regarding the need to keep stirring the items in the pot, and they strode toward the stove at the same moment. Maggie had a clear look at Sarah and saw that she, like her father, was pale. Her eyes were red-rimmed as though she had been crying.

"Sarah, are you okay?" Maggie asked. She never had been good at knowing the right things to say in such instances.

"Y-yes," Sarah replied in a trembly voice.

"Your father will be all right as soon as he rests up a little," Maggie said, knowing, after seeing the man, how lame her words were.

"Sure he will." But Sarah probably believed it no more than Maggie did. She took up the wooden spoon that her mother had propped on the rim of the pot and began stirring the shirts. "I'll take care of this, Maggie. But if you'd like, well, I haven't had a chance to gather the eggs this morning."

"I'll get right to it," Maggie said eagerly—mostly eager to get outside and away from the awkwardness in the house.

"Maybe when I finish that, I'll run up to the orchard and see if Colby needs help."

Sarah nodded and Maggie hurried out, hoping she made it before Mrs. Stoddard reappeared. It took her a little longer than usual to gather the eggs because the hens had hid a few, and she wasn't familiar with their hiding places, as she was at home with their chickens. She brought the basket back to the house. The women were busy with other tasks. She could tell Mrs. Stoddard was distracted because she offered no criticism about how Maggie had collected the eggs.

Maggie said she would head up to the orchard and help Colby. Mrs. Stoddard mumbled something, hardly even noticing Maggie, who had the feeling that her help was considered more of a curse than a blessing. She couldn't hold it against the woman though, for she had a lot on her mind.

Reaching the apple orchard, Maggie didn't see Colby, but noting a ladder propped against one of the trees, she headed there and found him straddling one of the stout branches.

"Hi, Colby," she said.

"Hi, Maggie—oh, I forgot you were coming today. I'm sorry." He reached forward and plucked an apple from the end of the branch. "I'm trying to get the last of the apples picked. Mother doesn't like any to go to waste."

"That's okay," Maggie said in response to his first statement. "You've got a lot to preoccupy your mind."

"Here, would you grab the basket and empty my sack into it?" he asked. He removed the cotton sack slung over his shoulder that was bulging with apples.

"Good crop of apples this year," Maggie commented, taking the sack and dumping the apples into the basket.

"Wish there was enough to sell. We could use the money."

"It must be hard with your father ill."

"I've been working like a plow horse." He continued to pick apples, balancing himself on the thicker branches to reach the high ones. Finally, having filled his sack again, he stepped onto the ladder and descended back to the ground. He took two apples from the sack, tossed her one, and took a large bite out of the other. "Mighty good apples!"

She bit into hers and agreed. "You know, if you have something better to do, I could climb up into the trees and get apples as good as you."

"Probably better 'cause you're smaller." He continued to chomp on his apple. "I sure appreciate your coming out to help."

"I can come as often as you need me until your father gets better," she offered.

He stopped chewing and looked at her. "He ain't gonna get better."

"Oh, surely not, Colby!"

"Doc was here early this morning—I had to go fetch him in the middle of the night because Dad was having trouble breathing. Anyway, that's what he said. He might have only a year to live."

Maggie gasped. The Stoddards were like family to her, just as was the entire community, so to hear this about Mr. Stoddard, whom she knew better than her own uncles, was shocking and sad.

"That must be why Sarah was crying," Maggie said.

"She took it pretty hard. Dad always doted on her. It's having a hard time sinking into my head. All I can think of is work, work, work. No time for much else." With what appeared to be frustration, he gave the core of his apple a hard toss into the bushes on the edge of the orchard.

"I'm so sorry, Colby." She didn't know what other words of comfort to offer.

"Guess I better get used to it—the work, I mean. It's not going to change, and before I know it, this place will be mine, and the work will never end—" His voice broke a little over the words. He swallowed and ran a sleeve over his face.

She had never seen Colby show such emotion before. Impulsively, she put her arms around him. It seemed a better thing to do than recite lame words.

"I'm just not ready to run a farm!" Colby lamented. "I don't want to work myself into an early grave like my father."

She still didn't know what to say, and she couldn't voice the fleeting thought that his words sounded a bit self-centered. Suddenly she felt the distinctive sensation of his lips pressing against the top of her head and forgot all else. She looked up at him, and before she knew it, he lowered his lips and pressed them against her own. As his arms tightened around her and the kiss deepened, she felt a tingle from her head to her toes.

All her dreams had come true! After years of pining for him and wondering what it would feel like, Colby was kissing her! She need wonder no more. It was a marvelous sensation. It occurred to her that she'd felt the same when Zack had kissed her, but it hadn't been love in Zack's case. She'd learned then there must be more to a kiss for it to represent love, though she hadn't figured out what that was. So as Colby's lips pressed against hers, she waited expectantly. For what, she did not know. Again, something seemed to be missing. It must simply be the poor timing, she rationalized. They were, after all, kissing while his father probably lay dying.

She surprised herself by being the first to push away. "Colby, I don't know . . ." she murmured.

"I'm sorry, Mags. I shouldn't have taken advantage of you," he said. "It was even more wrong because—"

"Now, you mustn't worry that you were betraying your father," she offered.

"Yes . . . yes, that's it. You must think me terrible."

"You just needed comforting."

"I'm really confused, Maggie," he said, almost as if it were a confession.

"Let's not think anything of what happened, okay?" But she was certain she would think of nothing else, even if she knew her heart hadn't been in that kiss as much as she had hoped it would be. Perhaps *especially* since it hadn't.

"I best get back to work," he said at length. "Would you mind finishing here in the orchard? I have some things to do out in the field."

"Your wish is my command," she replied, then felt silly for the glib words.

Colby smiled. "You better watch out. I can think of some pretty outrageous commands."

She laughed, trying to infuse some real mirth into the act, but the entire exchange with Colby was disturbing her more and more.

She watched him walk away and, when he was out of sight, gave a frustrated kick at the apple basket. Why did everything have to be so complicated? A kiss was a kiss, and it was dumb to analyze it so much. Colby had kissed her! That's all that mattered. Maybe he was falling in love with her at last. And maybe she was falling in love with him.

Maybe?

Of course she loved him. She had loved him for years. But a vague unease assailed her. She kicked the basket again when her grandmother's words about getting to know Colby invaded her mind. She was beginning to think that was the worst advice ever because she was getting to know him, and it wasn't helping at all!

To get her mind off all this, she threw herself into the work in the orchard. She enjoyed climbing into the trees to pick the last of the apples. Everyone always accused her of being a tomboy and enjoying climbing trees more than doing housework. Who cared? She was starting to enjoy stitching but still preferred what she was doing now.

That was something, wasn't it? Colby had given her this job. He didn't mind her preference for this kind of work over the usual womanly pursuits.

She picked as many apples as she could reach, filling six baskets, which she began hauling back to the house, one by one. She was bringing in the last basket, sweat dripping down her face from carrying the heavy basket of apples all the way to the house, when she saw Tamara hanging clothes on the line. Tamara saw her, as well.

"You look like you have been working hard," Tamara said.

"I think I got all the ripe apples picked." Maggie felt awkward, as if Tamara would be able to tell that the man she was falling in love with had just kissed Maggie. She set down the basket by the back door of the house beside the others, then ambled over to the clothesline. She supposed a conversation with Tamara was preferable, despite the awkwardness, to facing the mother of the fellow she'd kissed.

Tamara clipped a shirt to the line and then swiped a hand across her brow to push back a curl that had fallen into her eyes. "It amazes me how the work on a farm never seems to cease."

"You must be getting pretty tired of it," Maggie said. "I mean, you didn't come here to work yourself to death, did you?"

"I don't mind it. I told Mrs. Stoddard right at the beginning that I wanted to help, that I didn't want to be treated like a guest."

"Well, she took you at your word!"

Tamara chuckled. "I was growing so bored and discontented with my life in Portland. I like it here. It's refreshing and, I don't know . . . healthy."

Maggie thought of poor Mr. Stoddard. Maybe working a farm wasn't what was killing him, though most farmers would agree it was backbreaking, and often even soul-crushing, labor. And the rewards were often poor crops and empty larders, with still no letup in the work.

"You sound just like Evan. Believe me, farm life isn't as idyllic as you city folks think."

"Neither is having servants do it all for you," Tamara replied. "I fear turning out like my mother, whose life consists of one garden party after another. Here, I have had so much more purpose to my existence."

"I don't know. I can't picture you as a farm wife. You seem more like one who should be married to . . . perhaps a lawyer with a big-city practice. Say, like Evan." Even as she said this last, she realized it was nearly as halfhearted as the kiss with Colby had been. But she had promised Evan she would put in a good word for him, and this seemed the perfect opportunity.

"Evan is a dear, isn't he? But I realized long ago he wasn't for me."

"Not even if he got back into farming?" Maggie prompted. "He told me he was disenchanted with the law and the city and that he liked being here in the backwoods."

"That wasn't the real problem," Tamara said. "When I was with him, I didn't feel any passion. And he was always talking about things that, frankly, I find boring—books and philosophy, politics and geography. It was like being in school."

"Really? I think he's the most interesting person I know." Maggie's voice rose defensively. How could Tamara say Evan was boring? Maggie hoped Tamara had never said that to his face. It angered her that anyone should hurt him like that.

"Now, calm down, Maggie," Tamara said soothingly, "or rumors will fly that you like Evan, just as they are circulating about you and that boy who is in jail."

"Tommy? What rumors?" But she already knew the answer to that.

Tamara replied, "They—"

"Who are *they*?" Maggie demanded.

"I—uh—can't really say. But they've said you go into the jail to visit him and bring him gifts. They say you are in love with a half-wit and a murderer!" Seeing the obviously stricken look on Maggie's face, Tamara hurriedly added, "I don't mean to be hurtful, Maggie, I truly don't. I just thought you ought to know what is being said. Perhaps it might be easier to take from an outsider."

Her words sounded truly sincere, and that made it hard for Maggie to direct her anger at a seemingly innocent person. But she did anyway. "You are an outsider, so shut up about it! You don't know anything!"

Maggie was about to storm away when Tamara laid a gently restraining hand on her arm.

"Please, Maggie. I just thought it might help for you to know," Tamara beseeched. "I so want us still to be friends."

"Well . . ." Maggie relented a little. It was hard to be angry at Tamara, with her innately kind and gentle spirit. "You shouldn't speak of things you know nothing about. You don't even know Tommy."

"Is it true, then, what they say?"

Maggie stamped her foot. "No! It's not true! But I'd sure like to know who is spreading such rubbish."

"I wish I could tell you—"

"You know, then?"

"Oh no. I meant I wish I knew. That's all."

Maggie tried to calm down, but everything that had been said still seethed inside her. She knew more than ever that she didn't want to face Mrs. Stoddard just now. She had done a good morning's labor, so there was no shame in leaving early. "Look, I have to go home. Tell Mrs. Stoddard I'll try to come back tomorrow."

"All right." Tamara paused, then added hesitantly, "Can I still come to your house for sewing lessons? I have so enjoyed them."

"Come tomorrow morning if you want."

Maggie turned around, got her horse from the barn, mounted, and rode away, thankful that Mrs. Stoddard had not caught her.

# NINETEEN

Maggie continued to fume as she rode home, working herself into a lather all over again. She just couldn't help being furious. How dare her friends and neighbors say such things about her! She imagined it was probably even worse than Tamara had said because, as an outsider, she wouldn't have heard everything. And even if she had, she wouldn't have told Maggie everything, in order to spare her feelings.

How could they think she was in love with Tommy? That made her angrier than anything. It actually embarrassed her that they would think she could love someone like that. Oh, she'd heard vague rumblings of this before, but she had been able to ignore them. But now—what if Colby had heard these things and believed them? She thought he was joking about it at the picnic. What if he wasn't? What he must think of her!

She reminded herself that he had just kissed her. That must mean something. Or had it merely been a pity kiss?

Tears welled up in her eyes.

That's all it was, then. He felt sorry for her. He thought all she could get was a fellow like Tommy and had kissed her out of pity.

Who was spreading these rumors and ruining her life?

Dad had told her to be careful in her friendship with Tommy, but she had ignored him, as well. But she and Tommy were just friends! *She* felt sorry for *him*!

Then the most horrible thought of all assailed her. Maybe Tommy *was* all she could get. Maybe she was the fool for aspiring to snag someone like Colby. Look what happened when she had believed she could get Zack, the next best catch in the county. He had rejected her, too. Maybe she had too high an opinion of herself.

Tears now dripped from her eyes. She swiped a sleeve across them and sniffed. She was not paying attention to where she was going, letting the horse follow his natural instincts to carry her home. Thus her surprise when she glanced up and saw a rider within a few feet of her. It was Evan, of all people!

Too late to hide her emotion, she stared at him starkly and silently.

"Maggie, what's wrong?" he asked, riding up beside her.

"N-nothing," she replied, stifling a rising sob. When he responded with a skeptical look, she continued, her voice breaking over the words, the emotion only becoming worse as she tried to explain it. "I hate the people around here! They are nosy, stupid busybodies!" She sniffed loudly and was about to draw her sleeve across her eyes once more when Evan took a handkerchief from his pocket and held it out for her.

She wiped it across her eyes, then blew her nose into it.

"Do you want to tell me what happened?" he asked gently.

She was about to refuse. It was too humiliating to reveal to anyone. Then she realized that, of everyone she knew, Evan would be the one person to truly understand.

"Let's find a place to talk," he said.

He turned off the road, and she followed him down a broken path until they came to an oak tree in a pasture. This was still the Stoddards' place, but Colby was nowhere around. They dismounted, tied their mounts to a low branch, and sat in the grass under the tree. Maggie used the handkerchief once more. Her tears were abating. She knew God had sent Evan along at the perfect time.

"I was just helping out at the Stoddards'," she began. "I was alone with Tamara for a few minutes, and she told me something that made me angry. Mind you, I don't think she was being malicious. She really thought it would be helpful. But it makes me so mad—" The emotion she thought had slowed now seized her again. A sob broke through her lips, and she covered her eyes with her hands.

"There, there," he consoled.

She thought she would like him to comfort her with an embrace, as she had comforted Colby. In fact, she thought she would like it a lot, but he made no move toward her. Instead, he fumbled with his spectacles, and then, rather awkwardly, he reached out and patted her hand. She found she appreciated this gesture more than an embrace. Because of his shyness, even this was probably quite a stretch for him. She offered him a tentative smile in return.

Dabbing her eyes with Evan's handkerchief, she went on, "Tamara was repeating gossip, that people are s-saying I-I'm in love with Tommy."

"Who is saying such things?" he asked.

"Tamara said she didn't know, but I think she just didn't want to say. It doesn't really matter, does it? I don't know what is worse, that people are saying these things or that it angers me so. It isn't the first time I've heard people joke about me and Tommy, but I was always able to ignore it. It isn't true. You know that, don't you?" she implored, realizing it meant a great deal to her that he believed her.

"Of course I know it."

"What if Colby hears it? And just when I thought I might have a chance with him!"

"He probably has heard, Maggie."

Evan's hand had slipped around hers now and felt strong and comforting.

"But he should know better than to believe rumors, don't you think? Can't you just talk to him, make sure he knows the truth?"

"What would I say?" she probed. " 'Oh, Colby, I don't like Tommy, so it's okay for you to like me.' That just sounds silly and forward. What if he just laughs in my face?"

"If he did that—" Evan stopped abruptly. The tenderness momentarily left his voice, and it became uncharacteristically hard-edged. After a swallow and another fiddle with his spectacles, he added, "Would you like for me to talk to him?"

"I don't know . . . you wouldn't tell him about my feelings toward him, would you? That would be so embarrassing."

"I definitely would say nothing about that," Evan replied firmly.

"You two aren't the best of friends. I don't know if it would work."

"I'll be sure to be casual about it. In fact, my mother mentioned taking supper over to them tomorrow. I'll go along with her."

"That's so kind of you, Evan."

"I told you I would help you."

"I simply don't feel right making denials myself," she went on. "And I don't think I could say anything without getting all emotional again. The worst of it, Evan, is that when I deny it, it always comes out in my mind as, 'How could they think I'd love someone like Tommy?' And that is an insult to Tommy and a betrayal of our friendship. It would hurt him, too. Yet I do think it—and I hate myself for it! It's just as bad as actually saying it."

"What you think and what you say are different," he said. "And the fact that it tortures you so only proves the quality of your character."

"Thank you for saying so."

They were silent for a few moments. Then suddenly, as if he'd just realized he was still holding her hand when the need had passed, he quickly removed it. In that nervous way of his, he removed his spectacles and wiped them on a corner of his jacket.

Because she wasn't ready to ride home, she said, "I appreciate your stopping to talk with me. It really helped. I hope I haven't kept you from something important."

"I was just returning from St. Helens," he replied. "I went to see Tommy."

"Oh, I thought I would be helping you." She was a little hurt that he hadn't asked her to accompany him, but mostly she was disappointed she had missed another trip with him. The last time had been so very enjoyable, despite the mishap with the carriage, perhaps even *because* of it.

"I did stop by your house to see if you wanted to come, but your mother said you had gone to the Stoddards'. There really isn't a need for you to come every time I see Tommy. In fact, it is probably a good idea for me to see him alone occasionally so that he can build trust in me."

"I can understand that. How is he?"

"He's growing very restless. We talked for quite a while this time, and he opened up more to me. He began to tell me some things about his father—I never realized what a scoundrel that Tom Donnelly was. I believe if I can gather enough witnesses to Donnelly's bad character and to his physical abuse of Tommy, I can build a substantial case for self-defense."

"There'll be plenty of folks around here who can attest to Mr. Donnelly's lack of character," Maggie affirmed.

"I wonder if there are any, besides Mrs. Donnelly, who actually saw the man beat Tommy."

"I saw him backhand Tommy once."

"I don't want to put you on the stand. I don't know how much of our last conversation that deputy heard, but if any of it got back to the prosecutor, his cross-examination of you could be very damaging."

"That's too bad, because I could be a very good witness for Tommy."

"We'll find a way around it." He paused, then added with more optimism, "I did find out that Earl Cranston will be representing the county as prosecutor. I think he feigned illness before, simply not wanting to defend Tommy. I believe it is an open-and-shut case to him, and he didn't like the idea of losing."

"*Humph!*" Maggie grunted disdainfully. "He is still going to lose. But it's also good news that Mr. Cranston is the prosecutor, because he is the worst lawyer around."

"It would be a mistake to underestimate him. He may spend an inordinate amount of time in the taverns, but he will likely be sober for the trial. And he has tried a criminal case or two, while I have never litigated a real case. My previous experiences in courtrooms have been . . . well, not spectacular."

"Oh, you'll do cartwheels around him." A giggle slipped out from Maggie's lips.

"What?" He frowned, perhaps thinking she was making fun of him.

"I'm not laughing at you, Evan. But I did just get a picture in my mind of you doing just that. Old drunk Cranston standing there gaping as you turn one cartwheel after another."

He laughed with her. "So you think I'd look funny doing a cartwheel?" he said with mock offense.

"You are not exactly the cartwheel kind of person."

"I can do a jim-dandy cartwheel, I'll have you know."

"You cannot!"

"We'll see about that!" He jumped up, stripped off his jacket, and removed his spectacles, laying them on the coat.

He spread out his arms, leaped forward and, as she looked on in astonishment, flipped on his hands, propelling his body into a quite perfect cartwheel. Then, without a pause, he launched into another and another.

Maggie threw back her head and howled with laughter.

Breathless, he dropped back to the ground beside her. With a smug smirk on his face, he said, "So there!"

"I wouldn't have believed it without seeing it," she said. "Did you learn that at Harvard?"

His smugness turned sheepish. "No . . . I . . . uh . . . didn't really know I could do one until just a minute ago."

She laughed harder. "You are amazing, Evan!"

"It was worth it to see that smile on your face."

"You have made me feel so much better!" She paused. "And you know what? I am now more certain than ever that you will soundly defeat Mr. Cranston."

"Just because I did a cartwheel?"

"Because you were willing to." She gazed at him as a moment of silence descended upon them. A jumble of thoughts flitted through her mind. She tried to shake them away because they were things she wasn't prepared to deal with, things like: How could Tamara have rejected this wonderful man? How could anyone have ever ridiculed this smart, bright, witty person? And, would Colby have done a cartwheel just to see her smile?

Now she wished she had spectacles to fumble with. She was suddenly very nervous. Perhaps he saw, though it embarrassed her that he might have.

Suddenly he jumped back to his feet. "I told my mother I'd be home for dinner," he said.

She also rose to her feet. "Yes, I should be on my way, too. Thank you, Evan." It would have been so natural just then to give him a friendly, appreciative hug, but she restrained herself, not knowing exactly why.

They walked to their horses and before mounting, Evan said, "I'd like to speak with your parents about testifying for Tommy. Perhaps one evening when your father is home I could come by."

"Any evening would be fine. They are almost always home."

"Good, then I'll do that. The trial should be starting soon. I will be interviewing several potential witnesses."

"Let me know how I can help."

"Yes . . . I will."

Maggie thought it odd that the conversation between them had suddenly become so stilted, forced. She had no idea what caused it, and that disturbed her because their friendship had come to mean a lot to her.

Feeling quite bold, brazen even, she laid her hand on his arm. "Thank you, again!"

He glanced down at her hand, then straightened his spectacles, which didn't look crooked at all to her.

"I'm glad I was here for you."

They mounted their horses, and when they got back to the road, they turned and went in opposite directions. Mulling over the day in her mind, Maggie remembered she hadn't said anything to Evan about Colby's kiss. Since he was trying to help her catch Colby, he might have liked to know their efforts were paying off. She realized she had purposely withheld that information. She didn't want Evan to know about the kiss. How perfectly silly of her! He'd be happy about it. Perhaps that's what worried her.

# TWENTY

On Saturday Mabel Parker came to call. Maggie could not recall Mabel ever coming to visit. She'd only been to their house on rare occasions, such as the recent quilting bees.

As usual, she was dressed as if to meet the queen of England. Her frock was a mauve-and-purple print with a striped, pleated flounce at the bottom of the skirt. She wore a matching bonnet with a jaunty feather in it and white kid gloves. Maggie actually liked the dress quite a bit, for she was developing an eye and a taste for fashion despite the fact that she was, at the moment, wearing her old overalls. Well, she had just come in from cleaning out the horse stalls!

Mama, Grandma, and Ellie were working in the kitchen putting up apples, but they stopped their work when Mabel arrived. Mama hesitated just a moment before inviting Mabel to sit at the kitchen table. Perhaps she had been wondering if this was a "parlor" visit but decided in the end it wasn't. In Mabel's prissy way, just shy of brushing crumbs from the seat of the chair, she sat down. Maggie could not imagine two more different siblings than Mabel and Evan.

Mama and the others also took seats around the table.

"Let me fix some tea," Mama offered, rising.

"How kind of you," Mabel said while fastidiously removing her gloves.

Maggie exchanged a covert look with Ellie, who gave an ever-so-slight shrug. This was a visit that should have occurred in the parlor, but Maggie was glad Mama was trying to treat it as casual. Mabel may act as if she were special, but she was, after all, just one of the neighbors.

The women chatted politely for a few minutes. Mabel asked how Grandma was enjoying her visit, and the conversation turned to Deer Island and general county gossip. Maggie was never more thankful for Grandma's presence. She took up the slack in the conversation. Maggie had a feeling this visit was more than merely a social one. But they drank their tea and conversed for nearly a half hour before Mabel made her real intent known.

"I was wondering, Maggie, if I might have a word with you in private?" she asked with great delicacy. She glanced at Mama. "You wouldn't mind, would you, Mrs. Newcomb?"

"No, of course not," Mama said in a perfunctory manner. She probably did mind but could hardly say so. "Why don't you two use the parlor."

Maggie rose and led the way, her mind in turmoil. The last and only time she and Mabel had had a real conversation had been at Evan's welcome home party, where the seeds of the scheme to manipulate romantic events had been planted. Maggie was growing weary of the scheme and was wary of what new intrigue Mabel might have in mind.

After entering the parlor, Mabel paused and closed the door. They sat on the divan. Here, Maggie was more than ever aware of her overalls and felt terribly inferior to the prim and proper Mabel.

"Maggie, we must talk about the . . . um . . . situation we discussed at Evan's welcome home party," Mabel began without preamble.

"Yes?" Maggie prompted.

"It is not going at all as planned."

"What do you mean?" Maggie, for the most part, agreed with Mabel's assessment but wasn't ready to make an admission. What she ought to admit, Maggie didn't know, but the way Mabel spoke, it was apparent that Maggie was somehow at fault for the failure of the plan.

"It is making little or no progress," Mabel replied. "Just the other day, I encouraged Evan to go with Mother to bring supper to the Stoddards. I practically had to push him out the door. Then, when he was there, he made no attempt at all to socialize with Tamara, according to Mother. Instead, he and Colby went outside, and before anyone knew it, they were having heated words."

"Heated?" Maggie's stomach lurched. Could this have to do with Evan's offer to speak with Colby about Tommy? "What was it about?" Maggie forced herself to ask.

"I don't know. They wouldn't say. But from what I heard, they came just short of blows. I'm sure Evan must have backed down—I can't imagine him involved in fisticuffs, especially with someone of Colby's superior physical hardiness."

Mabel's insult of her brother sparked ire in Maggie.

Mabel went on, "I suppose on the positive side, if they were arguing over Tamara, that could be helpful. But even Evan must realize he will never win Tamara with physical prowess."

"I am sure you must be mistaken about the argument," Maggie said hopefully.

"Nevertheless, there is no doubt that no love is lost between Evan and Colby. Naturally Evan is worried about the growing closeness of Colby and Tamara."

"Closeness?" Maggie started to feel ill.

"I myself saw them the other day in the store, their heads together looking at yard goods, whispering and laughing. And why wouldn't they be getting close, seeing each other daily as they do?"

"Well, there is nothing to be done about that," Maggie replied defensively.

"In any case, Mother and Evan departed from the Stoddards' forthwith, and thus there was no interaction between my brother and Tamara. Evan denies that he and Colby were arguing." Mabel sighed. "I fear there is no way this can bode well for Evan. I have tried and tried to get him to pay visits to the Stoddards, but he always manages to make excuses, the biggest one being his involvement in Tommy's trial. I hear you were the one to instigate this, Maggie. I cannot say it was a wise move."

"Evan will save Tommy's life!" Maggie retorted.

"My brother?" Mabel came just short of laughing. "Surely even you can see he is inept to the point of being almost foolish."

"Mabel, how can you say such a horrible thing about your own brother!" Maggie exclaimed. Suddenly she perceived something that should have occurred to her before. Why was Mabel so interested in Evan's love life? They had never been close growing up; even Maggie had seen that. Mabel had always been accepted by her peers, while her brother had been an outcast. And she had never done a thing to draw him in. Now suddenly Mabel cared about Evan's happiness? It seemed very suspicious.

"I love Evan," Mabel said without enough passion to give her words veracity. "But he has always been his own worst enemy."

"Tell me the truth, Mabel," Maggie said, "why are you suddenly so interested in Evan's well-being?"

"He's my brother. I want to see him hap—"

"Oh, come now!" Maggie sharply interrupted. "There is only one person whose happiness you really care about."

"I am insulted!" Mabel huffed.

"Be honest with me, and maybe I can still help you." Maggie placed a special emphasis on the word *maybe* because she didn't want to commit to anything.

Mabel seemed to mull this over before speaking. "All right. It is very simple. I am engaged, but my mother has it in her head that it would be unseemly if I, the little sister, married before my older brother."

"What! That's ridiculous. Perhaps this might be a concern with two sisters, but between a brother and sister? I have never heard of such a thing."

"Whether it makes sense or not, it is true. My mother has always had a soft spot in her heart for Evan. Perhaps it's because he was born prematurely and almost died. I suppose it's like how one loves the runt of the litter more than the other puppies—" When Maggie opened her mouth to protest yet another insult of Evan, Mabel hurried on, "Oh, settle down! One would almost think you loved Evan the way you are acting."

Maggie snorted dismissively. "I just hate to see a nice person like Evan being insulted."

"Regardless," Mabel went on, "Mother has a special place in her heart for Evan. Lucky for me he was gone to his fancy schools so much of the time that it gave me half a chance. But Mother is afraid that if Evan doesn't marry soon, he will never marry because of his . . ." Mabel seemed to reconsider what she wanted to say when Maggie gave her a dirty look. "His somewhat backward manner. She hopes, I believe, that by forcing me to put off my marriage, it will motivate me to push him, which I am doing, or trying to do."

"I have never heard anything so conniving and unsavory," Maggie said with an indignant huff. "You are treating Evan like a pawn on a chessboard."

"It's only because he doesn't have the wits to help himself."

Maggie jumped to her feet. "That's it! It's time you left, Mabel."

Mabel did not move. She arched a brow. "Perhaps I should forget Tamara and set you up with my brother."

"Why don't you just butt out completely! Evan can take care of himself."

Mabel rose in a languid fashion, as though to emphasize that she was doing so on her own initiative, not because Maggie had asked her.

"I plan to marry my Stanley next summer," Mabel said. It sounded like a veiled threat. "Nothing is going to stand in my way. If I have to marry Evan off to Iris Fergus, I will. My earlier plan seemed to benefit more people, so I was willing to support it. If you care about Evan at all, you will continue to work with me in this." She slipped her gloves back on her hands, smoothing each finger with great care. "Maggie, I don't know what is going on in your little mind, but I suggest you try to grow up and act like a mature young woman. You will surely lose all around if you don't take some affirmative action in this matter."

Maggie didn't know what to say to that and just stared with her mouth slightly ajar. Perhaps in her deceiving, twisted way,

Mabel was right after all. But Maggie still didn't know what more she could do to help the situation.

When Maggie made no move, Mabel opened the parlor door. "I will see myself out."

Maggie watched her go. She heard Mabel bid the women in the kitchen good day before letting herself out. Maggie still did not move as she listened to Mabel drive her carriage out of the yard. Stupidly Maggie recalled the great time she and Evan had had in that very carriage.

Thinking of Evan made Maggie's dander rise again. She didn't mean to glare at her mother when she looked up to see her standing in the parlor doorway.

"What on earth went on in here?" Mama asked.

Maggie blinked and tried to rearrange her expression, but it was too late. "Now I know why you hate Florence Parker," she said. "Mabel is cut from the same cloth."

"For one thing," Mama countered, "I don't hate Mrs. Parker. Why would you say such a thing?"

"Oh, Mama, you know why. Everyone knows there is bad blood between you two."

"We are not the best of friends, that is true, but I do not hate her. I don't hate any living soul!" Mama was truly offended, and Maggie regretted raising this sensitive issue, especially when she had so many other sensitive issues to deal with.

"I'm sorry, Mama. Of course you don't." Maggie sighed. That still didn't help with her own problems.

"Maggie . . ." Mama put an arm around Maggie's shoulders. "I know you think you are grown up—" Maggie tensed, and Mama added, "You *are* grown up. But that doesn't mean you have to shoulder your burdens alone."

Maggie grasped eagerly at the olive branch offered by her mother. She'd been afraid of her mother's censure, probably because she knew she deserved it. But seeing Mama reach out to her made Maggie remember that she loved her daughter. And having been reminded of Florence Parker, Maggie also realized that her mother had once been young and besieged with dilemmas and romantic difficulties, whatever they might have been.

"Mama, I have made a mess of things," she confessed, unbidden tears springing to her eyes.

Mama nudged her over to the divan, where they sat, Mama still with her arm around Maggie.

"You can tell me about it, dear," Mama said. "I promise I will be understanding."

So Maggie told her everything. Well, most of it. She didn't tell about the kiss, because parents had a way of blowing such matters all out of proportion. And she didn't tell about the mud incident with Evan because it just didn't seem pertinent. Basically she told her how she had enlisted Evan in conspiring to keep Colby and Tamara apart so that they, Evan and Maggie, could have a chance with them.

"I now think I have made a deal with the devil," Maggie concluded.

"The devil? You mean with Mabel?"

"She was the one who instigated it all in the first place. Now she says she's going to get Evan married off before next summer with or without my help."

"You don't have to help her, do you?"

"No, but—" Maggie let out a frustrated breath. It all seemed so convoluted now that she was putting it into words. And silly, to boot! "I still want to win Colby, don't I?"

"Do you?"

"Of course! That's what this is all about." Maggie thought her mother could be exceedingly dense at times. "But without

Evan to distract Tamara, how will I ever have a chance with Colby? Tamara gets a chance every day to win Colby, while I get to see him just once in a while. And if Mabel starts to match Evan with someone else—well, that would be disastrous!"

Mama eyed Maggie. "Disastrous? That seems like a strong word."

"Mama, you said you would try to understand."

"Do you want to know what I think?"

Maggie wasn't sure she did, but she shrugged and nodded.

"I think that if you and Colby are meant to be matched, it will happen without all these machinations. You are every bit as fine a catch as Tamara is, and I am not just saying that because I'm your mother. You are a lovely girl with many desirable attributes. If you and Colby are meant to be, it will be."

"Did your mother tell you that when you and Mrs. Parker were tangling over the same boy?"

Mama smiled a rather mysterious smile. "So that is the story you have heard?"

"Is that what happened, Mama?"

"I am afraid I can't tell you what happened. Florence and I swore to take it to our graves unless we both agree to tell. And Florence never will agree to such a thing."

"Does it bother you that people are whispering behind your back?" Maggie was thinking of her own situation along these lines when she asked.

"I find it more amusing than anything. To think a plain old farmwife such as myself is fodder for the gossips!"

She chuckled, but Maggie didn't believe her entirely. She'd thought the gossip about Tommy had been funny at first, too, but it had grown hurtful.

"Folks talk about me behind my back, too, Mama. But I don't find it very funny anymore."

"What are they talking about?"

"Me and Tommy. And don't say, 'I told you so.' You wouldn't want me to be anything but a true and loyal friend. Even Dad can't dispute that."

"That's how we raised you."

True to her word, Mama was understanding!

"Your father and I see that you are probably Tommy's only friend besides Zack, and we couldn't be so cruel as to cut him off from that. But do be careful, Maggie. People talk, and reputations can be ruined. That is just a fact of life. Please make sure Evan or someone is always with you when you are with Tommy. It isn't that we don't trust him or you, but tongues wag."

"I know that, and I will be careful."

Maggie snuggled up closer to her mother, and Mama's arm around her tightened. It had been a long time since she had felt so close to her mother, physically and in her heart, as well.

# TWENTY-ONE

Ada gazed out the kitchen window. The slanting of the afternoon sun showed more clearly than ever that the leaves on the willow tree in the front yard were starting to turn. The seasons came and went with an unrelenting regularity. Sometimes she wished she could stop or slow them for a while, but where would she have stopped them? Would she return to last spring when she was worried about her daughters getting married? Or before then when the children were young and she worried about them getting good marks in school, getting along with their friends, and building a good foundation of faith? Perhaps she would go back to when they were babes in arms or wee toddlers?

Each season of life had its appeal, to be certain, but also its drawbacks. When her children were babies, Ada had had to work like a slave, caring for their needs and the unceasing demands of the household. She now realized she had not been able to fully appreciate her sweet babies because of all the work needing to be done. When they were in school, she and Calvin had borne the responsibility of making sure their children grew up to be decent, God-fearing adults. And now that three of them were adults, the burden remained, didn't it?

Of course they trusted God in all these things and derived strength and wisdom from Him, knowing He shouldered the burden with them. Yet they were still the parents, ordained by God to guide their children in life's journey.

Ada sighed.

"Is something wrong, Ada?" Mama Spooner asked, snapping beans for supper.

Ada had almost forgotten she was there. "There really shouldn't be," Ada replied. "I had the most wonderful exchange with Maggie the other day. It truly lifted my spirits. Perhaps it is just seeing the leaves start to turn and knowing that winter is on the way."

"You never did like winter much," Mama said. "I always enjoyed the brisk air, the rain, and especially the clean covering of snow."

"And the perpetually gray skies?"

"They make the evergreens more vivid," Mama replied with a smug grin.

Ada dried her hands on a tea towel and sat at the table across from where her mother worked. Her darning basket was close by, and she drew it to her. She would never dream of sitting without something to keep her hands busy. After pulling out a sock with a big hole in the heel, she threaded a needle and set her darning egg in place.

"Mama, I do appreciate how you always look on the bright side of things," Ada commented. "I suppose what I am really feeling is just how quickly time is passing. Boyd will be married in a few weeks, then Ellie will surely follow soon, even if it isn't by Christmas. And at the rate Maggie is going, she won't be far behind. Georgie turns fifteen soon and hardly needs me anymore. I'm not sure I am ready to be put out to pasture, to be useless. Is that how you felt when your children left home?"

"I expect every mother feels that way. Our children are the center of our lives."

"I've always regretted that we don't live closer to you, Mama."

"Well, it was your father and I who moved away. He couldn't pass up the deal he got on the Deer Island farm. I have been there nigh onto twenty years now, and it is home to me."

"I do wish you'd come live with us," said Ada.

Mama shook her head, but there was a tiny hint of regret in her expression. "As I said, Deer Island is my home now. Homer and Opal live near and would feel slighted if I moved."

"You've said they hardly ever come to see you," countered Ada.

"Opal is very sensitive about . . . well, most everything."

That was true. Mama's daughter-in-law was as touchy as a she-bear guarding a hive. But soon Mama would have to move in with one of her children, and it was a sure bet Opal would find an excuse not to have her. Perhaps then Mama would move back to Maintown. Calvin could build an extra room on the main floor so Mama wouldn't have to climb the stairs. Ada was surprised at how much she was looking forward to this, although it meant her mother would not be as healthy as she was now. Perhaps Ada was just hoping for someone to care for after her children left.

The knock on the front door gave her a start. She wasn't expecting visitors, though uninvited guests were not unheard of. She set aside her sewing and rose.

She wasn't surprised to find Evan Parker standing at the door. He was coming by often lately. Dancing lessons two weeks ago, a Sunday picnic, parties . . . It had perplexed Ada until her conversation with Maggie Saturday. Now she understood the reason for the visits.

"Good afternoon, Mrs. Newcomb," he said, doffing his Derby hat, which slipped from his hand. He tried to grasp it midair, missed, and lost his balance, nearly colliding with Ada before he caught his balance on the doorjamb. "Oh, dear me . . . please, excuse me . . . I'm terribly sorry."

Ada felt sorry for the young man. He tried so hard to be polite and proper. Too bad what he gained there he lost because of his two left feet. How had Maggie ever managed to teach him to dance!

"Come in, Evan," Ada said, stifling a smile.

"I don't wish to trouble you—"

"I know you must be looking for Maggie, but she isn't here." The stark look of disappointment on Evan's face surprised Ada. "Come on in. You have ridden a ways, and I can at least offer you some cider."

"Thank you very much."

He followed her into the kitchen and politely greeted Ada's mother, this time without mishap. He sat in a chair at the table, and Ada brought him a glass of cool cider.

"We have had a bumper crop of apples this year," Ada said. "And they are especially sweet."

Evan took a sip from his glass. "This is excellent."

"How is your family, Evan?" Mama Spooner asked.

"They are well. Thank you for inquiring. Mother had a touch of ague last week but has fully recovered."

"We are happy to hear it," Ada said. "All the excitement of so many parties lately must have overtaxed her."

"I don't remember Maintown being such a social hub of activity," he said.

"Nevertheless it must be rather dull here after Boston."

"I am enjoying it here immensely." He paused and took another drink of his cider. "Might I ask, that is . . . would Maggie be close by? I wanted to speak with her about Tommy."

"As a matter of fact, she isn't far. She and her sister are down by the east pasture picking huckleberries." When he brightened considerably at this, Ada added, "You could find them easily enough."

"I should like that—I mean . . . I might go down there . . . that is, if you don't mind."

"Not at all. I'll give you a bucket if you like, and you can help them." Ada rose, went to a cupboard, and took out a pail.

"Oh, okay, grand . . . wonderful." Evan drained off the last of his cider and took the pail. "Thank you very much." He rose, nearly knocking over his chair in his sudden haste.

But he managed to exit the house without further mishap.

Ada looked at her mother and gave an amused roll of her eyes. "I don't know how much time I spent when Boyd was young trying to get him not to make fun of Evan Parker. But, goodness! I can rather see why the boys did so."

"Looks to me like he is a bit taken with Maggie," Mama commented.

"What?" Ada laughed and felt suddenly quite pleased that she finally knew the way of things. "According to Maggie, Evan is smitten with Tamara Brennan."

"Humm," Mama mused. "I guess my old eyes are deceiving me."

Maggie looked into her pail and saw it was only half full. Huckleberries were tedious to pick, and Mama didn't like when there were a bunch of small leaves mixed in with the berries. But they were worth the work. Maggie liked them better than blueberries. Besides, she was happy to be out of doors. She could feel autumn in the air, and knew the warm days of summer were drawing to a close.

"So, Maggie," Ellie said, working beside her sister, "how are things going with Colby? We haven't talked about it for a while."

"There's really nothing to talk about." Maggie spied a nice ripe clump of berries and reached deep within the bush. "Nothing much is happening. Colby is so busy with the farm since his father became ill, I hardly have a chance to see him." She wondered if she should tell Ellie about the kiss, but as time had passed that seemingly momentous kiss had become almost insignificant. "I suppose romance isn't foremost in his mind right now."

"Not with Tamara, then, either?"

"I hope not. I am doing all I can without looking like a brazen hussy." Maggie dropped a handful of berries into her pail, then paused to remove several leaves. "Anything new with you?"

"Well, Zack and I decided for certain there will be no Christmas wedding."

"What? And you said nothing?"

"I'm saying something now." Ellie sighed. "I don't know why I didn't tell you a couple days ago after Zack and I talked about it. I guess I'm not entirely sure about it. Waiting is scary. A lot can happen in nine months till summer."

"You will never have to worry about Zack," Maggie said unequivocally. "He loves you completely. Seeing you two gives me hope to persevere with all this romantic business. To have what you have . . ." Maggie sighed dreamily, and oddly, no picture of Colby popped into her mind just then. Shouldn't she be daydreaming of him?

"There is another reason for us to wait," Ellie went on. "Zack is still seeking God about whether to enter the ministry. Everyone keeps telling him he should if he 'feels the call.' But he doesn't know if he feels it. I've been a Christian a long time, and understanding God's will is still confusing to me."

"It has always seemed to me," Maggie offered, "that short of a burning bush or something, the only way to know God's will is just to set about what you think you ought to do and trust God to lead you in the right direction. I remember something from one of Zack's sermons. It was that God can't direct a stationary object. You've got to be moving. It was a sermon he preached on faith."

"Well, aren't you a font of wisdom," Ellie said, partly with good-natured mockery but mostly with admiration.

"It's what Dad calls horse sense," Maggie rejoined, a little embarrassed but also pleased she had impressed her big sister.

Maggie heard the sound of a horse picking its way through the pasture grass and saw a Derby hat bobbing above the huckleberry bushes. A little thrill ran through her.

"Hi, Evan," she called. "We're over here."

Evan heard her voice and smiled, well, more like grinned foolishly. He hoped she hadn't seen, but he couldn't help it. He led his horse along the scruffy path around the bushes. He was getting more comfortable with riding but still had a time making his mount accept that he was the one in control. His classmates at Harvard had sometimes gone riding on the paths along the Charles River, but he had always been too busy studying, not that he was ever invited along. To them he was good only for tutoring, not for socializing.

When he reached the spot where Maggie and her sister were picking berries, he reined his mount, an ornery mare named Daisy, to a rather ungracious stop. He didn't know why she was unwilling to halt until he saw too late a bee winging toward them right in Daisy's line of vision. The animal whinnied and reared while Evan frantically tried to keep hold of both his seat and the reins.

"Whoa!" he jerked on the reins, perhaps too hard, for Daisy danced sideways and reared again.

Maggie leaped forward and grabbed Daisy's halter with a firm, sure hand, and the animal responded to her almost immediately. "There, there, girl," she said soothingly. "What's got your dander up?"

"I think a bee spooked her," Evan offered, hoping to deflect his humiliation onto the bee. He took advantage of Daisy's calm to dismount, trying to do so in a more polished manner than his entrance had been. His foot caught briefly on the stirrup, but he managed to reach the ground safely.

Maggie seemed to be stifling a smile as she answered earnestly, "I'm familiar with Daisy's reputation. Your mother has many stories of that animal's mischief."

Evan tied the rein to a stout bush branch and then doffed his hat, already sitting askew on his head. "Well, then, hello, ladies."

After greetings were exchanged, Maggie asked, "What brings you out this way?"

"Your mother said I might find you here. I have some news I just couldn't wait to tell you."

"Good news, I hope," Maggie replied.

"I think so," he said. "I have found someone who saw Tom Donnelly beat Tommy!"

"Oh, Evan, that is good news! I knew you were a genius!" Maggie dropped her berry pail and flung her arms around him.

Before Evan could get up the nerve to return the embrace, his arms dangling impotently at his sides, she had stepped back. Maybe he would never know what it would feel like to hold her in his arms. That dulled his enthusiasm over his news.

"Is something wrong, Evan?" she asked.

"No . . . nothing . . . nothing at all," he fumbled.

"So who did you find?"

"Hal Fergus. He said he went up there once because he'd heard Tom had won some money at poker in St. Helens, and he wanted to collect a debt Tom owed him before he spent the money. Anyway, he found Tom punching Tommy like they were in a fistfight, only Tommy wasn't fighting back. He had his arms up trying to protect his face. It was entirely one-sided, according to Mr. Fergus. For the first time since I took this case, I feel truly confident of winning."

"You will win, I have no doubt. Have you told Tommy?"

"I'll go into St. Helens tomorrow."

"Would it be okay if I went with you? I'd sure like to see his face when you tell him."

"I'd . . . that is . . . he'd love it, I'm sure."

"Do you have enough witnesses? You haven't spoken to my parents yet, have you?"

Evan realized then that he had intended to ask Mrs. Newcomb when he was there if she and her husband could speak with him regarding Tommy. But he'd been so flustered, so worried about making the proper impression on not only Maggie's mother but her grandmother, as well, that he'd completely forgotten Tommy. He still wasn't certain he had a prayer of winning Maggie, but he did know that if he did, it was only half the battle. Her parents would have to be won over, too, and that was going to be even more difficult considering the silly feud between Mrs. Newcomb and his mother. He knew that was why he got so clumsy and foolish around Maggie's mother, and probably why he had put off consulting with them about the case. Mrs. Newcomb had never done anything to indicate that the rivalry between the two women extended beyond them to their families, but the prospect of a Parker for a son-in-law certainly would not go down easily.

"I must do that," Evan replied with resignation.

"Say, Evan," Ellie spoke up. He'd almost forgotten her presence. "Why don't you come to supper tonight?"

"That's an excellent idea," Maggie said. "You can talk to them then, and tomorrow there might even be more good news for Tommy."

"Your mother won't mind an unexpected guest?" he asked.

"You know better than that," said Maggie. "Would you like to pass the time helping us pick berries?" She eyed the pail still hanging from Daisy's saddle.

"Your mother gave me the pail, and normally I would enjoy that," he said, "but I should probably go home and freshen up before supper. I have been riding all day speaking to folks about Tommy's case."

He left out the fact that the recent mishap with Daisy hadn't been the first of the day. He'd actually fallen off once when a garter snake had spooked her. It might not be immediately noticeable, but he felt somewhat worse for the wear. He wanted to be at his best for this supper. Though it wasn't his first meal with the Newcombs, it would be the first since he'd become certain that he loved their daughter. Impressing them was paramount, and he simply could not come to supper all dusty and sweaty from berry picking. Moreover there was the added pressure of having to prove to them that he was a success in his chosen occupation, especially when he wasn't even sure of that himself.

# TWENTY-TWO

The evening at the Newcombs' immediately got off on the wrong foot. The moment Evan stepped into the house and saw the other men—Zack was there along with Mr. Newcomb and Georgie—he knew he'd overdone his dress.

His black wool jacket and matching vest were cut short with narrow lapels according to the most current fashion, and with only the top button fastened on the jacket, his watch and chain, given to him by his father upon his graduation from Harvard, were nicely displayed. His trousers were a natty gray pinstripe. He'd labored long over his hair, using brilliantine liberally in an attempt to tame what he considered his most unprofessional curls.

While gazing at his reflection in the mirror at home he'd begun to wish he could have taken a classmate's advice back in Boston to grow a moustache. The fellow said it would help him look less like a rosy-cheeked youth and more like a formidable lawyer. But he'd never had much luck growing more than patchy facial hair, so he gave up the idea.

Mr. Newcomb, Zack, and Georgie were dressed in work clothes—they had cleaned up after their day's work, certainly, but they were still garbed in dungarees, coarse cotton shirts, and scuffed boots. Mr. Newcomb had on wide suspenders, and Zack wore a well-worn brown wool vest over his shirt. Evan suddenly felt like an undertaker next to them.

He silently vowed that he would forthwith buy some farm clothes. He would have done so before now, but since he was not making an income, he hated having to ask his parents for more than what they were already providing him—a roof and food. They were more patient with him than he deserved. They had spent a great deal on his schooling, which now appeared he might waste by eschewing the vocation he had trained for. He'd given his father at least some hope by taking the Donnelly case, but honor had propelled him to insist that Mrs. Donnelly pay him only for a successful outcome.

He said a silent prayer of thanks that the Newcombs were the kind of folks who did not judge people on appearances. They welcomed him warmly, though Georgie did stare a bit until his mother scolded him.

"Georgie, mind your manners," she said. "You'd think you'd never seen a decently dressed man." She smiled at Evan. "Let me take your hat and overcoat."

Georgie said, "Evan, you don't suppose I could try on that nifty hat of yours? Why, I bet the girls would like me fine if I wore the like."

"You are welcome to, Georgie." Evan didn't add that it had never helped him much with women, but perhaps it wasn't the hat's fault.

With thanks, Georgie took the hat upstairs where there was no doubt a mirror.

"Come on in and sit down," Mr. Newcomb said. He and Zack were seated on chairs in front of the big hearth.

"Supper will be a few more minutes," Mrs. Newcomb said and went into the kitchen.

He took a seat in a straight-backed chair that faced the kitchen as well as the other chairs. Ellie, Mrs. Spooner, and Mrs. Newcomb were busily making the last-minute preparations for the meal. Maggie was slicing bread, but she looked over at Evan and smiled. Immediately he felt heat rise beneath his collar. Embarrassed, he looked away. But that left him looking at Zack and Mr. Newcomb, and he could only wonder if they had noticed the red splotches on his neck.

"So, Evan," Zack said, "Maggie told me you are making some headway in Tommy's case. That's good to hear."

"Yes, we are moving in an encouraging direction," Evan replied, "but I am surprised how few folks are willing or able to speak on Tommy's behalf."

"You've got to understand," Mr. Newcomb said, "Tommy had fallen into many of his father's bad habits and thus did little to endear himself to his neighbors—"

From the kitchen Maggie interjected, "They just assumed he was like his father! No one ever took the time to get to know what he was really like."

"That may be," Mr. Newcomb replied patiently, "but it is based somewhat on facts. I myself often saw Tommy overcome by strong spirits. I have heard from others how they had to chase him off their property in the midst of stealing produce and such shenanigans. Arliss Briggs says he is almost certain both Donnelly men attempted to rustle some of his stock. That is pure hearsay, the legal term, I believe, but such stories have nonetheless shaped how folks feel about them."

"I have heard similar stories as I've gone around talking to folks hereabouts," Evan said.

"But he has a good heart," put in Zack. "I have talked to him often and can say that without a doubt. The thievery and few acts of vandalism were purely youthful mistakes, done only to find acceptance from his father."

Evan replied, "Someone—I won't mention names—said that Tommy once cut down a fence out of spite because the owner had made some unkind remarks about him."

"So he deserved it!" piped up Maggie.

"We are to do unto others as we would *have* them do unto us," Mrs. Newcomb said. "Not as they *do* unto us!"

"Your mother is quite right," said Evan, happy to have been given an opportunity to agree with Mrs. Newcomb. "Neither is it a viable defense in a court of law. For instance, you might say Tom Donnelly deserved to be killed for the awful things he did, but that doesn't give anyone a right to kill him."

"Then Tommy is doomed," Maggie said miserably.

"Unless we can prove self-defense," said Evan. "And I will build this case by showing Tom's past actions gave cause for Tommy to fear for his life."

"Would Hal Fergus's testimony about the beating be enough?" asked Zack.

"I need more than one witness to the man's violence."

"Maggie said you were hoping that Mrs. Newcomb and I would help in this," Mr. Newcomb said.

"You are probably closer to the Donnellys than anyone."

"Tom Donnelly was careful about his attacks on his son," Mr. Newcomb said regretfully. "I expect he didn't want to be shunned entirely by his neighbors. Most folks might believe in the rod as discipline for their children, but even the harshest disciplinarian would find it hard to abide the kind of beatings

I've heard Tom gave his son. Tom had to do business around here, so he probably tried to put up some cover of decency, thin as it was."

Evan hadn't planned to take up this unpleasant topic before supper, as he didn't want to cast a dark pall over the meal, so he was glad when Georgie came downstairs wearing the derby and distracting everyone.

Zack whistled. "Georgie, you look so good I might take to wearing one of those hats myself."

Georgie did indeed look good in the hat, which he had set upon his head tilted in a jaunty fashion. Evan usually wore it square on his head.

Mrs. Newcomb merely stared silently. Perhaps she saw how much more grown-up her fourteen-year-old son suddenly appeared. Maggie and Ellie offered effusive praise. Mrs. Spooner went up to Georgie, put an arm around him, and kissed his cheek.

"This is one female you have impressed," she said with a grin.

"Aw, Grandma!" Georgie started to blush.

"My hat never looked better," Evan said. "I think it was made for you. It even fits tolerably well." He paused, and it occurred to him how he could really make an impression on the Newcombs. "Georgie, would you like to borrow that hat for a while? I've got another, so I won't miss it."

Georgie shot a look at his father, who gave a slight nod.

"I'd like that a lot!" Georgie said. "Thank you very much."

Mrs. Newcomb smiled at Evan, apparently pleased that he had done something to make her son so happy. Then she said, "Supper is ready. Come to the table."

As Georgie headed to the table, still wearing the hat, Mrs. Newcomb added, "Though you look as handsome as a prince, son, we still don't wear hats at the table." Georgie obediently hung the hat on the coatrack, and everyone moved to the table.

Though Evan had overdressed for the evening, he was happy to see the meal was being treated as a usual family dinner. He liked that the Newcombs didn't feel they had to be formal for his sake. He might not fit in as well as Zack, who was treated like one of the family, but there was perhaps some hope for Evan. A simple meal of stewed chicken, carrots, onions, and turnips, with a side dish of boiled potatoes, was laid out on the table. They ate off everyday crockery.

Mr. Newcomb began the meal with a simple but sincere blessing, then the group burst into chatter as food was passed and conversation evolved. Everyone must have agreed that Tommy's trial was not an appropriate topic for supper, because they did not return to that subject. Instead, they talked about various events or news of the day. They questioned him about Boston and listened avidly to his tales of a part of the country none had ever visited.

Evan enjoyed these folks enormously. Meals at the Parker home were always far more formal and definitely less interesting. Mabel usually dominated the conversation, lately with endless talk of her fiancé and their forthcoming wedding. Mother engaged with Mabel, and sometimes with Evan, but seldom did she and Evan's father say much to each other. They did not have the easy camaraderie he noted between Mr. and Mrs. Newcomb.

Zack had been rather quiet during the meal, but when Mr. Newcomb finished a story about a breakdown at the mill that afternoon, Zack began to move about restlessly.

"You okay, Zack?" Mr. Newcomb asked.

"Well . . ." he hesitated.

Evan didn't know Zack well, but what he had seen of the man indicated that the one thing he didn't lack was confidence. His reticence now didn't seem much in character.

Zack took a breath and plunged ahead. "I've been wanting to say something but . . . I feel strange about it. It's about the minister's position. As you know, I have been praying and thinking about it lately. At first there was no way I'd have even considered it, so just for me to think about it is pretty amazing." He looked over at Ellie seated beside him. She smiled encouragement but her brow was knit as though she did not know what he was about to say.

"Go on, Zack," Mr. Newcomb said. "You are among friends."

"I know that, if I know nothing else! What I have struggled with is this whole idea of 'hearing God's Call.' Finally, last night a bit of a sermon I preached, or rather recited, came back to me. I never listened much to Reverend Markus's sermons while I was memorizing them or speaking them, but I guess they are hiding in my brain somewhere, because lines will pop into my head every now and then. What I remembered was something about stepping forward in faith, trusting that God will lead me in His ways."

"Why, Zack!" Ellie exclaimed. "Maggie was saying that very thing today. She remembered that sermon, too. She said the best way to know God's will was to move ahead, trusting God to direct you."

"Maggie, I should have come to you for counsel all along!" Zack said with a chuckle.

"Oh, it was nothing. Just horse sense, like Dad always tells us." She tried to sound casual, but her cheeks pinked as she spoke. Evan glanced around and saw the pride on her parents' faces.

Zack went on, "Today, I rode into St. Helens and had a talk with Reverend Barnett. He actually asked for a copy of that sermon so he could use some of it himself. But of course, I don't have one, since it got burned up in the fire at the Copelands'. Anyway, he has agreed to help me. He says if I don't mind his being of another denomination, I can apprentice to him for a period of time, both as training and as a kind of probation to be sure this is what God wants for me. He thinks that out here in the West where there is no seminary, an apprenticeship ought to be sufficient for me to eventually be licensed. So that's what I am going to do—if you think it is all right, Ellie. And Mr. and Mrs. Newcomb, I would greatly appreciate your counsel in this, as well."

The eruption of well-wishing and encouragement that spread around the table was doubtless a clear indication of where the Newcombs stood. Ellie's smile revealed her feelings on the matter.

"I feel certain the denomination headquarters will think this is an excellent idea," Mr. Newcomb said.

"Our prayers have been answered," Mrs. Newcomb put in. "We will have a minister once again."

"The pick of the crop, to boot!" added Maggie.

"But, Zack," Ellie said more earnestly, "you know my happiness is for you, that you are setting upon a path of your choosing. My affection for you would be the same regardless of what you did for a living."

Zack took her hand in his. "I know, Ellie. But I couldn't do this without your support and your desire to one day be a minister's wife. It is a ministry for both of us, I believe."

"I will be honored to serve God with you," she replied.

Evan was especially moved by the affection he saw between Zack and Ellie. The way Zack gazed at Ellie with such love and respect made Evan long for a time when he, too, could look openly upon the woman he loved with the same glow in his eyes. Now he had to studiously avert his eyes from Maggie. One look and he would have glowed, not only with love but with a face red as a beet. He was happy that for the rest of the meal he was hardly noticed at all. Everyone's attention became focused on Zack and his immediate plans.

When the main course was cleared away, Maggie went to the kitchen and returned with a pie.

"Huckleberry-apple!" She grinned at Evan. "But Grandma made it, so it's edible."

"Maggie, your baking is coming along very nicely," Mrs. Spooner said.

They had pie and coffee, and then Evan, Zack, and Mr. Newcomb adjourned to the hearth area, while Georgie excused himself, after more thanks for the hat, to go to his room to do homework. Mrs. Newcomb was about to help the women with the dishes, but Maggie shooed her away.

"Mama, I think Evan wants to talk to both you and Dad about Tommy," Maggie said.

Since there was plenty of help in the kitchen, Mrs. Newcomb removed her apron and joined the men. She sat on a stool by a lamp and took up her sewing while they talked. Evan asked Mr. Newcomb about the scene of Tom's death. Then Zack shared about meeting Tommy later at the Veronia lumber camp and how Tommy had willingly turned himself in to the sheriff in St. Helens.

"I'd be willing to testify regarding Tommy's character," Zack said, "but I have already been told my past would make me a bad witness. Maybe . . ." His voice trailed away with uncertainty.

"I wish I was already the minister. Maybe it would help boost confidence in my testimony."

"I might still call you to the stand," Evan said. "There are enough folks around who think highly of you."

"I will be willing to testify," Mr. Newcomb said. "Boyd would, too."

"I don't think there would be a need to pull him away from the lumber camp."

"He will be home soon enough when the rain starts," Mrs. Newcomb said. "And, of course, his wedding is only a few weeks away."

"The trial will start next week, and I hope will last only a couple of days," Evan said.

"Evan," Mrs. Newcomb began. Her hands paused in her stitching, and she looked up, meeting his eyes squarely. "I must confess something to you. I hope you can understand my reticence—" She shot a glance toward the kitchen, where Maggie had ceased her work and was listening to the conversation. "I hope you understand, as well, Maggie. In my defense, it was only recently that I realized the importance of . . . well, of seeing some of the goings-on at the Donnelly house. I saw Tom Donnelly strike Tommy. I happened upon the scene—" Her voice caught, but she took a breath and went on, "I yelled at him to stop, and then Tommy took the opportunity of my interruption to run away. Believing the boy to be safe, I left. I didn't even go to the house to visit with Jane, as I had planned. I have never said anything because Jane doesn't know, and I feared it might change something in our friendship. She might have been too embarrassed to be around me. I will testify if you think it will help Tommy."

"Mrs. Newcomb, that would be marvelous!" Evan replied enthusiastically, then realizing how difficult this was for her now and would be at the trial, he sobered. "Forgive my insensitivity. I know how hard this will be for you. But it could save Tommy's life."

Mrs. Newcomb's lips curved into a gentle smile. "I see now Maggie's wisdom in encouraging you to take Tommy's case. You will save his life, Evan. I have complete confidence in you."

Evan swallowed nervously and unconsciously fiddled with his spectacles. His insides quivered. Despite the fear her confidence instilled in him, it also heartened him in another matter. If Mrs. Newcomb had such high regard for him, why would not her daughter?

He decided then and there that he would end the farce of helping Maggie win Colby Stoddard. He was a worthy suitor himself and ought not fear rejection. He would tell Maggie how he felt about her. If she rejected him—well, then he would accept it as God's will. He would take a lesson from Zack. He must not stand paralyzed with fear. He must move in the direction of faith.

But when Maggie walked him out to his horse after the evening ended, he lost his courage because she mentioned going to the Stoddards' the next day to help out.

"I thought you were going to town with me to see Tommy," he said, trying to hide his disappointment.

"That's right. I forgot."

"I understand—"

"No. I'll go to St. Helens."

"You don't have to."

"Evan, I want to."

He couldn't tell if she meant it but argued no further. Maybe he'd find his nerve tomorrow to reveal his feelings to her.

## TWENTY-THREE

Maggie was excited about going to St. Helens. She hurried through her morning chores and ate breakfast so fast her mother scolded her. But she wanted plenty of time to dress. Not that she had many choices, certainly not a closet full of outfits like Mabel had. Her two best dresses were far too nice for town. The dress that had gotten muddy was ruined. She discovered mud didn't always wash out. It was now in Mama's scrap basket to be salvaged for quilts.

Maggie's remaining choices were her red shirtwaist and two older calicos. As she reached for the green calico, she saw Ellie's newer lavender paisley that was only six months old. When Mama had made this she had wanted to get dry goods for Maggie, as well, but Maggie had turned down the offer, preferring instead to buy some books Dolman's had just stocked. Maggie couldn't have dreamed then how her attitude about clothes would change!

She was greatly tempted to borrow Ellie's dress but then remembered that her clothes had not fared well around Evan and couldn't risk a dress she knew Ellie loved. So she put on the green calico. She fixed her hair by pulling back the sides with two nice tortoise-shell combs, leaving the back to fall loose to her shoulders.

As she was fussing with the combs, she questioned why she was so concerned about her appearance. She was only going to town to see Tommy, and only with Evan. She supposed she was just coming to enjoy dressing up like a girl, or rather, like the young woman she was.

Evan arrived promptly at nine in his family's carriage. The drive to town was uneventful—remarkable considering who her escort was. The conversation was pleasant, as it always was with Evan. Wistfully she wished she could have as interesting and lively exchanges with Colby.

At the jail they were given more good news for Tommy. His trial was set to start next Monday. He was in good spirits because of that and upon hearing about Evan's hopeful roster of sympathetic witnesses. Evan spent some time explaining how the trial would go. Tommy asked several times if Maggie would be there, and she assured him she would. He didn't seem to be interested in much else. Maggie thought he hardly listened to Evan.

After leaving the jail, Maggie and Evan went to Dolman's. For once Mama hadn't given her a shopping list, but Evan wanted to purchase a few things. While Evan made his selections, Maggie admired the yard goods. The clerk pulled out a couple of bolts she was especially keen on. Mama had mentioned she wanted to make her a new dress for Boyd's wedding. Was there still time? Maybe Mrs. Renolds would let Mama use her sewing machine.

She was debating between two fabrics, a rosy pink floral and a green paisley, when Evan came to the counter with his purchases.

"Let me buy one for you," he said. When she gaped at his boldness, he added quickly, "I owe you at least one dress for the two I ruined."

"Absolutely not!" Even she knew such a gift from a man would be unseemly. "Besides only one is ruined. However, you can help me decide which fabric to buy. Mama said I could get a new dress for Boyd's wedding."

He probably also realized the impropriety of his making such a gift, for he didn't argue; instead, he pointed to the pink. "This would bring out the green in your eyes."

"I always thought green did that," she replied.

"Yes, but you were wearing a similar color, though darker, when I met you at my welcome party, and you looked quite stunning in it."

First, it surprised her that he even remembered what she had been wearing when they met. But for him to say she looked stunning, well, she could hardly take that. She blushed as she attempted to laugh off the compliment.

"Hardly that!" she said.

But she told the clerk to cut her a length of the pink and put it on her parents' account. She was certain her father would not mind the fifty-cent charge for a dress for his son's wedding.

Then she noted Evan's items—two plaid flannel shirts like the lumberjacks wore, a pair of denim dungarees, and a felt slouch hat.

Fingering the shirt, she asked, "What's this?"

"I am a country fellow, so I thought it was time I dressed like one."

"Does that mean you won't move to Portland after you marry Tamara?"

He blinked and gave her a peculiar look. "I like it here," he replied softly.

Carrying their packages, they exited the store only to run into Colby and Able Jenkins.

Maggie was about to smile a greeting when Able spoke first.

"Hi'ya, Maggie," he said. "Did you come to town to visit your beau?" he asked with a grin.

Taken aback by the comment, she still reacted quickly. "Oh, shut up, Able. You don't know anything!"

"I know we're gonna start calling that jail the love nest. Ha ha!"

"Listen here, Jenkins—" she heard Evan start to say behind her.

But Colby broke in. "Able, apologize to Maggie, then get out of here!"

With a shrug Able mumbled, "Sorry," then strode away.

"Thank you, Colby." Maggie was pleased that he had so gallantly come to her rescue.

"He had no call to talk to you that way," he said. Pausing briefly, he went on, "But, Maggie, you gotta know folks are talking. You think it's wise to keep visiting Tommy?"

"How do you know I was—"

"We saw you go into the jail."

"I appreciate your concern, but I know what I'm doing," she replied curtly.

"And you, Parker," Colby said to Evan, "should not be encouraging her. It'll ruin her reputation, people thinking she is consorting with a jailbird."

"No one would ever think such a thing if they knew Maggie was the finest, most decent girl in the whole county!" Evan retorted. "And if you for an instant believe such a thing, you are no friend of hers."

"Don't tell me what I believe!" Colby snapped.

"It surely sounds like you agree with the likes of Able Jenkins—" Evan began hotly.

"Listen here, you two—" Maggie tried to interject but was cut off.

"It's getting hard not to believe," Colby retorted.

"Why, you two-faced churl!" Evan spat back, his neck reddening with anger. Somehow he had moved to within inches of Colby, their noses nearly touching.

"Take that back, you four-eyed fop!" demanded Colby.

"I will when you apologize to Maggie."

"I ain't got nothing to apologize about," Colby rejoined.

Maggie thought perhaps he did, but she was so stunned by the suddenness and fierceness of the exchange she could hardly find her tongue.

"You have besmirched Maggie's honor," Evan returned. "Even if you haven't gone so far as to spread the rumors about her. Though I begin to wonder about that, as well."

"I ain't taking any more of this! Get out of my way." Colby gave Evan a shove.

Evan dropped his package and shoved back.

"That's it!" Colby yelled, taking a swing at Evan.

His fist missed its intended target, probably Evan's face, but it connected with Evan's shoulder instead. Evan stumbled back but recovered quickly, raising his fists and charging. His attack had the effect of knocking Colby back a couple of paces, though it might well have been that Colby only stepped back to avoid the attack. In any case, Evan's attempt hardly fazed his opponent.

Maggie finally found her voice. "Stop it this instant!" she yelled. But they were not listening.

Evan took a couple of swings but completely missed Colby, who only had to jump back a bit to avoid impact.

"Quit while you are ahead," Colby railed. "Before I make mincemeat out of you."

Evan swung again, with more success this time, clipping Colby on the chin.

"I've had enough of you!" Colby declared as he went on the offensive. He swung his arm, powerful from bucking logs at the mill, baling hay, and plowing fields on the farm. His fist slammed into Evan's face like an axe against a stout tree trunk. The impact spun Evan around once before he crumbled to the boards of the sidewalk. Blood spurted from his nose and mouth. The force of the blow knocked his spectacles clean off his face, sending them flying onto the dirt road just as a wagon passed. The crunching sound of wire and glass being crushed by the wagon's wheel was almost as bad as the sound of Colby's fist crunching Evan's jaw.

"Colby!" Maggie screamed.

"He asked for it! You saw."

"How could you hit someone smaller than you and wearing spectacles no less!" she ranted.

Evan was starting to stir. He sputtered and spit blood and what might have been a tooth. "Lemme at 'em," he mumbled. He seemed to be having a hard time moving his lips. But he clawed at the boards trying to get up.

"Colby, just get out of here," Maggie implored, "before there's more trouble."

"Ain't gonna be no more trouble from that lily-livered milksop—"

"Go! Now!" Maggie ordered.

At that moment the sheriff showed up. "What's going on here?"

"Nothing," Maggie said quickly. All she needed was to have three friends tossed in jail. "Evan just . . . ah . . . ran into the post, is all."

The sheriff looked at Colby for confirmation. Colby shrugged.

"Okay, then. Move along," the sheriff said.

Colby obeyed, probably satisfied that he'd settled Evan Parker once and for all.

Maggie dropped down beside the still prostrate Evan. "Are you all right, Evan?" She took his handkerchief from his pocket and tried to mop up some of the blood dripping down his chin.

"Huh? D-did he a-ap . . . say sorry?" Evan sounded like he was chewing pebbles.

"Can you walk, Parker?" Sheriff Haynes asked.

"Sure . . . just don' know if I can stand," Evan replied. With the help of the sheriff and Maggie, he was able to get to his feet. "Thank you," he added, swaying a bit.

"Thank you, Sheriff Haynes," Maggie said. "We'll be okay now."

Haynes arched a skeptical brow but no doubt had more important matters to attend to than fussing over the bumbling lawyer and the troublesome Miss Newcomb. "Watch them . . . ah, posts, Parker. We gotta keep you healthy at least till I get that trial out of my hair." He then quickly strode away.

"Can you make it to the carriage?" Maggie asked Evan.

"Gimme . . . give . . . a minute." Evan tottered back and leaned against the wall. Then in a sudden panic, he cried, "I can't see! Everything's a blur!"

"Your spectacles came off," Maggie said.

His hand shot to his face, and he shook his head foolishly. While his hand was there he rubbed his jaw where a red welt was already turning black and blue.

"Is anything broken?" Maggie asked.

"Don't think so, but it hurts like everything."

"What were you thinking, trying to fight with Colby?" Maggie asked.

"Had to defend your honor."

"That is ridiculous. I can take care of myself, you know."

"But it's the man's place to protect the fair maiden."

She rolled her eyes. Then it suddenly occurred to her that two men had been fighting over her! She didn't know whether to be pleased or angry. Finally she decided upon anger, because even if she was starting to like dresses, she did not want to be perceived as a helpless female.

"I can protect myself," she said unequivocally. "Let's go home."

She started to walk toward the carriage and had taken just three strides when she heard some stumbling and then a crash. Spinning around, ashamed that in her anger she had forgotten Evan might still be disabled, she saw him doubled over a barrel that had been sitting on the sidewalk. Several crates, which Evan had probably knocked over, were strewn on the ground. Luckily the crates had been empty. She grasped his arm to help him, but he pulled away.

"I'm okay," he said stubbornly. "Just get my spectacles."

"Oh . . ." Maggie groaned. "Evan, your spectacles . . . Well, they are sort of broken . . . truth be told, they got a bit crushed by a wagon."

"I can't see much without them."

"I'll help you." She took his arm and then paused to pick up their packages.

This was the cherry on top of the humiliation of being knocked out by Colby. To be led around by a woman—by this woman, no less!—like a helpless babe. Everything Colby had said about him was true. Lily-livered, four-eyed milksop! That described him to a tee. He'd had several tries and hadn't been able to make serious contact with Colby even once. But only one punch by Colby had sent Evan to the boards!

Aided by Maggie, Evan climbed into the passenger's seat and slumped dejectedly.

"Do you have spare spectacles?" Maggie asked, taking the reins in hand.

"At home."

They sat in silence for several moments. He was too numb to speak, not in a physical sense, though his jaw ached and felt as if it was swelling larger by the moment. No, he merely had nothing to say except for self-recriminations, which he was afraid to speak out loud for fear she would agree with them.

He waited for her to drive the horses forward, but they remained still.

Then she spoke. "Evan, I'm sorry for being so harsh with you. I don't know why I got so angry."

"I know," he replied glumly. "It is because I went against Colby. I can't blame you for defending the man you love."

"What?" Her brow creased. "No, that's not why."

He read her words as a question rather than a statement.

"I guess I thought you understood me better than that, that you knew I don't want to be treated like some simpering, helpless female."

"You can't expect a man to just stand by and watch a woman he cares for be spoken of in such a manner," Evan replied. He knew she wouldn't realize how much courage it took for him to admit he cared for her. She would not perceive the depth with which he meant it.

"I am able to take care of myself."

Bitterly, he replied, "You didn't seem to mind when Colby defended you against Able."

"Colby didn't try to knock his head off!"

"I acted deplorably," Evan admitted. "But . . . I just couldn't bear for them to speak such lies about you! I had to defend the woman I love!" The words were out of his mouth before he realized he was saying them. Nevertheless, a huge wave of relief washed over him. He'd finally said it. There would be no more charades.

"You mean Tamara?" she asked, clearly confused.

"No. I mean you!" Let there be no more confusion.

"But—" For a moment her mouth moved, but nothing came out.

"Ah, there you are!" came a new voice, like an otherworldly sound that did not belong to the suddenly inflamed atmosphere in the carriage. Evan saw the blurry figure of a man standing by the driver's side of the carriage.

"Mr. Cranston," Maggie said, her voice pitched high with tension.

"I'm glad I caught you before you left town," said the lawyer.

"What can I do for you, Mr. Cranston?" Evan asked, forcing his voice to sound normal, calm, when his heart was still racing with the emotion of his admission to Maggie.

"What happened to you, Mr. Parker?" Cranston asked. "Walk into a wall or something?"

"Something like that," Evan replied vaguely. "How can I help you?"

"It is actually Miss Newcomb I wish to see." Cranston reached into his coat pocket and withdrew something white, a paper of some sort. This he handed to Maggie.

It was an envelope. She opened it and pulled out a paper. Even with his blurred vision, Evan could see the perplexed wrinkle of her brow.

"What's this?" She handed it to Evan, probably not realizing he was useless to decipher it without his spectacles.

"This," Mr. Cranston said, "is a subpoena for you, Miss Newcomb, to appear as a witness for the prosecution in Tommy Donnelly's trial." There was a certain smugness to the man's tone that Evan did not like at all.

"Me? Why me?" Maggie's voice was still unnaturally high.

"I understand that you are one of Tommy's closest friends," Cranston said. "I wondered why you were not on Parker's list of defense witnesses."

"Because I was loath to place such a burden on someone of Miss Newcomb's delicate sensibilities," huffed Evan with quite a bit of conviction, considering it wasn't the entire truth of the matter. He added irately, "And you should be just as loath, Mr. Cranston. Miss Newcomb is a young girl." He could see this ruffled Maggie but hoped she had the sense to let it go. It would be worth a wounded self-image if it kept her off the stand.

"She is at eighteen an adult woman and quite able to testify," Cranston rejoined smoothly.

For a man with a reputation for lazy drunkenness, he appeared quite in command of himself. Perhaps they had misjudged him.

Maggie grabbed the paper from Evan and shoved it back at Cranston. "Well, I don't want to take this!" she declared. "I won't witness against a friend."

"You have no choice," Cranston insisted. "The subpoena is legal and binding. You must appear in court."

Maggie turned helplessly to Evan. He thought how moments before she had gone on about being able to take care of herself, but such impudence had fled from her now. He felt no sense of victory but rather wanted to reach out and comfort her, protect her, defend her. He knew what it felt like to be helpless, probably more than she did herself, and he understood how it hurt.

"If that is all, Mr. Cranston," Evan said curtly, "we need to be getting home."

The subpoena was still clutched in Maggie's hand as she took up the reins and urged the horses into motion.

When they were a short distance down the road, Evan asked, "Are you all right to drive?"

"Y-yes," she replied, a tremor in her voice.

He'd never seen her so shaken. He was desperate to comfort her. "Maggie, the things Tommy told you are not necessarily as damning as they appear. We still can make a strong case for self-defense."

"Okay," she mumbled, but he knew she didn't mean it.

"Maggie, we must talk."

"Not now, Evan."

"But—"

She shook her head.

He couldn't imagine spending the two-hour drive back to Maintown in silence. That, however, only proved what a limited imagination he had. Though he tried a couple more times to induce conversation, he was met with silence. He even tried talking about something innocuous like the weather. Even that was ignored. In the best of times they were beyond such mundane topics.

He finally gave up until they pulled into the Newcomb yard. Then, making one last futile attempt, he implored, "Maggie, please talk to me!"

She turned to face him, and even with blurred vision he could almost see in her eyes the myriad of things she wanted to say. He waited hopefully.

"I can't talk right now," she said. She handed him the reins and scurried out of the carriage. In her haste her skirt caught on a step. She gave it an impatient tug. He heard a ripping sound, but before he could reach over to help, she had freed herself and was hurrying to the house. He thought how he owed her another dress but could find no solace in that.

She paused at the steps to the porch, turned and said, "Evan, put a mustard poultice on that jaw." Then she ran up the steps and quickly disappeared inside the house.

Only then did he remember his blurry vision and the reason she had been driving in the first place. But he was sick of his own helplessness, so he grabbed the reins and urged the horses forward, praying he wouldn't run over the dog or into a fence. He made it home safely because he had come to know well the road between his house and Maggie's. Would this be the last time he traveled it?

Why had he blurted out his feelings as he had? Before, at least, he'd had the excuse of the scheme to win Colby and Tamara as a reason to see her. Now he had nothing. There was the trial, but he could not let himself be distracted with thoughts of Maggie while he was trying to defend a man's life. He had to win this trial for Tommy's sake. But still, he could not let Maggie down again.

# TWENTY-FOUR

The house was unusually quiet when Maggie stepped inside. She wasn't certain she wanted to be alone right now; however, she knew she didn't want to answer questions, either. She'd had a nice talk with her mother the other day, but something told her that what had happened in town was not a matter she'd be able to discuss with Mama. She didn't know how Mama would react to the fact that Evan Parker was in love with her. He was Florence Parker's son. It would not sit well. Neither would Maggie's confused thoughts about the confession.

"Anyone home?" she called.

"Just me," came Grandma's voice.

Maggie felt as if she'd been given a reprieve, as if a prayer she hadn't even spoken had been answered.

Grandma was sitting at the table, sewing in her hands. Maggie caught a brief glimpse of her work before she folded the piece with the design inside and laid it on her lap. She thought she saw a flash of red-and-yellow material. There might be a reason her grandmother was being secretive about it, so she said nothing, despite her curiosity. Perhaps this was a wedding quilt for Ellie.

Maggie sat in a chair adjacent to Grandma. "Where's Mama?"

"She and Ellie went to help Mrs. Wallard and Kendra with some sewing."

That reminded Maggie of the package she had laid on the table. "I guess I'm too late with this."

"What's that?"

Maggie tore away the string and opened the paper. "I got some yardage for a dress, you know, for Boyd's wedding. I should have gotten it sooner, I guess."

"It's very pretty. I didn't know you liked pink."

Evan had said she would look stunning in that color. Even now, hours later and with all that had happened since, a color to match the dress goods still rose up her neck at the thought of Evan's compliment.

"It certainly does bring out the roses in your cheeks," Grandma said dryly, a twinkle in her eye.

Maggie clasped her hands against her cheeks, though it was too late to hide her reaction. "I was just told I would . . . ah . . . look nice in this color, that's all," she said defensively.

"And I think you will." Grandma fingered the fabric. "Your mother is going to be busy these next couple of weeks. Why don't I sew a dress for you?"

"Oh, would you, Grandma?" Maggie couldn't have been more pleased. Though Mama was an excellent seamstress, Grandma was even better. She would make a dress as beautiful as any in *Godey's Lady's Book*. In fact she would be able to look at a picture from the magazine and reproduce the dress exactly.

"I'd be happy to. We can look at some pictures right now and figure out what you'd like."

The prospect of the new dress had lifted Maggie's spirits momentarily, but the events of the day still weighed on her too heavily for her to be much good at choosing dress designs.

"Maybe later, but thank you very much," Maggie said. "I better go up and change. It's going to be milking time soon." But she made no move to go. Instead she ran her hand over the fabric that Evan had liked. He'd been so kind to her, protective and decent, and she had repaid him terribly, first yelling at him, then not speaking for two whole hours! He must surely hate her now.

But he'd said he loved her. *Loved!* No, it couldn't be. She must have heard wrong. Loved? Could it be?

"Maggie, dear, is everything all right?" asked Grandma.

Maggie had almost forgotten Grandma was there. Maggie gave a big sigh. "I didn't have such a great day in town. Nothing is going as I planned." Spying her sewing basket in the corner where she kept it, she jumped up, grabbed the handle, and brought it back to the table. She had six blocks done for her sampler. She lifted them lovingly from the basket. "Grandma, would you feel awfully bad if all this work was for nothing?"

"Me? It is your work, Maggie. My joy in teaching you is there no matter what." Grandma paused, running a finger thoughtfully across her lips. She studied Maggie a long moment. The creases between her brows were drawn and deep. Finally she spoke. "Tell me what happened in town, dear."

"The worst is that I am going to have to testify against Tommy," Maggie replied. "And there's nothing that can be done about that. Maybe there's nothing to be done about the other thing, either." She dropped the blocks into the basket and plopped back into her chair. "It is hard to give up something that has been so important for so many years. That's what I should have told Evan. That's why I was really angry and why I couldn't talk about it. But why is it hard to give up something I'm not even sure I want anymore?" She was hardly aware of her grandmother now and was simply debating with herself. Grandma must have realized that. She only sat and nodded with encouragement. "But it was like I was seeing Colby for the first time—and I didn't like what I saw. Sure Evan called Colby a couple of names, too, but I could see he didn't mean them. The things Colby called Evan, though, were just plain cruel. And I could tell he meant to hurt Evan with them. He just wasn't nice. And he didn't have to hit Evan so hard! He nearly knocked his teeth loose! It wasn't called for. Poor Evan couldn't even land one good punch. All Colby had to do was walk away. But, no, he knocked Evan senseless—"

"Is Evan all right?" Grandma cut in with concern.

"I think he lost a tooth. And his jaw looks like he has a real apple in his cheeks. His spectacles were crushed—oh, my goodness! I forgot he couldn't see. I let him drive home alone!" Agitated and worried, she started to rise. What could she do now? She could saddle a horse and ride after him and see that he got home okay.

Grandma laid a hand on Maggie's arm. "I'm sure the horses will get him home safely. They have made the trip between the two houses often enough lately."

"They probably won't come back here again!" she declared glumly.

"Sounds like that bothers you more than what you learned about Colby?" There went Grandma with her questions!

"It all bothers me!" Maggie exclaimed. "Did I want Colby all these years without really knowing him? What did I see in him?"

"He's a charming, handsome young man. Even my old eyes can see that. How much time did you spend with Colby until now? Or perhaps it is merely that you are measuring him against another and he has come up lacking?"

Maggie gaped at her grandmother. This last comment of hers went beyond her usual questions. It was more like second sight or something. Maggie realized she had often compared Colby to Evan. What she hadn't realized, or let herself see, was how many times Colby had lost in such comparisons.

"That can't be, Grandma," Maggie breathed.

"What can't be?"

"You know what!" Maggie shook her head in denial. "I simply can't accept that. He's a Parker, for heaven's sake!" Again she gave her head a shake. "This time, Grandma, the answer to all your questions is no. I don't care how Evan feels."

"How does Evan feel?"

"Oh no, you don't, Grandma! No more questions!" She jumped up. "I have to bring in the cows."

Maggie went upstairs, changed her clothes, and slipped outside without taking any more questions from her grandmother. Then with great force of will she diverted her thoughts from both Colby and Evan. Anyway, she had something far more important to worry about—Tommy's trial.

Fortunately, the cows knew it was time to come in, and she didn't have to give them much thought when she brought the two milk cows into the barn. And she certainly didn't have to think about the milking. So her mind picked away at the problem of the trial. It didn't take long for her to decide that she had to lie. It would be her word against the deputy's, if indeed he was the one who had clued Mr. Cranston in on her secret. Not exactly just his word, now that she thought about it. Evan knew. Would Cranston question Evan? Could he question the opposing lawyer? Tommy also knew, but he wouldn't contradict her.

Lying was her only choice. But she wasn't very good at lying. Mama might have told her often that she had a cunning way of sidestepping the truth, but that applied only to harmless fibs. This was pretty big. She was intimidated by the sheriff and probably would be by Mr. Cranston, as well. What if she babbled or couldn't get her story straight?

Perhaps the best approach would be to just say she couldn't remember. It had been a couple of months. They couldn't expect her to remember a conversation that far back, could they?

She imagined the scene as she milked Bessie.

*"Miss Newcomb, did you have a conversation with Tommy Donnelly regarding his desire to 'get back' at his father?"*

*"I don't recall."*

*"Come now. Surely you would remember when someone threatens their own father."*

*"I can't remember."*

*"Your Honor, this girl is obviously lying. She must go to jail!"*

Dismayed at her own dismal rendering of the courtroom scene, she yanked too hard on Bessie and was nearly knocked off her stool.

"Sorry, Bessie, but I don't know what to do! I can't lie, yet I can't betray Tommy. And no matter what Evan says, I think when folks hear what Tommy told me, they will think twice about self-defense. What would you do? You and Blackie are close. Would you send her to the slaughterhouse? No, you'd lie to protect her, wouldn't you? It's the decent thing to do. Sometimes lying isn't wrong if it's done to protect someone. Right?"

Besides Evan, there was only one other person Maggie could talk to about this. But Zack was really busy lately, spending much of the little spare time he had in St. Helens with Reverend Barnett. Even Ellie didn't see him very much. When Zack had been a fake minister, he had counseled Maggie to keep quiet about what Tommy told her. He probably would have had no problem back then to also agree with her about lying. But now that he was about to become a real minister, would he feel the same?

She knew she was grasping at straws to even ask the question. There would not be a single person, except perhaps Tommy himself, who would counsel her to lie, especially in a court of law where the consequences would be dire. But wasn't that what friendship was about, making sacrifices for your friend? Wasn't that called "the greater good" or something? A lie would save a person's life. That had to be the greater good.

Her head started to ache with these deep musings. She was glad when Georgie came in to help with the chores. He began forking hay into Jock's and Samo's stalls.

"Are Mama and Ellie home?" Maggie asked Georgie as she began milking Blackie.

"I didn't see 'em when I went in to change," Georgie replied. "Hey, Maggie, next time you see Evan tell him how much I like that hat of his."

"Why don't you tell him yourself?"

"You see him a lot more than I do. Tell him that Cissy Fergus thought I looked right natty in it."

Georgie's interest in Cissy was certainly persisting. Well, at least Cissy was not at all like her homely, somewhat uncouth sister Iris who, at twenty-two, was probably going to end up an old maid. Cissy was pretty with red curls and freckles. She giggled a lot, though basically she was pleasant company. But Georgie was too young to be so serious about one girl.

She glanced at her brother and was more aware than ever at how grown-up he was becoming. He would soon be fifteen and was as tall as Dad, if not taller. The rigorous farm work was building a muscular physique on him. In a few years he would vie with Colby in good looks. And now she realized Georgie would surpass him where character was concerned, too.

Seeming to prove this observation, Georgie said, "You know, that Evan is a real nice person, not at all like his snooty sister or his mother. Must take after his dad, or maybe it was because he was away from home so much. Are you sweet on him, Mags?"

"What?" Had Grandma put Georgie up to this?

"Well, he's here a lot. I was just wondering."

"Of course not!" she said with more force than was needed.

Shrugging, Georgie went about his work, saying no more. Maggie returned her attention to the milking, her thoughts wandering again. She tried to think of the trial, but that went nowhere except to the moral question, which would only be answered when she took the stand at the trial. So, try as she might to concentrate on serious matters, she kept thinking about Evan. She thought of their first meeting when he tripped on the carpet and spilled his punch all over her. She thought of his accidentally letting the chickens out, then grinning as together they chased them down. She thought of his stepping on her toes as she tried to teach him to dance. And of the time he slipped down into the muddy ditch, pulling her after him.

All those thoughts made her smile. Evan made her smile. Not because he was funny and clumsy, but because every time she was with him, she felt happy. Even the time she had felt most miserable about the rumors, he had literally turned cartwheels just to make her smile.

Then she remembered how badly she had treated him today. She felt a sudden impulse to saddle one of the horses and ride to his house right then and there to tell him how sorry she was.

Yet what would be the point? If she could not respond favorably to his words of love, would he want to see her? He'd risked a great deal to say them. He'd risked rejection certainly, when he no doubt still felt the sting of Tamara's rejection. And he'd risked their friendship. She knew Evan well enough to know he wouldn't have done so lightly. He'd meant what he'd said.

How could she face him if she did not feel the same way? She cared too much for him to risk breaking his heart, as Tamara had.

# TWENTY-FIVE

The courtroom in the St. Helens courthouse was small but seemed even more so now with perhaps a hundred folks crowded in the room. Maggie didn't know even half the people. She thought many were simply seeking cheap entertainment. Well, the county had no theater, and few acting troupes ever graced the community, so the folks had little else but this kind of amusement. The level of noise and activity in the room resembled a fair more than a serious legal proceeding.

Though Evan had described some court protocol to Maggie, she still felt as though she had entered foreign territory. She thought Dad and Mama felt the same way as they stood beside her at the doorway, hesitant to proceed farther into this strange and forbidding world. There were some familiar faces. Several neighbors who could get away were present, but she suspected most were there to testify, not to be mere spectators. She saw Zack on the other side of the room and waved. Ellie had stayed at home with Grandma and Georgie to do all the chores that could not wait till the end of the trial. Dad, Mama, and Maggie would stay in town for the duration rather than make the arduous drive twice a day for who knew how long. Evan thought two or three days.

The spectator seats were filled to capacity, with many folks standing in the aisles. A railing separated the litigators' tables and the judge's bench from the assembly. The first row of seats was almost empty, obviously being saved. Maggie saw that Jane Donnelly was the only one in the row. Just as Maggie wondered if she and her parents could be so bold as to take these vacant seats, the only seats left in the room, Mrs. Donnelly turned and waved for them to join her.

"I saved the seats for you folks," she said to Mama. "I wanted friends close by."

"I'm glad you did, Jane," Mama replied, taking the seat next to Mrs. Donnelly. Dad took the next seat and Maggie the one beside him. "We are here to support you," Mama added with a caring smile.

Maggie knew that Mrs. Donnelly had no family close by because she and Tom had migrated here twenty years earlier from California. No sisters, no brothers, and no parents—it was almost as if Tom had wanted to drag her away from all her loved ones. But seeing Mama clasping Mrs. Donnelly's hand, Maggie realized that the horrible man hadn't been entirely successful. Mama and Mrs. Donnelly were almost as close as sisters.

"I can't believe so many people have turned out for this," Dad commented.

"Morbid curiosity," Mrs. Donnelly said, her lips tightening with her disapproval. Naturally she'd be upset that her son should be the object of such a thing, that folks wouldn't have come if they thought everything was going to turn out happily. Some were probably even hoping the spectacle would culminate in a hanging.

There had never been a legal hanging in the county, and Evan felt strongly that Tommy wouldn't hang. But he might go to prison, and from what Maggie had learned about the state prison, going there was a fate worse than death. One way or another Tommy's life hung in the balance here, and she became more and more determined to lie about what Tommy told her.

Soon the attorneys entered the courtroom. Mr. Cranston had a strut to his step. He grinned at the spectators. She had never met the man before the events involving Tommy had occurred and had only known his reputation for being drunken and lazy. But he looked quite in command of himself now. He must realize that winning a trial like this could be a huge boost to his career. Not only was there a reporter from the local newspaper, the *Oregon Mist*, but someone had said a reporter from the Portland newspaper, the *Morning Oregonian*, was also present.

Maggie knew Evan had not taken this case out of ambition, but she saw now how winning could favorably affect his future. Maybe it would boost his confidence to the point where he would feel able to return to the law firm in Boston. She knew his mother was pushing him in that direction. Maggie didn't like this line of thinking. He had to win this trial, yet it made her stomach queasy to think of him leaving.

Evan's entrance was far more thoughtful than his opponent's. He looked directly at Mrs. Donnelly and offered her an encouraging smile. Maggie thought he looked pale, more so than his usual city pallor, which had been darkening since he was spending more time outdoors. Though the swelling of his jaw had subsided, an ugly bruise remained. Perhaps that's what gave his skin such a greenish cast.

Maggie tried to get his attention with her eyes. She was only three seats away from Mrs. Donnelly, but his gaze did not reach her. She wondered if he was purposely avoiding her. She smiled in his direction, desperate to communicate to him—what? That she was no longer mad at him? She didn't know except that she wanted things to return to the way they had been. She wanted to return to their easy, enjoyable friendship. She should have followed the many impulses she'd had since that terrible day of the fight to go see him. She needed him now more than ever as she faced the possibility of betraying Tommy. Even if she had planned to lie, Mr. Cranston might somehow ferret the truth from her. Evan would never support her lying, so she needed to hear his assurance that all would be well if she told the truth.

In another moment Tommy himself entered the courtroom, led in by Sheriff Haynes. Tommy was dressed in his Sunday suit, and his hair was neatly brilliantined and combed. He didn't look like Tommy at all. He looked small and helpless sitting at the table beside Evan. He glanced briefly at his mother and smiled, but his lips shook a little. He was very nervous, probably more at having to be the center of attention than he was at the prospect of hanging. He was so simple and harmless. How could anyone think he'd maliciously hurt anyone? All he wanted to do was fish and hunt in the outdoors he loved. He did not deserve any of this.

Her thoughts were interrupted by the bailiff's strong voice calling, "Order in the court!" He had to say this once more before the noise dwindled to a halt. Then he announced, "All rise for the Honorable Judge Lionel Olsen, circuit judge for the Fifth District."

Maggie rose with the rest of the crowd, and for the first time that day, truly felt the seriousness of what was about to happen. She could not help being a little awestruck by the impressive presence of the man in a flowing black robe who strode to the raised bench at the front and took his seat. He looked like an

Old Testament patriarch, perhaps Moses or Aaron. He even had a beard, though his was shorter than the long white beard she'd seen in Bible pictures. But his beard was almost as white, contrasting sharply with his shrewd black eyes. She had hoped for a benevolent grandfather type to be Tommy's judge. This man was far from that. The words *hanging judge* popped into her mind. Not that she'd heard these applied to Judge Olsen, but he looked as if he could be such a one. Evan had said he was firm but fair, and she clung to that now, though her hands trembled as she clutched them together in her lap.

After everyone had been instructed to sit, Judge Olsen spoke. "Let us begin the proceedings in this action, the State of Oregon versus Mr. Thomas Donnelly."

The judge introduced the lawyers and instructed them to begin the process of selecting the jury. Maggie realized then that many of the people in the spectator area were prospective jurors. Cranston rose and questioned the first juror, asking him his name and where he lived, if he knew Tommy, and if he could be fair and impartial. The man answered yes to all the questions. Cranston accepted the man.

Then it was Evan's turn to question the man. As Evan rose, the hem of his jacket caught on a stack of papers sitting before him on the table. The papers were swept off the table, scattering all over the floor. Maggie saw red creep up Evan's neck.

"I beg y-your pardon, Y-Your Honor!" he said, bending to collect the papers. Maggie saw his hands were trembling almost as much as hers.

"Bailiff, help Mr. Parker," ordered the judge with a hint of disdain in his voice.

In a few moments the papers were back in place. Maggie hoped they weren't immediately important because they were now totally out of order. She said a quick, silent prayer for Evan.

Though she knew he was competent, she feared he'd lose what confidence he'd had before this small mishap. He approached the juror and questioned him in what appeared to Maggie to be an intelligent manner, despite his voice having started out more high-pitched than normal. Completing his questioning, Evan dismissed the man "for cause." Maggie thought that was some kind of legal maneuver, probably a way for Evan to gain an upper hand in the proceedings, especially after his initial blunder.

One by one, additional people were called to the stand and questioned in the same manner as the first. Some people she knew; many were strangers. When they recessed for dinner at two in the afternoon, only five jurors had been selected. Evan had mentioned that the trial could go on for a few days, but she had never imagined just how tedious a process it was. She had been primed and ready to give her testimony. Now she probably wouldn't be called till tomorrow or later. Her courage and resolve were already wavering.

Her parents had arranged for them to remain in St. Helens during the trial, staying with a cousin in town. Maggie thought at most it would be an overnight arrangement but now realized they might be here for days. She wished she'd brought more clothes.

They ate their midday meal with their cousins and then returned to the courtroom. Maggie had wanted to see Evan, but he had gone directly to the jail with Tommy and Mrs. Donnelly. Dad would not let her go there. She tried to argue that he'd let her go to the jail before, but he was adamant. She had a feeling he'd heard the most recent rumors about her and Tommy, so she did not press the issue.

The rest of the afternoon was spent choosing more jurors. Just ten had been chosen by the time the session adjourned for the day. This process would drag on for part of the day tomorrow, before the real trial could begin.

As they were exiting the courtroom, Maggie sidled up next to Tommy's mother. "Mrs. Donnelly, are you staying here in town during the trial?"

"Yes. I'm at the boardinghouse."

"Is Evan there, as well?" she asked, trying to sound casual.

"No. He's at the hotel."

"Oh." Maggie was disappointed to hear this. It would be inappropriate for her to visit him there. If he'd been at the boardinghouse, Mrs. Donnelly would be able to act as a chaperone. That did seem silly, considering all the times she'd been alone with Evan in the last weeks. But now it was different. He'd declared his love for her.

Perhaps Mrs. Donnelly, despite her own inner turmoil, had noted Maggie's chagrin, because she went on to say, "Evan will be taking supper with me tonight at the boardinghouse. You may join us if you like."

"I'd like that very much!" Maggie said enthusiastically, then was ashamed because this was too somber a time for such elation. Making her tone more in keeping with their austere surroundings, she added, "I wanted to discuss some matters with him regarding the trial. Did you know I am to be called as a witness for the prosecution?"

"Yes, I had heard. And don't you worry. Tommy and I understand that you had no choice in the matter."

"Do you know why I was called?"

"I can guess." Mrs. Donnelly patted Maggie's arm reassuringly. "You must do what you must do, dear. There will be no hard feelings."

"I don't know what to do," Maggie confessed. "That's why I need to see Evan. Well, one reason, at least."

"We'll have supper at eight."

"Thank you so much, Mrs. Donnelly."

Maggie's parents weren't happy about her declining to have supper with their relatives, who had been kind enough to open their home to the Newcombs. But they conceded the importance of her discussing her testimony with Evan. And Cousin Martha, a kindly woman some years older than Maggie's parents, seemed to understand, as well.

Maggie thought she would simply burst with impatience for eight o'clock to arrive. She changed into the better of the two dresses she had brought. She fixed her hair by pinning the sides back and tying them with a ribbon into ringlets at the back of her head. She marveled at how adept she was becoming in fussing with her appearance. She marveled even more at why and for whom she was going to such trouble.

When she saw Evan in the boardinghouse parlor, a little thrill ran through her. *Oh, for once in your life quit being silly!* she silently chided herself.

Evan received her politely. He had just found out that she would be joining them for supper. He did not appear angry with her, but his formality, which seemed more pronounced than his usual Boston manners, discomfited her.

They took supper at a large table with all the other residents. It was awkward at first because everyone wanted to talk about the trial, and they showed little regard for Mrs. Donnelly's emotional state. Maggie was impressed by the way Evan stepped in immediately to quell the conversation.

"Ladies and gentlemen," he said, "though we would like nothing more than to discuss the trial with you, we are forbidden to discuss it outside the court proceedings. However, I can offer you a few insights about another trial I am sure you have all heard of." He then launched into a description of the trial of President Garfield's assassin. This seemed to appease their hunger for sensationalism and take the focus off Tommy.

After supper, as Maggie exited the dining room with Evan and Mrs. Donnelly, she leaned toward Evan and said, "I wanted to talk to you about my testimony, but I guess I can't if it is forbidden."

He grinned and said in a voice only she and Mrs. Donnelly could hear, "I'm afraid I told a little fib. It's only the jurors who are forbidden to discuss the trial. I figured no one else would know that."

Mrs. Donnelly thanked him. Maggie smiled not only in response to his humor but because he seemed more relaxed, more the way he usually had been around her. She took courage from that. Perhaps he couldn't stay angry at her just as she couldn't stay angry with him.

Since many of the diners adjourned to the parlor for after-dinner conversation, Evan suggested that the three of them visit on the front porch. It was chilly outside and Maggie and Mrs. Donnelly had to don their wraps, but it was otherwise a pleasant night. The boardinghouse was off the main thoroughfare, on a quiet street away from the evening rowdiness of the three taverns. They visited for a short while. Then Mrs. Donnelly rose and, pleading fatigue, bid them good-night. Evan assured her he would walk Maggie home.

The previous awkwardness suddenly returned when Maggie and Evan were left alone. She searched in her mind for some way to break down the wall that had formed between them. Only an apology seemed appropriate, and while she was willing to take that step, she felt she'd been somewhat justified for her actions the other day. Yet far more important than that was her desperation to have Evan back as a friend.

"Evan—"

"Maggie—"

They both spoke at the same moment. They laughed together, and this made a small breach in the wall between them.

"Ladies first," Evan said.

She wished he wasn't so polite, such a gentleman, but that's one thing she loved—liked!—about him, his slightly out of kilter demeanor.

"Okay," she said with resolve. "I treated you badly the other day, Evan. I should never have become angry at you for defending me, and I certainly should never have met your . . . well, your *words* with silence." As she spoke, she realized she had been entirely wrong, that her actions had not been justified. He'd acted with his usual consideration. "Evan, you are so dear and kind. You mean so much to me. You are—"

He jumped up from the wicker chair where he was seated adjacent to the settee upon which she sat.

"Don't say it, Maggie!" he ordered. "Say anything but that."

"I was only going to say you have become my dearest friend," she replied, her brow knit, not understanding his response.

"*Humph!* Only one notch better than 'like a brother'!" he snapped.

Of course! Now she remembered the words Tamara had used to reject him, and her heart sank. That is what she feared most—hurting him as Tamara had. Yet now it appeared there was nothing she could say to appease him—short of a profession of love, of course.

"Evan, sit down and compose yourself," she gently chided. "Don't you see what kind of position this leaves me in? You mustn't be so intractable."

"Do you think one rejection has made me more amenable to another?"

"I only know that your words came at me totally unexpected," she said. "I had no chance to consider them, and in the last few days, though I have thought of little else, I am still confused. I have invested considerable time in my quest for Colby. Well, most of the time I just pined, as he barely knew I was alive. Then, in the last few weeks my hopes arose when he finally showed an interest in me—"

"Of course," he cut in sharply, "you want to see how that plays out before you respond to me!" His tone came out bitterly sad.

"I don't want Colby anymore!" Maggie admitted. "He finally showed his true colors to me, and I saw he is not a man I could admire or respect. Can you see how my emotions are now in complete disarray? I may not want Colby, but can you understand how hard it is for me to give up what I have long desired, or thought I desired?"

He nodded reluctantly.

"I do admire and respect you, Evan. You are the finest man I know. Is that love? I don't know. I don't know anything about love except that what I felt for Colby wasn't love at all. That's all I know. So I don't know how to respond to you."

He had resumed his seat, and now, at her eye level, he lifted his gaze to peer directly at her. "I think I am beginning to understand, Maggie. Forgive me for putting such pressure upon you. I will refrain from doing so in the future. In fact, let us agree that I will say no more of the matter. I will leave it to you whether to pursue or not pursue in your good time."

"It hardly seems fair that it's all up to me," she protested, though she knew he was being extremely fair and patient. She thought of something else. "What do we do in the meantime? I hate this awkward formality between us."

"I don't like it either," he replied, "but my words can't be unsaid." He paused thoughtfully. "Certainly we can call a truce of sorts. It won't be too hard to slip back into our old comfortable habits, will it?"

"I guess we can try." She held his gaze. All sorts of odd things were happening inside her, things that in the past had only happened when she looked at Colby. Now she knew such feelings were not love. Nevertheless, they still befuddled her mind!

"We'll get a fresh start after the trial," he said with an encouraging smile. "When our nerves are settled and Tommy is safe."

"Okay. It's a deal," she said, trying to match his assurance.

"Now I best get you home. It is late."

"I still need to talk to you about my testimony."

"Shall we talk as we walk to your cousin's house?"

She still felt the tension of past emotions between them but prayed that would diffuse with time. As they walked, she expressed her fears about her testimony.

"Maggie, I cannot impress upon you enough the importance of telling the truth on the stand," he replied when she finished.

"Couldn't I just say I don't remember?"

"That would be a lie," he replied unequivocally. "Let me put it this way. A lie will definitely hurt you. A person who commits perjury under oath can be imprisoned."

"They wouldn't!"

"You might escape such a punishment because of your tender years. But there would still be consequences, perhaps a stiff fine, which I doubt your parents could easily bear. And beside the consequences for you, think of Tommy. If you are discovered lying about him, it will only make him look that much more guilty. You must tell the truth."

She felt he'd been able to read her intent, and she was glad it was too dark for him to see the guilt on her face.

"Tommy will hate me for betraying him," she said miserably.

"After he is free, he won't even give it a thought."

Again Maggie found herself taking strength from his confidence.

# TWENTY-SIX

Evan leaned against the wall in the alley behind the jail. Perspiration beaded on his forehead, yet he felt icy cold. His insides roiled. He'd already lost what little he'd been able to eat for breakfast and still felt like his seemingly empty stomach would expel even more.

With shaky hands he removed his precious pocket watch and saw that court would convene in a few minutes. The watch felt heavy in his hands, heavier than its gold plating accounted for. This watch represented his family's pride and faith in him, while at the same time it seemed to mock him for his failure. How he had hoped that the weaknesses he'd experienced in Boston would not be repeated here. He'd tried to convince himself that he would feel more at ease in front of hometown folks. That was not to be.

Yesterday, before the trial had begun, he'd had to rush from the jail after seeing Tommy and making a hurried excuse to the boy and his mother. He'd barely made it to the privacy of the alley before his stomach heaved. He'd told himself then that it was just opening day jitters.

What was he to tell himself now? This was the second day of the trial.

He debated if he should tell his client about his weakness. Tommy and his mother might reconsider his capability to defend Tommy if they knew. But it would be horribly demoralizing for Tommy if the trial were postponed yet again. He and his mother were depending upon him.

His stomach lurched again, and he bent over just in time to avoid soiling his clothing. At least he knew how to vomit properly!

I also know the law! he argued with himself. I know how to try a case, and I have put together a very good case on Tommy's behalf. The firm in Boston had wanted him before they had chanced upon him vomiting before a court appearance, and that only for a minor case the firm had felt a freshly minted lawyer could be entrusted with. He'd been so humiliated, he had avoided further courtroom appearances.

They were even willing to overlook his weakness because he was new and green. But he had known this was not the whole reason for his problem. He'd experienced it in school, as well, not only during moot court exercises but even for oral exams and such. Getting up in front of an audience simply made him sick, and he didn't know what to do about it. He'd handled the problem at the Boston firm by quitting. It was obvious he wasn't cut out for this. Perhaps he could specialize in legal areas that did not require courtroom appearances, such as estate or contract law.

Yet like many young lawyers, he'd been enticed by the challenge of the courtroom and by the desire to help those in need, innocents brought before the court for deeds they had not committed. He did not care for the prospect of making his living helping the rich find ways to become richer. So he'd allowed himself to be enticed once more, this time by Maggie's faith in him, to help Tommy. He'd even let himself forget just how ill he'd become in the past.

He supposed he should be thankful that when he stood before the court he'd been able to comport himself with some dignity, aside from spilling his papers and cracking his voice. He thought he'd hid his inner turmoil fairly well once he got going. Certainly no one could tell that moments before he'd been in an alley losing his breakfast. Once or twice during the proceedings yesterday he thought he might have to make a quick escape to the courthouse alley, but by sheer force of will he had curbed his nausea and continued.

"Evan, is that you?"

Evan nearly jumped a foot. Guilt and shame sent flames of heat up his neck. It was Zack.

"Are you all right?" Zack asked.

It was quite futile to hide it, so Evan shook his head.

Zack walked into the alley a few steps, took in the scene, and stopped. "Maybe you don't want me here," he offered.

"It doesn't matter," Evan mumbled.

"Can I do anything?"

"Nothing to be done." Evan closed his eyes and let his head bang against the wall. The pain of the impact did no good. He thought to brush off his illness by telling Zack it was just a temporary stomach complaint. Then he remembered that Zack had once been a minister, true only a fake one, but from what Evan had heard, he'd been well thought of. And it appeared he had recently been called by God to become a real minister. Perhaps he had some God-given wisdom that could help. So he confessed, "I get sick every time I must appear before an audience."

Zack's eyes strayed to the mess in the dirt as if for confirmation. He nodded. "Must be a terrible feeling. I once knew an actor in San Francisco who got terribly sick before every performance. He called it stage fright. Do you think that's what you have?"

"Something similar at least. Were you ever nervous before preaching?"

"At first, but I sort of warmed up to it. For me it wasn't getting up in front of a crowd that got to me. It was worrying about remembering my 'lines.' " Zack went on, "I kind of enjoyed preaching. I hope that doesn't change when I do it for real."

"Then you can't understand what I am experiencing."

"No, I'm afraid I can't, but if I needed to experience everyone's pain before I could help them, it'd be almost impossible to minister to them. Now that I think of it, I do know how to help you. How about we pray together right now?"

"I've been praying about this problem for a long time," Evan said. "I have begged God to cure it, and it still hasn't gone away. I have almost decided to give up my chosen profession."

"Maybe it doesn't need to go away. You seem to comport yourself well once you are before the court. My actor friend was a very good actor. He got rave reviews despite that small weakness."

"I commend him," Evan replied glumly. "Imagine having to face every day something that made you physically ill. I don't know if I could do that."

"Yes, that would be hard—Wait a minute! This reminds me of something I heard—probably something I preached myself. Someone in the Bible had an ailment, and he prayed and prayed for it to go away, and it never did."

"I believe that was the apostle Paul."

"That's right. I was preaching a sermon on grace." Zack rubbed his chin thoughtfully, then brightened as he recited, " 'My grace is sufficient for thee.' "

"Yes," Evan said. "I memorized that verse when I was a child. It goes on to say, 'For my strength is made perfect in weakness.' " Evan smiled ironically. "I am the perfect example of that! At least the weakness part of it."

"Tell me, Evan, did you get sick like this yesterday?"

"Worse."

"Then you are an example of the rest of the Scripture, as well," Zack said triumphantly. "Despite being sick, you got in front of the court and spoke and questioned the jurors. And you did a mighty fine job of it, too."

"By God's grace!"

"Doubtless!"

"Thank you for reminding me of these things," Evan said. "There have been times when I've gotten angry at God for giving me this 'thorn in the flesh.' I would beg Him to take it from me. I see now I should have been thanking Him for allowing me to perform regardless. I was ready to toss aside the gifts He's given me in my education and my abilities. Now every time my innards roil, I will use it as an opportunity to praise God."

"Now, there's an interesting picture," quipped Zack. "And it is still a beautiful one."

"I would still like you to pray with me if you have a moment," Evan said. He slipped his watch back into his pocket. This was more important than getting to the courtroom on time.

Maggie was worried because Evan was late for court. She looked over at Mrs. Donnelly, who shrugged. She'd said earlier that Evan had left the jail a half hour ago, presumably to come to the courthouse. She had no idea why he hadn't made it.

When he finally made his appearance, Maggie noted that he looked pale again and a bit green. Was he feeling poorly? Yet there was buoyancy in his step this morning. He was closely followed in by Mr. Cranston. The jury was then hustled in, and finally the sheriff brought in Tommy. The judge was last, and everyone rose as he took his place behind the bench.

Judge Olsen cleared his throat and said, "Before we begin, I must emphasize to all concerned that I expect my sessions to begin on time. I will tolerate no further delays in this proceeding." He was looking directly at Evan as he spoke. Evan turned an odd shade of plum green.

As the morning progressed, normal color returned to Evan's skin. But Maggie's worries were not over, for she now began to fret in earnest about her imminent testimony. The rest of the jurors were selected and then each of the lawyers presented their opening statements. Mr. Cranston said he intended to show that the defendant, with malice and aforethought, did willfully kill his father. He went on for quite a bit about the law and the rule of justice. Maggie's mind wandered halfway through the monotone ramble.

Evan started off a bit shaky. It didn't help that as he rose and started forward from his seat, he snagged his foot on the table leg and nearly tripped. His speech was brief. He said he intended to show that the defendant acted in self-defense out of fear for his life, a fear rooted in years, even a lifetime, of abuse by his father. His words were not polished to a slick shine like Mr. Cranston's, but they were full of sincerity and, toward the end, passion.

After the speeches, Mr. Cranston began calling witnesses. Evan said Cranston had about a dozen witnesses. Maggie groaned inwardly when she was not among the first called.

Mr. Cranston's witnesses offered nothing that surprised Maggie. The sheriff was questioned first, and he had little to say except to describe the scene he found in the woods where Tom Donnelly had been killed. He also related that Tommy had fled the scene and was on the run for nearly two weeks before he was arrested. Cranston managed to make it appear as if Tommy had been a dangerous fugitive. When Evan cross-examined, he made it clear that Tommy had turned himself in and had committed a heroic act in the process by helping to save Zack's life from some hoodlums. When the defense presented its case, Zack would have the opportunity to elaborate on this, but for now, Maggie thought this round was at least a draw for both sides.

The next two witnesses questioned were unsavory sorts, not from Maintown, and strangers to Maggie. They told how Tommy had often accompanied his father to the St. Helens taverns and also to other unsavory activities. In cross-examination Evan was able to impugn their characters—he actually got one to admit to cattle rustling! When this fellow finished his testimony, the sheriff led him away. By the time Evan finished with those two, no one believed anything they said.

The next witness was a Maintown man, Donald Weller. Maggie didn't know him well. He didn't attend her Brethren of Christ church, but her father probably knew him because he worked at the sawmill and owned a small farm. He testified that he had once caught Tommy stealing some of his chickens. Maggie glanced at Tommy and saw him sink down in his chair a couple of inches. It must be true, then.

Well, she'd known Tommy wasn't the best behaved boy in the county. However, probably all the boys, maybe even Boyd and Georgie, had tried to filch a chicken or two, just for the thrill of it. But Mr. Weller had caught Tommy red-handed, and though he had let Tommy go, the crime was now coming back to haunt him.

Weller was an upstanding citizen, and Evan could do little to nullify his testimony. But he did coax Weller into admitting that the attempted theft had occurred nearly five years ago, and he'd been able to leave the jurors with the idea that a boy can change in five years.

A couple more witnesses testified before lunch in the same vein. Maggie came to realize that Tommy had lived what seemed a double life. One was the person she knew—an easygoing kid who loved to fish and hunt more than anything and who didn't mind a girl tagging along. The other was the person Tommy became when with his father—a more sinister character who stole chickens, visited taverns and, worst of all, possibly rustled livestock from their neighbors. In her heart Maggie knew Tommy did these things to please his father, a misguided attempt to be accepted by the harsh, cruel man. Yet it was not the kind of picture that would make a jury acquit him.

Evan did his best to punch holes in all this testimony, but it appeared these people were telling the truth, or what they believed was the truth, as in the case of those who didn't actually see Tommy commit acts but had guessed from various clues at their disposal. The most Evan could do was make it apparent to the jury that the testimony was hearsay, and thus put doubt in their minds.

Maggie was quite deflated when the midday recess came and she still hadn't been called to testify. Her new resolve to tell the truth was wavering, especially after hearing some of the incriminating testimony. She needed more reassurance from Evan, but before she could get to him, Mr. Cranston waylaid him. The two lawyers spoke quietly for a few minutes. Maggie thought Evan was turning green again.

He finished with Mr. Cranston and was hurrying toward the door. Maggie fairly ran after him.

"Evan!" she called.

He paused and turned. He looked as if he'd swallowed a huge green frog. "I can't talk now, Maggie!" he said abruptly and started forward again.

She was about to go after him when she felt a hand on her shoulder. She spun around with an angry glare on her face. "What!" she blurted impatiently. It was Zack.

"Maggie, let him go," he said.

"I have to talk to him."

"He's pretty busy," Zack said with far more patience than she had displayed. "He probably has many things to prepare before the next session."

"But this is important!" Then, against the advice of one of the smartest people she knew, she hurried away.

She thought Evan might have gone to his hotel to work, but since the jail was closer, she decided to look there first. The sheriff said he hadn't seen Evan since the recess. Outside, she began to question her impulsive behavior. It was selfish of her to foist her problems on Evan when he had much larger things to worry about. Besides, she already knew what he would tell her. She had to tell the truth. There simply was no way out.

If only Mr. Cranston would call her soon so she could get over her suffering!

She was about to head back to her cousin's house for a bite of dinner when she heard a peculiar sound coming from the alley behind the jail. It sounded like a sick animal. Turning into the alley, she saw a human figure bent retching. She also recognized the person.

"Evan?"

Though the midday sunlight didn't fully penetrate the alley, there was enough light for her to see his face when he looked up at her. Her heart quaked at the misery she discerned in his expression.

"Evan, what's wrong?" She started toward him.

"Go away!" he rasped.

"But you are not well—"

"Leave me alone!"

"But—"

"Please!" he begged, then bent over again.

She was torn. Foremost was the urge to go to him, put her arms around him, and comfort him. But she also had enough sense to know a man wouldn't want to be observed in such a humiliating position. The sound of his voice as he beseeched her was proof of that.

When he finished and dabbed his lips with a handkerchief, he said in a thin, strained voice, "I'll . . . be all right. Please, just go."

Dear Evan, so polite even when he was beyond distressed. She could not argue further. She just had to trust it really wasn't anything serious. She turned and exited the alley, cringing when she heard that retching sound again as she walked away. Leaving him there alone in his misery was one of the hardest things she had ever done.

## TWENTY-SEVEN

Maggie had never been much of what Mama called a "prayer warrior." Of course she believed in prayer. She just wasn't faithful about it like Mama or even Ellie. Yet, as the trial began again that afternoon, she found herself silently praying over and over for Evan. She all but forgot her worry about her own testimony.

She quickly saw what had probably upset Evan. The first witness for the prosecution after the recess was none other than Colby! She was fairly certain that was not what Evan had expected. He had told her about the prosecution's witnesses because, as was customary, both sides revealed their witnesses before the trial began. Evan would have told her if Colby was going to testify. Maggie wondered if that's what Mr. Cranston had spoken to Evan about before they left the courtroom. It smelled of a dirty trick to Maggie, and she knew a little about being devious. Cranston surely knew of the altercation between Colby and Evan and about Evan's humiliation in losing that fight. What better way to disconcert him during the trial than to unexpectedly spring an adversary upon Evan, whom Mr. Cranston must know was already quite nervous.

Worse still was the fact that Colby was an "unassailable" witness, as Evan would have termed it. He was the son of one of the most respected men in the community. Every word he spoke would be believed. Moreover, Colby may have his faults, which Maggie was becoming more and more aware of, but she knew he was not a liar.

Colby told the court of an incident that occurred a year ago in which Tommy Donnelly tried to sell a horse to the Stoddards. Albert Stoddard knew enough not to have any dealings with Tom, but it was Tommy who did the negotiations, and Albert had a soft heart and could not shut down the boy despite his misgivings. Turned out the horse had been stolen.

Maggie noted that, as before, Tommy reacted to Colby's words with signs of guilt. His cheeks colored, and he sank down in his chair. Maggie sighed inwardly.

"Now, I'm not saying Tommy himself stole that horse," Colby testified. "Tommy *said* his father had bought the horse from a drifter who needed some quick cash. But Tommy said"—the way Colby spoke that word *said* had skepticism all over it—"he lost the bill of sale. My dad wanted to give the kid the benefit of the doubt. He told me, 'That boy needs a break. Maybe the money will do the boy and his family some good.' "

"Objection, Your Honor," Evan cut in. "Again, the prosecution is presenting hearsay testimony."

"Overruled, counselor," the judge returned. "I am going to allow it because I understand that Albert Stoddard is ill and cannot be here to testify in person."

With a pointed glance at Evan, Mr. Cranston asked, "Mr. Stoddard, were you present during this transaction?"

"For most of it."

"Then your testimony is, for the most part, a firsthand accounting of the incident?"

"Yes, sir."

"Can you tell the court what young Tommy Donnelly's reaction was when he heard the horse had been stolen?"

"He denied knowing anything about it. But my father is a pretty good judge of people, and he could see Tommy really did know—"

"Objection!" exclaimed Evan.

"Sustained," the judge replied almost wearily.

Maggie had a feeling he didn't think much of Evan, and it worried her that he might be conveying this attitude to the jury.

The judge added, "Mr. Stoddard, please confine your answers to facts."

"Well, Your Honor, it's a fact that there was no bill of sale!" Colby declared triumphantly.

"I have no further questions," Mr. Cranston said.

Evan remained seated, looking as if he was weighed down by a lead ball. His skin still had a grayish green tinge. Maggie prayed harder.

"Mr. Parker, do you wish to cross-examine the witness?" asked the judge.

"Not at this time, Your Honor, but I request that the witness remain close in case there is need to question him later," Evan replied.

At first, upon hearing Evan's response, Maggie thought he had capitulated, giving in to his fear. But upon further thought, she realized this was the only move he could have made. There was no way he could discredit Colby's testimony in the eyes of the jury, so instead he probably opted to give him no further opportunity to speak. Hopefully his short testimony would be lost in the mix. Maggie thought Evan would be pleased at how she was beginning to think like a lawyer.

The afternoon dragged on with more prosecution witnesses of the same ilk. Maggie began to think her testimony was going to be put off another day. According to Evan, the most important witnesses were questioned early in the day when the jury was fresh. So Mr. Cranston might be saving her for the morning. If she was called today, it could indicate her testimony wasn't as significant as she thought. There was one other possibility. It came to her around four o'clock in the afternoon when her name was suddenly called. What if she was the prosecution's finale? Mr. Cranston might rest his case after she testified, leaving her words echoing with a kind of finality in the jury's collective mind.

"I call to the stand," Mr. Cranston said, "Miss Margaret Newcomb."

Her knees were shaky as she walked toward the witness box and her right hand trembled when she placed it on the Bible and swore to tell the truth. All thought of lying fled from her in that moment.

"Miss Newcomb," Cranston began, "please tell us your relationship to the accused."

"He's a friend. We went to school together," Maggie replied. She tried to block from her mind the awful rumors that there was more to their friendship. But her stomach knotted in fear that Mr. Cranston might try to exploit this.

"But you have been out of school for over a year, have you not?"

"Yes, sir."

"Yet, you have still maintained your friendship."

"Yes. I'm friends with everyone I went to school with," Maggie said smugly.

"Of course," Cranston replied dryly. "We have established in this court, if nothing else, that Tommy Donnelly was not the most respected or trusted person in the community . . ."

He paused, perhaps expecting an objection from Evan. But there was none.

Cranston continued, "Therefore, I must ask, why is it that you remained friendly with this boy who could not have been the best influence? Did your parents support this . . . ah . . . friendship—"

"Objection!" Evan jumped to his feet.

"On what grounds?" the judge asked.

"Well . . . I just don't like the sound of his voice," Evan replied.

His tone was hesitant. He probably realized belatedly that the last thing he ought to do was draw attention to the rumors to which Cranston was obviously making a subtle reference.

"Overruled. But, Mr. Cranston, do please watch your *tone,*" said the judge, his own tone sounding rather snide.

"Of course, Your Honor. I certainly don't wish to bring aspersion upon my own witness." There was amusement in Cranston's voice. He'd made his point and nothing would wipe it from the jury's memory. "So, Miss Newcomb, your parents approved of this friendship with Tommy?"

"Not exactly. But—"

"You continued to interact with Tommy despite their displeasure?"

"Yes. But—"

"Objection!" Evan exclaimed, again springing to his feet. "Why doesn't the prosecution let the witness complete a sentence? She is his witness, isn't she?"

"Overruled. As I understand it, she is a hostile witness," the judge replied.

"Is that why the prosecution must manipulate her answers?" Evan asked.

"You'll have your turn with the witness, Mr. Parker, but in the meantime please watch *your* tone," reminded the judge. "Now, please sit."

Cranston resumed. "How close were you and Tommy Donnelly?"

"Objection!" Evan cried again.

"Mr. Parker," the judge said with undisguised displeasure, "please refrain from these unfounded objections. One might think she was a defense witness, the way you feel you must protect her."

Evan slumped back in his chair, an almost imperceptible pout on his face.

"Would you please answer the question, Miss Newcomb?" the judge requested.

"I saw him once or twice a week," Maggie replied. "He told me I was his only real friend. And I liked his company because he didn't mind that I liked fishing and hiking better than stitching and cooking."

"What activities did you pursue when you were together?"

"We mostly went fishing when the weather was nice. Or hunting. We both liked the outdoors. That was all!" she added, almost daring the man to contradict her.

"Did you talk?" Cranston asked, ignoring her final remark.

Maggie wished he would just get to the point and quit dragging her through the wringer like this. She had a feeling it was as much to agitate Evan as it was to interrogate her.

"Some," Maggie replied. "Tommy isn't a big talker. We mostly just fished and enjoyed the peace and quiet. Sometimes we talked about news and such and occasionally about our problems."

"I can't imagine a well-brought-up girl such as yourself could have many problems, at least that would be pertinent to this case. However, I would be interested to hear what problems the defendant revealed."

Maggie looked desperately at the judge. "Your Honor, do I have to tell things that were told me in confidence?"

"Yes, Miss Newcomb. Only a doctor, a lawyer, or a man of the cloth has the privilege of confidentiality. Answer the question please."

"Well, then . . ." She hesitated. As much as she wanted to get to the point, she was also dreading that moment. "Tommy talked about things that happened at home."

"Can you be more specific?"

"His father." Maggie had tried studiously to avoid looking at the defense table, but out of the corner of her eye she saw Tommy stir and Evan lay a hand on his arm.

"Yes . . . ?" prompted Mr. Cranston.

"He'd tell me about his father beating him and calling him names."

"Did you ever see the father beat his son?"

"No. But—"

"That's good enough." As Cranston spoke, Maggie noted Evan was now about to make a move, but a sharp look from the judge forced him to refrain. Cranston added quickly, "So you have only the defendant's word regarding the abuse?"

"He had a fat lip once or twice!" Maggie said quickly before the man could cut her off again.

Cranston smiled. "I suppose Tommy never fought with anyone else in the community."

"Sure he did! The other boys were always making fun of him and egging him on."

"So those wounds you saw could have been from these fights, could they not?"

Maggie groaned inwardly, realizing her error. Gamely she replied, "Maybe, but—"

"Now, then—"

Frustrated with his constant interruptions when she wanted to explain an answer that could be misunderstood, she now assertively talked right over Cranston. "But I know the bruises were from his father!" she blurted.

Cranston arched a brow. "Please, Miss Newcomb, a simple yes or no is adequate unless *I* ask for more elaboration."

"Your Honor," Evan put in, "the way the prosecution is handling this witness is a travesty!"

"Your protest is duly noted, Mr. Parker," said the judge, only as a matter of form, she was certain, not because he agreed. "Continue, Mr. Cranston."

"Miss Newcomb, let's recall the day of June twenty-first of this year. There was an altercation that day between the defendant's father and the supposed minister, whom we now know as Mr. Zack Hartley. Can you tell the court what happened on that day?"

"I wasn't there to see it," Maggie said smugly. "So it would be hearsay." She risked a glance at Evan, and he offered her a faint smile.

"But you can tell us what the entire community knows of the incident."

Maggie shrugged. She may as well not fight it. "That day Zack called at the Donnelly house, and I guess Mr. Donnelly tried to kick him off the property. Anyway, it ended up in a fight in which Zack knocked Mr. Donnelly out cold."

"The defendant saw the altercation. Correct?"

"Yes. He told me about it later."

"What else did he tell you?"

Maggie took a breath. She had to practically force out every word. "He told me he had never believed his father could get beat—"

Tommy instantly sprang to his feet. "Maggie, no!" he implored. A murmur rose from the spectators. This was the kind of drama they had come to see.

"Mr. Parker," ordered the judge, "restrain your client, or the court will be forced to do so."

"Tommy, sit down," Evan pleaded, grasping his arm and giving it a tug.

Tommy wrenched his arm away. "Don't you say nothing, Maggie, or you ain't my friend no more!"

"Tommy, sit down!" Evan said with more authority. "Now!"

Tommy hesitated a moment before slumping back into his chair. He continued to glare at Maggie, however. Evan leaned over and whispered something in his ear. Whatever it was seemed to settle him a little.

"I'm sorry, Tommy," Maggie murmured.

"Did Tommy say anything else about that incident?" Mr. Cranston asked.

"Yes." Let him drag it from me, Maggie decided.

"Tell the court what Tommy said."

She glanced toward the defense table. Tommy's hostility made her heart quake, but Evan offered her a look of encouragement. She had to trust that he would somehow make everything all right.

"Tommy told me . . . well, that he wasn't afraid of his father anymore after seeing him get beat. He said . . . the next time his father pushed him, he was going to push back." Maggie couldn't look at Tommy, but she could feel his angry glower.

Her words caused another buzz of voices to ripple through the spectators.

"Order!" demanded the judge, and when there wasn't immediate quiet, he banged his gavel on his bench and said louder, "I will have order in the court, or the spectators will be removed!"

That brought the desired effect. Quiet descended.

Maggie realized her words also created the desired effect. That is, the effect the prosecutor hoped for. Everyone, including the jury, would have to consider her testimony as a real motive for murder.

"And," Cranston said, "less than a month later, Tom Donnelly was dead—"

"Objection!" cried Evan. "Counsel is—"

"I know what the prosecution is doing," the judge interrupted. "That last comment is to be stricken from the record, and the jury is instructed to ignore it."

Mr. Cranston had made his point nonetheless. "That will be all, Miss Newcomb," he said.

"The defense may cross-examine," said the judge.

Evan rose. "Good afternoon, Miss Newcomb," he said formally. Maggie had expected nothing less. "I will try to make this brief. The day is waning, and I am sure everyone is growing weary. But can you tell me something regarding the defendant's remark about not letting his father push him anymore? Was that the first time he ever made such a statement to you?"

Good question, Evan! Maggie silently cheered. "No, as a matter of fact it wasn't. He often said how he'd like to hit his father back."

"So this most recent statement didn't seem any more serious to you than the others?"

"No, not at all."

"As our learned prosecutor so aptly pointed out, nearly a full month passed between the conversation you described and the untimely death of Mr. Tom Donnelly. Did you have opportunity to see young Tommy in that time?"

"Yes, though not as much as usual. It was a . . . uh . . . kind of a busy time." Maggie hoped Evan didn't question her about this because she really didn't want him to know that she'd been busy throwing herself at the new minister. "I saw him at church," she added, thinking this ought to help Tommy.

"What did his demeanor seem like at this time?"

"Objection," Cranston said. "The question requires a subjective judgment from the witness that she has no real expertise to make."

"But, Your Honor," Evan argued, "it has been established that Miss Newcomb was the defendant's close friend, and by his admission, his only 'real' friend. I would think she'd be the best person to make such a judgment."

Judge Olsen nodded. Maybe he was a fair judge after all!

"I'm going to overrule the objection in the interest of illuminating an important aspect of these proceedings. I believe Miss Newcomb is a fair and honest young woman and will give the court a true assessment of her observations. But I will instruct the jury to keep in mind that these are, in fact, only subjective observations. Answer the question, Miss Newcomb."

She almost forgot what the question was, then just as Evan was about to remind her, she remembered. "Oh yes, his demeanor. He was pretty normal."

"He did not appear more embittered or sinister than in the past?"

"Goodness, no! He never was any of those. I mean he may have complained about his father, but he never was white-hot mad. When he did get a little angry, it was gone in a few minutes, and he was back to talking about the catch of the day or something. Tommy has always been a pleasant, good-natured person." She felt great relief at being able to say her piece uninterrupted. She silently thanked Evan for that.

"You mentioned that he had started attending church," Evan said. "How was his attitude there?"

"He was glad to attend. His father was very hostile about church, and that was one of the reasons he beat Tommy. If Tommy went to church, he was sure to expect a thrashing later." Maggie brightened as she realized something. "That was the true result of the incident between Zack and Mr. Donnelly. It gave Tommy the courage to defy his father and attend church. To do the *right* thing instead of all the bad things his father made him do. Tommy wanted to go to church because he wanted to be a better person."

Though Evan was maintaining a serious, formal façade, Maggie could see a brief glimmer of pleasure flit across his expression. Perhaps she was now actually helping Tommy more than her previous testimony hurt him.

Evan put forth a few more questions about Tommy's actions in the weeks and days before Tom's death, then he thanked Maggie, and she was excused from the stand.

Then, as she suspected, Mr. Cranston, with great flourish, said, "Your Honor, the prosecution rests!"

"The afternoon is nearly gone," Judge Olsen said, "so we will hear the defense's case tomorrow. Court is adjourned for the day."

After the judge exited and everyone was dismissed, Maggie found herself immediately surrounded by friends and family, all praising her and telling her how proud she had made them. Of course she was pleased, especially by her parents' support, but all she really wanted to do was get to Evan, who, much to her disappointment, hadn't joined the well-wishers. In fact, he had quickly gathered his papers into his leather satchel and all but raced from the courtroom.

How she wanted to run after him! But she couldn't be rude to these people who were showing her such kindness. Yet that wasn't the biggest reason for her not following her impulse. She could not forget the scene earlier in the alley. Evan had been humiliated, and she didn't want to risk a repeat should she find him in similar circumstances. Moreover, tomorrow he would begin to present his case. He needed to focus. He did not need to be distracted by her. But she found more and more that she greatly missed those lovely days when she and Evan had been easygoing friends.

# TWENTY-EIGHT

Evan took two days to present his case. His witnesses were a varied list of friends, mostly Mrs. Donnelly's, and neighbors who generally painted a picture of Tommy as a troubled boy with bad habits influenced by a father who was far less than an ideal model. They all agreed he was respectful to his elders and did not display violent tendencies except when defending himself against the taunts of his peers.

Since these witnesses were all upstanding, mostly churchgoing citizens, the prosecution had a difficult time tarnishing their testimony. Cranston did make such an attempt with Zack, but Zack withstood the barrage against his character with grace and forbearance.

Dad's testimony was the best because he made it clear he did not approve of Tommy's behavior or of Tommy's friendship with his daughter. But he never truly believed Maggie was in danger around the boy. He was also one of three people who had examined the scene of Tom's death immediately after the incident. Boyd was another, as was the sheriff. But Dad brought out something that the sheriff had failed to mention. There were several trees in the clearing in the woods where the killing had occurred that were badly chewed up by gunfire, trees behind the area where Tom's body had been found, and trees behind a spot where another shooter appeared to have stood. The marks were random, almost haphazard, as if fired wildly. This, along with Dad's description of a couple of empty jugs of moonshine, supported the suspicion that a drunken melee had taken place there.

Cranston, of course, tried to discount these observations. But Evan recalled the sheriff to the stand. He was forced to agree with Dad. Maggie thought Evan did marvelously and had made one of the most important points of the trial. The gunplay was wild and would certainly give a person reason to fear for his life. Also, the parties involved were most likely drunk and not in complete command of their actions.

Mama's testimony was the most difficult to hear. Evan had previously called two witnesses who described having seen Tom whip his son. He had induced them to give detailed, fairly graphic, descriptions of what they'd seen. It obviously pained Evan to draw this testimony from the two men, but he was especially distressed to do so with Mama.

"I heard a noise behind the Donnelly barn," Mama testified. "Maybe I should have minded my own business that day, but it sounded like distress, and I just couldn't turn my back on it."

"What did you discover?" Evan asked.

"Tom was beating Tommy."

"He was punching him in the face and body?"

"Not exactly."

"Describe what you saw, Mrs. Newcomb," Evan prompted, his voice strained, his eyes conveying apology.

Mama glanced at Mrs. Donnelly. Mama knew every testimony was gut-wrenching for her friend. She'd lost her husband, and now she was on the brink of losing her son, as well.

"Mrs. Newcomb, I know this is difficult, but the court needs to hear what you saw that day," Evan urged.

Mama licked her lips. Maggie had never seen her mother so reticent to speak her mind. "Tom had a piece of firewood in his hand and was striking Tommy with it. Poor Tommy was crouched on the ground trying to protect himself, but Tom kept hitting him and hitting him . . ." Mama paused, trying to control her emotions. "I yelled at him to stop. When Tom saw me, he halted in surprise, and the look on his face was fearsome. I thought he might come after me with that wood. In those few moments of reprieve, Tommy jumped up and ran away. Knowing I could do no more, I left the farm without even visiting with Jane, as I had intended."

"Tell the court, Mrs. Newcomb, was Mr. Donnelly simply striking Tommy on the backside as a father might when 'taking the rod' to the child?"

"Many of those blows would have struck Tommy's head if he hadn't been protecting it with his hands," Mama answered. "His hands and arms were bloody."

In cross-examination Mr. Cranston tried to twist Mama's testimony to make it appear that she had overreacted to a mere spanking, implying that her female tender sensibilities might have clouded her perspective. Those in the audience who knew Mama chuckled at this implication. While Mama was tenderhearted, she was in no way fainthearted, and everyone knew this.

After the midday recess on the second day of the defense's case, Evan called his final witness, Tommy himself. Maggie knew he had debated about doing this. Testimony by the defendant was, as Evan said, a "double-edged sword." It would give Mr. Cranston an opportunity to chip away at Tommy's story and his self-confidence. It was also tricky because of Tommy's mental slowness and his propensity to say what he was thinking with little restraint. But Tommy was the only witness to the death of Tom Donnelly. He needed to have a chance to tell his side of it. Evan trusted that Tommy's account was completely true and that Cranston would be unable to impugn it.

First, Evan questioned Tommy about his father's treatment, the beatings, which Tommy said happened almost daily, the name calling, and the constant criticism.

"Why did you stick around?" Evan asked. "Many boys your age would have run away long ago."

"I saw my pa strike my ma only once or twice," Tommy replied. "But it was pretty awful, and I knew that if my pa didn't have me to knock around, he'd light into my ma."

"So you stayed and took the beatings to protect your mother?" Evan repeated, no doubt to impress this fact upon the jury.

"Yeah, 'course. Wouldn't you do the same?"

"Did you ever strike your father back?"

"I tried a couple times. But did you ever see my pa? He was big, and let me tell you he was strong. I didn't get none of his size. I was pretty puny next to him."

Next, Evan asked him to describe the day of his father's death, and Tommy related the events in the same way he'd done several times since it had happened. He had to be telling the truth, Maggie believed, because he wasn't bright enough to get his story straight over and over again unless that's what really happened. He told how they had gone bird hunting, and Tom had brought a couple jugs of moonshine. They started into those and soon both of them were quite drunk. His father started railing at him for going to church, yelling that religion was making Tommy into a "nancy boy," a "pansy," a "sissy." Then his father got it into his head that he was going to make a man of Tommy. That's when the shooting started. Tom might not have wanted to shoot Tommy, but he was so drunk there was no telling what he was likely to hit.

"Then he started to shout, 'I'd be better off with a dead son than a girly boy!' " Tommy said. "That's when I really got scared. I could see it in his eyes . . . he wanted me dead. Then he tripped and fell and dropped the rifle. I grabbed it."

"Tommy, are you saying you had no rifle of your own that day?" Evan asked.

"Nah. Pa came and got me when I was workin' in the field. It would have been too much trouble to go back for my gun. We'd just share his. I figured if this was like most hunting trips, there'd be more drinking than hunting."

"So you had no gun of your own?" Evan reiterated.

"No, sir."

"Now, tell the court what happened after the shooting started?"

"Well, like I said, he tripped and I got the rifle, but then he got hold of a fallen branch and came at me with it. I was yelling at him to stop and leave me alone." Tommy's voice started to tremble. His eyes welled with moisture. With difficulty, he went on, "I yelled and yelled, and the next thing I knew the rifle was firing. Like my fingers had a mind of their own, you know? It went off several times 'fore I realized my pa was down again. This time he didn't move. I saw blood on his shirt, and I ran."

"Did you run because you had murdered your father?"

"I never thought 'bout that. I just ran because I knew Ma would be mad at me for what happened."

"Did you know what you had done was wrong?"

" 'Course! It was a horrible, horrible thing I done shooting my own pa. I . . . I still can hardly believe it happened. Except I know it did 'cause for the first time in my life I finally feel safe. I don't gotta wake up every morning dreading the beatin' I was sure to get that day."

"Thank you, Tommy." Evan turned to the prosecution. "Mr. Cranston, your witness."

Mr. Cranston tried hard to tear apart Tommy's story but without success. He spent much time dissecting Tommy's statement about not realizing he was firing the rifle until he saw his father fall. Though Evan objected, Mr. Cranston implied that Tommy was too level-headed and too adept with firearms to fire one in a daze of passion.

When Cranston finished his questioning, Evan quietly said, "The defense rests."

The trial concluded with closing remarks from each lawyer. Mr. Cranston harped about premeditation, though he'd made a weak case for it. But he was fairly convincing in attacking Tommy's word regarding not knowing he was firing the rifle. It was a critical point, because if Tommy knew he was shooting, the case for murder strengthened. Self-defense could still apply, but it did raise an important question.

Maggie thought Evan was absolutely eloquent in his closing remarks. First he outlined the facts of the case, emphasizing the fact that Tommy had not even taken a gun into the woods that day, so how could there be premeditation? Evan then drew a poignant and heart-wrenching picture of a boy taunted and abused by his father, a boy who wanted to be a better person but who fell into unsavory actions in order to find acceptance from a cruel, and heartless father.

Maggie was crying by the time Evan finished, and a glance around the courtroom revealed other women with moist eyes. The all-male jury was dry-eyed, but she saw many creased brows and sympathetic expressions among them.

The jury then exited the courtroom for their deliberation. Maggie's prayers, and she was certain those of many other supporters of Tommy, followed them. It was in the jurors' hands now and in God's hands.

Tommy was taken back to jail, and Evan hurried from the room. Maggie didn't even try to go after him. Though it was hard for her, she had to give him time to get over his humiliation, if that was the problem, or just time to concentrate on the remainder of the trial. Tommy needed Evan more than she did anyway. Waiting for the jury's decision would be excruciating.

Exiting the courthouse, she saw Colby standing on the sidewalk. She was going to ignore him when he called.

"Hi, Maggie. That was some spectacle, wasn't it?"

She gave him a cold glance and, without a word, walked on. She felt he was the enemy now and wondered that she had ever desired him.

She and her parents had a very quiet and subdued supper with Cousin Martha and her family. No one wanted to discuss the trial or ponder the possible outcomes. If the trial had been a contest, even Maggie, who was definitely prejudiced, couldn't say who had come out ahead. Evan had told her once that a quick verdict often favored the prosecution, while a more prolonged one was good for the defense. Thus, she felt as good as she could when no word had come about a verdict after supper. The jury might deliberate through the night, maybe even for days, though that didn't seem likely. Those men had farms and families to tend, and though they wanted justice done, they were also practical men.

Maggie passed a sleepless night. When she did manage to doze off, her dreams were unpleasant enough to wake her.

Everyone returned to the courtroom at nine in the morning. If the jury had reached a decision during the late evening or night, the judge would have held off to announce it until morning. This, in fact, had been the case.

When all were in their proper places, the judge turned to the jury and asked, "Has the jury reached a verdict?"

"Yes, Your Honor, we have," said the spokesman. He passed a paper to the bailiff, who handed it to the judge.

The judge read the paper. "Will the defendant please rise?"

Today, both Evan and Tommy looked sick. But Tommy stood and Evan stood beside him.

"In the matter of the State versus Thomas Donnelly, the jury finds the defendant . . . not guilty."

The entire courtroom erupted into a spontaneous outburst. There were cheers and perhaps some less than supportive sounds, but Maggie only heard the words "Not guilty!" Then she surged forward with her parents and others to congratulate Tommy and Evan.

She tried to embrace Tommy, but he turned away from her. When she approached Evan, he wasn't as obvious in his rejection, but he ignored her, as well. He seemed to be distracted by someone else, thus avoiding her overture. Heartsick, she stumbled back on the fringes of the well-wishers.

The judge tried to call order so he could properly adjourn the court but finally just rose and exited. In all the hullabaloo it was easy for Maggie to slip out of the courthouse unnoticed. She tried to choke back the emotion that rose in her. If she was going to cry, she'd prefer it was in private, but she didn't know where to go to be alone here in town. Somehow she made it to the alley behind the jail—a perfect spot to unburden one's misery, as Evan had proved.

She sank down on the ground and let the tears flow. She wanted to be happy that Tommy was safe and that Evan had proven his worth to everyone who had ever maligned or doubted him. How she had wanted to embrace them and shout a cheer for them!

That they had rejected her was bad enough; that she deserved it was worse yet. She had betrayed Tommy, though some of her testimony may have helped him. She had humiliated Evan, but she had not intended to do so. She had lost two dear friends. And perhaps in Evan she had lost far more.

# TWENTY-NINE

The next few days after the trial Maggie moped around the house—at least that's what Mama called it.

"Maggie, why are you moping around the house?" she said more than once. "Before that trial I hardly ever saw you. Now you are getting peaked from staying indoors so much."

Maggie would merely shrug and concentrate on her stitching. She had ten blocks finished for her quilt and only two more to go before all were complete. Twelve blocks with sashings would make a nice-sized quilt. Though her purpose in making this quilt had become completely muddled since she had started it, she still wanted to finish it. She wanted one finished quilt that she had made herself in her hope chest. At the rate her romantic pursuits were going, she might still end up with all twelve like Ellie.

However, she couldn't spend all her time stitching. Boyd's wedding day was fast approaching, the Sunday after next! Reverend Barnett had agreed to officiate, and Boyd had asked Zack to take part, as well, by saying a prayer and perhaps a few words. The wedding would be at the Wallards' house, but Mama was going to help with the food for the reception. They had been baking all kinds of goodies to put away for the big day. When Maggie had come home from the trial, Grandma had surprised her by having finished her dress for the wedding. Maggie had been thrilled but also sad, though she tried not to show it. That dress would remind her of Evan. He had helped pick out the material.

Would he see her in the dress? Although he was invited to the wedding, would he decline the invitation for fear of seeing Maggie?

She didn't understand why such a relatively small thing like her seeing him upchuck in an alley would have set him off so. However, she got an inkling there was more to it than met the eye when Ellie let something slip.

"Zack says stage fright can be a serious thing," Ellie had said one day when Maggie finally confided what had happened. It was the time they often talked—at night in bed with the lamp turned low.

"What do you mean stage fright? What does Zack know of this?"

"Oh!" With a little gasp, Ellie covered her mouth with her hand. "I can say no more—"

"Not on your life! Tell me what you know!" Maggie demanded. She'd feared there was more to this, and if there was, she wanted to know so she could do something about it. She'd been waiting for Evan to take the first step, trying to give him time to get over his humiliation. But it might be up to her. Something had to be done. She was miserable without his friendship.

"Maggie, I can't. Zack may not be an official minister yet, but since he is sort of an apprentice, he has to abide by certain ministerial rules."

"Whatever it is, he told *you*. That doesn't sound right."

"I'm his fiancé. He ought to be able to tell me, as long as I follow the rules, too."

"Tell me!" Maggie ordered.

"Girls," Mama called from across the hall, "it's late. Time to settle down."

Quietly, Ellie asked Maggie, "Why are you so agitated about this, Maggie? Do you care for Evan?"

"Of course I care for him. He's a good friend!" she quickly replied, barely able to keep her voice low as she emphasized the word *friend*.

"No more?"

"How do I know, Ellie?" she replied miserably but honestly. "Still, I can miss a friend, can't I? Doesn't mean it's . . . well . . . ah . . . love or something!"

A moment of silence passed before Ellie responded. "Ask Zack. Okay? He will be the best judge of whether he ought to tell or not."

Maggie talked to Zack the very next time she saw him, but he wouldn't divulge what he knew. He did suggest she be patient with Evan because he was a mature, level-headed man who would soon get over what shame he might be feeling.

Evan knew he was behaving abominably. He should not have ignored Maggie after the trial. Yet he'd been so ashamed that she had caught him in his awful weakness. The forward steps he had taken after talking to Zack had nearly melted away after the encounter with Maggie.

Now that several days had passed and he was able to think more rationally, he realized how ridiculous that was. Heavens! She certainly must have already known how weak and inept he was. She'd seen him trip and fumble around like a circus clown.

Watching him bumble around the courtroom couldn't have been more shocking than watching him vomit behind it. Besides, how was she to know that it wasn't an isolated incident?

Oh, she would guess. She knew him that well at least.

The incident in the alley, no doubt, was the cap on everything else. The nail in the coffin of his heart. She had already rejected him, so the alley scene surely must have cemented her decision.

As for himself, the incident had simply weakened his already faint courage. Before that had happened, he'd thought he would keep trying to win her. Did he have the strength now to keep bashing his head against a wall? His love for her had grown each day, each moment. He thought of her constantly, he missed her desperately. In the last two days he had decided several times to ignore his pride and go see her. He'd gone as far as to saddle his horse a couple of times. But he couldn't mount because the fear of another rejection from her was more than he could bear.

One might think that events following Tommy's trial would have bolstered his confidence. For two days following the trial, he'd been swamped with potential clients. It surprised him how many pending legal matters there were in the small county—people needing contracts reviewed, wanting legal counsel for land deals, for drawing up wills and a plethora of smaller items. Nothing criminal, which suited him just fine, for it meant he wouldn't have to appear in a courtroom anytime soon. He'd heard that winning an important public trial could make a name for a lawyer, but he'd not even considered that until the potential clients began pouring in, a couple from Astoria and even some from Portland. He saw that he could make a nice living here in Columbia County practicing what he was trained to do. He need not shame his family or give up something he fairly enjoyed, courtroom nausea aside. His father had told him how proud he was, and his mother . . . well, one cannot win every battle. His mother still wanted him to reach for the power and prestige offered in Boston.

Evan truly desired to remain in Maintown, if only he had a reason to keep him here. But how could he stay if that very *reason* thought him a fool and had rejected him?

On Friday night Zack came to see him.

"Listen, Evan, Maggie is asking about what happened in the alley," he said. "She knows there is more to it than just a simple stomach upset. She thinks I might know something of the matter. I assure you I didn't say anything to her. I'm afraid I did tell Ellie—I'm sorry about that. You'll understand one day when you love someone and she is your best friend and confidante. But she promised to keep your confidence. Yet they are very close, and something might have slipped."

"I never told you to keep it a secret," Evan replied.

"Yes, but—"

"I appreciate your concern about keeping my shame quiet," Evan cut in quickly, realizing Zack would be too circumspect to say exactly what he was thinking.

"That's not it at all," Zack replied, seeming upset that Evan would assume such a thing. "I never once thought you had anything to be ashamed of. I merely feel that since I plan to become a minister, I have to be careful in talking about my interactions with others. In any case, Maggie is upset, and that is why I have come to you."

"Upset?" That shouldn't have surprised Evan. He knew she was a caring woman. It was one of the reasons he loved her.

"She says you haven't spoken to her since the trial. You two had become good friends, and you saw each other often. Even I could take your silence and absence as unusual. Perhaps it is not my place to interfere," Zack added. "I just felt you ought to know."

"It was selfish of me to ignore her as I've done," Evan admitted miserably. "But Zack, she saw me vomiting in the alley. I was so humiliated! That doesn't excuse my behavior. But . . . how can I face her when she knows just how weak I am?"

"God doesn't care about your weakness. Why should Maggie?"

"Because she is human."

"Do you truly believe her to be so petty?"

Evan reached for his spectacles, pushed up the bridge, and then straightened the earpiece. But he couldn't avoid the truth that was so blatant before him. "It has nothing to do with her, or even God. It is all me! I thought when you and I spoke that day all would be better—it wasn't you either, Zack! You gave me a new perspective on my . . . uh . . . problem, and that helped me through the trial. But when Maggie saw me, all my strides forward were lost. I had wanted her to see me as a warrior—a courtroom warrior, at least, because I had already proven I wasn't a warrior on the battlefield. I suppose you know now that Colby whipped me a couple of weeks ago."

"I heard."

"Well, Maggie saw that, too. I thought if she could see me doing something Colby couldn't do—but all she saw was a man stumbling and vomiting."

"She saw you win a case and save a man's life!" Zack insisted.

"Too little, too late."

"Not for Tommy. And it is a sure bet, it's not for Maggie, either."

"It wasn't as much my courtroom prowess that won that case as it was the obvious facts of the case."

"I wonder if you will ever give yourself credit, Evan. I think you are your own worst enemy."

"Don't I know that!"

"You're in love with Maggie, aren't you?"

Evan nodded reluctantly. "And like a fool I told her so."

"Ah!" Zack looked as though a shutter had been opened in his brain and light had suddenly been shed on a mystery. "Did she reject you?"

"Worse. She said I was her dearest friend, *but* . . ." Evan placed enough emphasis on that final *but* so that he didn't need to say more.

"That must have hurt."

"I don't know how I can face her now."

After a long pause, Zack said, "If you care for her, Evan, you must put aside your own pain and think of Maggie. She is devastated because she has lost two friends since the trial. Did you know Tommy has turned from her, as well?"

"I didn't know." Evan felt as if a fist was squeezing his heart. He knew what these friendships meant to Maggie. Thinking of her pain almost made him forget his own. "I will talk to Tommy."

"And to Maggie?"

Evan knew he must do that. He had told her they would remain friends, and it would be selfish to go back on his word. If she needed his friendship more than his love, then love demanded that he give her whatever he could, whatever she needed.

While Maggie was practicing patience concerning Evan, perhaps the most she had ever practiced it in her life, she had another disconcerting visitor.

It was Saturday morning and the family was getting ready to go to Scappoose to see Grandma and Grandpa Newcomb.

They would spend the night there and attend church with them on Sunday. Maggie was glad to get back to familiar routines. It made her feel that life was back to normal. She hoped it would fill the hole left by the loss of her friends. Maybe it would, but as thoughts of Evan flitted uninvited into her mind, she wasn't very sure.

Carrying her things out to the wagon for the trip, she looked up and saw Colby ride into the yard. It surprised her that he would show his face at her home after the cold shoulder she had extended him.

The family was going in and out of the house loading up the wagon, and Colby exchanged greetings with everyone; then he asked Maggie if she would mind taking a walk in the yard with him.

"Maggie," he began when they had strolled over to the stone wall by the vegetable garden, "I know you are mad at me for testifying against Tommy, and I hope you can forgive me. I hope we can be friends again." He spoke with sincere apology in his voice. The very words she had been longing to hear from Evan were quite unexpected coming from Colby.

"I was really disappointed in you, Colby."

"I did what I felt I had to do, just as you did."

"Mr. Cranston forced me to testify," she said defensively, knowing that made her betrayal no less hurtful. Tommy hadn't come to see her, either, deepening her sense of loss.

"Well, regardless of what we did," Colby reasoned, "Tommy got off, so it all came out okay in the end."

"It might not have. He might have hanged."

"Aw, come on, Mags, can't you give me an inch?" He offered her a lopsided, rather pathetic smile.

Her heart didn't leap as it once might have, but she still thought what a handsome fellow he was. "I guess I can forgive you," she relented. She'd lost too many friends over that trial to be hard-nosed about it.

He grinned his full, stunning grin, and his eyes sparked with playful charm, causing Maggie to remember all the time she had spent pining for Colby Stoddard when he had been so unreachable. She recalled that unexpected kiss in the apple orchard.

"I'm glad to hear that," he said. "You've become kind of special to me."

"I have?"

"Didn't we share a real nice kiss that day in the orchard?" His grin was just a bit devilish now. "I wouldn't mind sharing another."

"Oh, Colby!" She couldn't help herself, but she actually giggled.

"I couldn't win Ellie, but now I got a chance with you. That's not too bad, eh?" he said.

"Not too bad?" Her brow creased. If he had intended his words to woo her, he was heading in the wrong direction.

"You know what I mean. You two are practically two peas in a pod."

"Practically?"

"Let's quit talking." He slipped his arm around her waist and drew her close.

Maybe it was out of pure habit, but she was about to melt into the kiss he offered. Before she did so she had to clarify one thing. "Are you saying one Newcomb girl is just as good as the other?"

"Yeah, that's it! You are almost as pretty as Ellie, and you got a lot more spirit." He leaned closer.

Maggie stepped back and removed his hand from her waist. "Colby, your sweet talk is just about to give me vapors!" she said snidely. "Every girl wants to hear she is *almost* as pretty as another girl."

"Come on, Mags. You know I'm no smooth talker. I got no fancy education like that Parker. Give me a chance."

"A chance at what?"

"My parents say I have to settle down. My father is ailing, and it probably won't be long till I am running the farm. They want me to get married."

"I didn't think you did what your parents told you." By "parents" they both knew they meant "mother."

"Well, it seems the right thing to do. I'm smart enough to know I'm not gonna go out and make my fortune in the wide world. Being a farmer in Maintown is what I'm fated to be. Why fight it? If that's my destiny, then it may as well be with you."

"So you are proposing to me?"

"Sure. Why not?" He grinned, as if he had just offered her the world.

She laid a hand against her forehead and simpered, "I do declare! My head is spinning with your vows of love!"

He laughed. "Like I said, you have spirit! And I do like that. So you gonna say yes? I mean, if you don't, it's gonna have to be Tamara. She is fine but only my second choice. You are my first choice—"

"Wasn't Ellie your first choice?"

"Oh . . . well . . . sure . . . but that was—"

"Colby Stoddard, get out of here right now—before I forget I forgave you."

He looked shocked. Well, she thought, being rejected by one Newcomb girl was just as good as being rejected by another.

As he started to turn, Maggie added, "And, Colby, if you do propose to Tamara, do it on bended knee and try not to make her feel like you are looking to buy a cow."

She added that only out of consideration for Tamara, whom she had grown to like.

She waited until Colby rode away before she returned to the house. When she saw everyone, she wanted to shout, "Colby Stoddard just proposed to me, and I turned him down!"

That would have been silly. Nevertheless, she did feel a certain victory. More than that, she felt as if she had shed one of the last vestiges of her childhood. How many times over the last couple of years had she complained that everyone treated her like a child? Now she realized she had been just that, clinging to youthful fancies, scheming to get her way, pouting and sulking when she didn't. While grasping for adulthood, childhood had continued to pull her back. For the last year or so she'd been mired in some in-between world, as though caught in a huge spider's web and trying to claw her way out. Suddenly she felt that she had broken through.

What it all meant, she didn't know. Would it make her a better person? Would she not argue as much with her mother? Would she make better choices? Would she suddenly enjoy housekeeping?

She wanted desperately to talk to Ellie and get her insights on the matter, but when Maggie returned to the house, everyone was coming out, ready to board the wagon. Maybe once they got to Scappoose there would be a chance to get Ellie alone. Maggie needed to know how to navigate in this new adult world. She had to know what to do next. This first step into being a grown-up hadn't cured her impatience. She couldn't just sit and let it happen. She still had to do something about it.

On Saturday, Evan went first to the Donnelly place and had a long talk with Tommy. Evan felt Tommy better understood the position Maggie had been in and that it had pained her deeply to testify against him in court. Tommy said he'd go see Maggie real soon and clear things up.

Then Evan went to the Newcomb place but found it deserted. He sat on the front step and waited, hoping someone would return. Finally, two hours later, he rose dejectedly and left. Back at his house Mabel said she'd heard that the family had gone to Scappoose for the weekend to visit their grandparents. Mabel also said that it was a beautiful day, and instead of his moping around the house as he had been doing lately, he should ride over to the Stoddard place. Tamara had asked about him the other day.

He just looked at his sister as if she was speaking gibberish. But she couldn't possibly know that he had not thought romantically about Tamara in weeks.

# THIRTY

Tommy came to see Maggie the next week. She was pleased to see him, though she couldn't help a small pang of disappointment that he wasn't the person she had been hoping and praying would come.

It had rained all day and the sun had just come out, so Maggie had decided to take advantage of the bit of late afternoon sunlight to sew. She had just a little more to do on her final block. Then she could sew the blocks together, and she would have her first finished quilt top. Maybe she would still show it to Mrs. Stoddard, though it really no longer mattered what she thought. Maggie was proud of her work, regardless.

"Well, look at you!" Tommy said, striding up to the porch. "Sitting and stitching just like your ma. A fellow's in jail just a couple of months and everything changes." He grinned to show he was teasing.

"It's really good to see you, Tommy!" Maggie replied with a welcoming smile. "Come sit and visit for a while."

He sat on a porch step, leaning against a post facing her. He removed his hat and fiddled with it a moment before speaking. "Maggie, I'm sure sorry I got riled at you in the court place."

"I understand," Maggie said earnestly. "You had every right—"

"No, I didn't. That's just it. Mr. Parker, he explained it all to me and made me realize you had to tell the truth. He said you prob'ly helped me more than anyone else."

"I don't know about that—"

"Mr. Parker pointed out some of the good things you said. 'Course I heard 'em, but didn't really listen at the time 'cause I was mad." Pausing, Tommy scratched his head thoughtfully. "I also heard all the bad things other folks said 'bout me. I guess I saw for the first time just what a no-account fool I was. I told Mr. Parker and Zack that I ain't gonna do no bad things no more."

"That's real good, Tommy."

Tommy studied his hat for a few silent moments. Maggie put a few more stitches into her block. As she had said in court, she and Tommy didn't often have long conversations, so it was no wonder there was some awkwardness now. Other than that, she felt things were healed between them, or at least on the way.

Then Tommy spoke. "Maggie, when I was in jail, I had nothing but time to think and think—you know I ain't much good at thinking. I thought lots and lots 'bout you. I made myself think I was sweet on you—"

"Oh, Tommy," Maggie said sadly.

"Now wait," he said. "I know it ain't so, not really. And that you aren't sweet on me. Maybe that's why I got so mad like I did. Anyway . . ." He paused and wrinkled his brow. "You ain't sweet on me, are you?"

She opened her mouth to reply, but he cut in, "No, 'course you ain't. But can I ask why not?"

"I don't know," she said gently. "There is just no telling why a person cares for one person in that way and not another." She wanted to tell him she cared for him as she did one of her brothers, but she knew better than that, so she said no more.

"Well, I'm glad if it ain't gonna be me, it's Mr. Parker," Tommy said.

Maggie stared, unable to speak, especially unable to deny Tommy's statement.

"He's a very fine fellow," Tommy went on. "Why, I'd say I think almost as much of him as I do Zack."

"He is a fine person," Maggie finally said. A grin slipped across her face. "Oh, my goodness! I do care for Evan. I am sweet on him!"

"I knew it!" Tommy smiled. "You and him will be fine together. But once you and Mr. Parker hitch up, will you still go fishin' with me?"

"We both will, Tommy. You'll get two friends for the price of one!"

"Price? Well, I don't got much money—Oh, I get it!" Tommy laughed. "Mr. Parker will be my friend, too. That'll be nice."

Maggie chatted with Tommy for a few more minutes.

Then he rose to leave. "I gotta get back to the farm. There's loads of work to do. Zack did the best he could helpin' Ma while I was gone, but he couldn't do everything. I'm gonna be able to take care of my ma now."

The last few minutes before Tommy left, Maggie had a hard time sitting still. Her heart was racing, and her feet were itching. She could barely wait to go see Evan and tell him her astounding revelation. The moment after Tommy left, Maggie began packing away her sewing into her basket. Before she finished, her mother rode up on the saddle horse. She had been to the Wallards' to help with wedding preparations.

"Maggie," Mama said, dismounting and tying the reins to the hitching post. There was a high-pitched, almost nervous quality to her voice and a crease in her brow.

"Mama, is everything okay?"

"Maggie," Mama said again. "Oh . . . Maggie."

Maggie jumped up. "What's wrong? Is it Dad—?"

"No, everyone is all right," Mama said quickly, but she didn't seem fine herself. She came up the steps and put an arm around Maggie's shoulder. "I have some disturbing news. Let's go inside."

"Mama, what is it?" But Maggie curbed her impatience as she went in with her mother's arm still around her. If the family was okay, what else could be so awful? Though Maggie's tendency would have been to insist her mother tell her without all this fanfare, she wasn't anxious for bad news to ruin the elation she felt with her realization about Evan.

Once in the kitchen, Mama said, "Perhaps you should sit down, Maggie."

Grandma and Ellie were there, too. Seeing Mama's expression, they were looking just as concerned as Maggie.

"I don't want to sit down. Just tell me what's wrong," Maggie insisted, impatience finally getting the better of her.

"When I was at Nessa's today, Mabel stopped by—"

"Something's happened to Evan!" Maggie exclaimed, her heart clapping hard against her chest.

"No, Maggie," Mama said. "Mabel told us . . . well, that Colby and Tamara are engaged."

Maggie blinked. She felt as if she had braced for a thunderstorm and received only a sprinkle. She looked at her mother, expecting more, something really terrible.

"I know this is difficult for you, dear," Mama said tenderly.

"Is that all?" Maggie asked.

"You're devastated, aren't you?"

Then Maggie smiled.

Mama looked confused. She glanced at Grandma then at Ellie. They had peculiar looks on their faces, too—"the cat who swallowed the canary" looks.

"What's going on?" Mama asked.

"Mama," Maggie said, "Colby proposed marriage to me before we went to Scappoose, and I turned him down. I don't care to marry him."

"You don't?" Mama's voice came out in a small squeak, confusion deepening on her face.

"Mama, perhaps *you* should sit down," Maggie entreated.

A little giggle escaped Ellie's lips. She probably already guessed what Maggie was going to say.

Just as stubborn as Maggie, Mama remained standing.

Maggie continued. "Mama, I don't love Colby. I barely even like him anymore." Maggie paused. Though she was sure of her feelings, they were so new. It would be the first time she had spoken them aloud. "Mama, I'm in love with Evan Parker." Oh, that felt so good to say!

"Evan . . . Parker?" Mama squeaked. Then she did sink down into a chair. "Evan . . . ? You love Evan . . . ?"

Ellie clapped her hands as Grandma came and gave Maggie a hug. "I just knew you were trying to impress the wrong mother!" Grandma laughed.

"Grandma," Ellie said, "didn't I tell you we had to get busy working on—just a minute." Ellie went to Mama's chest by the hearth, opened it, and took something out. With Grandma's help they opened it and revealed a quilt top, the one Ellie had been working on earlier in the Sister's Choice pattern.

"You finished the top!" Maggie exclaimed.

"I got Grandma to help. I knew there wasn't going to be much time, that you were very close to making your *choice*. Now you'll have at least two quilts for your quilting bee—this one and your sampler."

Mama found her voice at last, though it was still a little shaky. "You should have twelve, you know."

Maggie sat in the chair facing her mother and grasped her hands. "Are you okay with this, Mama?"

"Evan's a fine boy." Mama spoke as if in a daze.

Well, no wonder. It was obvious this was the last thing on earth Mama expected to hear. And most likely it hadn't sunk into Mama's head yet that this would also mean that she and Mrs. Parker would soon be related. Maggie decided to leave it at that, to let Mama come around in her own time. Maybe Maggie and Evan would be a modern Romeo and Juliet, bringing together feuding parents, though in a much happier manner.

She did think she ought to prepare her mother more in another vein, a little better than she herself had been prepared for the realization that she loved Evan. "Mama," she said in a soothing tone, "I don't think there is going to be time for twelve quilts."

"Oh my!" Mama fanned herself with her hand, flapping it vigorously.

"Now I have an important errand to run," Maggie said. "I'll take your horse, if that's okay, Mama?"

Then Maggie excused herself, anxious to accomplish another important mission that day.

She was halfway to the Parkers' when she saw a riderless horse chewing grass on the side of the road. It was the Parkers' horse, Daisy.

"Daisy, where is your rider?" she said, dismounting. She rubbed Daisy's nose.

"Here," came a familiar voice. "I'm down here."

"Evan!" Maggie cried. "Did Daisy throw you?" She carefully climbed down the muddy ditch.

"No . . . not really . . ."

"You've got to quit riding that ornery animal before she kills you!" Maggie scolded.

When she got to the bottom of the ditch, thick with brush and blackberry bushes, she saw Evan scramble out from the middle of one of the bushes. He had a few scratches from the thorns. Leaves and twigs were stuck in his hair and clothes—a plaid shirt and denim dungarees he had bought the last time they had gone to St. Helens. She had never seen him dressed like this and thought he looked every bit as wonderful as he had in his expensive Boston suits. And since he was on his feet, he was apparently unharmed by his spill.

"I couldn't let her get the better of me," Evan replied defensively. "I did get her under control after the snake spooked her. But I dismounted, thinking to walk her until she calmed down. I lost my footing in the mud and went down."

"You fell in the bush?"

"My spectacles did. I was looking for them."

"Still, that animal can't be trusted," Maggie declared. "I'd feel terrible if anything happened to you."

"You would?"

"Of course I would!" She gave her head a shake. "I care about my friends, you know! But I've come to tell you—"

"Maggie, wait," Evan said in a rush. "I was on my way to see you, as well. Please, let me say what I have to say. I have been practicing all morning, and I want to get it right."

She nodded.

He took a breath and continued, "Maggie, I know I am not the best catch in this county. There are a dozen better-looking fellows and dozens who are more adept at . . . well, at everything. They don't fall off horses, slip in the mud, trip over carpets, or get queasy stomachs when they do their jobs. But, Maggie, you will never, ever find a man in this county, even on this earth, who loves you more than I do, who adores every little thing about you, or who would do more than I to make you the happiest woman in the world. I thought I could love you best by letting you go to the man you wanted. But, Maggie, I know in my heart that Colby will never love you as much as I do nor make you as happy. I know I don't deserve you, but I can't let you go because I am sure you and I are meant to be. And you know I don't often get this sure about many things."

"I know we are meant for each other, too, Evan," Maggie said with a grin.

"You do?"

"I love you, Evan!" Her grin grew wider. She could hardly contain her joy.

"You do?"

"But one thing, Evan, I don't want to hear anymore of this business that you don't deserve me. You deserve every good and wonderful thing, and if that's me, then so be it. You are the finest man around and the best looking, too, if you ask me!"

Then she did what she had been wanting to do since he had climbed out of the blackberry bush. She flung her arms around him and pressed her lips against his. It took him but one stunned instant to lift his arms, wrap them tightly around her, and return the kiss.

Pulling back slightly, he grinned, wider and broader than when he had been chasing chickens. And though the kiss had momentarily paused, he continued to hold her and she him.

"Maggie, might I be so bold as to propose marriage to you?" he said with his impeccable manners.

"You better be so bold!" she laughed.

"Do you think a Christmas wedding is too soon?"

"I think that'll be enough time to get our mothers to accept this."

He laughed. "I forgot about them. My mother is also going to have to get used to the idea of my being a lawyer here in Columbia County."

"You have decided to keep practicing law?"

"It is what I am best at, aside from the minor inconvenience of internal upsets. And despite all my failings, God has shown His faithfulness to me in so many other ways. Above all, He has taken a misfit and allowed him to fit perfectly with the woman of his dreams."

"He has done the same with me, Evan. We fit together like two peas in a pod. I am so glad I finally realized it!" She hitched up on her toes and kissed him again. Christmas seemed a long way off. Perhaps she could talk her mother into a Thanksgiving wedding instead.

## Sister's Choice Pattern

This block will finish to 10 inches. I'll give the directions using light and dark, but I have seen this pattern in many pretty variations using lights, mediums, and darks, so be creative!

Fabrics: Background or light (BG) and dark (D)

Cutting: From background fabric
Eight $2\frac{1}{2}$" squares
Four $2\frac{7}{8}$" squares, each cut once on diagonal
From dark fabric:
Nine $2\frac{1}{2}$" squares
Four $2\frac{7}{8}$" squares, each cut once on diagonal

Sew together the BG/D triangle pieces so that you have eight half-square triangle units.

BG
D

Arrange these units with the squares of BG and dark as indicated below, then sew together in rows.

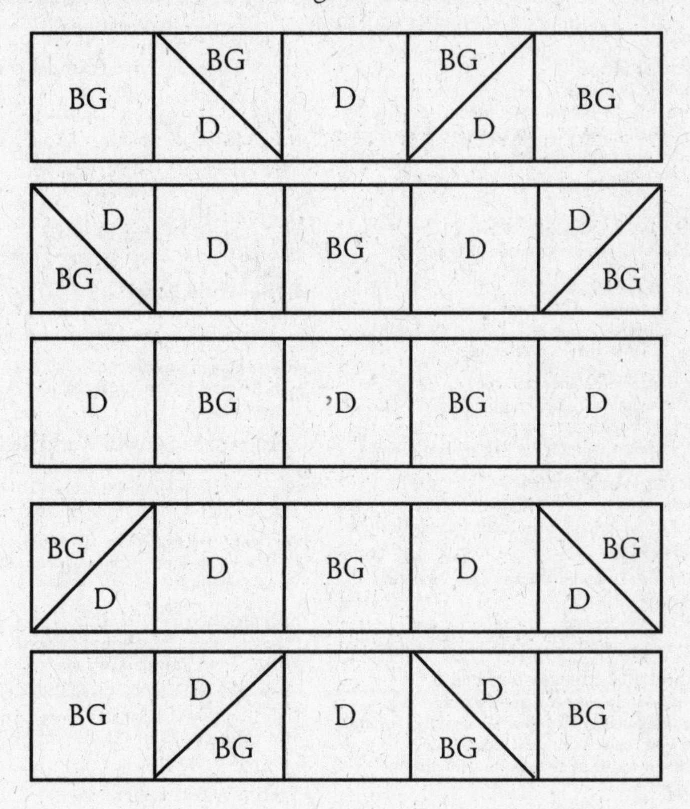


Enjoy your block! Alone, it can make a nice pillow or front of a tote bag. Or make several for a wall hanging or larger quilt.

# Quilt Drive

In honor of Judith Pella's newest series, PATCHWORK CIRCLE, Bethany House Publishers is hosting a quilt drive for those in need. The following is a list of charitable organizations that accept quilt donations. **If you would like to donate a quilt to one of these, visit *www.judithpella.com/quilts* to make a Good Faith Commitment and receive a free Bethany House novel!** Be sure to let us know which organization you will send the quilt to. We will post a virtual quilt block to Judith's Web site to recognize each donation.

### Convoy of Hope

A Christian compassion organization that meets physical and spiritual needs: mobilizes resources, and trains churches and other groups to conduct community outreaches, respond to disasters, and direct other compassion initiatives in the United States and around the world.

Vineese Childs
330 S. Patterson, Springfield, MO 65802
417-823-8998 • www.convoyofhope.org

### Home to Home, Inc.

Equips "local churches and pastors to minister through friendship, outreach, evangelism, and discipleship to our local Jerusalem in the name of Jesus."

Wayne Wingfield, Affiliate Director
326 Habersham Rd., Suite 103, High Point, NC 27260
Email: info@hometohomehp.org
Go to www.hometohomehp.org for more information.

### Lutheran World Relief

Distributes quilts to people around the world: those fleeing conflict, suffering from a disaster, living in chronic poverty, or refugees.

Brenda Meier, Director for Parish and Community Engagement
Email: bmeier@lwr.org
Go to www.lwr.org/parish/quilts.asp for more information.

### Oklahoma Campers on Mission

A Christian camping organization whose women sew for needs in the communities where their men build, restore, and remodel buildings, especially churches. Your quilts will go to children who are victims of recent diasters.

Fran deCordova
Trinity International Church
1329 NW 23rd, Oklahoma City, OK 73106-3617
Email: kidscomfyquilts@cox.net
For more information go to www.bgco.org/com, then click on the "kids comfy quilt" link.

### Sewn-N-Love

Provides quilts to cancer patients and their families.

Sandy Wilson, Co-founder
Email: info@sewn-n-love.org
Go to www.sewn-n-love.org for more information.

### United Methodist Committee on Relief Sager Brown Depot

Dispatches tons of supplies worth millions of dollars to points around the world, domestic and international.

Kathy Kraiza, Executive Director
Phone: 337-923-6238
Email: director@sagerbrown.org
Go to www.sagerbrown.org for more information.

### Wrap Them in Love Foundation for Children

Collects donated quilts and distributes them to children in need around the world.

Ellen Sime
2522 A Old Hwy 99 S, Mt. Vernon, WA 98273
Phone: 360-424-9293
Email: admin@wraptheminlove.org
Go to http://wraptheminlove.org for more information.

### Boise World Relief

Your made-with-love quilt will welcome a refugee family to a new life in Idaho, cheering their hearts and their homes.

H. Renee Hage, Director
6702 Fairview Avenue, Boise, Idaho 83704
hrhage@wr.org

### Minneapolis-St. Paul World Relief

Reaches out to refugees and immigrants; partners with churches to provide tangible help to needy families while embracing them with God's love and care.

Woubejig Shiferaw (Docho), Volunteer Coordinator
1515 East 66th Street, Richfield, MN 55423
Email: Minnesota@wr.org

### Sacramento World Relief

Provides refugee resettlement for family reunification, including case management, donated home goods and clothing, immigration services, and tutoring.

Betty Eastman, Assistant Director/Fiscal Officer
4721 Engle Road, Suite #11, Carmichael, CA 95608
Email: BEastman@wr.org

### Seattle World Relief

Their mission is to be the hands, feet, and face of Jesus Christ to refugees and immigrants. Your quilt will go to a recently arrived refugee family.

Kelly Pearson
Web site: www.wr-seattle.org
Email: kpearson@wr.org

### Tri-Cities World Relief

Assists new refugees with basic needs such as food, blankets, and furniture.

Scott Michael
2600 N. Columbia Center Blvd., Suite 206
Richland, WA 99352
Email: SMichael@wr.org

### World Relief – Spokane

Works with church partners to help refugees and immigrants begin new lives.

Linda J. Unseth, N.W. Regional Director
1522 N. Washington, #204, Spokane, WA 99201
Email: lunseth@wr.org

**For more information on regional World Relief offices, go to www.wr.org and then to "Where We Work."**

# More Heartwarming Fiction from Judith Pella

**Don't Miss Book One!**

When the ladies of Maintown hear the new minister is a bachelor, they and their daughters decide to make him a welcome quilt. But the project turns into a fierce competition as each young woman vies for the attention of the young minister. And so taken is the town with the handsome preacher that they don't notice how especially inexperienced he seems to be....

***Bachelor's Puzzle*** **by Judith Pella**
**PATCHWORK CIRCLE #1**

**Bestselling Series!**

Amid the chaos of World War II, newspaper tycoon Keagan Hayes finds himself strangely powerless as his three grown daughters get caught up in the explosive drama of a world at war. As each girl sets out on a path certain to dismantle a family already fragmented by turmoil, long-held secrets shimmer just beneath the surface...will the trauma of war be the catalyst for peace?

**DAUGHTERS OF FORTUNE:**
***Written on the Wind, Somewhere a Song, Toward the Sunrise, Homeward My Heart***

**A Beloved Tale**

Philip de Tollard is the illegitimate son of a powerful English lord and given no claim to an inheritance. Gareth, the legitimate son, is cruel and abusive and falsely accuses Phillip when their father suddenly dies. Escaping with only his life, Philip devises a dangerous plan for vengeance. But love and hate have consequences, and he must face the truth that God will not be ignored.

***Mark of the Cross*** **by Judith Pella**